D1326961

BRONZE SUMMER

BRONZE SUMMER

NORTHLAND: BOOK TWO

STEPHEN BAXTER

GOLLANCZ

LONDON

The right of Stephen Baxter to be identified as the author of
this work has been asserted by him in accordance with the
Copyright, Designs and Patents Act 1988.

First published in Great Britain in 2011 by Gollancz
An imprint of the Orion Publishing Group
Orion House, 5 Upper St Martin's Lane,
London WC2H 9EA
An Hachette UK Company

A CIP catalogue record for this book
is available from the British Library

ISBN 978 0 575 08922 8 (Cased)
ISBN 978 0 575 08923 5 (Trade Paperback)

1 3 5 7 9 10 8 6 4 2

Typeset at The Spartan Press Ltd,
Lymington, Hants

Printed and bound by
CPI Group (UK) Ltd, Croydon, CR0 4YY

The Orion Publishing Group's policy is to use papers
that are natural, renewable and recyclable products and
made from wood grown in sustainable forests. The logging
and manufacturing processes are expected to conform to the
environmental regulations of the country of origin.

www.stephen-baxter.com
www.orionbooks.co.uk

For Brian Aldiss

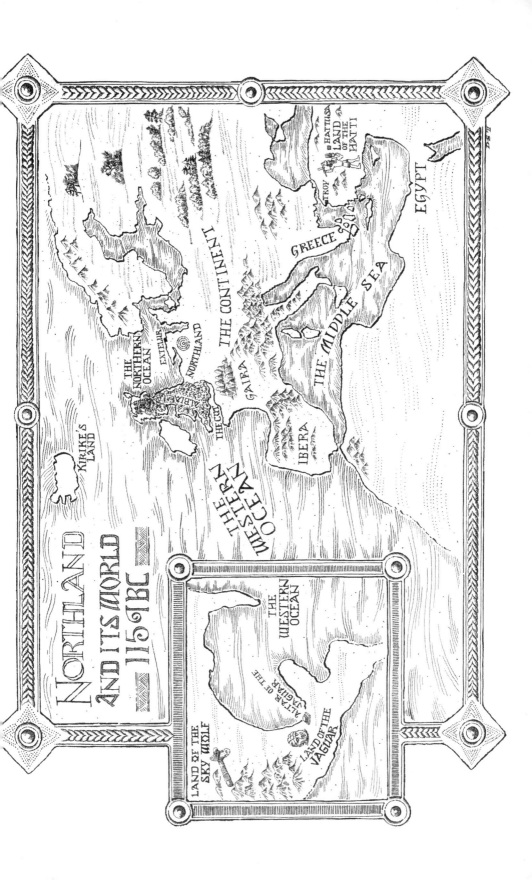

ONE

1

Once the ice had covered continents. The silence of the world had been profound.

Eventually, grudgingly, the ice retreated to its fastnesses in the mountains and at the poles. Humans spread northward, colonising the recovering land. They lived sparsely, their lives brief. Soon the ice was remembered only in myth.

Yet the world around them continued to endure significant changes. The land rose and flexed as it was relieved of the burden of the weight of the ice, and meltwater flowed into the oceans and pooled in hollows on the land. Rising seas bit at the coastlines of Northland, the great neck of land that still connected the peninsula called Albia to the Continent. Perhaps that neck would have been severed altogether – if not for the defiance of Northland's people, who, tentatively at first, with crude flood-resistant mounds, drainage ditches scratched in the ground, and heaped-up dykes of stone and earth, resisted the ocean's slow assaults.

Meanwhile, far to the east, other new ideas were emerging. People had long tracked wild sheep and goats and encouraged the more nutritious cereal plants. Now, as people sought more reliable food supplies, that practice intensified. Herds were corralled, fields planted. Populations bloomed.

But the ice was not done with mankind. A remnant ice cap over the western continent collapsed, and chill waters poured down the river valleys to the ocean. Sea levels rose in a great pulse. Northland survived this too, its already ancient network of sea walls and dykes and soakaways resilient. But the drastic injection of chill meltwater caused ocean currents to fail, and the world suffered a cold snap that lasted centuries. The eastern farmers, driven out of their homes by climate

3

collapse and over-exploitation, spread west along the river valleys and ocean coasts, taking their animals and seeds with them. In a slow wave that rolled across the Continent, forest was cleared, and threads of smoke rose from new farming communities.

After two thousand years the farmers' culture reached the shore of the Western Ocean – but here the wave broke. If the Northlanders had not existed, perhaps the farmers and their culture would have colonised the shore lands and islands of the ocean fringe. But Northland, though still a culture living off the produce of the wild earth, was literate, technically advanced, strong, self-confident. The Northlanders traded and learned, but farming held no interest for them.

Again the climate shifted, with a spasm of drought heralding a new age of warm, dry conditions; again humanity's fragile cultures flowed and changed in response. In the east the farming communities coalesced into a new phenomenon: towns and cities, major gatherings of population, centrally controlled, dedicated to the great task of maintaining complex nets of irrigation channels in increasingly dry landscapes. Empires bloomed like fungi on a log. Soon trading routes spanned the Continent, carrying amber from the north, silver from the south, timber from the west, tin and lapis lazuli from the east. Bronze was everywhere, in cups and ornaments and statuary, in the body armour and swords of the new warrior kings. The traders and warriors probed west and north, seeking profit and conquest. But again the old Northlander culture stood strong, and older ways were preserved.

And still the earth would not rest. Over an ocean on the far side of the world, elaborate cycles of heat and moisture collapsed, resumed – changed. The consequences rippled across the continents, in more waves of flood and drought, famine and disaster.

And under a mountain on an island in the Western Ocean, molten rock surged, seeking escape.

2

Milaqa climbed the staircase cut into the face of the Wall. She took big deliberate strides, reluctant to think about her dead mother, whose rotting corpse lay out in the open on the roof.

The growstone surface by the staircase was covered in scratched graffiti, swirls of circles and arcs in flowing Etxelur script: 'HARA LOVES MEK.' 'GAGO OF THE HOUSE OF THE VOLE OWES ME A DEER HAUNCH. DO NOT TRUST HIM . . .' Here, she was intrigued to see, was a line scraped in the angular alphabet of the Greeks. She knew the language and picked out the words with ease: 'I PALLAS CLIMBED THIS WALL AND DEFIED THE NORTHERN SEA, IN THE NINTH YEAR AFTER THE STORM.' A sightseeing trader or princeling, she supposed, and boastful like all of his kind.

Her steps were slowing, her attention too easily snagged by these scribbles. She forced herself on.

As she reached the roof, under a grey sky, her view of Old Etxelur opened up, the earthworks and flood mounds, the houses clustered over the lump of Flint Island. Beyond, the flat, misty expanse of Northland stretched to the southern horizon, the grey-green landscape cut into a neat patchwork by the tremendous straight lines of tracks, canals, dykes, holloways and gullies. A cloud of birds, redwings perhaps, descended on a distant swathe of grassland. When she looked to the north the Wall's own sharp horizon hid the sea from her sight. The Wall, it was said, was as tall as thirty adults standing one on top of the other, and about half as thick. But she heard the growl of the sea, and felt cold spray on her brow.

The wind shifted, and there was a reek of rot, of decay, of death. She wrapped her cloak closer around her body. She longed to run back to the warmth and light of the galleries of the Scambles, the bright chatter of her friends. But she could not.

She walked along the spine of the Wall, following the sparse line of monuments that dominated this tremendous roof. The oldest were slim monoliths, slabs of granite and basalt, gifts from the austere sky-watching communities of Gaira. And then there were the more recent Annid heads, images of Etxelur's leaders carved by sculptors from across the Western Ocean: blocky faces as tall as Milaqa defiantly facing the rage of the waters, just as the Wall itself had for hundreds of generations. Her own mother's face would soon be joining that row of bleak, sightless watchers. A memory surfaced like an air bubble from a still pond: a summer's day when Kuma had lifted her up, Milaqa had been only five or six, and whirled her in the summer sunlight. Milaqa was now sixteen years old. She pushed the memory away.

And she approached her mother's lying-out platform. It was a simple wooden frame surrounded by busy, swooping gulls that scattered, cawing their irritation. Her mother's corpse was just one of a row of prone bodies on the frame, many of them small, the crop of children taken by the recent winter, just as every year. The bodies lay under worn-out thatch nets that kept their bones from being scattered by the birds. Kuma, Milaqa's mother, still wore her bronze breastplate, gleaming in the watery day-light, the ceremonial armour of the Annid of Annids yet to be removed, to be given to her successor. The breastplate was damaged, Milaqa noticed, with a neat slit punched in its front.

And a man stood beyond the lying-out frame. Bulky, wrapped in a featureless cloak, silhouetted against the northern sky, this was her uncle Teel – come to make her face her mother's death, and, she supposed, other unwelcome realities.

Milaqa walked forward. The Northern Ocean was revealed to her now, big muscular waves flecked with foam. The grey water was only a few paces below the lip of the Wall; the level of the sea was higher than the dry land behind her. Sea birds rode the ocean swell, and further out she saw a litter of fishing boats.

'An eagle,' Teel said.

'What?'

'I saw an eagle – a sea eagle, I think – wheeling away over there.' He pointed out to sea. Teel was not a tall man but he was bulky, given to fat, and he habitually shaved his head to the scalp. Milaqa knew he was around thirty years old, but he looked younger, his face oddly round, like a baby's.

'I wouldn't be surprised,' she said. 'The eagles nest in crevices in the Wall's outer face. Lots of birds do. And on the inner face too.'

'Wearing away the Wall bit by bit, with each peck of a curious chick, each streak of guano on the growstone. Well. We can leave it to the Beavers to fret about that.' His blue eyes were running in the cold breeze. 'Thank you for coming up.'

'Did I have a choice?'

'Well, I didn't drag you here, so yes, you had a choice. I know how difficult this is for you. To lose your mother in your sixteenth year, the year of your House choice – you'll have to face the whole family at the equinox gathering—'

'Don't give me advice about my feelings, you ball-less old man.'

He laughed, unperturbed. 'Ball-less, yes, I grant you. But not that old, surely.'

'Let's get this over.' She walked deliberately to the sky burial platform. A couple of gulls had landed again; they fled into the air. Milaqa lifted her cloak so it covered her mouth. Teel had a linen scarf, grimy from use, that he pulled over his mouth and nose. And Milaqa looked closely at her mother's body for the first time.

It had only been a month since Kuma had been brought home from the Albian forest where she had met her death. A fall from her horse had killed her, her companions had told the family, an aurochs chase that went wrong, the back of her skull smashed on a rock – an accident, it happened all the time, there would be no point hunting the great cattle in their tall forests if it wasn't dangerous. Only a month. Yet Kuma's head had already been emptied of its eyes, her gaping mouth cleansed of tongue and palate. Scraps of flesh and wisps of hair still clung, but enough bone had been exposed for Milaqa to be able to see the crater-like indentation in the back of the skull, the result of that fatal fall. *This is my mother.* Milaqa probed for feeling, deep in her heart. She had not cried when she had heard her mother was dead. Now all she seemed to feel was a deep and savage relief that it wasn't her lying on this platform, her flesh rotting from her broken frame. Did everybody feel this way?

'It works so quickly,' Teel said, marvelling. 'The processes of death. Look, of the body's soft parts there's not much left save the big core muscles.' He pointed to masses of dull red meat beneath Kuma's ribs. 'The birds and the insects and the rats, all those little mouths pecking and chewing—'

'Is this some kind of test? I know what you're like. I grew up with you setting me tricky challenges, uncle.'

'All for your own good. I wanted to show you something.' He pointed to the flaw in the bronze breastplate. 'Look at that.'

The breastplate, supposedly a gift from the tin miners of Albia to some Annid many generations back, was finely worked, incised with the rings and cup marks of the old Etxelur script. The damage was obvious close to. She inspected the rough slit, the flanges of metal folded back to either side. 'What of it? When the next Annid takes the plate, this will be easily fixed.'

'Perhaps so. But how do you imagine it got there?'

Milaqa shrugged. 'During the accident. She fell from her horse, when it bucked before the charging aurochs.'

He nodded, and mimed a fall, tipping forward. 'So she landed hard, and – what? A bit of rock punctured her breastplate?'

'It's possible.' But she doubted it even as she spoke.

'But she fell backward. That's what we were told – that's how

she got her skull stove in. You can see the wound, at the back of the head. So how, then, was the plate on her *chest* punctured?'

'Come on, uncle. You never ask a question if you don't already know the answer.'

He lifted his cloak back over his shoulder, revealing a mittened hand holding a bronze knife, and he began sawing at the net strands over Kuma's torso. 'Actually I don't know the answer – not for sure. But I have a theory.'

He quickly cut enough strands to be able to peel back the netting, itself sticky, from Kuma's chest. Then he reached under the breastplate to cut into its leather ties. Carefully, respectfully, he lifted the plate off Kuma's body. It came away with a sucking sound, to reveal a grimy linen tunic. He slit through the rotting cloth and peeled that back to reveal Kuma's chest, scraps of flesh and fat and muscle over ribs that gleamed white. Flies buzzed into the air, and there was a fresh stench, sharp and rotten.

Teel pulled off his deerskin mittens and handed them to Milaqa. 'Hold these for me. This is going to be messy.'

And he dug his fingers into Kuma's chest, in the gap between the racks of her ribs. Bone cracked. He pushed and probed, spreading his fingers into the soft mass beneath. He was looking for something. His expression was grim; Milaqa knew he had his squeamish side. Then his hand closed. He looked at Milaqa. He withdrew his hand, and held out his fist; black fluid and bits of flesh clung to his skin. He opened his hand to reveal a small object, flat, three-sided, evidently heavy and sharp, coated in ichor. He rubbed it on his cloak, and held the object up to his eye.

'It's an arrowhead,' Milaqa said slowly.

He nodded. '*Somebody shot your mother* – right in the heart. That's how she died. The head injury surely happened as she fell from her horse, or was maybe faked later.'

'But it must have gone right through her armour, her breastplate.' Milaqa seemed to be thinking slowly, plodding from one conclusion to the next. 'What arrowhead can pierce bronze?'

'One like this,' he said, holding out the point to her. 'Iron.'

9

3

Far to the east, a generation-long drought gripped the land. People abandoned their failing farms and wandered in search of succour, or turned to raiding the rich trade caravans and ships. But the collapse of trade only worsened the crisis, when there were no more caravans to rob.

Eventually whole populations were on the move, by land and sea. And ancient empires crumbled.

Qirum heard the approach of the column long before it arrived at the city walls. The neighing of horses, the rattling of wagon wheels, a distant crowd murmur – all these disturbed his sleep, as did the bear-like snoring of Praxo in the next room. But it was the blare of bronze war trumpets that finally penetrated his ale-sodden head. The Hatti, of course, the great power of Anatolia, it was the Hatti who would be coming with mobs of captives from the cities they sacked, the countries they emptied.

And when booty flowed through Troy, and booty people, there was opportunity for a man like Qirum.

Qirum guessed it was close to noon. The room was windowless, and stank of farts, stale wine, piss and sex, but the walls of packed mud were cracked, nobody had bothered to repair them since the great fire set by the Greeks, and they admitted slabs of bright daylight. He sat up, pushing the thin linen blanket off his torso. The whore lay sleeping beside him, or feigning sleep at least. He found a pouch of wine, and one of water; he took draughts from one and then the other, and poked at the whore's backside with his foot. 'Get up and get out.'

She stirred reluctantly and sat up, rubbing her eyes. 'I need sleep.' She was dark, with tousled black hair and brown eyes. She was only about fourteen; though her body was full, her face was small, round, like a child's, and her mouth, bruised around the lips, had an habitual pout.

He thought she was a Kaskan, from the north. He didn't know her name, or care. 'You've been asleep since dawn.' The last time he'd managed it. 'Now it's noon. Up and out with you. Praxo! Wake up, you fat slug.' He rummaged for his clothes on the floor, amid the stale, half-eaten loaves, a spilled cup of wine.

The girl pulled the blanket over her small breasts. 'You want me tonight?' She forced a smile, but her eyes were like a hunted animal's.

He'd seen that look before in his women; they wanted his money, but feared the strength of his lust. This girl hadn't satisfied him but he supposed it wasn't her fault. He needed an athlete, to match him. A Spartan maid! Rummaging in the heap of stuff he found a tiny goblet, a miniature as you might make for a baby prince. It had lost its base and was badly dented, but it was silver, and it would keep this girl fed for a week or more – and her family, her babies, whoever controlled her, whatever shadowy figures lay behind the child-woman he had taken a fancy to in the street last night. 'No. I won't want you again. Here.' He threw the cup over to her.

She grabbed it, sniffed it, tucked it under the blanket out of his sight, gone in a flash. She smiled again. 'You were strong. Like bull of legend—'

He swept the back of his hand towards her, and she flinched. 'You won't get any more out of me. Out. Now. Oh, and empty the night soil bowls on your way.' He turned his back and pulled on loincloth, tunic, boots. He heard her move around, finding her clothes. Then she was gone, and he knew he would never think of her again.

He stood, fully dressed. The sudden movement brought a sharp pain to the base of his skull, a relic of the lousy wine which was all you could find in this town these days. He stretched and bent, tensing his muscles. He felt familiar twinges, the scar tissue on his back, the broken cheekbone that had never quite healed right, the burned patch on his arm – each a souvenir of a fight fought, and won. He found his bronze sword and swung it a couple of times, and he let out a roar. Blood pumping, lungs drawing in the foul air, he could feel the day's recovery starting. It never took long. He was no bull, no war god, he wasn't prone to flattery of that sort. But he thought of himself as a healthy animal in his prime, and if the Storm God favoured him he would stay that way until a decent death spared him the humiliation of illness and age. Refreshed, he slipped his sword into its scabbard and picked up the rest of his gear, his bronze dagger, his leather belt with its pouches.

Still Praxo's snore rattled the walls, despite the gathering din of the approaching caravan. 'Praxo!' Qirum raised a boot and started to slam his heel into the wall. It smashed in a shower of lathes, dried mud, wicker and plaster, and there was a faint smell of soot and smoke. Before the fire this had probably been quite a grand house, even though it was a long way out from the Pergamos. Now it was a crumbling wreck. He kept kicking the wall until he had made a hole big enough to step through.

He loomed over Praxo, who lay on his belly under a scrunched-up blanket that barely covered his hairy backside, his head tipped sideways, his mouth open, his big fleshy nose squashed, his snoring like an earthquake. Qirum's closest companion was only a couple of years older than Qirum himself, only twenty-five, but the jowls and folds of his fleshy face made him look a good deal older than that. Praxo's own whores – he preferred two at a time if he could afford them – had long gone, though at first glance it didn't look as if they had had the nerve to rob the sleeping sailor.

Qirum picked up a slat from the walls, and laid about Praxo's back and arse with vigorous blows. 'Up! Up, you beached whale. The day's half gone, and there's booty coming to town.'

Praxo stirred, snorted, coughed, and rolled onto his back, leaving a puddle of snot where his nose had been. He had a monstrous waking erection that stuck up like a ship's mast. He opened one eye. 'Clear off, I need a piss.' But then the martial trumpets sounded again, and a broad grin spread over Praxo's grimy face.

'Do what you have to do, my friend, but get on with it.' Qirum pushed through the remains of a doorway and emerged onto the mud track outside. Once this had been a fair-sized street. But now it was greened over by weeds, and cluttered by huts, shacks and lean-tos, smoke trailing through their roofs. If you stood still for too long the kids came swarming out with their little hands out towards you, chattering, begging for food. Living like rats on a midden.

Behind him he heard Praxo swear and strain at his stool.

Qirum walked away up a low rise. From here he looked out over the ruined lower town towards the Pergamos, the citadel, with its ring of cracked walls, the palace with its fallen towers and smashed-in roof. Once this view would have been cluttered by crowding buildings, winding alleyways; now it was all but clear. This was Troy. Qirum had been born here – he had been conceived during the disastrous night of the fire that had ended the Greek siege – this was his home city, and always would be. But he had travelled widely; he had seen Mycenae and Hattusa and Ashur, he had seen what a city should be. Maybe Troy would recover some day, maybe it would get back to the greatness it had enjoyed. But not while drought and famine stalked the land, and populations fled and princes toppled everywhere. And he, Qirum, was meant for better than this. He dug a leather pouch from his belt, and absently sprinkled himself with scent, of lilies, roses, saffron crocuses. In a stinking world, a stinking city, smelling good was a sign of wealth, of posterity. Troy was the past, the place he had begun his journey in life, not the place he would end it.

Praxo emerged at last, dressed in a tunic that looked more stain than cloth, with his weapons on his back, his battleaxe and heavy sword. He carried a sack with the bits of booty they carried to pay their way around the city. 'That last stool was a beauty. I feel like I gave birth to a tree.'

'Of all your revolting habits, your boasting about your bowel movements is the worst.'

'I try to please.'

The trumpets pealed again. Looking east over the outer city's walls Qirum glimpsed movement, a river of people, the glitter of bronze, banners fluttering in the languid air. Hatti! He felt as if he could smell the gold. 'Come on.'

Praxo said, 'You have an admirer.'

Qirum glanced down. A boy, skinny, naked, no older than eight, turned and bent, showing his bare arse. Qirum turned away, disgusted.

But Praxo lingered. 'Oh, aren't you going to give this little one a ride? Just for old times' sake. After all he's got to start some-where in the world. Selling the only thing he's got, just like you did. Come on, be a sport!'

Qirum stalked away from the boy, from Praxo, emptied his head of the goading, and focused his gaze on the glitter of Hatti bronze.

4

On the day of her mother's interment Milaqa woke early in her cell, deep in the belly of the Wall, in the District known as Great Etxelur. It had been an uneasy night, of dreams of dead iron punching through ribcages. It was a relief when the flickering torch glow around the door of her room was at last dimmed by the cold grey of dawn.

She clambered off her bed, a pallet of soft deerskin on a growstone platform, heaped with blankets of aurochs wool and cloth. Moving quickly in the cold, she stripped off yesterday's tunic and loincloth. She drank water from the bowl she had brought in last night, and emptied her bladder into a channel that led her urine away to the fullers' tanks somewhere deep in the fabric of the Wall. She voided her bowels into her night bowl, cleaned herself with a handful of dried moss, and pulled on fresh clothes, leggings and boots. She took her cloak, picked up the night bowl, and pulled back the heavy linen door flap.

And for a heartbeat she paused, and looked back at her room in the glow from the passage torches. This was a new apartment, freshly cut into impossibly ancient growstone. The bed, table, shelves were all made of the original growstone too, lumps of it left unremoved by the artisans who had carved out these rooms. Such apartments, brand new, exclusive and very expensive, were owned by the House of the Owl, the Annids, and were really meant for clerks and other officers of the Annid order, or were used in a pinch by guests of the government of Northland. Milaqa had been loaned it as a favour by her mother, the Annid of Annids, and her stuff, her clothes, the little pouch with mementoes of her mother, sat in the alcoves chipped into the walls. Well, Kuma was dead now, and once the interment was done Milaqa would have to give up the apartment. But when the Annids came to throw her out, at least they would find the place tidy and clean, dignified. She let the door flap fall closed.

She walked out along the passage towards its open end, and the gathering light of the spring sky. She passed other doors on the way, and heard human sounds, people softly moving about their morning business, a baby crying. The corridor gave onto a gallery cut into the Wall's growstone face. She made her way a few paces along to a vertical gutter incised into the face, where she dumped her night soil. The ordure slithered down the gutter, heading for a heap at the Wall's base, where it would be collected by workers of the House of the Beetle to be dug into the soil far from the Wall.

The waking world below the Wall was a plain stretching off to the far distance, punctuated by sheets of water and soft low hills. From here you could make out the artifice of the whole world, from the flood mounds on which the big communal houses sat, to the dead-straight lines of the main tracks and the great diagonal canals, a framework which contained patches of forest and marsh in its tidy quilted pattern. Fires sparked everywhere, and smoke rose up through the morning mist. Already people were making their way towards the Wall along the main tracks, bringing fish, meat, eel, wildfowl – the fruit of the marshlands brought to feed the communities of the great growstone heap. Along the canal banks people were out too, throwing offerings of broken bronze tools or pottery or scraps of food into the water, praying for the beneficence of the little mothers.

And over all this loomed the face of the Wall, within which she stood. It curved inwards, subtly, a tremendous concave flank to match the stout belly of its sea-facing side. Thanks to the curve Milaqa could make out much of the detail of its nearby face: the etching of the galleries where lamps flickered and people walked, the ladders and netting hanging from the

16

balconies, and a huge, rickety scaffolding of wood where workers were already out fixing a deep crack in the face with fresh growstone. Up above, on the Wall's roof, she could make out great frames with sails that turned languidly in the breeze; day and night the invisible muscles of the wind lifted pallets of excess water from the foot of the Wall and dumped it into the ocean. There were birds too, a few early arrivals already colonising cracks and crevices in this huge human-built cliff. Later in the year the boys would be climbing across the Wall's face, clinging to crevices with fingers and bare toes – searching for eggs, just as she and Hadhe, her cousin and closest friend, used to when they were a few years younger.

This was Great Etxelur, the District that was the very heart of the Wall, looming over the huddle of Old Etxelur below. But beyond the nearby clutter the Wall went on and on, to east and west, until it became a pale line in the misty air that stretched to the horizon, inhabited all along its length, the Districts strung out like shells on a bracelet. Children often grew up believing the Wall went on for ever. The truth was almost as staggering; the Wall had its limits, it did come to an end, but not until it had spanned the whole of the northern shore of Northland, a reach of very many days' travel.

And all along that length, and across hundreds of human generations, it kept the ocean at bay. It was deliciously scary, if you were snuggled up safe in your bed at night deep inside the Wall, to think that the sea level was far above your head.

The day was growing lighter while she stood here. The time of her mother's interment, at noon, was not far away. She ought to go to the great meeting chamber known as the Vestibule, the entrance to the deeper warrens that led to the Hall of Interment. She ought to be talking gravely about her dead mother to aunts and nieces, to her mother's colleagues in the House of the Owl.

Or she could run off and see if Hadhe was up yet. Hadhe, Milaqa's cousin, had children, two of her own and one adopted, and her little one was ill, which was why she was spending the winter in the shelter of the Wall, on the outskirts of the

17

neighbouring District, the Scambles. Her own home, a house in a place called Sunflower down by the Brother River, would have been too damp for a sickly little boy.

The kids would have got Hadhe up by now.

Impulsively Milaqa turned to her left, to the east, away from the Vestibule, and began to run lightly along the galleries, the roughened growstone secure under her feet. She greeted people she knew, and nodded to strangers, and grinned at the children who were already swarming everywhere, even so early on a cold day. On the big scaffolding platform the workers stirred their huge ceramic pots of growstone, pouring in crushed rock and lime and water. These members of the House of the Beaver, mostly men, called out to her as she passed, every word obscene, and she made fist-pumping gestures back at them.

She ducked inwards, into the body of the Wall. She climbed staircases and hurried along torchlit corridors cut through the growstone itself. As she ran on the nature of the galleries and passages subtly changed. Here, for instance, marigolds from the marshland, early bloomers, had been gathered and stuck in pots cut into the walls. The Wall was not the same everywhere, and nor were the people living in it, its Districts as different as the villages of the plain, each unique if only in small ways. And the further you went, the more different the people became, even in the way they dressed and spoke. Milaqa, who had a talent for languages as much as for anything, knew that a Wall-dweller from the western end, near the Albia coast, could not communicate with an inhabitant from the eastern end, near the estuary of the World River. And yet they all inhabited the same Wall, the one immense building; and they all worked together to maintain the Wall and the lands it depended on.

She loved this place, the crowded communities, the corridors and galleries, the taverns – even the graffiti on the walls, layers of it, the sharp-cut recent additions obliterating the older marks beneath, some in forgotten languages. It was probably the nearest she was ever going to come to the cities of the east that the traders and travellers told of, where people lived in great heaped-up stone piles. Northland, her homeland, with its canals and landscapes and its smattering of people, with its emptiness and austerity and duty, wasn't enough for her. But the Wall itself was something else.

She soon came to where Hadhe was staying, in a chalet in the growstone loaned her by a fisher family who were wintering on Kirike's Land. Milaqa was greeted by the sight of a ten-year-old boy calmly standing by a waste duct with his tunic pulled up, urinating into the air. His young bladder was strong, and the pale liquid arced far out into the void.

'Jaro, stop that,' she said, stalking up. 'Use the gutters like everybody else. How would you like it if you woke up to find somebody pissing on your head?'

He turned to face her, his penis in his hand still dribbling. 'Are you looking at my cock, Aunt Milaqa?'

'Looking for it, maybe, little boy. Put it away before I throw you over too.'

'All right, all right.' He tied up his loincloth, dropped his tunic and ran off, disappearing into the maze of galleries.

'Hello, Milaqa.' Her cousin Hadhe came out along the passage, carrying a double armful of bowls of soil. One was full of vomit.

'Let me help you with that.' Milaqa took the vomit-filled bowl. 'Little Blane, is it?'

'Poor mite's not been right all winter. The priests can't do anything for him. Coughing all night, and he keeps Jaro and Keli awake too, and what he does eat he throws back up. I'm surprised we've not had to put him up on the roof already . . .' Side by side the cousins tipped the bowls of soil into the waste gullies cut into the Wall face. 'As for Jaro, a right pest he's turning out to be, and as randy as his father, from what I remember of him, even if he doesn't know what to do with his little man yet. He shows it to *me* the whole time, and I'm the nearest thing he's got to a mother.' Hadhe sighed, and brushed a lank of dirty hair back from her face.

Milaqa saw how tired her cousin looked, how ill, her face slack and grey, her shoulders stooped, her breasts heavy with

19

milk. She was fifteen, a year younger than Milaqa. 'It was good of you to take in Jaro. You already had your hands full after you lost Jac.'

Jac, Hadhe's husband, had been a fisherman, whose first wife had died when Jaro was small. Then Jac had got himself caught in a storm and killed just after getting Hadhe pregnant with little Blane, her own second child.

Hadhe shrugged. 'Everybody has kids. Half the kids die, or if they don't their parents do, and you have to take in the orphans. This is the way we live our lives, isn't it? Except *you*, up to now, anyway. Even *you'll* have to settle down sometime.'

'And be like you?' Milaqa snapped. Hadhe recoiled, and Milaqa reached out her hands. 'I'm sorry. I didn't mean that.'

'Yes, you did. Oh, forget it. You're not yourself; I've seen that since your mother died. Speaking of which – when is her interment? Oh, it's today, isn't it? So why are you here?'

'I . . .' Milaqa didn't really know.

From along the gallery, a child started crying.

Hadhe sighed. 'That's Blane. He needs me. And your mother needs you. Go, Milaqa.' And she picked up her bowls and turned away.

5

Outside Troy's broken walls, the land under a harsh noon sun was dusty, rocky, bare, marked by a few abandoned dust-bowl fields. Roads radiated away from this place, roads that had once carried the seaborne produce of Mycenae and the other Greek cities overland to much of Anatolia – roads now becoming invisible beneath the drift of the dust, the product of decades of drought. Qirum felt his mouth dry, his skin desiccating, and he pulled a soft felt hat from his belt to shield his brow from the spring sun.

Qirum and Praxo were not alone in coming out of Troy to greet the train. Alerted by the war trumpets, vendors drifted up to offer the troops water, food, trinkets, whores, and slavers came out to take a first look at the fresh merchandise.

And Qirum heard a deep rumble of thousands of voices. Here came the march.

They climbed a ridge to see better. The caravan was revealed as a tremendous column stretching back along the road from the east as far as Qirum could see, thousands of feet raising a long yellow dust cloud. Somewhere behind the column itself must come the baggage train, ox carts bearing the senior officers and a Hatti prince or two in command, and heaps of booty, gold and silver and defeated gods, and the tremendous quantities of food and water required to keep this shuffling crowd alive. There would even be cattle and sheep, stolen herds driven along the trail.

But the people came by first. The Hatti infantry walked in files alongside the main column, their officers on horseback. They were Hatti warriors, each with a loose shin-length robe tied around by a leather belt, and a conical helmet, spear and sword, and that oddly shaped shield of theirs, a slab of wood and leather with rounded corners and indents to either side. They all wore their hair long and plaited so it hung down their backs, and Qirum, who had fought Hatti, knew that this thick tail afforded a little extra protection to the neck. The walk had clearly gone on for many days; the soldiers looked footsore, their pace a dull plod. But their officers looked reasonably alert. From horseback they scanned the country for bandits and robbers, and watched the column of marchers they shepherded.

And that column was made up of ordinary folk, not soldiers, two or three or four abreast, men, women and children alike, shuffling in dull misery.

Qirum stared curiously at the booty people. He had seen such columns before, but you never got used to the sight. Here was the population of a town, or maybe even a whole country, emptied out once the fighting was done, the warriors killed off, the buildings looted and torched, grain stores and farms picked over – and the people rounded up and driven out. Most of the captives had their hands tied up with rope. Some were hobbled, and walked with difficulty. Most were clothed, some in the ragged remains of what might have been fine clothes, but some went naked, perhaps after some act of spite or punishment by their guards, or even after being robbed by their fellow captives. And many walked barefoot, with splashes of dried blood about battered feet and legs. Qirum saw few old folk, and nobody obviously lame, and few little ones, toddlers too heavy to carry but too young to be able to sustain the pace. The marches were a great winnowing, and their trails were always littered with corpses. As always some of the more attractive women and girls had evidently been used by the soldiers; you could see it in the way they walked, the state of their clothes, the bruising and the blood. Was there a lack of young men? They were always the most trouble, but the most valuable on the slave markets.

Most trudged in silence. Qirum realised now that the crowd

murmur he had heard came mostly from the soldiers. This tremendous column was actually quiet, for its numbers.

Praxo nudged Qirum, for coming past them now was a group of young women – six or seven of them, no more than girls really, it was difficult to tell their ages under matted hair and caked dirt. They wore similar clothes, or the remains of them, tunics of pale linen edged with what looked like gold thread. Most walked with their heads down, as if they neither knew nor cared where they were. One had a kind of bag over her head, obscuring her face. A taller, perhaps older woman walked behind them, her long robe a shapeless rag, her face hidden by a dusty hood.

'Come on,' Praxo murmured to Qirum. 'Let's do some shopping.'

'I doubt you're going to find many fresh apples in that barrel, friend.'

'They always keep some whole to get a better price from the slavers.' He nudged Qirum's back. 'Go on. Pick a couple for us. You do the talking . . .'

They fell in pace with the column. Qirum nodded in a friendly fashion to the nearest soldier, a tough-looking veteran of maybe thirty who walked with a slight limp. He regarded Qirum and Praxo with blank contempt, as all soldiers regarded those who were not soldiers. But his interest quickened when Praxo dug a pouch out of his sack and threw it to him.

'Wine and water,' Qirum said, trying his Mycenaean Greek. 'Keep it.' The soldier took the pouch but looked blank. You never knew with Hatti soldiers; their empire was a conglomerate of many peoples, of vassal kingdoms and dependencies like Troy itself, all ruled by the kings at Hattusa. Qirum switched to the language the Hatti used themselves, which they called Nesili, supposedly the language of their old kings. 'Wine and water,' he repeated.

This time the man nodded grudgingly. One-handed, holding his spear, the soldier flipped out the stopper and took a deep draught. 'Thanks.' He held out the pouch.

Qirum waved it away. 'I told you, keep it.'

The soldier shrugged and passed the pouch to the fellow behind him. One or two of the prisoners looked on longingly. The soldier looked Qirum up and down as they walked by the column. 'What are you, a sailor? I can tell by the stink of salt under the woman's perfume you're wearing.'

'We're traders. A bit of this, a bit of that – you know. Who are this lot?'

'Arzawans. Always a troublesome bunch. This action should keep them quiet for a while. We'll sell some to the slavers from Egypt and Assyria. The rest are going to be used to rebuild some city up in the north.'

That, Qirum knew, was the way of the Hattusa kings – to move whole captive populations around the country, to sell them on, or recruit them into the armies, or use them in the fields, or to repopulate empty cities or countries. The strategy of an empire always short of manpower.

The soldier eyed Qirum. 'As for you, I can guess what you're sniffing around.'

'Just one of these beauties in the robes,' Praxo said in his own rough Hatti, and he licked his lips. 'One for me and my buddy to share.'

The soldier looked faintly disgusted. 'Not this lot. Temple maidens. Or court servants. Something like that. Should fetch a high price.'

Qirum grinned easily. 'Your sergeant will get the profit, not you. You've come all this way, you're at the gates of Troy itself, the city of traders. Why not make it worth your while? I know it's against the rules. But look along the line.' The soldier turned his head. All along the column the traders from Troy were doing bits of business with the soldiers. 'Everybody's at it. Nobody's watching. Nobody's going to miss *one*.'

'These girls are special. They'll have been counted.'

'Then say she fell to a scorpion bite in the night. Oh, come on.' Qirum dug into Praxo's pouch and dug out a broken silver necklace. 'Look at that. Egyptian. Made for the wife of a pharaoh.'

24

In fact, that was true. 'You and your pal could have a fine night in Troy for that. Believe me, it's not a pricey town.'

The soldier's comrade saw the necklace, and murmured something.

The soldier laughed. 'All right. Just get her out of here quick before the officers notice.'

Qirum handed over the silver chain.

The soldier reached back for the girl with the bag over her head, grabbed the bonds of thick rope that tied her wrists together, and pulled her away from the others. One of her companions called out. Maybe this was a sister, Qirum thought, or a friend, about to lose a companion she would never see again, but the soldier glared, and she shrank back. Praxo grabbed the girl's bound wrists in one huge fist, and squeezed her rump with the other hand. The girl stumbled, instinctively trying to pull away. She turned her bagged head fitfully, this way and that.

Qirum frowned. He had caught a whiff of corruption. 'There's something wrong.' He had been sold sick slaves and whores before, or insane ones; you had to be careful.

'Yes. There is something wrong with her.' The voice, speaking Nesili, was commanding, clear – and a woman's.

Qirum turned. It was the older woman who had been walking behind the girls, her hands tied as theirs were. Now she shook back her hood to reveal a face of fine command, despite streaks of dirt and blood and a shaven scalp. Like an eagle, Qirum immediately thought. A downed eagle.

The soldier who had spoken to Qirum strode over and aimed a punch at her.

Qirum called impulsively, 'No. Let her speak.'

Praxo was holding the girl by her wrists at arm's length. 'What's wrong with this one?'

'See for yourself,' the woman said. 'Pull back that bag.'

The soldiers looked at each other, and shrugged.

Praxo pulled the bag from the girl's head. Flies swarmed out, buzzing, and Praxo flinched, gagging.

Qirum put his fingers under the girl's chin and raised her face. Her eye sockets were pits of black corruption; he saw maggots squirm.

'This is what we do,' the older woman said.

' "We"?'

'She tried to escape. She flirted with the guard in the night. He loosened her bonds and she ran. Every night, some run – sometimes hundreds. Better the parched land than slavery, I suppose. Most are caught. They are punished like this – with blinding. It does not harm their capacity to walk, you see. Or to work, in some circumstances. In a mill, chained to a wheel. Or pulling an oar on a ship like yours, trader. Or a brothel. But it is a punishment that makes further escape impossible, and deters the rest, of course.'

'You said, "we". What did you mean?'

'Take me and I will tell you.'

Now Qirum laughed. 'A wizened old stick like you?'

'I am thirty-two years old. Take me – buy *me*, not one of these girls.'

'Why would I do that?'

'I am not like these others.' She broke out of the line and pushed past the soldiers. The one negotiating with Qirum went to grab her, but she shook him off. She stood before Qirum, filthy, hands bound, head held high. 'I am not Arzawan. I am Hatti. I am of the royal family, of the family of the first Great King Hattusili, who reigned five centuries ago having descended from the Annita kings before him.'

Praxo snorted. 'Everybody in Hattusa is related to a king.'

She ignored him and kept her gaze on Qirum. Her eyes were an extraordinary pale brown, almost yellow. 'My name is Kilushepa. I am Tawananna.'

Praxo frowned. 'What does that mean? Tawananna?'

'Queen,' Qirum said. His heart was pounding at this utterly unexpected turn of events. 'It means queen.'

'I was delivered into this bondage by my enemies. You can free me from it.'

26

'Why should I?'

'I have a plan. I will return to Hattusa. I will save it, with your help – and you will be rewarded.'

Qirum felt he ought to be laughing at these grandiose claims from a woman in a queue of booty people. 'Why me?'

'Because I see something in you, trader, sailor. Pirate, are you? Raider? Well, such are the times we live in. I see a spark. A potential. Something I can work with. And because—' with an extraordinary flash of humour, '—I don't have much choice, do I?'

Praxo shook his head. 'Even if this woman's telling the truth, you're a trader, brother. You're not a king, or a kingmaker.'

Qirum snarled, 'You don't know what I am, or could be. You don't know anything about me.'

'You're a street kid from the ruins of Troy!'

'Shut up.' He met the woman's steady gaze.

Bound as she was, helpless before the men who surrounded her, she seemed utterly fearless. 'What is your name?'

'Qirum. I am Qirum.'

'You have dreams, don't you, Qirum? Dreams that burn you up at night – or nightmares—'

'That's the future. What can you promise me now?'

She stepped closer, and he could smell the dust of the arid plain on her breath. 'I was a queen. For a decade I entranced a king, until his enemies, and mine, struck him down. Tonight I will entrance you.'

'No,' Praxo called. 'This isn't good. This isn't right. I can feel it. No good will come of you coupling with this witch. Qirum, there are any number of girls here, some of them tupped only once or twice, probably. Pick another. Not her!'

But Qirum could not draw his gaze from her pale brown eyes, windows to the future.

6

Teel met Milaqa as she entered the Vestibule. He wore his ceremonial robe of leather stitched with owl feathers, and cap adorned with the beak and talons of the bird, the Other of his House, the Annids. The ground-length robe hid his excess bulk and made him look imposing rather than fat. 'You're late,' he said. He wrinkled his nose. 'And you smell of sweat. You've been running, I suppose. Well, you're here now . . .'

He led her to the stone table on which her mother's remains lay, a jumble of bones under the bronze breastplate.

The dignitaries solemnly gathered around, lit by lamps of whale oil that flickered in alcoves cut into walls rubbed smooth by generations of passage. All the great and ancient Houses were represented here. The Annids, of course, in their cloaks of owl feathers like Teel's – all women save for Teel, for few men would pay the price of joining the Order of those who governed Northland. Then there were the priests with their mouths made grotesque by the teeth of their own Other, the Wolf, and the Beavers and the Voles, workers of Wall and land, and Jackdaws, the traders – even a few representatives of the lowly but essential House of the Beetle, who cleaned drains and dredged canals and shipped waste, resplendent today in their carapaces of polished black leather. Most exotic of all to Milaqa's eyes were the Swallows, the wayfinders, the sailors and navigators and surveyors, men and women who mapped the world in their heads and knew the shape of it. Her own uncle Deri, Teel's brother, was a Swallow, but today he was out on the ocean. Of all the Orders, Milaqa longed most of all to be a Swallow, to be standing there in one of those black shaped capes, so like graceful swallows' wings. But her strength was languages, speech, not numbers and maps.

None of these dignitaries would speak to her. Milaqa had a right to say goodbye to her mother, Kuma Annid of Annids. She had a right to be here. But she was not an Annid, and never would be, and so nobody gave Milaqa more than a passing glance.

None save Voro. The young Jackdaw, tall and ungainly, approached her, shyness and self-doubt covering him like a shadow. 'Hello, Milaqa.'

'Voro.' She puckered her lips and blew him a kiss.

He almost crumpled, blushing. She tried not to laugh. This boy had had a crush on her, she knew, since they had both been younger than Jaro. He was easy to chase away. But today he stood his ground. 'I'm sorry about your mother.'

'Well, that's why we're all here.'

'You know I was there. When she died in Albia.'

'There was nothing you could do.'

'Perhaps we could talk about it. I always thought—'

'No.' She felt impatient, irritated. Her mother's interment was no time to be dealing with what sounded dangerously like it was going to be some kind of declaration of affection. She wheeled away, leaving him standing.

Teel walked with her. 'What did he want?'

'Nothing important.'

'All right . . . There are some family here. There's my father, your grandfather Medoc.' A big man with a booming laugh, dressed in walrus fur. 'Come all the way from Kirike's Land to say goodbye to his daughter. You should talk to him.'

'All these people, all this finery – all for my mother. It's a shame she couldn't have been here to see it. I heard what they said about her when she was alive.'

'That's a mark of greatness, the quality and number of your enemies.'

'I have no enemies. I suppose I will never be great.'

'But you must find your place. "Everyone in Etxelur is a hunter and a scholar." You know that's the rule, Milaqa. You know it's your duty, you must find your place. And if you haven't made your House choice by the appropriate Family Day, which I remind you is the spring equinox of your sixteenth year and will be here soon, the choice will be made for you.'

He was right, of course. Northlanders were comparatively few, and their very land survived only through continued and dedicated maintenance. Everybody had to play a part. 'You sound like my mother.'

'Good. My sister was a great Annid of Annids.'

A priest stepped forward now, murmuring a prayer to the little mothers, and the babble of conversation hushed. The priest scattered a salty incense over Kuma's shrunken corpse. Then, gently, he lifted the damaged breastplate away from her chest, and handed it to a member of the House of the Owl. The plate would be passed on to the next Annid of Annids, when she (or, just possibly, he) was chosen. Now the priest reverently wrapped up Kuma's bones in a cloth blanket and lifted her up. Milaqa saw her mother's head loll, the fleshless jaw gaping. Carrying the corpse the priest made for the door. There he was met by a senior Annid, a severe older woman called Noli, and a procession began to form up behind them.

'Walk with me,' Teel murmured to Milaqa.

The two of them took their places at the rear of the group of Annids, who in turn led the priests and the wayfinders and the others, with the humble Beetles bringing up the rear. Then, to the soft beat of a drum, they shuffled forward, along a candlelit passage that led deeper into the Wall. They turned corners, and soon the last of the daylight was excluded. The corridor was musty and dry. When Milaqa glanced back she noticed the Beavers looking around, sniffing the air for damp, instinctively checking the walls for crumbling and mould. One of them carried a pot in which liquid growstone sloshed.

30

'We're walking very slowly,' she whispered to Teel. 'I wish we could get this over with.'

'Have you not been to one of these ceremonies before?'

'Not since my father died, and I was very small then.'

'Not even for the family?'

'I always chose not to come. I suppose you'll say that's me running away from my responsibilities again.'

'There are men and women younger than you who are already in their Houses of choice, training as wayfarers or builders – even as priests and Annids.'

'I have no skill.'

'Your languages are good. Everybody says that.'

'I only learned them because of getting drunk with traders and sailors in the taverns in the Scambles, and nobody approves of that.'

'It doesn't matter how you learn. What matters is ability. With a skill like that you could become a Jackdaw.'

She sniffed. 'Like Voro? Haggling over tokens of clay? Travelling to mines in Albia, or stinking farms on the Continent? I don't think so.'

'Nevertheless you must do something. Actually I have an idea,' Teel said. 'Something that might help you decide.'

'I'm wary of your ideas.'

'You're probably right to be. Call it an assignment.'

'What assignment?'

But he had no time to reply, for they had reached the Hall of Interment.

In the weak glow of smoky lamps this long, shallow room extended out of sight to left and right. The wall opposite was a smooth growstone surface with small alcoves cut into it in rows. Milaqa was reminded of a sandy river bank, the burrows of sand martins above the water. All the alcoves nearby were open, those further away blocked off, their shapes clearly visible in the discolouring of the growstone. There was a soft breeze. Somehow air reached this place, feeding the lamps, and the people who quietly spread out into the room.

The priest stepped forward, lifted the slight bundle in his arms, and slid it into an alcove at chest height. He chanted a series of numbers: 'One. One. Five. Four. Four. Two. Four. Two. Three. Five. Two.'

A mason, clad in a cloak of beaver fur, armed with a shaped chisel, stepped forward. Briskly he stamped the priest's number into the wall below Kuma's alcove, using the ancient concentric-circle number symbols of Etxelur. The priest began to chant, in a language so old it was unknown even to Milaqa.

Teel murmured, 'Do you remember this place from your father's ceremony?'

'I remember the holes in the wall. They scared me.'

'Yes . . . The priest has recited the number of the day. Do you know about that? We began the counting from the very day Prokyid saved us from the Second Great Sea. Prokyid left us a system of cycles, based on the number five.' He spread his hand in the gloom. 'For five fingers. The last of the priest's eleven numbers was two; we are in the second day of the current eleventh cycle of five days. The second last number was five. We are in the fifth element of the current tenth cycle of five fives, which is twenty-five days. The third last number was three. We are in the third—'

'The traders talk with a system based on tens. Hundreds, thousands.'

'Well, so do the common folk, mostly. I'm told the priests' count of days has reached somewhere over five thousand years.'

It was an incomprehensible number. 'We've been counting the days that long?'

'Oh, yes. But our history goes back even before that, and we plan for a future stretching far ahead, and our calendar accommodates that. Remember, we have *eleven* cycles. The first cycle is five fives of fives of—'

'What language is the priest using?'

'It is said to be the language spoken even before Prokyid, perhaps in the time of Ana, who built Etxelur.'

'Ana is a little mother. So is Prokyid.'

'Yes, but they were both human too. Gods made incarnate. Don't you know any of this? You aren't cut out for the House of the Wolf, are you? The priest is consigning your mother to the endless sleep of the little mothers. The Wall is built not just of rock and growstone but of the bones of all our ancestors, back to the days of Prokyid, even the mythical time of Ana, who defied the First Great Sea. All our ancestors sleep in the stone that defies the sea.

'The priest is reminding your mother that the Wall is not still. As the sea wears the Wall away at its front, we build it up at the back. Thus the Wall itself is like a slow tide, that marches slowly back across the land. And Kuma is learning that the day will come when the alcove of stone in which she lies will be opened by the sea, and then she will have a new flesh of stone, and muscles of air, and she too will join the endless war against the sea . . .'

Another mason came forward with his bucket of growstone. With a shining bronze spoon he began to ladle it into the hole, sealing in Kuma until her liberation by the sea, in the far future.

Milaqa thought about Teel. She had lost her father when she was very small, and her uncles, Teel and Deri, loomed huge in her memories of her childhood, these brothers of her mother, then young men with faces like her own. While Deri had taken her sailing in his fishing boat, Teel had played elaborate games with her, testing her mind, making her think. Now that her mother was gone, she reflexively looked to Teel for guidance. Yet there had always been something opaque about Teel. She had grown up not quite knowing if she understood him, or if she could trust him. She wished Deri was here. Or better yet her mother.

She whispered, 'What assignment were you talking about?'

He pressed something into her hand. In the uncertain light of the wall lamps, she saw it was the iron arrowhead.

'Find out who killed your mother, and why.'

7

Qirum decided that a queen should not enter Troy by climbing through a generations-old hole in city walls smashed by marauding Greeks. No, she would enter by the gates, like royalty.

So he walked her around the walls. He'd had Praxo cut the shackles on her ankles, but at Praxo's dogged insistence they kept the ropes on her wrists. Kilushepa must have been exhausted; if so, she did not show it in her face, or her gait, and as she walked on doggedly she gazed around, imperiously curious. Praxo followed, silent and resentful.

As they skirted the city, to their left was what remained of the wooden outer walls and the double-ditch earthworks, built to keep out war chariots, now clogged with twenty years of debris. To the right was the shore, a long, sandy beach, the lagoon beyond swampy and plagued by mosquitoes. Ships were pulled up on the strand, each the centre of an impromptu camp, and sailors, traders, wives, children and whores followed rough trails between the ships and the city. It was the sea that had always given Troy its commanding position; the city dominated the sea lanes between Anatolia and Greece, and controlled trade with the rich lands of Asia to the north.

Qirum said to Kilushepa, 'The currents are strong here. Takes some skill landing. The traffic is not what it was twenty-five years ago, before the Greeks sacked the place. But it is a valuable site for all that.'

'Of course. The logic of land and sea is unchanged, no matter how much men may loot and burn. Troy will recover. And is this the gate?'

It was a break in the wall, flanked by two imposing stone columns carved with the image of the god Appaliunas. The god-stones had survived the fires, but the gates and wooden curtain wall had not, and traffic flowed around the standing stones, rough carts drawn by oxen and horses, people on foot, a few on horseback. Within the walls the city stank of dung and piss and rot. Kilushepa stared around without comment, at rubble and shacks and half-collapsed walls. The Pergamos still rose up, dominating the lower city, a citadel within a city. Hattusa itself was laid out like this; it was the Anatolian fashion. But this citadel's watchtowers were smashed and fallen, and you could see the ruins of the palace, and the temples and abandoned mansions that surrounded it.

'Once this area was crowded with houses,' Qirum said to Kilushepa. Oddly he felt as if he was apologising for his city. 'Shops, traders' posts, markets. There was a big slavers' market just over there, and that big ruin was a granary. The houses crowded right up to the city walls. And there were tight little alleyways where you could barely see where you were going, and you'd always get lost. So they say . . .'

As they stood there, children began to emerge from the rubble. Dust-covered, they were the same colour as the fallen houses. Kilushepa did not seem to see them, though they stood before her and plucked her robe. They came to her, Qirum saw, responding to her regal aspect, despite her own filthy clothes, and the dirt and blood on her face, and the bonds that still tied her wrists. Maybe she really was a queen.

Qirum led Kilushepa to the broken-down house he had been sharing with Praxo. At least there were no whores hanging around looking for repeat business. He took her to the room he had been using, the one room that still had a roof on it. Kilushepa stood amid the debris as if she belonged to some other reality.

'Sit.' Qirum indicated the pallet on the floor.

Elegantly she settled down. Some of the tension seemed to

leave her body. The room was warm, the light that flooded through the doorway bright.

'Are you hungry?'

'I have been walking rather a long time. But my thirst is greater.'

'Praxo. Water and wine. Go fetch some.'

Praxo hovered in the doorway, huge, scowling. 'No good will come of this, Qirum. Hump her, get it out of your system, and have done with it.'

'Water!'

Growling, Praxo went off.

'He is jealous,' Kilushepa said with a smile. 'I notice that, among young men who fight side by side.'

'Forget him,' Qirum said.

'Yes. Forget him. Here we are, the two of us, alone. Surely the gods have brought us together to serve their purposes. Let us tell each other who we are.'

'You are really a Hatti queen?'

'I was the senior wife of King Hattusili, who was the fifth of that name in our history. He in turn had taken the throne from his cousin Suppiluliama, the second of that name, who almost lost Hattusa at the height of the uprising.'

'What uprising?'

'The one we are still putting down. It is the famine, Qirum. Hungry people do not listen to princes or priests. They move to where they think the food is. They storm cities for their granaries. And then provinces and vassal territories rebel, and our neighbours make war and invade. Hattusa has always been surrounded by enemies, within and without. Some of our historians say it has been a wonder of diplomacy that we, my family, has managed to maintain the realm across five centuries . . . Of course we are not alone – even the Egyptians are suffering from the famine, and the Greeks' petty kingdoms are falling like rotten fruit from a dead branch.

'My husband Hattusili was able to take the throne from his cousin because he was able to promise a new source of food. We had been relying on grain from southern Anatolia and from Egypt, but the trade routes were precarious. And our access to our source of tin, too far to the east, was always uncertain. But my husband, as a young man, had travelled, and he forged a trading link with an empire far to the west of here, called *Northland*.' She said this word in a tongue with which Qirum was unfamiliar. 'They send us tin from their own sources. And they send us food, great barrels of it, by the shipload. In return we send them wealth of various sorts. I think they see us as useful, because we help keep the pirates and raiders – people like you, Qirum – away from their ships, and ultimately their own lands and their allies.'

'What kind of food? Grain, meat?'

'Not that. Food made from the produce of plants we have no knowledge of. And they do not send us the seed stock so we cannot grow it ourselves. Northland is a strange country that nobody has ever been to and nobody knows anything about.'

'And you were involved with this?'

'I was senior wife of Hattusili the Fifth. I was involved in the negotiations with the Northlanders. But Hattusili died. Some say it was plague.' Her face was blank. 'He was succeeded by his nephew, Hattusili the Sixth, who is a callow boy much under the influence of another of his uncles. In our court, you may know, a queen who survives her husband has influence. I was Tawananna. I *am* Tawananna. I had priestly responsibilities, and was involved in diplomacy and affairs of state. It is our way.'

'But Hattusili the Sixth—'

'Or his uncle.'

'Found you in the way.'

'I was asked to help organise a major military expedition against the Arzawans, of western Anatolia, who as you know have always been a problem. But this was a ruse to get me out of Hattusa. Once I was alone with the King's soldiers, away from the palace bodyguards, I was taken. Hands were laid on me.' She paused. Qirum could imagine what had followed. 'I was thrown among the population of a captured city. Those around me did not believe I was who I said I was. So I was brought here. And then I met you.'

'And in me, you saw . . .'

'A chance.'

'What do you want?'

'Ultimately, to return to Hattusa in triumph. To remove the fool Hattusili from the throne along with his obnoxious uncle, and to install my own son in his place – if my boy survives.'

Qirum was astonished; in this saga of palace politics and betrayal this was the first time she had mentioned she had children.

'And, incidentally, I will save the Hatti kingdom from drought and famine, and secure our future for all time, so that we may fulfil our service to the great Storm God Teshub.' She was exhausted, he saw, barely able to sit up straight. Yet her words were strong and clear.

He had to laugh, though. 'Is that all? And how will you achieve that?'

'By using my knowledge of Northland. My links with it. I will go there. *We must acquire the seed stock behind their strange food.* We cannot remain dependent on the goodwill of a country so far away. I have thought on this for a long time. It was a project I pursued before I was deposed, in fact. It remains a valid strategic goal. And with that treasure I will buy back my influence and position at court.'

All this sounded impossible, a fantasy. He had only a hazy idea where Northland actually was; although he had travelled far compared to most, he could not even imagine such a journey. 'The Northlanders won't just give such a prize to you. Look at you – you're in rags – you have no power to speak for the King in Hattusa. What could you possibly have to trade?'

'In these turbulent times, they and their allies will receive the partnership and the protection of the mightiest empire the world has ever seen.'

There was a guffaw from the doorway – Praxo, laden with sacks of water. 'Trojan, you need to stop up that mouth of hers

38

with your pork sword before she makes me piss my pants laughing.' He threw down the sacks.

Qirum set a sack before Kilushepa, and loosened the bonds at her wrists so she could drink.

'I won't tell you how much this water cost me,' Praxo said, settling to the floor. 'There's a secret pipeline, you know. Laid down in previous generations by wise rulers, to keep the town watered during sieges. There's a sort of cabal that knows where it is, and runs it. About the only place you can get clean water in Troy nowadays. I hope what you've got between your legs is worth it, oh queen.'

She did not reply. She merely drank, steadily.

Gently, Qirum took the sack away from her. 'Take it easy. Your stomach needs to get used to being full. You're expecting me to help you achieve this dream you speak of?'

'As I said, I don't have much choice.' She turned that startlingly pale gaze on him again. 'But perhaps the old gods favoured me. For I saw something in you, Qirum. Something you may not know is there yourself. A hunger. I think you will rise up from this squalor, the ruins of a devastated town . . .'

Praxo swigged wine and laughed. 'You've got it wrong, lady. If not for this squalor he wouldn't exist at all.'

'Be still, Praxo.'

'No, it's true. He was conceived on the very night Troy fell to the Greeks. I don't suppose he told you *that*. His mother was a highborn, supposedly, but everybody in Troy these days says they are descended from highborns—'

'Shut up!'

'And his father was a Greek. It was a rape! A quick in-and-out, and the lad goes on his way for a bit more plunder and mayhem, and if he still lives he probably doesn't even remember it. Just one more hole to plug, in a long line of holes.' He gestured at Qirum. 'And here's the result. Neither Greek nor Trojan, unintended, wanted by nobody, dumped by his mother as soon as she could manage it, and left with nothing to sell but his little pink arse!'

Qirum bunched his fist, longing to strike the man. But his anger was overwhelmed by a deep ache of humiliation.

Kilushepa watched him steadily. 'We will put this right, you and I.'

These words drew him in like a fish on a line. 'How?'

'By winning. In the morning we will start.'

'And tonight?'

She held out her arms. 'If you untie me, and send away this oaf – and allow me to clean myself, to make myself as I once was – I will show you, as I promised, how I captivated a king.'

Praxo laughed, and stood clumsily. 'Well, you'll find me at the whorehouse as usual. Enjoy the night, friend, for it's all you're going to get out of that old stick.'

'Go!'

Kilushepa held out her bound arms. Entranced, fearful, Qirum reached for his knife.

8

The men hauled the skin boat safely up the beach from the rushing surf.

Tibo, exhausted by the rowing and the sun, got his father's permission to take a break. Stiffly, unused to the land after so long at sea, he walked away from the boat, up to the softer sand above the waterline. It was morning still but the sun beat down from high in a cloudless sky, and his skin prickled with sweat and sand and salt, slick with the oily unguent the men had given him to keep from burning. He climbed a shallow dune and flung himself down, panting.

He had crossed the mighty Western Ocean. He was far from home. He was fifteen years old.

From here he could see more of the landscape of this distant continent, a bank of sandy hills, a forest like a wall, remote mountains. The forest was dense and mysterious, and he saw rustlings in the green – heard a cry like a distressed child. Soon he would have to penetrate that strangeness. To his left, to the south, he saw a stream of clear-looking fresh water, gushing down a gully in the open, sandy earth and to the sea. Beyond it he saw more such streams, and further out the ocean itself was discoloured. This, his father Deri had told him, was an estuary, the outflow of a tremendous river that drained the heart of this strange country.

It was no accident the boat had landed here. Traders from Northland had been coming to this remote shore since time beyond memory, voyages recorded in graceful swirls and loops in the Archive in the Wall. With Deri's detailed periplus and the knowledge and experience worn deep in the heads of the older sailors, they had made their way here without any difficulty, hopping down the long and convoluted coasts of these western continents, foraging and trading for provisions. But it was all extraordinary to Tibo, even though he had spent much of his young life travelling with his father between Northland and his father's family home on Kirike's Land, an island in the middle of the Western Ocean.

Looking back, he saw the sailors were getting on with the chore of unloading the boat. They dumped out the oars and leather sail and mast, their packs of clothing, dried food, water sacks and fishing gear. Then they turned over the boat itself to allow it to dry out, exposing a hull of tanned ox-hide crusted with barnacles. Most of the men had stripped down to their loincloths. They looked like winter animals, bears perhaps, muscular and hairy, out of place on the hot sand of the beach. A cousin of Tibo's father's called Nago, comparatively skinny, of few words but a leader when the oars came out, ran down to the sea, pissed noisily, and hurled himself into the water.

His father Deri walked up. He carried two light packs, and bronze swords in their scabbards. He sat on the dune crest, and handed his son a flask. 'We'll fill these up in the stream. You look thoughtful.'

'Look at the lads on the beach. We're a long way from home.'

'I know it's all strange,' Deri murmured. 'But we of Kirike's Land are at home here, we know our way around. You'll see.'

Deri was not yet thirty. He wore his red hair long and tied back from his face; his skin was paler than his son's and burned easily, but in the months of the journey it had weathered to a leathery texture, the creases around his eyes prominent where he had been squinting against the sun. He looked strong, at ease. Tibo couldn't believe he would ever be so effortlessly confident. And yet Deri had been younger than Tibo was now when he had become a father.

'So,' Deri said. He held out one of the packs to Tibo. 'You ready to go?'

'Go where?'

'To find the Jaguar people, of course.' He stood in a single, supple movement. 'We'll just follow the estuary inland, and into the green. You won't believe their country until you see it. And there we will beg the services of their king's sculptor.'

Tibo stood unwillingly. 'Now? We only just arrived.'

'But this is why we came.' He helped Tibo hitch the pack on his back; it was cloth and leather sturdily sewn, and it sat comfortably on a frame of willow. 'Let me tell you something. I was born on Kirike's Land but grew up in Northland, because my mother, your grandmother, came from there, and then I went back to Kirike's Land to raise my own family. And in Northland we are forever looked down on by those leathery old snobs in their great Houses, the Annids, the Wolves. We're just boatmen from some rock in the middle of the ocean, and that's all Kuma was to them. If you're low-born, you stay low-born. But now everybody agrees your aunt Kuma was one of the best Annids who ever lived.

'*That's* why we came here – we, the family of Kuma herself – you and me. We will find the sculptor who will create the greatest honour of all for Kuma, by which she will be remembered for all time.' He ruffled Tibo's hair. 'Nothing to it. Just watch where you step. Oh, and keep away from the water.' He led the way down the beach to the stream, where he bent to fill a water flask.

Tibo had no choice but to follow.

The estuary was fringed by a muddy plain, itself bordered by walls of forest. Working their way inland, father and son followed roughly defined paths that followed the edge of the forest, or cut in among the trees. Out on the mud birds worked in great flocks, exotic types that Tibo didn't recognise and Deri couldn't name. In the deeper water Tibo saw fish swim, bronze and gold, unfamiliar, and what looked like eels, and stranger shapes, long and sleek with crusty backs. Once he saw a long, flat head that seemed to be all jaw, opening and yawning,

ᴣ rows of teeth. These beasts were why, Deri said, you
be careful of going in the water, or even near it.

ᴊwards the end of the day they cut away from the water and
ᴊshed into the jungle. The trees were impossibly tall and green
and laden with vines and lichen, and the ground was choked
with undergrowth so thick you had to slash your way through
with your bronze blade. Deri knew the forest to some extent,
having travelled here at the death of the last Annid of Annids a
decade earlier, and he knew which fruit was safe to eat. You
could find rabbits and deer here, he said, brought over the ocean
in the deep past by Northlanders. And there were other sorts of
animals to hunt, such as big clumsy creatures like huge rats that
fled at their approach.

But there were other, still stranger forms lurking in the forest.
Once Tibo heard a cry, almost human, and he saw a shadow
flitting through the high branches, like a child, a thing that
clambered and swung. And, late on as the light faded, he saw
two yellow eyes peering out of the green gloom around them – a
black face, a slim muscular form. But when he looked again it
was gone.

He told Deri what he had seen. His father grinned, his teeth
white in the gloom. 'Perhaps it was a *jaguar*.' The word was
strange, not of the ancestral language of Northland. 'The god-
animal of the Jaguar folk. You are honoured; the jungle is
welcoming you.' But after that Deri kept his bronze sword
drawn and in his hand, and stayed subtly closer to his son.

Deri called a halt for the night at the edge of a wide area of
swampy land. They found a dry space away from the water, and
spread out a cloth over the ground, and hung another from a
tree branch to discourage the insects. While Deri gathered dry
wood, Tibo started a fire using a flint and a striking-stone from
his pack.

Then, before the light vanished completely, Deri beckoned to
Tibo and led him to the edge of the water. Here an extraordinary
tree grew right out of the water, a complex tangle of trunks and
branches draped with vines. Deri took off his shoes and stepped

carefully into the water, leaned down and dug in with his bare hands, scooping out crabs that he threw up the bank to Tibo. Then he took a knife and began prising off oysters and mussels that clung to the tree roots. 'This strange waterlogged tree is the whole world to these creatures.'

Tibo, avoiding the crabs' snapping claws, smashed their shells with rocks. They heated a stone slab over their fire, and cooked the crab meat in strips, and popped open the mussels and the oysters.

Night seemed to fall quickly here. Tibo was grateful for the light of the fire, which kept the looming forest shadows away.

When he woke the light of day was seeping through the seams of their thin tent. His father was still asleep. Tibo slipped on his boots and pushed his way out of the tent, naked save for his loincloth. The dawn was not far advanced, but the sky was already bright, the air already hot, and the jungle was full of birdsong and the distant cries of animals. He walked down towards the tree with the crabs and loosened his grubby loincloth. He disturbed birds that flapped away, huge and unreasonably colourful, squawking their protest.

And as he was pissing against a root he saw the girl. He jumped, and felt warm liquid splash against his leg. He had no weapons, not so much as a blunt knife.

The girl was standing on a low rise, watching him. She was naked save for a skirt of dyed cloth loosely tied around her waist. Her skin was brown, her bare breasts small. She was slender, shorter than he was. He couldn't tell how old she was. Her hair was tightly tied up, and adorned with brightly coloured feathers. She was holding a bag of knotted string, within which a small creature was curled up, like an oversized rat.

She grinned. Her teeth were grooved, he saw, striped with some red-orange dye.

She didn't offer any threat, Tibo told himself. He had just crossed an ocean to speak to these people. He smiled back. 'Hello.'

But she flinched, spat something guttural, and from nowhere produced a stone knife that she held out, pointing its tip at him.

ı right.' Deri stood beside him, as near-naked as Tibo
nese people have their own ways of speaking. To her, you
being threatening, or rude. Or both.'
ı didn't mean to—'

'Follow my lead.' He smiled at the girl, covered his eyes with
his fists, and bowed. Then he straightened up, opened his hands
palms outward so that it was as if his hands were his eyes, Tibo
saw. Then he carefully lowered his hands so his true eyes were
revealed. 'I saw her with my body, then my spirit. You aren't
real until you're seen properly. To her, it was as if you were a
corpse that just sat up and spoke.'

Tibo copied the hand-eye movements as best he could.

The girl seemed to relax. She tucked the knife into her leather
belt, and made the eye gesture, first to Deri, then Tibo.

'Try not to do anything else to alarm her. And put your cock
away.'

Tibo hastily rearranged his loincloth.

The girl jabbered something in an alien tongue, full of clicks
and stops.

Deri shook his head. 'I don't understand all that . . . *Ki-xi
wes-tar.* Deri.' He gestured. 'Tibo. *Ki-xotl t'xixi . . .*' The girl's eyes
widened, and she looked puzzled. Evidently the way he spoke
wasn't always clear, and he stumbled over the clicks with his
tongue.

In the end she grinned again, showing those grooved teeth.
'*K-xa!*' And she turned and ran off.

Tibo frowned. 'Where has she gone? What did you say to
her?'

'The only thing I know how to say. That we're from Northland, and the Annid is dead. If we're lucky she'll have gone off
to tell somebody about it.'

'And if we're not lucky?'

He sighed. 'I'll just have to try again. Or *you* can try. I'll teach
you. All those tongue-clicks are hard work. Now come on, let's
get cleaned up here and get moving.'

9

With their packs on their backs, their swords in their hands, they pressed into the jungle, the way the girl had gone. Soon they came to a narrow track through the dense green, so faint and meandering it might have been made by animals rather than people. To his relief, Tibo saw that the jungle was clearing, the land rising, and the tree cover above began to break up to reveal a sky sparsely littered with clouds.

They came to a ridge of earth, grassed over but clear of trees that stretched away through the green to left and right, a dead straight line.

Deri snorted in triumph. 'The work of the Jaguar folk!' He strode forward boldly and clambered up onto the ridge.

Tibo followed, and found himself standing on the bank of a dyke, a tremendous drainage gully that cut through the forest. Paths were laid out on both banks, tracks of wood pressed into the earth.

Deri stepped out along the path.

'This is big,' Tibo said, hurrying after him. 'Bigger than anything I've seen at home.'

'The great works in Northland dwarf anything on Kirike's Land, which is after all a small island. And they'd dwarf this too, but this is respectable. We're approaching their heartland now . . .'

They reached the edge of the forest and broke out into the open air, still following the spine of the dyke. It wasn't as hot here as at the coast; a wind blew from the north, chill and faintly damp. Tibo saw they were crossing the flood plain of a mighty river, sparsely scattered with stands of trees. In the far distance loomed mountains, the angular blue hills he had glimpsed from the sea. And at the feet of the mountains the land rose up into a plateau, edged by ridges and gullies, like a tremendous sculpture.

The whole of this landscape swarmed with people. Smoke rose everywhere, especially from that dominating plateau, and houses sat squat on the plain. Deri said the plateau was called the Altar of the Jaguar.

They came upon a party of people waiting for them, gathered around a kind of wheeled cart. Tibo recognised the girl from the river; she grinned, excited and happy, still holding the basket containing the little animal. Others stood with her, a handful of adults, dressed like her in practical-looking loincloths and with bright feathers in their hair. Her family, perhaps, her people. They smiled, evidently proud.

Two people stood on the cart's platform. One man was tall, slim, bare to the waist, his lower legs wrapped in an intricately woven cloth. He wore a mirror of bronze from a strap around his neck, and Tibo was disconcerted to see his own face looking back at him. The other was a child, standing on a kind of box and holding leather straps – no, Tibo saw, looking closely, not a child, a man, a dwarf, with a wrinkled face and an oddly misshapen skull and a vestment as expensive-looking as the other man's. The straps he held led to the heads of the two horses that drew the cart . . .

Not horses. Tibo stared, astonished. These were four-legged beasts with thick woollen coats, their legs were slim, and their necks were *long*, long and flexible and mounted by small heads. One turned to look at Tibo. It had large eyes, a kind of topknot of hair, and an oddly disapproving expression on its face.

The taller man stepped forward. He made the seeing-hand gesture to both the newcomers, and spoke in clear Etxelur-speak. 'My name is Xivu.' *Shi-voo.* 'My rank is the Leftmost Claw on the Front Right Paw of the Jaguar King.'

Deri and Tibo hastily went through the ritual with their

palms. Deri said clearly, 'We are honoured you have come to meet us. We are honoured you speak our tongue.'

Xivu gestured. 'This girl who found you ran like the wind to bring me your message . . . It is my honour to be the one to greet you. It was my predecessor who greeted the last party from Northland. I regret the death of your Annid of Annids. Kuma's name and her heroic exploits rang across the ocean.'

Deri thanked him. 'Then you know what we have come to ask of you.'

Xivu inclined his head. 'Alas, it may be difficult to help you. But you are our guests.' He produced a small bag and pressed it into the hands of the hunter girl. She opened it, and gasped at the sparkling stones that fell out into her palm. 'Thus, her reward, and we need consider her no more. Please.' He gestured at the cart.

Deri jumped up onto the cart. Tibo, bemused, followed.

'Hold the rail,' Xivu said gently. Then he spoke softly to the dwarf.

The dwarf snapped at the draught beasts, who raised their heads and ran at a clip, and the cart lurched forward. When Tibo glanced back, he saw the hunter girl and her family waving at them. He waved back.

The cart followed the dyke for some distance, then cut away onto a broad, straight, clean road paved with stone that led straight to the plateau that dominated the landscape.

The country was laid out in a neat grid. People toiled, labouring at fields thick with crops. Tibo saw more of the long-necked animals, some herded in pens, some drawing carts with expressions of aloof disdain. In other pens Tibo saw what looked like tremendous rats, or huge fat dogs. A few children looked up as they went past, skinny, dark, and they ran after the cart, waving. In one place a group of young men were playing a fast, complicated-looking game with a ball that bounced high when they threw it.

'Farmers,' muttered Deri. 'Just like the farmers on our

49

continent – except, of course, not. They grow dogs for food as our farmers raise cattle and pigs. And see how the plants in the fields are all mixed up? *Our* farmers grow one sort in each field, and pluck out the rest as weeds.'

'Which is the best way?'

'How should I know? Farming is nothing but a short road to a bad back, bad teeth, and an early grave.'

'I don't know how this dwarf driving the cart can see where he's going.'

Deri eyed him. 'Don't let Xivu hear you say that. Dwarfs are holy people in this country. It may seem odd to you and me, but our stories of little mothers and ice giants may seem odd to *them*.'

'There are lots of them, and they are very powerful. I can see that. What did they ever want from us?'

'Bronze for a start. When the first of our ships came here these people had no metal-working at all, save for a few lumps of iron that fell from the sky. And writing. They use our script to keep control of their country and its people. And we brought these long-necked animals, which they call "Northland horses". They are neither horses—'

'Nor from Northland.'

'No. They come from mountainous country to the south of here. We have reached it with our ships; these people are cut off by barriers of land and sea.'

'And in return we have taken their sculptors.'

'Well, we borrow them. And a few precious items – jade, for example. But we got potatoes and maize, long ago, and that's much more important. Actually potatoes came from the south-ern highlands, where the Northland horses came from.

'Look, son, be careful what you say. We're just two rascals from Kirike's Land, but they don't know that. To them we *are* Northland, you and I. Luckily there are only a handful like Xivu who understand what we say. Always remember you are talking to a people who believe they are in our debt.'

Now they were approaching the plateau. The cart turned onto

a road cut into the shoulder of the slope, rising steadily as it wound around ridges and gullies. Below them the plain opened out, a quilt of farmland stretching to the bank of the great river and the edge of the forest. Even the plateau slope turned out to be populated, with farms crowded onto neatly shaped terraces. When they heard the rattle of Xivu's cart the people came running out of houses of mud and daub, and hastily made the palm-seeing gesture to Xivu as he rolled past. Xivu was evidently a man of some importance.

Finally the cart rolled up onto the plateau itself. On this broad, open expanse, tremendous buildings stood on platforms of earth. One massive structure had pillars of rock holding up a heavy roof, and walls of packed clay. Tibo thought he could never walk into such a thing without fearing he was about to be crushed. Standing on the open ground around the buildings were monuments – ornately carved blocks of stone, pillars, sculptures of humans and animals and birds and fish, the parts mixed up as if in a fever dream – and tremendous heads, faces nearly as tall as Tibo was, glowering sternly over the plain. It was as if the toys of a giant baby had been dumped on a vast tabletop. The few people out in the open here all appeared lavishly dressed, all with great bronze discs at their necks, and they walked in a stately fashion among the monuments.

The great stone faces, of course, were the reason the men from Northland had come so far.

'I was here once before,' Deri muttered as the cart rolled on. 'Not much more than your age. Never felt so frightened in my life.'

The cart pulled up before a relatively modest house, of stone walls and wooden roof. A young man came hurrying out, hastily fixing a skirt in place around his bare waist. Xivu cuffed the man's head hard enough to make him stagger, barked out orders, and the man hurried away into the larger structure.

'Fool,' said Xivu in the Etxelur tongue. 'Lazy dolt! He was not expecting me back – he was sleeping, or fiddling with his

51

genitalia as usual. There is no food prepared for you, no drink. No matter! I have sent him to fetch the girl for you. Then we will eat and drink, and if you need to sleep or bathe I have servants to assist you. This evening you will prostrate yourselves before the King's youngest son. You are honoured visitors! Please, sit.'

He waved at a shady area under a broad veranda, littered with pallets of woven cloth. Tibo sat on one of these; it was stuffed with what felt like hair.

Deri asked, ' "Girl"? What girl do you mean?'

Xivu smiled, rueful. Now he was at rest, sitting in the shade, he didn't look much older than Tibo was himself. 'She is the one you have travelled so far to find – and she is the problem we must address between us . . . Ah, here she is!'

The girl, shadowed by Xivu's cringing servant, stood before the veranda. She looked younger than Tibo – thirteen, fourteen. She was naked to the waist, her legs wrapped in an ornate skirt. On her breast she wore an immense mirror of some polished stone, not bronze like Xivu's, and she had a bit of stone, like polished jade, pushed through the flesh between her nostrils. She just stood there. She seemed dull, incurious.

Deri asked, 'And this is your sculptor?'

Xivu sighed. 'Her name is Caxa.' *Ca-sha.* 'You can see the problem. She is young, so young! But this is our way. The master sculptors are a family line that goes back to the last creation, when the gods gave the sculptors their genius as a tool to separate the . . . the *categories* of the world, of dead from living, human from animal. Each master sculptor selects from the next generation of his extended family the most gifted, the one through whom the gods speak most clearly. The priests have various tests to help establish this. The master must do this before completing the carving of a fallen king, of course.'

Tibo asked, 'Why?'

Xivu looked at them blankly. 'Forgive me. I forget how little you people can know. When the sculptor completes the head of the King, he is laid in a pit in the ground, and the monument is placed over the pit . . . It is obvious why this must be so. Hands that have carved the face of a king could never be used for other purposes. But it is clearly essential that the successor should be in place first. In this case, unfortunately, the orderly process was disrupted.'

'Disrupted by what?'

'Factions within the master's family. Each pushing a favoured rival. Even poison was used, or so it was suggested. Murders!

'Caxa was surely the most gifted of her generation. She has produced model heads, I have seen them, which . . . disturb. She was in fact the daughter of the master. But she was so young, and so difficult. However, by the time the infighting was done, none was left standing, or without blood on his hands. None save Caxa. Her mother had died some years before – she only had her father—'

'Who she saw buried alive under a stone head,' Deri said grimly. 'A fate that will be hers, some day.'

'After she returns from Northland, having performed her duty, and after she carves the face of the King. After a lifetime of duty and privilege. Let's hope her children aren't quite as cracked! You can see why we're reluctant to let her travel to Northland.'

'But she must come. It has been the custom for generations. Perhaps if her family came with her—'

'She has no family left.'

'Her guards then, her priests. You yourself, Leftmost!'

'*Me?*'

While they argued, Tibo stepped forward, curious about this slim girl on whose shoulders rested the expectation of two cultures. She wasn't pretty, her face was too narrow, too unhappy. She didn't even seem to see him. Something fell to the ground, from her right wrist. A drop of liquid, bright red.

'She's bleeding.' Without thinking Tibo grabbed her hand. There was a neat slash across the wrist. He searched the girl's face. 'Did you do this?'

She gave a small cry, pulled her hand away, and ran off.

Tibo found himself running after her, despite his father's calls and Xivu's protests.

10

The Year of the Fire Mountain: Spring Equinox

On the morning of the spring equinox – Family Day – Milaqa walked with Hadhe and her children to Hadhe's home, a community south of the Wall called Sunflower. They were going to spend the day dredging a canal, for their spiritual benefit. Well, Milaqa had spent the night in the Scambles, and as a result she had been catastrophically slow getting ready this morning. Hadhe, one hand hanging onto little Blane, sternly disapproving, missed nothing.

The grand avenue leading to Sunflower was a dead-straight avenue twenty paces wide, lined by willows carefully coppiced and shaped, the earth packed hard by walking feet and swept scrupulously clean. Looking ahead Milaqa could soon see the track leading to the broad hearthspace that was the centre of the community. It was a grand prospect. But this particular avenue had been designed as a tribute to the sun of the spring equinox, and was aligned to salute the position of the sun at noon on that day – and it was nearly the equinox, and nearly noon, so the sun was right before her and blasting straight into her pounding head, and the thought of spending the day dredging a canal with aunts and uncles filled her with dread.

North of Sunflower, Teel was waiting for them. He wore a floppy leather hat over his bare head, an old tunic that stretched over his ample belly, and long leather leggings. 'You took your time, didn't you? Ximm's being patient enough, but there've been a few comments.'

'There are always comments. That's what our family does best, isn't it? Comment, comment, comment. I don't care what they comment.'

Teel glanced at Hadhe, amused. 'What's wrong with her?'

'Drunk.'

'No,' Milaqa said. 'I *was* drunk.'

Teel laughed again, took Milaqa's other arm, and with Hadhe escorted her the last few paces into the hearthspace. 'Traders, I suppose?'

'A bunch of Dumnoes. Met them in the Scambles. Tin traders from Albia—'

'I know Dumnoes. They know how to party, don't they?'

'I can still taste the honey from the mead.' She couldn't actually remember much. She didn't even remember getting back from the Scambles. This was the District nearest to Great Etxelur, to the east. To the west, in the direction of the austere forest-land of Albia, lay the Holies, a realm of temples and religious academies; the east was the way to the Continent and the farmers, and perhaps as a result of the attraction of that spiritual pole the Scambles was a cheerful mass of taverns, inns, music houses and bawdy shops that got plenty of business from the grand folk of Etxelur, and indeed from the Holies and the grand Embassy District further west . . . Suddenly anxious, she fumbled at the tunic at her throat, and felt the dull, heavy shape of the iron arrowhead she wore around her neck. Not lost, then, or stolen.

'Ximm's not a bad sort,' Hadhe said. 'He won't mind.'

'It's his wife that's the problem,' said Teel. ' "You want to keep away from those cattle-folk and their swill of rotting wheat . . ." '

The high-pitched impersonation made Milaqa laugh, and then she wished she hadn't.

They reached the hearthspace of Sunflower. Jaro and Keli, Hadhe's older children, ran ahead. The big houses with their dark green seaweed thatch were spaced evenly around this circular area, dominated by a flood mound topped by the big communal house, and before it the common hearth that smouldered fitfully. Everything was clean and neat – even the midden heaps were tidy, the broken tools, animal bones, and spare scraps of cloth and other bits of discarded rubbish waiting for a fresh use. This big clear space was the hub of Sunflower, which was actually a network of connected communities. From here you could see down the avenues that radiated away to north-east and south-west, links to smaller satellite settlements. The avenues were separated by stands of willow and alder, carefully tended and coppiced.

A bird flying high overhead, Milaqa thought idly, would have seen concentric bands of trees and hazel scrub surrounding this central hearthspace, a map like the classic Etxelur circles-and-bar symbol, like the ancient earthworks of the Door to the Mothers' House that stood beneath the Wall itself. The whole of Northland was like a map, a landscape Northlanders had written on all the way back to the divine Ana who, it was said, had first refused to allow the sea to overwhelm her coastal homeland.

And today all of Northland seemed to be full of her cousins and aunts and uncles, all adults judging her, or so it seemed, while the children and the dogs swarmed in the spring sunshine, flocking like birds.

'Here comes trouble,' Teel murmured.

Ximm was approaching them. He was a short, stocky man, older than most at somewhere over forty, and though he wore sensible working clothes he had a cap of polished black leather on his head, indicating his membership of the House of the Beetle. Behind him his wife Enda was glaring at Milaqa, harsh and judgemental.

And, trotting up beside Ximm, Milaqa saw Voro, the young Jackdaw.

'Oh, by the mothers' milk, not Voro. Not today. If he does all that puppyish stuff . . .'

Teel laughed. 'It's not his fault he likes you. I think he's here to talk to you about your induction prospects. He's doing well, you know, the Jackdaws tell me—'

'I'll throw up over him.' Milaqa was serious.

'*Don't* do that. Look, Hadhe – I see Riban over there.' Riban, another remote cousin, was in the House of the Wolf, training to become a priest. 'Maybe he can give her something for her head. And her gut.'

'Ah,' Hadhe said. 'Good idea. Not that she deserves it. Come on, little one.' Hadhe jogged away, trailed by Blane.

Ximm and Voro came up. Voro, twenty years old, was lanky, clumsy in his ill-fitting tunic. 'Hello, Milaqa.'

Milaqa looked away.

Ximm had thick red hair, a family trait, frosted now with grey. His face was broad and kindly, but his look was sharp. 'You're very welcome, niece.'

'Am I?'

'Well, you *were* supposed to have been here not long after sun-up.'

'She hadn't even gone to bed by sun-up, by all accounts,' Teel said.

Ximm held out his arms and beamed. 'But never mind. You're here! And it's your day, Milaqa, the Family Day in your sixteenth year. The day the clan comes together, to celebrate the House choice you are to make.'

She shrugged. 'If I could make a choice.'

'Well, it's not easy for everybody.' He winked. 'And I've swum in a few buckets of mead in my time too. But we're proud of you even so, Milaqa. Proud of what your mother achieved – to become the Annid of Annids! And her with a grandfather who hunted seals on Kirike's Land. Why, I dare say there hasn't been such a step up since the days of Prokyid. We're going to celebrate *you* today, no matter how you feel about it.'

Family Day was a loose Northland tradition centred on the spring equinox, when a clan would come together to commemorate their origins with a day of honest work. And in every family, Milaqa thought sourly, you'd find someone like Ximm, coming to the fore on such a day as this. The forgiver. The jolly one. The growstone that held the family together.

58

Ximm had been born in Kirike's Land, and though he had left that remote island at the age of five she thought she could still detect the twang of a Kirike accent in his voice. She imagined how the House elders back in the Wall would laugh at him if they could hear him speak. He was a good man, but he was also a walking reminder of the family's humble roots.

He was waiting for her reply, she realised.

'Thanks,' she said.

'Here.' Hadhe returned with a small leather pouch, stopped with a bit of bone. 'Riban got it from a trader from the east.'

Milaqa took the pouch, opened it, sniffed and recoiled.

Hadhe said, 'It's made from the bile of a—'

'Never mind,' said Teel sternly. 'Just drink it.'

Milaqa braced herself, lifted the pouch, and poured the thick liquid into her mouth in a single swill. It burned her throat as it went down, and she coughed, her stomach heaving as if she would throw up after all. But then a warmth started spreading through her belly.

Ximm had gone back to the centre of the hearthspace, and people were forming up around him, bearing tools of wood, stone and bronze, buckets of leather, water bottles, food packs. Any children old enough to walk had to carry their own little burdens; the older kids, above eight or nine, would be expected to work with the adults.

'Well, we're starting late,' Voro said to Milaqa. 'But we can still put in a few hours. Can I walk with you? If you're not feeling well. Look, I even brought you a shovel.' It was slung on his back, a willow shaft with a blade shaped from a reindeer scapula.

She wanted to laugh at him. 'Let's go dredge that canal.' She set off after Ximm, tailed by Voro.

Teel followed her, while Hadhe called for her children.

They were heading for a branch of one of the five great canals that dominated the landscape, named for the three little mothers and for Ana and Prokyid. The day was bright and warm, though

59

an edge of coolness in the shadows was a reminder of the winter just over. As she walked, her arms and legs working, her lungs pumping, Milaqa began to feel better, though whether because of the air and sunlight or Riban's potion she couldn't have said.

And today the butterflies were showing, she saw, yellow-green, or spectacular black and orange. In open water frogs croaked greedily as they mated. Early flowers like celandine and dead nettle peppered the grasslands, vivid yellow and red, and bees buzzed, preparing for their own long work season. This was the point of Northland's grand design. Within the network of the roads and canals, a frame had been necessary to save this landscape from the sea, the wild was allowed to flourish.

A hare bounded across the track, and children scampered after it noisily.

Voro walked beside her. He said abruptly, 'You could do worse than be a Jackdaw.'

'Oh, what now, Voro?'

'I know you're having trouble with your House choice. Come into the Jackdaws. I've suggested it before. Look, we're traders. We travel far. You'd enjoy that. I've drunk mead with tin miners too, but I went to Dumno itself to do it. A bit further than the Scambles! . . . Maybe you're like me, Milaqa.'

'I do *not* think so.'

'A wanderer, I mean. Restless. As I always was.'

That surprised her. 'You? I never thought of you as restless.'

'Then you got me wrong,' he said mildly. 'And I'm not doing so badly at it either. Ask anybody. I've even made a trip to Gaira with Bren himself.' Bren was among the most senior in his House. 'Look, Milaqa, I know you think I'm some kind of idiot. But when we were kids, when we were growing up – you were a bit younger than me—'

'Nothing was ever going to happen between us,' she snapped. Then she regretted it; her hangover kept making her say things she shouldn't. 'I'm sorry.'

'That's not what I'm trying to say. I always thought we had a lot in common. I thought we might be allies. If something deeper had developed – well, fine. But you were always too . . .'

'Arrogant?'

'I wouldn't say that.'

But he didn't need to. Had she really misjudged him so badly, over the years? After all – look at him now. *He* had made his life choice, and evidently a good one.

He said, 'I think you genuinely don't know what you want, do you?'

She sighed. 'No. I just know I don't want *this*.' And she opened her arms to indicate the carpet-like landscape of Northland, the people marching with their shovels, the laughing children. 'I keep thinking there must be more to life. Even getting drunk with some greasy Dumno miner with wandering hands is *different*.'

'Then be a trader,' he said. 'See the world. See Hattusa and Mycenae, see Egypt . . .'

Ximm looked back. 'Serious talk's for tomorrow,' he said briskly. 'Today we've got a canal to fix – and here we are.'

Before them, the people were spreading out along the bank of a drained canal, dropping their packs of food and water, taking their shovels from their backs.

Irritated, Milaqa snapped, 'Oh, give me that shovel, Voro, and show me where to dig.'

11

They were to be supervised by a senior of the House of the Vole, the water engineers, who unrolled a complicated map drawn in red and black on a sheet of bark. The canal system had been dammed and diverted at some point upstream from this stretch, which was a branch of the main canal called the Sky. The duct here had been left to drain and dry out for the best part of a month, ready for the family to take it on.

So, with Ximm and the others cheerfully calling out orders, the adults and older children grabbed their shovels and buckets and clambered over the banks of hardened mud and earth down into the empty channel. Though it had been drying out for some time the mud at the bottom was wet and deep and clinging and cold. Milaqa, up to her calves in it, wondered how long it had taken this thickness of muck to build up – how long since this particular stretch had been dredged, five years or fifty?

The people got their bearings quickly. They formed up into rough lines, the adults and older kids in the deeper mud of the bottom, the smallest children and nursing mothers and old folk walking along the banks, looking down and calling encouragement. They began to dig away at the mud with shovels of bronze and bone, passing it up by a bucket chain. The glistening stuff was dumped to add another bit of height to the banks that lined the canal – and indeed, it was this endless digging-out that had created the banks in the first place.

There were a few surprises. They turned up broken pots, what might have been a child's doll of wood and bone – even a broken bronze sword. Offerings to the gods, to the little mother of the sky, to Ana and Prokyid. You were supposed to make such offerings by one of the five great canals, but people driven by sufficient hope or despair would make their small prayers wherever they could. Ximm always made sure that such finds were pressed back into the deeper mud, to be covered over and lost again. Then some of the children got excited at the sight of a sunken boat, a few hundred paces further down the channel. They ran off to investigate, followed by cries of exasperation or envy from the toiling adults.

Milaqa had Hadhe and Teel to either side of her, Ximm just ahead, and Voro hanging around somewhere just behind her. She threw herself into the work. There was no real choice; this was what Family Day was all about. And she didn't want any comments about how hard she worked, or not. Besides, though the mud was heavy and sticky, she found the simple repetitious work warmed her muscles up. Somebody began singing, a rhythmic comic song about the only ice giant who didn't like fighting. People joined in, up and down the stretch of the canal, as they dug and lugged their way through the mud, growing steadily filthier.

'This is the life,' Teel said, working beside Milaqa.

She eyed him sceptically.

'Good honest work. Building the world, spadeful by spadeful. The way it's been since Ana's time. It's the Etxelur way. When our family came here from Kirike's Land, this work was all we could do, all we could understand. But we were welcomed into the House of the Beetle, and we worked hard, and did it better and better. And look at us now!'

'What, still up to our knees in muck?'

He grinned, his face a muddy mask. 'I felt the same way when I was your age. Younger, probably.'

'What way?'

'Like I didn't fit. Our world here, the Northland way – it's fine, and it works, but it is *rigid*. It's a world where you are expected to find deep spiritual joy mucking out a canal.'

'So what did you do?'

'You know what I did. I gave up my chance of ever becoming a father, for the sake of a greater ambition. And it was all the fault of Prokyid the Second, the nearest to a king we ever had here in Etxelur, about a thousand years ago. Did you know that? *He* did just what all these other petty kings and princes do on the Continent – strutting and posing, picking fights with others of his kind, starving his people to wage war on others. And for a generation the important stuff, the engineering, was neglected. When he was toppled, the Annids decreed that no man could ever again join their number, for generally it's men who cause trouble of that sort. And so now—'

'It's women only, or eunuchs.'

He shrugged. 'I made my choice years ago. It's as if a different person made it for me. I jumped off a cliff. I had no way back, and I have none now.' He glanced at the children playing on the bank. 'Like you, I wanted more.'

'And was it worth it?'

'Oh, yes. I got what I wanted, which was to see how North-land works from the inside. But that's what worries me now. Northland is ponderous and slow-moving – frankly, the Houses are usually too busy infighting to look outside. And yet there are new things in this world. Things that need to be looked at. An arrowhead that can pierce bronze. The nestspills who come trickling into our country from their failing drought-ridden farms—'

'I've seen some of them.'

'In the east people are starving, dying, marching. Ancient kingdoms are collapsing. Even the Hatti are in trouble. The world is changing. And if it's to survive Northland must change too. Change and adapt.'

'How? You just said the Houses are too busy fighting each other.'

'But the Houses you know about aren't all there is.'

'Now I really don't follow you,' she grumbled, pecking at another patch of hardened canal mud. 'What other House is there?'

He dug under his shirt and pulled out an amulet – a crow's foot, dried and suspended from a loop of leather.

She stared.

'Keep digging,' he murmured.

She bent over her spade. 'I never heard of a House of the Crow. Besides, you're an Owl. You sacrificed your balls to become one! How can you be in two Houses at once?'

'It just evolved that way . . . Milaqa, like most things in Northland, the House of the Crow is very old. Somebody far back in our history realised that we have this basic problem of getting stuck in our ways. And that every so often the world changes, something new happens, and we have to be able to cope with it. So the Crows emerged. Like the other Houses, you can only join if you're invited. And you're only invited if you have the right kind of mind.'

'What kind?'

'The kind that doesn't fit anywhere else. The whole point of the Crows is to be the ones who deal with the new, the unexpected, the challenging.'

She felt her heart beat faster. 'The exciting.'

'The dangerous,' he warned. 'Look, Milaqa, I'm just offering this to you as a way forward. I already showed you something unexpected. Something strange.'

'You mean the arrowhead.' She pulled it out from under her tunic, as he had his crow's foot.

'What have you done about it?'

'Nothing,' she said slowly. 'I . . .' She had felt reluctant to face the fact that her mother must have been murdered. Somehow asking questions about it would make her seem even more dead. It was easier to dive into the clamour of the Scambles and forget everything.

'I know it's complicated,' Teel said. 'But that arrowhead isn't just lethal, it's *new*. Maybe if you can find out where it came from, what's different about it—'

'Nice pendant.' Ximm was only a pace behind them. Teel hastily tucked away his crow's foot. Ximm reached out to cradle the arrow in his palm. 'I know a bit about iron.' He frowned. 'An arrowhead? Funny sort of ornament.'

Milaqa took a breath. 'It's not just an ornament. This *works*. It's been fired.'

'You saw that, did you?'

She stayed silent, hoping she wouldn't have to lie.

Ximm turned. 'Here, Voro, take a look at this.'

Voro straightened up from the mud and strode over. 'Iron?'

'Not just iron. Hard and true iron, good enough for the bow, according to the lady here.' He tapped the head on the shaft of his shovel. 'How come? Iron falls from the sky, doesn't it? No use for anything but showing off,' and he cackled.

'I heard rumours,' Voro said. 'About the Hatti. You know how it is – we send them potato and maize mash, and tin for their bronze. We get iron goods back from them in exchange, among other stuff, and so we know something of their techniques. I heard they have a way of working iron that makes it harder. Better than bronze, so they say. I may be meeting some Hatti myself. Some of their high-ups are coming to the Giving in mid-summer. I'm supposed to go with Bren to meet them in Gaira and escort them here.'

Teel pulled Milaqa away, and murmured, 'Maybe this is your way forward.'

'To do what?'

'Follow the thread, Milaqa. If you can find out where this arrowhead was made and how it got to Northland, maybe you can find out who pulled the bowstring. If there's some connection with the Hatti—'

'I don't know any Hatti. I don't know anything about them.'

'What, you don't bump into any in the Scambles? Then it's time you found out, isn't it?'

12

The midsummer Giving at Etxelur was, Qirum had learned, a custom more revered than all the ceremonies of Egypt, more ancient than the rites of vanished Sumer and Akkad. And as the solstice approached people travelled from across half the planet to attend the Giving, like a great drawing-in of breath. Now Qirum was going to Northland for the first time, he was going to a Giving. And he would have a queen of the Hatti at his side.

The long journey began as they pushed off from Troy's long gritty beach. The rowers dragged on their oars under Praxo's gruff leadership, and Qirum worked his steering oar as they navigated the treacherous currents of the strait.

Kilushepa was fascinated by Qirum's ship. She paced the length of it, picking her way between the eight rowers' sweating torsos and the bales of food, water, wet-weather clothes, folded sails, bailing buckets, bundles of weapons and other junk that crammed the narrow hull. Her balance was good, as the ship pitched and creaked in the offshore swell.

'Twelve paces long.'

'About that.' Qirum, sitting at his position in the high stern, was unfolding the periplus for this stretch of coast. He was amused by the way the rowers were distracted by Kilushepa's slim figure brushing past them, and by Praxo's clenched, furious expression under his salt-stained felt cap.

She sat down at the prow, running her fingers along the hull beams. 'Your paintwork is flaking.'

He laughed. 'Probably. We never were the smartest ship on any of the oceans. But it's pitch, not paint.'

Praxo growled, 'Smart or not, she's the fastest and most feared of all – right, lads?'

The only answer he got was a couple of uninterested grunts. Most of these rowers had been signed on in the dingy taverns of Troy, and most looked as if all they wanted was to work off last night's mead or wine or beer. At least they seemed to be an experienced bunch, however; they could handle their oars, and none of them was throwing up as the sea swelled under them.

'Oak,' Kilushepa said now. 'These planks are of oak, are they not?' She picked at the withies that bound the planks, the caulking. 'And these lengths that bind them?'

'Yew. And then it's all caulked with moss, beeswax and animal fat. The hull is sealed to keep out the water.'

'You know, we Hatti generally don't have much time for ships. Even though we rely on the fleets that bring us our grain from Egypt. Everything this ship is made of was once alive, wasn't it? The wood, the wax, the moss, the leather – all these bits of trees and plants and animals, sliced up and stitched together. The living stuff of the land moulded to defy the sea. It's wonderful when you think about it.'

'Is it?'

'Yes! As if the ship is itself alive, a creature bounding across the waves.'

'Praxo says she has a mind of her own, that's for sure.'

His only response from Praxo was a scowl.

They were putting out from the land now. Troy diminished to a shabby blur on the eastern horizon, and a breeze was picking up, fresh with salt. Sitting at the prow, Kilushepa turned and looked out to the open sea, breathing deep. She was remarkably composed, Qirum thought, not for the first time, considering her circumstances – considering she had been the booty of her own people's army so recently, and now here she was alone on the ocean with ten violent, lusty men.

'So we sail for Northland,' Kilushepa called back. 'Will we be out of sight of the land altogether? How remarkable *that* would be – the world reduced to an abstraction of sea and sky.'

'Only for brief stretches,' Qirum replied. 'We'll do some island-hopping before we get to the Greek mainland. Basically we're following the coastline.' He held up his periplus, a linen scroll. 'From Gaira, we'll work our way up the river valleys and over-land to get to Northland.'

'Would you get lost, out of sight of land?'

Praxo hawked and spat over the side, a green gobbet on the grey-black water. '*He* would. There are clever sorts who have tricks to find their way around on the open water. Such as to see how high the sun rises at noon, and from that you can work out how far north or south you are.'

She frowned. 'What sort of divination is that? Sounds like the Greeks to me. Always full of tricks, the Greeks, clever-clever, like clever children. What is that scroll, Qirum? A map, is it?'

He unrolled the periplus carefully, passing the fragile fabric from one spindle to the other, holding it up so she could see the writing, the little sketches. 'This is my periplus. A guide to the coast. It cost me half my fortune when I bought it from an old seaman down on his luck. And he bought it in turn from somebody else, long ago. I've been adding to it since. See, the three different writing hands?'

She came back down the boat to see. 'I can't read your script. But yes, I see the differences. And this faded writing must be the oldest.'

'It's a kind of description of the coast. Of landmarks, dangers like shoals and shallows – and dangers of a human kind. You see, there are little sketches to help you understand. Good ports, safe places to beach, the prevailing winds. Look at this.' He ravelled the scroll back. 'Here is an old description of how it was to come upon Troy, before the Greeks burned the place. A sketch that shows how it might have looked from the sea.'

She studied the picture solemnly. 'You have crossed it through.'

'I hadn't the heart to erase it.'

'This little scroll is shared wisdom. You treasure it, don't you?

A sailor would have to be desperate indeed to sell such a thing. How would you feel if you had to part with it?'

'I hope I never have to.'

Her gaze was steady. 'You hope to have a son, don't you? A family. You don't want to be doing this all your life, fighting all day, whoring and drinking all night . . . You want a legacy. A son to have your periplus, when you're done with the sea.'

Praxo, at his oar, was staring at the two of them.

Qirum felt unaccountably embarrassed. 'That's all for the future.'

'You aren't wrong to dream,' she said, her voice like a rustle of linen. 'I saw that in you when I met you.'

Praxo guffawed. 'And did you see his father the rapist?'

Qirum threw a water jug at him. He ducked, it hit the man behind him, and Praxo laughed.

By mid-morning they had picked up a breeze blowing offshore. Under Praxo's brisk instructions the men shipped their oars, fixed the mast to its socket, and unfolded the leather sail. Soon the sail billowed out, and they were driven east with a creak of wood and leather. This was another new experience for Kilush-epa. As the rowers stretched and took food and water, she sat in the prow, letting the wind ruffle hair that was growing back after its brutal shaving by the Hatti soldiers.

Praxo came to sit beside Qirum in the stern. They shared a leather flask of wine mixed with water. 'This is a stupid plan,' Praxo said. 'To meet up with Hatti traders and officials in North-land?'

'She sent letters to arrange it.'

'But the Hatti threw the woman out, remember! Why will they accept her now?'

Qirum shrugged. 'She says it will work.' Hattusa itself was a big place, Kilushepa had said, and the reach of the Hatti kings stretched much further. Traders out on the edge of the world might not even know Kilushepa's name, let alone know of the intrigues in court that had deposed her. If she simply *claimed* to be back in power, even if they suspected her, how could they prove her wrong?

'Get rid of her,' Praxo said bluntly. 'I mean it. She's trouble. She's getting into your head.'

'We wouldn't even be making this voyage if not for her,' Qirum said. 'At least she has a plan. Face it – before we met her we were sailing in circles, going nowhere, you and I. She's given me a direction, Praxo.'

'She's given you a hard-on, that's all. Well, that's my advice, and you can take it or ignore it, I'm past caring. Now I'm going to get some sleep before the wind dies.' He handed Qirum the wine flask and slumped down with arms folded over his belly, his old felt cap pulled down over his eyes.

If Kilushepa had heard any of this conversation, she showed no sign of it.

13

In another boat, crossing another ocean, it was Caxa who was the first to glimpse Kirike's Land.

'Smoke!' she cried.

Tibo, buried in a heap of furs, thought he was dreaming. 'Hmm? What?'

The Jaguar girl nudged his ribs.

They were side by side in the stern of the boat, like two fat seals in their layers of furs, under a sky that was deep blue but streaked with pink cloud to the east, the sign of the coming dawn. There was the usual morning stink of greasy human flesh, farts, fish guts, and the stale brine of the bilge water. Around them the men were waking, more bundles of fur from which peered human faces, thick with beards and smeared with fat to keep out the night cold. On Caxa's other side the priest Xivu lay curled up, still asleep. Caxa was the only female in the boat, and these men had been away from home for a long time; Deri had made sure that whenever they slept the girl was walled in by Xivu on one side, Tibo on the other.

Tibo was falling asleep again. She nudged him. 'Smoke. Smoke!'

He struggled to sit up. 'No. Not smoke.' In the course of the long voyage he had been trying to teach her the rudiments of the Etxelur tongue. She was a slow learner, or an incurious one. 'We didn't light the boat's fire last night, remember? It was raining.' Another night of salted fish, wet furs and cold. 'There can't be any smoke. Do you mean "clouds"?'

'Not clouds.' This time the nudge was hard enough to hurt,

despite the thickness of the furs. 'Know clouds, know smoke. Smoke!' She thrust out an arm and pointed beyond the boat's prow.

He peered to see in the dim light. And he made out a black column that rose up from the north-east horizon, billowing, spreading into a layer at the top, flat and tenuous. He thought he saw a flicker of light in the column – like lightning, like a storm.

The men saw it; they stirred and muttered. Deri was already awake, sitting up, one hand loosely holding a rope rowlock. He was watching the smoke too.

'What is it, father?'

'Home. That's Kirike's Land. We're due to come on it today, tomorrow at latest.'

'And what's that smoke? Fires?'

'Not that. A different kind of smoke. I saw it once before, years ago – before you were born. It might mean nothing. And, see the way it's climbing straight up? Not a breath of wind. No point unfurling the sail this morning. Come on, lads, time to get moving, this boat won't row itself.'

The men, seven of them plus Tibo and Deri, stirred, grumbling. The boat rocked gently as one after another knelt up to piss over the side, or to bare his arse and dump his soil. Deri got to work dragging up the sea anchor.

And a noise like thunder came rumbling over the sea, from the north-east, from the direction of Kirike's Land.

'Told you,' Caxa said, her thin face almost ghostly in the dawn light.

They came upon Kirike's Land after noon, approaching from the south. Snow-capped mountains and glaciers, bone-white, showed first above the horizon, and then the green of the lower lands, the meadows and birch woods. The men grew animated at the sight of home, and they pointed out landmarks to each other, massifs, cliffs and headlands.

The southern coast was long and with few harbours, and as

soon as Deri got his bearings he directed the crew to row west, towards the big bay called the Ice Giant's Cupped Palm. There was a touch of breeze now, blessedly coming from the east, and the men gratefully hoisted their leather sail and let the little mother of the sky guide them home through these last stages. They passed through the usual fleet of fishing boats, and were greeted with hails and waves and obscene cries. One fast little boat raced ahead of them to the Cupped Palm, so a welcome would be made ready for them. Caxa stared out curiously as the island's shore slid past – gaunt, rocky, yet with birch forest lapping down almost to the sea in some places, and the flanks of mountains beyond striped with ice. It was late spring. The winter always lay heavily on this land.

And that smoke pillar towered over the island. When the wind shifted it brought a smell of ash and sulphur. Deri said it seemed to be coming from a mountain called the Hood, in the south of the island.

Xivu was uneasy. 'We have such mountains at home,' he said in his stilted Northlander.

'Here, the land often stirs,' Deri said evenly. 'We believe the little mother of the earth comes to this island to sleep beneath the ground when she flushes with heat, as many old women do. There is rarely any harm in it.'

But Xivu was not reassured. He was deeply reluctant to be here in the first place. Tibo didn't know how it had been finally decided that Xivu would be the one to accompany Caxa on this long trip across the ocean. Perhaps he was the best speaker of the Etxelur tongue; perhaps he knew Caxa the best – or perhaps it was just that he was the least skilful at avoiding an unpleasant chore. Anyhow here he was, and he had been complaining since his first bout of seasickness, and the strange smoke column wasn't helping his mood.

They sailed into the Ice Giant's Cupped Palm, and for their final approach into harbour the men folded their sail and wielded their oars. Tibo felt a surge of relief to be home, as he looked around at the houses, the rising smoke, the boats littering the water, and the looming ice-striped mountain in the background. But the smoke column from the Hood cast a kind of pall over the sky, staining it a faint orange, and that smell of sulphurous burning lingered.

When the boat pulled into the shore, Tibo leapt out with the rest to haul it above the high-water mark. There was a party waiting, cheerful wives who threw themselves at their husbands, a few traders hoping for trinkets from the Land of the Jaguar. Children came swarming, as children always did, great mobs of them outnumbering the adults. Xivu and Caxa looked taken aback. Luckily the children seemed to find these exotic folk strange rather than interesting, and they were as wary as the Jaguar folk themselves.

And here came Medoc, Tibo's grandfather, huge in his furs, striding along the strand towards them. 'Deri! So you managed not to sink the boat, son. And Tibo! I swear you grow a bit more every time I see you.' He held Tibo's shoulders and shook him hard enough to make his head rattle on his shoulders. Medoc's tremendous grey-flecked beard was studded with fish bones, and his walrus fur stank of smoke. 'Look at you now, arms like tree trunks, neck as thick as an ice giant's cock! Well, I'm just back from Etxelur myself, and I'll tell you all about it.' He turned on Caxa, who flinched. 'Oh, and who's your lover?'

Deri took his father's arm. 'This is our sculptor.'

Medoc's eyes widened. 'What – bound for Northland, for the Annid's carving? The last master sculptor I saw was a fat old man.'

Xivu said precisely, 'Vixixix was the master a decade ago. The last to visit Northland, for your Annids are blessedly long-lived.' He stepped forward. He had shucked off his loaned furs, despite the relative chill of the afternoon, and he stood proud in his kilt of exotically coloured linen, his torso and arms bare, his mirror of bronze hanging from his neck. 'This is Caxa. The granddaughter of Vixixix. She is the current master sculptor.'

'And she is not,' Tibo said, 'my lover.'

'Well, you're welcome here, Xivu, whatever the reason

you've come . . .' Medoc was distracted by his own reflection in the mirror on the priest's chest. He plucked half a fish-head from the depths of his beard and popped it into his mouth. 'Wondered where that got to. Well! Come with me.' Crunching bone, he led the way from the shore towards the houses.

They walked past tremendous racks of drying fish, set up so that the prevailing breeze carried the stink away from the houses.

Caxa seemed curious. 'Sacrifice?'

'Not a sacrifice,' Tibo said. 'Well, we apologise to the fish when we catch them . . . We dry the fish. And then we send it home.'

She looked puzzled. 'Home?'

'I mean to Northland. I was born here. This is my *home*. But everybody calls Northland home.'

'Fish would stink on boat. Go rotten.'

'That's the secret. If you dry them out the right way, the fish keep for months. We trade them in Northland. They call it Kirike-fish.'

Medoc's house, one of half a dozen arranged around a rough hearthspace, was set on a grassed-over mound of earth. Children swarmed around, and Deri and Tibo bent to greet nieces and nephews and cousins.

Vala, Medoc's wife, came pushing out of the house through the door flap. She carried a pot of meat and herbs she was mixing with a wooden spoon. Her face was sturdy but pleasant, and she wore her greying dark hair tied back. She smiled at Xivu, and managed to give the wide-eyed Caxa a gentle embrace without the girl recoiling. Not yet forty, she was Medoc's second wife, a cousin of his first, long dead; she was stepmother to Deri, step-grandmother to Tibo. She greeted Deri and Tibo with kisses and brief hugs, and she called out her own children, a lively boy called Liff and a toddler girl called Puli, both of whom Deri swept up for a huge embrace. A willowy twelve-year-old called Mi, daughter of Vala's by a previous marriage, stood back more shyly.

Medoc grinned expansively at this family scene. 'We share the island, you know,' he said to Xivu and Caxa, 'with neighbours of yours. From across the ocean. Well, originally, that's where their fathers came from, and it's said that Kirike himself brought them here. We call them the Ice Folk. Maybe you'll know some of them.'

'Father,' Deri said patiently, 'they're hardly likely to know one another. The Ice Folk come from the Land of the Sky Wolf, which is many days' sailing north of the Jaguar country. These are whole continents we're talking about.'

'Oh, pick, pick, pick, you're just like Vala. I'll take you up country,' Medoc said to Xivu. 'Before you have to go on to Etxelur. I'll show you the Ice Folk – our forests of birch and pine – it is a beautiful island, surprisingly rich. We could set off right now, if you like—'

'Oh, no, you couldn't,' Vala snapped. Still cradling her bowl of spiced meat, she put her free arm around Caxa. 'You come with me. I'm sure you'd like to change those brine-stained clothes; I know just what salty leather against your skin feels like. Mi! Come and see if you've got some clothes this little one can borrow. Would you like something to eat? Other than fish, I mean . . .'

Deri followed, then Xivu, and at last Tibo.

'Tomorrow for the walk, then,' boomed Medoc, oblivious to the fact that everybody was ignoring him, and he trailed into the house after the others.

14

It took only a few days' sailing before Qirum's boat reached the mouth of a river called the Na by the local people, and thus recorded in his periplus. This was the southern shore of the western country called Gaira. They arrived on the afternoon of a warm early summer day.

They came to a fishing village sprawled untidily along a rocky strand. The shore above the waterline was cluttered with over-turned boats, and small squat wooden houses, racks of drying fish, a big open-air hearth that smoked languidly. Beyond the beach, forest rose up, dense. More boats were out on the deeper ocean, to the south.

A child playing in the surf at the water's edge was the first to spot their sail. Naked, no more than four or five years old, she ran up the beach to the houses, calling out. Soon adults emerged to watch Praxo's crew furl their sail and row in towards the shore. One man came down to the water where they would land, but others hung back.

'Take care,' Praxo said to the rowers. 'Let me do the talking. I can speak the local jabber, a bit of it anyway. See how they're hanging back from the shore? See that mother gathering in her children? We've come a long way west, and these parts aren't as infested by sea raiders as back east, but they have their prob-lems, and they're wary. By the way, this isn't Troy. You can't assume that every woman you meet is a whore. You'll get your share in time, have no fear, lads. But not yet.'

The ship pulled into the shore, and they all jumped out at Qirum's command, Kilushepa included, splashing in knee-deep surf. The men lined up and hauled the ship until its flat base scraped over the beach. Then they relaxed, panting, and reached for their water flasks.

The man who'd come to meet them stood before Qirum and Praxo. He was young, under twenty, and he wore a tunic of coarsely spun linen, a short cow-hide cloak, and boots covered in fish scales. He was dark, his face round, his hair black. He tapped his chest. 'Vertix,' he said. 'Vertix.' He spoke on in his own coarse tongue, but there was Greek, Egyptian and even Hatti in the mix, Qirum could tell. 'Show? Show way? Food, water? Guide?'

Praxo started to negotiate with the man. Kilushepa stood with Qirum. 'What does this fellow want with us? Can you understand any of what he's saying?'

'He's asking to be taken on as a guide. A navigator.' He pointed up the river valley, which narrowed as you looked inland, cutting through a forested landscape. 'We're going across land. Otherwise we'd have to go out through the strait, out of this Middle Sea, and brave the Western Ocean – a much tougher journey, and a longer one. We'll go north-west, *that* way, following the valley of this river as far as we can. We'll have to walk as far as the watershed, I'm afraid.'

'I did plenty of walking in the company of those Hatti soldiers, as you will recall. My soles are like leather.'

'After the watershed we'll follow another river further to the north and west, until we come to the land of the Burdi, as the people there call themselves – different from this lot by the way, and speaking a different tongue altogether, I'm told. We should be able to barter for a boat to take us down the lower reaches, and into a great estuary called the Cut. From there we'll reach the southern coast of Northland. And there, I hope, we'll meet the Hatti trading party you wrote to.'

'Who will escort us the rest of the way to the midsummer Giving at Etxelur.'

'We'll be there in time, with a fair wind and a little help from this local fellow Vertix, who seems to know his business.'

'And he knows his value,' Kilushepa said drily, as they watched the man pick over the goods Praxo had to offer as payment, bits of silver and bronze, carved bone and wood, shaped stone.

Soon a deal was done. Praxo returned to Qirum. 'We start at first light tomorrow. Come on, you men, you'll be sleeping on dry land tonight, let's get set up.'

The men hauled the ship's sails out on the beach to dry, and spread blankets and sacks on the ground. Two of them set off up the valley in search of firewood, and straw or grass to stuff sleeping pallets. Praxo went up the beach with Vertix to negotiate for some fish and meat and water.

Kilushepa said, 'Would you walk with me into the forest, Qirum? I'd be interested to see what herbs grow here. Perhaps we can flavour the fish supper we will soon be sharing.'

The idea of exploring a forest glade with a queen appealed to Qirum greatly. They walked together up the beach to the edge of the forest, followed by Praxo's baffled, irritated gaze.

In the morning, at first light, Vertix came down the beach to meet them, laden with a heavy pack of his own.

Praxo had picked two men to stay behind here and watch the boat. These two were going about their morning chores sleepily, banking down the big fire they'd built, kicking sand into the holes they'd dug as latrines. Nobody bothered saying goodbye. The rest of the crew were gathered beside the boat, all of them, save only for Kilushepa, wrapped in their cloaks with packs on their backs or heads.

Vertix grinned at them all. 'Nice day, nice forest, nice walk,' he said in broken Greek. 'And then land of Burdi, and then – Northland! Now walk.' He turned and led the way up a narrow track that led along the eastern side of the river valley.

Praxo, laden by his own immense pack, marched ahead with him. The men shuffled after them. Kilushepa and Qirum brought up the rear, treading side by side along a path not much more than an animal track. Qirum listened to the men's grumbles, amused. For days they had been complaining about their sore backsides on the ship's rough benches, and their blistered hands; now, right from the start of the trek, they complained about their feet.

Kilushepa murmured, 'That man is my implacable opponent.'

'Praxo? He's a good man. He does his job—'

'What hold does he have over you?'

He turned his head in surprise. 'He has no hold. I lead.'

'Yet you defer to him.'

'That's not true.'

'I say it is. Tell me about him – how you know him.'

He hoisted his pack more comfortably on his shoulders. 'He's a Trojan, as I am.'

She said softly, 'Though I suppose he would say you are merely half-Trojan.'

'He was a child at the time of the Greek siege – only two years old, less perhaps. But his family had money. They bribed a Greek officer to let them escape before the final assault, the fire. I'm not sure where they ended up. From what he's said I think it might have been Patara.' A city on the southern shore of Anatolia, in another Hatti dependency. 'He doesn't talk about that much. Anyhow he always seems to have been a tough kid.

'As soon as he was old enough to steal one of his father's horses, he rode out of there and made his way back to Troy. That's where he's been based ever since, as far as I can tell – making a living by trading, mercenary fighting, sailing—'

'Piracy. Banditry.'

'That's the nature of the times.'

'Tell me how he met you.'

'He saved my life.' He paused. 'There was a fight in a tavern. I was fourteen. I was on the losing side. But when Praxo waded in, he was only sixteen but already twice my size, the odds changed. We've been friends ever since. At first he was dominant, of course; he was older, more street-tough, stronger. But with time—'

81

'You hesitate. What haven't you said? Go back. This "tavern". Was it really a tavern?'

Suddenly he feared her, her sharp mind, her probing words.

'Praxo told me what you had to do to survive. There is no shame—'

'It was a brothel.' The words came in a rush, but softly, so the others could not hear. 'One man refused to pay me. He— I was thrown out into the street, for I did not have the bit of silver that was the barman's usual fee. The man was waiting, with his friends. They grabbed me. Five or six of them. They were farmers, I think, strong as oxen. They got me in a ruined house. I . . .'

'They took it in turns, I suppose.'

'They were crushing me. I could not breathe. They would have killed me, I think, before they finished. But Praxo had seen me, saw the men pull me into the house.'

'He saved you.'

'I think he just felt like a fight. They were drunk and foolish, and, though strong, they were farmers, not warriors. He pulled them off me, broke the arm of one of them, the rest ran off. One against five or six, and he won.

'I was barely conscious. He sat me up against a wall until I could breathe properly.' He remembered the ache in his bruised chest, the burning pain of his ripped rectum, the foul taste of semen. These were memories he had put in a sealed pot and buried in the dark undersoil of his mind. How had this woman dragged them out of him so quickly?

She was staring at him as she walked, studying his face as he scrutinised his periplus, squeezing meaning out of it. 'You shouldn't be ashamed. You couldn't help any of it. You were a victim.'

'No.' He hated the word, and anger flashed. 'Not a victim.'

'All right. *But that's not all.* Is it? What else happened? Go back again. Praxo sat you against the wall. You were recovering. What then?'

'He was laughing. Full of fire. He'd just won a fight that he would talk about for years. The men had brought some mead, and he took that and he drank it. And he said I should pay him for saving me. Years later, you know, he spoke of that night. He apologised, he said we would never speak of it again, that no man would know, and that . . .'

'How did you pay him? . . . Ah. With your only coin.'

'He doesn't lie with boys, not Praxo. Not to his taste. But that night, he was full of himself, he said the fight had made him hard. I used my mouth. He closed his eyes, and shouted the names of women he had lain with.'

'So that's it,' she breathed. 'And yet you stayed with him?'

'He was ashamed, I think. Well, he was once he'd slept off the drink. He said I could go with him. I didn't have to go back to the brothel. I could stay beside him, learn to fight. I think he meant this as a gesture of pity, he thought I wouldn't last. But I learned fast, and bulked up, and we were soon an effective team. Then we rowed our first ship together.'

'And that's the hold he has over you.'

'No. He has no hold! I told you, as we grew older, and it became clear I was the smart one—'

She was whispering now, into his ear, intense. 'I know how it feels, Qirum, believe me. I was used by Hatti soldiers. I remember their faces, every one. I remember their filth. I learned their names when I could. When I return to Hattusa in my pomp I will seek them out, and their families.' She smiled. 'You, though. You are the victim who kept his rapist close, haven't you?' And she walked ahead of him, cutting off the conversation.

Qirum strode on, angry, humiliated, as he had not felt for many years. Up ahead he heard Praxo's voice, telling some joke to the men, his booming laughter, his gusty singing resuming once more.

15

The Year of the Fire Mountain: Late Spring

The elders of Etxelur gathered for their convocation: the process of selecting the new Annid of Annids in succession to Kuma. It was almost a month before midsummer and the Giving, when the new appointment would be announced to the world and celebrated.

They had come to the central mound of the great earthwork called the Door to the Mothers' House. The Door, a very ancient complex of earthworks, was the navel of Northland history. In this age a ring of lodges had been built atop the central mound, one for each of the great Houses of Northland. And today, in the space encircled by the lodges, the House leaders, the Annids themselves, and the Jackdaws, Beavers, Voles, Swallows and the rest, with the priests mediating and counselling, were arguing in the open air, in tight, bickering groups, or sitting on pallets stuffed with dried reeds. In among the Annids were representatives of Districts far from Great Etxelur itself, the Markets to east and west, austere librarians from the Archive, engineers and craftsmen from the Manufactory, even a few cheerful-looking innkeeper types from the Scambles.

The leaders of the Houses wore their ceremonial robes, and fur, feathers, polished leather gleamed. They looked like a flock of birds, Milaqa thought idly. Big fat exotic birds. As one of a loose band of advisers and supporters, she sat on the grassy sward with Teel and Riban and others outside the central circle. She had been here for three days already, the proceedings had gone on all day, it was mid-afternoon, and it was insufferably tedious.

At least the setting was magnificent. The sun, still high in a clear southern sky, bathed the face of the Wall with light, the sweeping surface with its galleries and ledges, the climbing nets and ladders dangling from the roof, the huge scaffolding structures of the Beavers. It looked like something natural, she thought idly, like a great hive, rather than something made by people.

But the talking went on and on. The core of the confrontation seemed to be between Bren, leader of the Jackdaw traders, and a group of Annids. His principal opponent was a severe older Annid, a woman called Noli. Bren was pushing his own candidate for the office of Annid of Annids, a young, slightly confused-looking woman called Raka. The debate was passionately argued, but it was all very formal. The participants always spoke to each other via a neutral speaker, one of the priests, they used an archaic form of the Northland tongue, and every word they spoke was transcribed on a linen roll by a Wolf scribe. In his late thirties, Jackdaw Bren's face was handsome, but it was oddly too symmetrical – too perfect – and it was severe, Milaqa thought, with deep-grooved lines around his mouth and on his forehead. He was the sort of man it was impossible to believe had ever been a child. Somehow it didn't surprise Milaqa to find out that Raka, his candidate, was actually Bren's niece.

Milaqa glanced at the sky, where gulls wheeled so high they were almost out of sight, and she smelled the sea on a soft breeze from the north. She imagined she wasn't stuck in this dull session of talk, talk, talk but swimming in the cold sea, or flying up in the air as free as the gulls . . .

An elbow poked her ribs. She jolted upright.

The elbow had been Riban's. Her cousin, a young acolyte in the House of the Wolves, was grinning at her. He was taller than she was, even sitting cross-legged on the grass; he had a dark, open face whose good humour was not ruined by his mouthful of wooden teeth. 'You were snoring.'

'I wasn't.'

'You were about to. Mind you, you wouldn't be the only one. Half these fat old fools have spent the whole day dozing away, dreaming of their evening feast.'

Milaqa snorted a laugh.

There was a rustle around her, of swallow feathers and stitched vole hide, as the elders reacted.

'Hush, you two. You're showing the family up.' Teel sat with them on the grass, but bolt upright, almost like a hare, Milaqa thought, a bald fat hare, totally intent on what the elders were saying.

At long last the day's sessions ended. Bren and his opponent bowed to each other, and to the Wolf speaker. The scribe scattered sand over her parchments to dry them, and stowed away her ink and her bone pens. Servants emerged from the lodges bearing plates of snacks, eel and oyster and clam and snail, and flagons of water, juice and tea, no doubt some of it laced with the mead that was so popular throughout Northland, even if it did come from the despised farmers. The elders, gobbling food and drink, loosened heavy robes that must have been ferociously hot at the peak of the day, and they stretched and walked.

Milaqa and Riban stood easily, but they had to help Teel up. 'My leg is fast asleep,' he complained. He walked in a little circle, pressing his foot to the ground.

'Your leg is as bored as I am,' said Milaqa, and Riban guffawed.

'Oh, how can you be *bored*? By the mothers' tears, the tension out there is agonising. Can't you feel it? Bren is taking on the Annids – he's trying to force his own candidate on them as next Annid of Annids, even though she's from outside the House of the Owl, which is rare enough but not unprecedented. He's locked horns with Noli for nearly a whole day now. Like two rutting stags! And you have to remember this isn't just a domestic battle being played out, for many of the great Houses have allies in the world beyond. If it's drama you want, never mind the hunt, never mind the spear-chucking at the Giving – *this* is where the excitement is, with the whole future of Northland itself at stake.'

But Milaqa could only yawn. 'I suppose it's a matter of taste.'

He glared at her. 'You do disappoint me sometimes, Milaqa. You should listen. Think. Make connections . . .'

A serving girl came by, no more than twelve years old, barefoot but wearing a tunic adorned with jackdaw feathers. She bore a tray of treats, and Riban picked off goodies. 'Look, why don't you just leave me the tray?' He smiled, showing his wooden priest's teeth. The girl blushed, gave him the tray, and hurried off.

Teel disdained the treats. Milaqa, though, pecked like a bird. 'Mmm, burned sheep.'

'Lamb, actually.' Riban chewed a mouthful of meat. 'Flash-roasted and flavoured with something – pepper certainly – and another spice?'

Milaqa picked up a slab of bread, thinly cut, lightly toasted, and smeared with a bit of honeycomb. When she bit into it the honey dribbled down her chin. 'I didn't know I was so hungry.'

'You're not,' Teel said sourly. 'You shouldn't be eating that rubbish. It's unnatural. And all part of the wily traders' long-term game to seduce us into the farming business. No!' He strode over to another servant, and grabbed a handful of raw eel flesh. 'This is good enough for me. Good old-fashioned Northland catch.' He crammed it in his mouth and began chewing assiduously.

Still eating, they walked to the mound's south-facing crest. The great grassed ridges of the Mothers' Door swept around this central mound, their surfaces carefully restored, and water glimmered in the channels between the ridges, shadowed by the afternoon sun. Further out Northland itself stretched away, a blanket of land and water overlaid by misty air, with the smoke of early fires rising from the green domes of houses. The world hummed with the sounds of springtime, even from this elevated remove, the buzzing of bees, the singing of birds, the laughter of children.

Riban, staring down into the shadowed trench below, stopped chewing and pointed. 'Look down there.'

A party of men walked the track around one of the Door's circular channels, looking around curiously, at the earthworks, up at the Wall. One man seemed to be staring straight up at Milaqa. She thought she saw the dull glow of bronze: armour or weapons.

'Greeks,' Riban said simply.

'What Greeks?' Milaqa asked. 'There are lots of kinds of Greeks, with different tongues. I've met some of them.'

'The Mycenaeans are the toughest, but they are just the strongest dogs of a squabbling pack.'

Teel said, 'Maybe you haven't heard. Mycenae has collapsed. The oldest and grandest of those warrior-kingdoms – gone, like a bad dream.'

'Hmm,' Riban said. 'Well, they're all hungry dogs, in this time of drought and famine on the Continent.'

Milaqa looked at Riban, interested. She'd grown up alongside him, another of her gang of distant cousins. A couple of years older than her, he'd always seemed curious about everything, and obsessed by gossip and intrigue; even as a boy he would hang around with priests or Annids rather than play. 'You're going to make a funny sort of priest, Riban. You're much too interested in this world rather than any other. And the way you flashed those teeth of yours at the girl to get her tray off her—'

'Well, there are lots of rooms in our holy House,' Riban said easily. 'One sect studies the teachings of Jurgi, who is supposed to have been priest at the time of Ana – or possibly he was her father, her lover or her son; the legends vary. *He* said you find the gods through other people, rather than in smoke-filled dreamers' huts. That's the side of the work I'm interested in.'

'But you're still to be a genuine priest?'

He grinned. 'Oh, yes. I had to let them pull out my teeth to get this far.'

Teel said now, 'You're right to speak of hungry dogs. That's why this particular convocation is so important. We've always had trouble with the farmers. The problem is there are so *many* of them, in their dense little communities, all the way across the Continent. We've found ways to keep them at bay. They've always needed the tin we mine in Albia, for their bronze. And as they've grown hungry with the famine we've started to buy them off with potatoes and maize, or their products. We encourage the farmers in Albia and Gaira to grow this stuff, and then sell it on to the empires further east. Yes, it's hypocritical – we turn one lot of farmers against another – but it works. But now, as the famine in the east worsens, this delicate web of trade and intrigue and manipulation is coming under pressure again. There are strong disagreements about how best to deal with all this. Between the Houses, and I dare say within them. Bren believes we should take a much more aggressive stance towards the farmers – make closely binding deals with them.'

Milaqa was shocked. 'My mother would never have agreed to that.'

But Teel just looked at her. *You should listen. Think. Make connections . . .*

What connections? Well, her mother was no longer here. Was the opposition she would have raised to Bren's schemes the reason *why* she was not here? And now here was Bren forcing his own candidate on the Annids. Webs of suspicion formed in her mind. She plucked at Teel's sleeve and drew him away from Riban, who strolled off with his plate of treats. She whispered, *'Was it Bren?'*

'Hush.'

'No, listen – that Jackdaw, Bren. It all fits. As a trader he had access to the Hatti and their special iron. If he wanted to push through this treaty with the Hatti he had a motive to remove my mother, to force this convocation – to create a gap to have his own niece installed as Annid of Annids. He *killed* my mother—'

'Or some puppet did, more like,' Teel murmured sadly. 'I've come to suspect this myself as the convocation has unfolded, and Bren has made his intentions clear. I wanted you to work it out for yourself. It's why I've been trying to get you to pay attention to the discussions, child! But it's one thing to suspect, another thing to prove it.

'I'll tell you what we do know. That Bren's certainly got his iron from the Hatti, for only they make the stuff strong enough for it to be used in weaponry – and some of *them* have long wanted a closer relationship with us, so maybe they have some hand in this. Milaqa, listen to me. There's a party of senior Hatti traders and diplomats, coming from the east for the Giving. Isn't Voro supposed to be going with the party to meet them?'

'So what?'

'You must go with that party of Jackdaws. Meet the Hatti. We talked about that before. You must follow the thread. Voro is your way to do that.'

'They won't say anything in front of me.'

'You can translate. Offer your services. Interpreters are invisible; they'll speak as if you aren't there, you'll be surprised. Look – this is your chance.'

It made sense. Yet she hesitated, as she had since her mother's interment, to become entangled in her uncle's webs of deceit and intrigue.

The sun was dipping, the mist thickening over the great damp quilt of Northland. On the mound behind them a din of raucous laughter rose up as the assembled leaders of Northland started on the evening's mead.

16

The Trojan party, travelling ever deeper into the great country of Gaira, followed the valley until the river dissolved into its feeder tributaries. Then they climbed a long rise and emerged from the forest, to find themselves on an island of higher ground in a landscape coated by thick oak woodland. They had come several days' walk from the beach where they had landed. Smoke rose here and there, but otherwise there was no sign of people.

Praxo approached Qirum and Kilushepa. 'Vertix says we're near the watershed. There's a community of farmers a bit further on. We can trade for food and shelter. They know folk who will guide us to the big river that will lead us north and west to the land of the Bardi. And then – well, then we can start looking for a sea-going ship.'

Qirum nodded. He would not meet Praxo's eyes. He had found it impossible to speak to the man since his conversation with Kilushepa some days earlier.

Praxo waited for a response. When none came, he just laughed and walked away.

Vertix led them down to lower land and back into dense forest, where they followed a track so narrow and winding it might have been made by deer. The men pushed along, grumbling.

As the day approached its end, at last they broke through into a clearing. Perhaps a hundred paces across, it was walled off by tall oaks with knots of hazel at their feet, and the open ground was studded by saplings. A handful of houses sat here, Qirum counted four, five, six, with frames of oak trunks covered by a thatch of leaves and reeds. Half the clearing seemed to be given over to a crop, wheat growing sparsely. In a pen of woven wicker a few scrawny sheep grazed apathetically. The rest of the clearing looked to Qirum like a hunters' camp, with joints of a recently killed deer hanging dripping from a frame, a skin stretched out to dry, and heaps of spears, arrows, bows, amid the usual middens. A big open-air hearth crackled, smoke rising, with a huge pot suspended over it on a trestle. In one doorway a woman sat with her child on her lap, watching, uninterested.

A man came out of one of the huts, bare-chested, hobbling, leaning on a stick. He must have been well over forty. Vertix went to greet him, and they spoke.

Praxo, standing with Qirum, listened in. 'He's saying the men are away hunting, with most of the older kids. Just a few mothers here, with infants. There's a big man who will talk with us when we get back . . . This old one will bring us water. Not very quickly, probably.'

Kilushepa was peering around at the camp with contempt. 'What a shabby place. Do these people think they are farmers? This isn't a farm! This is a scrape. At Hattusa we have farms that stretch to the horizon. And in Egypt, along their great river – you could lose all of this in a single one of their fields.' She walked to a house and kicked its support. 'Call this a house? I have seen bigger hearths.'

And Qirum saw the compact little farm as she saw it, with eyes accustomed to the glories of cities like Hattusa, immense monuments of stone.

Now there was a commotion: a growl, a slap, a baby's wail. A couple of the men, growing bored, had gone over to the woman nursing the baby. Now she was standing, her baby crying against her chest, and one man held a hand before a bloody mouth. 'I only wanted to play with her spare titty! What's wrong with that?' The old man emerged from his hut again, shouting and waving his stick. Vertix hurried over, calling for calm.

Praxo growled, 'I'd better go sort it out.'

'No,' Kilushepa said simply.

'No?' Praxo turned to her, huge, a dangerous expression on his face. 'No, you say?'

'Why deal with these people? Take the food you want. Have that woman. Have the old man if you want. Are you afraid of women and old men?'

Praxo glowered. 'It's not a question of fear. We're here to trade with the Northlanders. That was my understanding. Not to burn our way through the forests of Gaira.' Behind him a shoving match was developing between the old man and the rowers, while the baby screamed. 'Tell her, Qirum.'

'Praxo, you don't tell me what to do,' Qirum said, his anger seething, inchoate, directionless.

'Evidently he does,' Kilushepa murmured softly. 'Or he thinks he does. Why do you think he speaks to you this way, Qirum? I wonder how he sees you – as the beaten boy on his knees before him?'

'Enough,' he snarled.

'If you won't start it, I will.' She strode to the big hearth, picked a brand out of the fire, and prepared to hurl it at one of the houses.

'No!' Praxo strode across and grabbed her arm. 'You do as I say, woman.'

'And you will not defy me!' Qirum's words were a bark that sounded in his own head as if they had come from somebody else's mouth, from the muzzle of a dog. He ran forward, and his right arm reached for the sword in its leather scabbard on his back, as if of its own accord.

It was over before he understood what he had done. His sword protruded from Praxo's back, its tip thrusting from his front, ripping his tunic.

Praxo dropped to his knees and looked back at Qirum, astonished. He tried to breathe, and a pink froth bubbled from the wounds on his back and chest, and then a darker fluid gushed, almost black. He fell forward.

Qirum looked around. Everybody in the clearing was staring at him, the men from the boat, Vertix, the old man, the woman.

'I—' I did not do it. It was not me. Yet it was my hands, my arms, my sword.

Kilushepa, breathing hard, still held the burning brand. 'That's the end of that complication. Now let's get on with things.' She dropped the brand into the dirt, where it burned out harmlessly.

17

So Milaqa, submitting to Teel's urging, attached herself to the party of traders led by Jackdaw Bren to meet the Hatti embassy. The meeting point was in a country called Kanti, in the south of Albia. They had to travel the length of Northland over the higher ground of the First Mother's Ribs, by canal, horse carriage and on foot, until they reached the south-east corner of Albia, where the peninsula met Gaira and the Continent. Kanti was not like the open plains of Northland. Here the hills and valleys came in waves, small and closed in. After days of following river valleys and tracks through this shut-in landscape – and with the oppressive company of the traders, five of them including Bren and Voro – Milaqa longed for a glimpse of horizon.

It was a relief when the Kanti farmstead came into view on the higher ground. At least the farm was an open sprawl, on a hillside above a river bank. Around a big central house, long and square-cornered, fields were roughly scratched in the earth, storage pits, animals in pens, and the usual dumps of ordure and waste. Other, smaller buildings were scattered around. The animals were cattle, stunted-looking creatures much smaller than the graceful aurochs Milaqa was used to in Northland, and sheep and goats, long-legged, hairy creatures, exotic imports from the east. People worked in the fields, mostly women and children, poking at the chalky soil with sticks and pulling up weeds. The farm as a whole was encircled by stones, each as high as Milaqa's waist and spaced a few paces apart.

And all of this was surrounded by the endless forest of southern Albia, the tremendous oaks with their long straight trunks.

Milaqa could see there had been burning at the forest edge, where huge fallen trunks lay blackened and scorched, and bright new growths of saplings and hazel pushed into the light. The farm looked poor to Milaqa, the ground desiccated and weed-choked. Maybe the drought that was famously afflicting the Continent was breathing on Albia too – and, indeed, she knew that a number of nestspills from Albia had come to Northland in their distress.

The folk in the fields were distracted by the new arrivals, and stood and stared as they walked up towards the big house. One woman stood apart, at the head of the rough track by the house. Tall, slim, dressed in a robe of some ornate cloth, her hair close-cropped, she looked utterly out of place in this scrubby farm. A handful of men stood behind her, dressed like well-off Hatti, as Milaqa recognised. They all stood silent. You could see they were utterly dominated by the woman.

And Bren was suddenly excited. 'It is her. Her! Queen Kilush-epa! The last time I saw her was at a feast in the heart of Hattusa itself – years ago, oh, a world away. And here she is, the Tawananna herself standing in this grubby Albian farmstead! I never thought I'd live to see the day . . .' He hurried towards her.

A couple of the farmers approached now, a man and woman. Handsome, not tall, their hands grimy with farm dirt, they spoke in their own strangulated Kanti tongue. The man ostentatiously displayed a bronze dagger at his waist, probably his most precious treasure.

Bren just brushed past them to get to the regal woman. He switched to the Hatti tongue. 'Tawananna. When the runners told me you were here I could not believe it. It is an honour to be in your presence once again.' He bowed before the woman. A man of position in Etxelur fawning over this representative from a distant empire – before cattle-folk, as a Northlander would say. Milaqa was faintly disgusted.

The woman looked down at him. 'Oh, get up, man, there's no need for that.' Her Nesili was richly accented and fluent. Milaqa, who had been studying the Hatti tongue since becoming attached to this expedition, had trouble following it. But it was just another farmers' tongue, like Greek; they all sounded the same to outsiders. 'I'm pleased the runners got through, to inform you of my approach. But evidently they did not give you the full story. I am no longer Tawananna – not, at least, in the eyes of the man who usurped me, and who now occupies the throne of the Hatti.'

Bren stood straight and stared at her, evidently shocked, and yet Milaqa saw calculation in his narrow face. If she'd learned one thing about Bren, who was in some ways typical of the clan of traders he led, it was that he was constantly looking for advantage in the endlessly fluid world of human affairs. And in this sudden revelation he saw opportunities and threats. He said carefully, 'Then much has changed since we last met.'

'Oh, it has indeed,' she said drily. She glanced at Milaqa and Voro, and the other junior traders.

Bren hastily introduced the youngsters. 'Voro is one of our less foolish young Jackdaws. I have instructed him to make it his special task to ensure that all your needs are met during your time in Northland. Milaqa here is no trader. However, she is the daughter of our late Annid of Annids, and she has some skill with languages.'

Kilushepa turned to Milaqa, her interest briefly engaged. She must once have been very beautiful, Milaqa thought, looking up at this tall, slender woman. She had fine high cheekbones, a strong nose, a firm chin, a full mouth. But there were lines around her mouth and eyes, small scars on her forehead, and her skin looked taut, weather-beaten. And her pale gold-brown eyes were eerie. Without pity. It was like being eyed by some huge bird of prey. Milaqa suppressed a shudder.

'I never met your mother,' Kilushepa said now. 'She was called Kuma, was she not?'

Milaqa said carefully, 'It's an honour for me to meet you now.'

'We did correspond, however. Myself and your mother. A

correspondence which is now stored away in some archive in Hattusa. We did not always agree. Indeed I thought of your mother as an opponent. Yet our correspondence was always courteous and constructive. I suppose one can't ask for more than that.' Kilushepa straightened up, pressing a slim hand to her back. 'Oh, will you walk with me, trader? Standing for any length of time makes me sore, yet I cannot bear to sit for long in the hovels of these people.'

'We are at your disposal,' Bren said hastily.

'Even though,' Voro muttered to Milaqa, '*we* just walked most of the way from Etxelur.'

They fell in beside Kilushepa as she began a slow march around the edge of the fields. The other Hatti followed, and the two farmers trailed after, ignored by all concerned on their own land. Milaqa heard the other Hatti murmuring, when they thought that Kilushepa could not hear, and that the others could not understand. They complained how they had not come here to support this Kilushepa, but for very different reasons, now utterly ignored. It was just as Teel had predicted; as a mere interpreter she was invisible to them, and they spoke freely despite her presence.

'The Trojan and I are staying in that hut on the left,' Kilushepa said, pointing. 'With the rest of the party, who were sent from Hattusa. Not that *they* matter. There is room for you, trader. Sooner a hut like that than to stay in the big hall, which these people share with their cattle in the winter, imagine that! I mean, look at this place. They don't even use bronze to blade their hoes!'

Bren said gently, 'Bronze is expensive. And flint, as you can see,' he said, kicking the dirt, 'is plentiful in this country. You only have to dig it up.'

'But they don't plough the fields properly, they don't mark the land – it seems to me they only spend half their time at the proper work of farming, and the rest drifting off into the forest to chase deer. And that,' she said, pointing a finger at Bren's chest, 'is *your* fault, Northlander. It has been this way ever since the Trojan and I reached the hinterland of your country. If not for you, this would be sensible farming country, just like the civilised world of the east.'

'Of course we think of ourselves as civilised, in our way.'

'I suppose you do. So tell me of the new Annid of Annids, who must have been selected by now?'

'Oh, yes. A fine candidate. In fact a protégé of mine, from the House of Jackdaws. She met with some controversy, but so does every Annid selection.'

'And do you think she will be easy to work with?'

'Unlike my mother?' Milaqa snapped.

Kilushepa glanced back at her with a humourless smile. 'Feisty one, isn't she?'

'Not necessarily a bad trait in the young,' Bren said.

'As long as it's beaten out of them before they are grown.'

'Your mother and the Tawananna did have their differences, Milaqa,' the Jackdaw said. 'Kuma wanted only what was best for Northland, as she saw it. But our two countries have been closely linked for so long – our destinies are intertwined – I don't think your mother saw that. And I don't think she saw the greatness of the Tawananna here, who, working behind the throne of Hattusa, kept an empire intact in a time of famine and drought. Planning military interventions. Restoring irrigation and water storage systems. Ensuring flows of food into the desiccated heartland—'

'And the last is where I relied on our traditional links with Northland,' Kilushepa said. 'And the miraculous foods you ship to us in such massive loads. If not for that, yes, I believe the Hatti empire would have collapsed by now. Even Hattusa itself burned and abandoned, perhaps.'

Milaqa said, 'If Northland's foods were so valuable to you, why the differences with my mother?'

'I didn't just want shipments of mash. I wanted the *secret* of that food, the seed stock, for which I was prepared to pay a very high price. Hattusa and Etxelur are close allies; I could see no reason why a sharing of such resources should weaken the bond between us rather than strengthen it. Yet the partnership I offered was rejected by the Annid of Annids . . .'

Milaqa studied Bren as she described this. Was this Bren's plan too, this heady scheme, this integration of Hattusa and Etxelur? Was this the reason her mother had had to die? And was this why Hatti iron had been used to kill her mother – did Bren somehow think it was appropriate, or just? And who was Bren to discuss such issues with the representative of a foreign power?

They came to the stone circle that surrounded the village. Kilushepa sneered. 'Oh, look at this wretched effort. It would be dwarfed by some of the tremendous structures we have seen in Gaira! And I am told some in Ibera are even more dramatic.' She led them to walk within the circle. 'In any event my failure to make headway with this child's mother surely contributed to my fall.'

'Which was a disaster for the Hatti, and for the whole world,' Bren said soothingly. 'But a disaster I hope we can put right, in the days and weeks to come.'

'That,' said Kilushepa firmly, 'is what we must discuss.'

18

When the conversation began to break up, Milaqa made for the hut Kilushepa said had been given over to their use. Maybe she could clean up in there, have something to eat and drink. Such was her mood of impotent fury at Bren and his lethal scheming, just to get out of sight of people for a while would be a good thing.

But as she approached the hut she heard a belch erupting from it, thunderous, liquid, drawn out, delivered with relish.

A man came strutting out of the house. Aged perhaps mid-twenties, he wore a tunic of grey wool that just reached his knees, leather leggings, strapped-on sandals, a scabbard with a bronze sword on his back, and a breastplate he laced about his body as he emerged into the light. He was shorter than she was, muscular. His head was bare, his dark hair cropped short and tousled, and his face was smoothly shaven. Even from a distance he smelled of spices, of perfumes she couldn't identify, and of ale.

When he saw Milaqa his hand was on the hilt of the sword in an instant. He was a man used to sudden threats, she saw, a warrior. She took care not to move a muscle, showing her hands were empty.

He grinned, dropped his hands to his sides, and said something in what sounded like poor Greek.

'Excuse me?' she replied in Hatti. 'And by the way, you stink of ale.'

'Oh, you speak the tongue of the longhairs, do you?' he said, reverting to that tongue. 'Passably well, too.'

'It's what I study. Languages.'

'Really? You *study*?' He looked her up and down. 'A girl like you doesn't need to be studying anything at all. Except maybe how to twist her hips.' And he gave his own pelvis an obscene wiggle. His arms were bare, heavily muscled, and striped with small scars. He was stocky, but he moved with an animal grace – he was a slab of muscle, with not an ounce of fat on him.

Revolted, appalled – fascinated – she snapped back, 'Not too respectful, are you, to the daughter of an Annid? Well, you won't get any hip-twists from me.'

'Daughter of an Annid? So you're a Northlander. The first I've met in fact. Explains the skinny frame, the complexion like water, the arrogant ways. As for stinking of ale . . .' He raised a hand to his mouth, breathed, sniffed deeply. 'It will wear off. Anyhow, what do you know about beer? Got a husband who likes a drop, have you?' When she hesitated, his grin widened. 'Oh. No husband. Well, that makes the situation more interesting. Like a drop yourself, do you? You want to join me? I've a cask in the back, barely touched. Kilushepa sips a little, leaves the rest to me. Not bad stuff – not made by these dirt-scratchers here, but bought from a village a couple of days away where they specialise.'

She felt like jabbing at him. 'Queen Kilushepa told us about you. Or at least, she let slip that you existed. She calls you "the Trojan".'

He grunted. 'My name is Qirum. She has other names for me, when we're alone in the dark, as we have been nightly, ever since I *bought* her.'

She tried to understand the sudden swirl of emotions inside her. This repulsive man, this arrogant, dirty, hard-drinking bully of a soldier was the opposite of everything she respected. What did she care if such a woman as Kilushepa lay with such a man as this, or not?

He was staring at her, as if he could see into her head, her heart. He took a bold step forward. 'The daughter of an Annid – you know, I've never lain with a Northlander—'

'And you're not going to now.'

'What, is it the drink you're worried about? Think it will hinder my prowess?' And he stepped back, performed a back-flip that left him standing on his feet, and drew his sword from the scabbard on his back and slashed at the air. His body had moved in one piece, as if carved from oak; the strength of his core muscles must be remarkable. 'See? Not even sweating. Tell you what – fetch me some of the nettle tea the farmer women serve up, and come and join me in here. It's warm and dark . . .'

'No, thanks.' She walked away.

His laughter pursued her. 'I'll see you later, little girl, daughter of an Annid. See you later!'

That evening the farmers built a tremendous bonfire at the heart of their village. Sheep were slaughtered for the roast, as was a boar trapped that day in the forest, and there were mounds of the coarse bread the farmers made from their grain. In return the visitors handed over gifts: bronze and amber from the Northlanders, and from Kilushepa's party exotic artefacts of glass, copper, tin, even a creamy white substance that turned out to be from the tooth of some tremendous animal whose description Milaqa didn't quite believe, and *iron*, ornaments and tools made of the precious stuff.

It was a clear starry night. After the feasting, while Bren engaged Kilushepa in deep conversation, the Kanti farmers began a ritual of their own. They tracked around their circle of stones, trampling flat a kind of walkway as they did so. Every so often the elders lay on the ground and took sightings of stars along lines of the stones, sometimes right across the village space, while the children danced and sang.

When she got the chance, Milaqa pulled Voro aside.

'Bren speaks with Kilushepa of alliances between the Hatti and Northland. But he is not the Annid of Annids. He is not even of the House of the Owl. He does not speak for Northland!'

'Yet his favoured candidate is now installed as Annid,' Voro murmured back.

'And I heard the other Hatti talking. If what they're saying is true it's an astonishing story. *They* are the embassy from Hattusa – not her! She found them, and just – well, she took over.'

Voro smiled. 'This is how the world works, I think. An ambitious Jackdaw, a disempowered queen, with knowledge and ability and cunning, in the right place and the right time – such people can change everything.'

As long as obstacles like Milaqa's mother were removed. 'It's not right. If my mother were alive—'

'But she is not,' Voro said firmly. 'Anyhow I thought you were the famous rebel, Milaqa. It's hard to believe you're demanding that things be done by the rules now!' He was grinning at her. *Mocking* her. Voro, the puppy dog!

Furious at him, at Bren and Kilushepa – furious at her mother for being dead – she stalked away and found a place to sit alone at the edge of the clearing, beside the tipped-up root of a great fallen tree.

Of course it was the Trojan who found her first.

'Go away.'

'Oh, come on.' He settled easily to the ground behind her. His lips shone with the grease of the meat he had eaten, and he carried a skin flask. 'I brought you some of my ale. You want to try some?'

'No.' But now she felt graceless. She lifted a flask of her own. 'I have this. Fruit, honey and water.'

'Suit yourself.' He took a draught of his ale, and let out a satisfied belch. 'We didn't get off to the best of starts, did we? My fault, I admit it.'

She fingered the iron arrowhead at her neck – a nervous gesture; she dropped her hand. 'And this is your way of having another try at me, is it?'

He laughed. 'I'm not that subtle. Believe me – I'm really not. We're going to be stuck with each other all the way across Northland. And besides, you've a choice of talking to me or that streak of gristle over there.' He meant Voro, who was hovering by the fire, trying not to be seen to be watching them. 'He's no doubt a decent fellow. If you want me to clear off so you can call him over—'

'No,' she said impulsively.

He laughed again and drank more ale. 'Or of course you could talk to some of these farmers, if you know the tongue.'

'They aren't the savages Kilushepa believes them to be.'

'Of course they're not. Do you know what they call themselves? The People of Venus. The wandering star is their principal goddess. And the way these stones are lined up is something to do with how Venus drifts around the sky. Don't ask me to explain. All this is locked up in the memories of their elders. They're a deep people – as all people are.'

'How do you know all this?'

'Because I keep my ears open, and my eyes. Because I too am deeper than you might think. Certainly than Kilushepa suspects, and that suits me fine. Mind you, I wouldn't go into that big central hall if I were you.'

'Why not?'

'Because among these people, when grandmother dies they cut out her guts and her brains and hang her up to dry out in the rafters, over the fire. It's nothing but corpses in there, dangling. Their feet knock your hat off.'

She snorted laughter.

'Here's what I think, daughter of the Annid. I think you and I have a lot in common.'

She remembered Voro saying something similar. Somehow she believed it of Qirum. 'How can that be? I never met anybody like you before.'

'Like me?'

She looked at him, his slab of a body, his scars, his arrogant bearing. 'A fighter.'

'So nobody fights in Northland?'

'Not the way you people do.'

He grinned. 'That fascinates you, doesn't it? And that's *why* we fight, you know. Deep down, underneath it all. The glamour. The thrill of hard muscle, the stink of blood. The finest sport anybody ever invented – war! You Northlanders don't know what you're missing.'

'Then why do you say we have something in common?'

'Because we're both outsiders. We're neither of us here for our own reasons, are we? I'm here because of what the Tawananna wants to achieve, which is to rebuild the Hatti's relationship with Northland, use that to win back her own position at home, and skewer her enemies. And you are here because – well, I'm not sure. You're no trader, are you? Must be something to do with your famous mother. And that nice Hatti arrowhead you wear around your pretty neck.'

She frowned. 'You don't know anything about me . . . How do you know it's Hatti?'

He reached out and cupped the arrow-point in his fingers. The back of his hand brushed her bare flesh, as he surely intended, and she tried not to show how it thrilled her. 'Only they can manufacture iron hard enough to use as a weapon.' He glanced across the village space. 'So here we are in the presence of an exiled Hatti queen, and a Northland trader who seems hungry for a little power himself, and a bit of weapon-quality iron. How does it all fit together, do you think?' He pulled back. 'Listen, daughter of an Annid – let's you and me stick together. We each need an ally.'

She said grudgingly, 'As long as it's convenient.'

He laughed. 'I wouldn't expect anything else. Well, I'd better go have a nap before it's time to service the Tawananna again. Goodnight, Annid's daughter.' He leaned over and kissed her cheek, quite gently. Then he got to his feet in a single bound, and walked off to the house he shared with Kilushepa.

She wiped away the meat grease he had left on her cheek. And then she touched the place he had kissed her, again.

19

The Year of the Fire Mountain: Midsummer Solstice

The visitors from the Land of the Jaguar were staying at Medoc's home, a place called The Black, a few houses, sheep and cattle pens and potato fields tucked into the lee of the Hood. This place had taken its name from the layered black rock that protruded from the ground hereabout. Deri liked to go whale-hunting from the little natural harbour on the coast below.

On midsummer morn itself, and despite the rolled eyes of his wife Vala, Medoc decided it would be a good idea to take Tibo and Caxa for a walk up to the summit of the Hood. A unique chance to see a fire mountain in its pomp!

It was almost noon by the time Tibo met Medoc with the Jaguar girl, at the head of the track leading out of the little settlement. Already The Black was alive with its own celebration of midsummer, the day of Northland's Giving. A party of boys, both Northlanders and Ice Folk, went from house to house, handing over gifts of food, leather, carved stone, fine bone fishhooks, and receiving gifts in return. They were followed by a procession led by the village's chief priest, singing songs of earth and sky in a mixture of tongues. It was noisy, pleasant chaos. And nobody seemed bothered by the tremendous column of smoke that loomed into the sky from the mountain just to the north, or by the steady drizzle of ash that turned everything and everybody a faint grey, coming down in the brilliant sunshine of the year's longest day.

As Tibo arrived, Medoc was loading a pack on his back the size of a mountain itself, stuffed with water and food. Caxa stood beside Medoc, with sturdy boots on her feet and a leather cap on her head to keep the drifting ash out of her hair. She looked bewildered, as so often since she'd arrived on this island. But today she had particular cause, Tibo thought. Medoc was explaining to her what was going on. 'See, we're a mix of Northland folk and Ice Folk, each with their own traditions. But we merge them happily together. To us, the whole world is a gift of the little mothers, and today we give back in return. And where the Ice Folk come from there's nothing to eat but animals and fish and the beasts of the sea, and they know that an animal will only give you the gift of its flesh if it is willing. So today everybody gives back, you see, in thanks for the gifts of others. And at the end of the day there'll be the Burial of the Bladders. The hunters keep the bladders of every single sea animal they kill during the year, all the way since last midsummer, and tonight they'll climb this slope to bury them. It's quite a sight, I can tell you, and quite a stink too . . .'

Caxa just listened to all this, expressionless. There was a rumble, like distant thunder, and Tibo thought the drizzle of ash fell a bit more heavily.

Medoc hitched his own pack on his broad shoulders, turned, and began the walk up the steep path out of the village. 'Keep up, you youngsters. You'll soon warm up.'

Tibo followed, grumbling, with Caxa at his side. 'We're hardly cold, grandfather. And we're walking up a fire mountain . . .'

That column of smoke towered before them, black at the base and feathering in the air. Birds swooped around the column, distant specks of darkness themselves.

'Ravens,' Medoc said. 'The Ice Folk believe they are the souls of the dead, guarding an entrance to the underworld. Whatever you do don't kill one, or you'll spend the rest of your life apologising to the gods for it. Step out, you two!' He strode boldly on.

They breasted a shallow rise, and the Hood was revealed before them. It was a bleak, ridged formation that loomed above the greener lowlands, streaked with flows of black rock – a lifeless thing, Tibo thought, like a skull emerging from the living earth. And after a few more paces, it seemed to Tibo that the ground was growing warm beneath his feet.

Milaqa's party of Northlanders, Hatti and one Trojan reached Etxelur and the Wall in the early morning of the midsummer solstice itself. Their journey had been long and arduous, and to make it here for the special day they had had to finish the journey overnight, hurrying along the last few tracks in the eerie light of a night that was never quite dark.

Bren brought them to his own home, one of the famous Seven Houses of Etxelur, an ancient neighbourhood of properties demolished and rebuilt many times, that overlooked the Bay Land itself. Inside they dumped their packs, drank nettle tea, and hastily smartened up for the day. Bren and Voro donned their ceremonial cloaks of jackdaw feathers, cheerfully complaining about how heavy and hot they would be to wear. Qirum polished his bronze armour clean of dust with a corner of his tunic.

Kilushepa meanwhile borrowed some garments and a bolster of cloth from Bren's wife and used Qirum's knife to make some brisk modifications. The result, when she emerged into the light of day, startled Milaqa. The Tawananna wore a sweeping gown that left her arms bare but covered her legs to the floor. Her growing hair was brushed back into a tight bun, and she wore a necklace of iron pieces borrowed from the traders. Picking at a stray thread, she noticed Milaqa watching her. 'How do I look?' she asked in her own tongue.

'Like a queen of Hattusa,' Milaqa replied honestly.

Kilushepa snorted. 'Well, since you've never been near Hattusa I won't take that remark too seriously. But your words are meant kindly, so I thank you.'

Now Qirum emerged from the house, alongside Bren. Strutting, Qirum had his armour on and his horned helmet jammed on his head. As usual he looked as if he was spoiling for a fight.

He saw Milaqa and winked at her. Then he sniffed the air. 'Can I smell something? Like smoke, ash?'

'Some of the Swallows, the travellers, say there's a mountain spewing fire on Kirike's Land.'

'Where's that?'

'Across the Western Ocean – a long way from here. But it's not unknown for ash and dust to be carried far across the sea. Anyhow I think it's more likely you're smelling meat cooking up on the Wall.' She gestured. 'Take a look.'

The party turned, and Qirum and Kilushepa looked upon the Wall, at close hand and in full daylight, for the first time.

They were only a few hundred paces from its base, where its tremendous growstone flank met the Wall Way, the rough roadway that ran along its length from east to west. Towering over the houses that clustered at its feet, the exposed face shone brilliantly in the sun, but today great cloth panels hug over wide sections of the face, alive with colour, many of them adorned with the concentric-circle design that was the root of the symbolism of Northland. The huge scaffolding structures for the endless repair work were abandoned today; nobody worked at midsummer. But the staircases and galleries chipped into the sheer face swarmed with people walking and eating, leaning on balconies to look out over the country, and children ran along the corridors. For the Giving, people travelled from across Northland – from across the world, indeed – and on first arriving almost all of them made straight for Great Etxelur, the ancient heart of the Wall. If you listened closely you could hear a merged rumble of voices, the calls and shouts and laughter of the tremendous vertical crowd.

Qirum took off his helmet and scratched his scalp. 'It just deepens the mystery for me. Why, if you people can conceive of a tremendous monument like this, you would choose to live in wooden barns, like animals.'

Bren said portentously, 'We are all, perhaps, a mystery to each other. It will soon be midday, and before then we must find our way to the Chamber of the Solstice Noon. I am not as agile a climber of the staircases as I once was . . .'

As they formed up into a little procession behind the trader, Qirum looked blank. 'What chamber is that?'

Milaqa murmured, 'There will be beer.'

He grinned. 'Whatever tongue you use, Milaqa, you always speak my language, and for that I'm grateful!'

Medoc had led them high up the flank of the mountain, high above the last of the green, and Tibo walked on a carpet of ash like fallen snow, studded with the stumps of burned-down trees. The ground was hot enough now to feel uncomfortable through the thick soles of his boots, and they passed pools of mud that bubbled and steamed, the stink of sulphur strong. Nothing lived as far as he could see, no creatures walked here save Medoc, Tibo and Caxa – even the belching mud pools lacked the green mosses that usually grew there, even the ravens wheeling overhead did not land. It was a dead country, a place of rock and fire and ash, a place for the little mother of the earth, perhaps, and her alone. It was too hot, the air was thick and increasingly hard to breathe, and there was a continuous rushing roar, like falling water.

And now, it seemed to Tibo, the land actually *bulged* under their feet.

They passed a dead goat, on its back, its limbs sticking up into the air.

'This isn't a place for us,' Tibo muttered.

'What?' Medoc did not break his stride. 'What did you say, boy? Keep up, keep up.'

'I said,' he called, shouting over the noise, 'we shouldn't be up here. It's too dangerous.'

'Nonsense. Though I can't remember the mountain being quite as restive as this before. Maybe nobody in the world has seen what we're seeing! We are explorers, like Kirike the ancient who found this island, and then crossed the ocean to be the first to the Land of the Sky Wolf.'

'We're not explorers.'

'Nonsense! Anyhow it's just a little further to the summit. We can't turn back now . . .'

Tibo slowed, and walked alongside Caxa. 'Are you all right?'

The Jaguar girl walked on doggedly, keeping up the pace, coated with ash, grey as a corpse. 'My people too live in the shadow of fire mountains. We run from the heat, not towards it.'

'So do we – most of us – most of the time . . .' He saw that she was staring at flickers of flame that emerged from the rocks. 'What are you thinking?'

'About fire. Keeps you warm. But too close, you burn. Yes? And even as it warms, cold on your back. The unending cold, just beyond.' She shivered.

'You are . . .' He had no idea how to say what he wanted to say, in words she might understand. 'You have many layers.'

'Layers?'

'I see a fire. You see life and death. All in the same thing. Maybe that's why you're a sculptor. You think strange thoughts, with layers.'

She grabbed his arm. Her grip, through his sleeve, was surprisingly strong, the grip of a sculptor, belying the slenderness of her body, her thin face. 'Let me stay.'

'What?'

'Not go with Xivu. Not back to land of Jaguar.'

He was bewildered, a rush of emotions flooding him – fear of the consequences of this, a kind of tenderness that this girl should ask *him* for help. 'They need you there, don't they? Who else can carve the King's face? And before that you have to go to Northland, for the Annid.'

Caxa said softly, 'Sculpture finished, Caxa finished, I die.' She shivered, despite the heat of the fire mountain.

He didn't know what to say. He had no idea how he could help her.

'Aha!' Medoc had reached the summit. He stood silhouetted against a wall of rising steam, hands on hips, panting hard.

Tibo clambered up the last few paces, with Caxa at his side – and faced a bowl of fire. It was a wound in the summit of the mountain, deep-walled. A kind of liquid pooled in it, red hot and crusted over with a black scum that crackled and creaked as it flowed. Plumes of fire rose up, and sprays of hot rock, cooling as they fell. Steam rose from cracks in the rock at the rim of the containing bowl. The noise was different now, like huge, fast exhalations – chuff, chuff, chuff. There was a sense of huge energies, as if they stood on the shoulder of some immense, angry animal.

Medoc laughed, exhilarated. 'I've never seen the like – never seen it before, or heard of it. It's one for the grandchildren, Tibo.'

Tibo turned around so he looked down the flank of the mountain, to the lower land below with its pockets of forest and farmland, and then the line of the coast, the impossible blue of the sea beyond. 'We should go back.'

Medoc shook his head. 'Sometimes you sound like your grandmother.'

The ground shuddered. Caxa grabbed Tibo's arm.

There was a tremendous bang, and a rush of boiling-hot air hurled Tibo backwards.

20

The party led by Noli and Bren was not alone in being late to get to the Chamber of the Solstice Noon.

As they clambered up the staircases scratched into the face of the Wall, people crowded with a kind of stiff dignity, all trying to get to the ceremonial hall before the crucial moment of midday arrived. And it was an exotic crush, Milaqa thought. In among the robed seniors of the Houses of Etxelur there were representatives of many of the Wall's own Districts, and country folk from Northland in simpler shifts, and foreigners, men from the Albia forests in their bearskins and bull's-head caps, and women from the World River estuary in seal skin, and men dressed much like Qirum, as warriors or princes of the eastern empires, with armour and helmets adorned with horns and plumes and bones. Milaqa wondered if there were more of them than usual; maybe the drought had driven them here in hope of a dole of Kirike-fish or potato for their starving peoples. Some of the more elderly or overweight nobles, having trouble with the stairs, were carried in litters, and the big structures with their teams of sweating, stumbling bearers only added to the crowding and confusion.

Milaqa was relieved when they finally got to the Chamber. This was a wide, shallow room, entirely contained within the structure of the Wall. The room was already crowded, and above a murmur of conversation in a dozen tongues Milaqa heard the sing-song chanting of a priest, and the rhythmic rattle of a shaker. The place was lit by whale-oil lamps burning in brackets, and daylight admitted by a single shaft that pierced the smooth-faced growstone wall, high above all their heads.

Bren and Noli were senior enough that they had a right to a place at the front of the crowd, a favoured position, and they led the rest through. Kilushepa looked around with amused contempt. At the front Voro was already here. He greeted Bren, his superior, and nodded at Milaqa.

At the heart of the Chamber, surrounded by the crowd, was a growstone plinth, seamlessly moulded to the floor, with its tilted upper surface carefully placed, Milaqa knew, so that it faced the south. The surface bore the Etxelur concentric-rings symbol, carved growstone plated with a gleaming bronze sheen. The sunlight from the shaft cast a spot on the wall just above and to one side of the plinth, the beam easily visible in the dusty air, sloping down from the shaft straight as an arrow-shot.

The ceremony had already begun. The new Annid of Annids, Raka, stood by the head priest, looking nervous and self-conscious, weighed down by Kuma's big bronze breastplate. More priests stood by, chanting in unison through mouths distorted by wolves' jaws. Young Riban stood with them, working the shaker; it was the skull of a deer, its eyes stopped up, containing rattling scraps of creamy Etxelur flint, a very ancient treasure.

And here was Teel. Wearing his own robe as a member of the House of the Owl, he sidled up to Milaqa. 'Hello, little Crow.'

'Don't call me that . . . I don't feel as clever as a crow at all.'

'Tell me what you've found out.'

She quickly outlined what she had heard of Bren's history of plotting with the Hatti. 'And *that's* why my mother had to die. Just as we suspected. She was in the way of his scheme to sell our secrets to the Hatti. I don't think Kilushepa or any of the Hatti had anything to do with it directly. But Bren used the advantage of the iron his allies gave him.'

Teel thought this over. 'Do you have the arrowhead?'

She handed over the bit of iron, warm from her body heat. 'Why? What are you going to do?'

'Leave it to me.' Her uncle slipped away.

Noon approached, the unseen sun shifted in the sky, the

beam of dust motes swept slowly through the air, the spot cast on the wall neared the plinth, and the priests continued their song.

Bren leaned over to speak to Qirum and Kilushepa in his workmanlike Hatti. 'We are privileged to be here, to witness this. Lucky that today is a cloudless day! The shaft has been carefully arranged so that at midsummer noon, and only at that moment, the sun's light will shine down on this spot – this plinth, its very heart, the centre of the circles. This marks a spot where, we believe, Ana herself once stood when the Wall was first built, long ago. You understand that we build the Wall continually, repairing the sea-facing surface as best we can, but continually building up the landward side. And as the Wall has thickened and grown, generations of master builders from the House of the Beaver have ensured that the shaft has been properly extended so that the miracle of the instant of solstice is always captured, this moment of exquisite symmetry, this point in space and in time on which the whole year pivots . . .'

As the spot of sunlight neared the centre of the circular ridges the priests' chanting became more rapid, and Riban's skull-shaking more excited. Behind Milaqa, people leaned and muttered and strained to see.

Qirum leaned over to Milaqa. 'You promised me beer.'

'So I lied. But you're in for a show, I think . . .'

There was a collective gasp. The priests' chanting cut off in confusion.

For, as Milaqa saw, the spot of solstice sunlight, now precisely centred in the growstone circles, picked out, not bronze, but iron – the arrowhead she had worn around her neck.

Teel stepped forward. He stood before the plinth, so that the solstice light fell squarely on his face, as he surely intended. And he held up the arrowhead, on his palm.

'Here!' he said. 'Look on this. *This* is how Kuma, Annid of Annids, died. Not from some accident on the hunt, not from a fall – from an arrow driven into her chest.'

Noli frowned. 'What is this, Teel? What proof do you have?'

116

'I dug it out of her chest with my own hands when she was lying out on the roof. And her daughter Milaqa saw me do it.'

Faces turned to Milaqa. She was overwhelmed. She felt a hand on her shoulder: cousin Riban, the priest. She was glad of his silent support.

Teel shouted, 'An arrowhead of iron, hardened as only one people can make it – yours, queen of Hattusa.' Holding the arrow, he pointed at Kilushepa.

Bren was frantically murmuring in the ear of the Tawananna, and Milaqa wondered how faithful his translation was. Kilushepa calmly looked back at Teel. Qirum was grinning at the fuss.

'Hatti iron,' Teel said now, 'but it was no Hatti who pulled the bowstring – there was no Hatti within a day's ride when Kuma died. *It was one of her own* who did this – one of her own people, one of those close enough for her to trust them with her life, on the hunt. Which of you?' He glared at them all. 'Do you dare lie, here and now, at the moment of solstice in this holiest of places? Will you lie before the spirit of Ana herself? Which of you?' Now he confronted Bren. 'You, Jackdaw?'

Fear and shock were evident in Bren's eyes. But he was always quick-thinking. He looked around at the faces of the people – the angry priests, Noli and the furious Annids, the bemused foreign guests. Then he stepped forward. 'Yes. All right, Teel, you pompous old woman. I got the arrows from a Hatti contact who was glad to help. It was not I who pulled the bowstring. You will never know who it was,' and he glanced at Milaqa with a kind of cold cruelty. 'But, yes, I planned it.'

Riban gripped Milaqa's shoulder hard, holding her back.

But Voro gasped, 'no.' He turned to Milaqa in horror. 'I didn't know. I was there – if I'd known, I would have stopped it – I didn't know, I swear!'

At Voro's evident distress Bren's expression flickered, as if guilt stabbed briefly. But he snapped, 'There was no choice, boy!' He glared around at the rest. 'No choice! Kuma was an obstacle to progress, in these times of universal change. As are you fusty Annids, all of you, as stuck in the dark as the owl you claim as your House's Other. The world is changing, and North-land must change with it. If we do, if we work with allies like the Hatti rather than keep them at a distance, we may become the greatest power the world has seen. If we do not, we may be wiped from the face of the land. And if we do survive,' he said, growing in confidence and raising his voice, 'if we survive, I, Bren, will be remembered by history, rightly, as the greatest hero since Prokyid himself!'

Noli stepped up to him, her nose a fraction from his. 'Not if I can help it.' The Annid looked over to the priests. 'Bind him.'

There was uproar. The Annids present began to jostle with the Jackdaws, who tried to surround Bren. The foreigners, awed or amused, began their own pushing and shoving.

Qirum laughed out loud. He said to Milaqa, 'I'm sorry about your loss. Truly. But I had no idea your people are so divided . . .'

'Quiet,' said Teel. When the din did not cease, he went back to the plinth. 'Quiet!'

At his commanding bellow, the commotion stilled. Noli and Bren, surrounded by their followers, turned to him uncertainly.

'Listen,' said Teel. 'Just listen.'

And Milaqa heard a distant rumble, like thunder carrying across the sea, though the day had been still and cloudless – thunder audible even here, deep in the growstone heart of the Wall.

21

'Tibo. Tibo!'

Hands at his shoulders, shaking him. The air hot. More heat coming from the hard ground under his back. A roaring sound like a wave on the shore. The ground shuddering. He tried to open his mouth. His lips were gummed up, dry, and when he tried to lick them his tongue rasped on a kind of grit, sharp-tasting. Ash.

'Tibo!'

He opened his eyes. He was lying on his back, on a slope, his head lower than his feet. Shreds of white mist fled across the sky. He remembered the wall of ash and smoke coming at him, the hot air that had hurled him back with a casual flick.

Caxa's face loomed over him, streaked with ash and dirt. Her right cheek was blistered, and a trickle of blood ran from her nose, dripping from the jade bead stuck in there. She pulled at his shoulder. 'Hurt? You can walk?'

His spine had been bent backward over his pack. When he tried to rise his head pounded, with a sharp ache at the back of his skull from the blow from the rock or tree stump that had knocked him out. But he was able to sit up.

And he saw the ridge-summit of the Hood, only paces away. Steam and smoke thrust up into the air all along the ridge, studded with flecks glowing white-hot. That angry chuffing rock-breath noise had gone now, to be replaced by a continuing, deafening roar. He could feel the dry blistering heat on his face and hands, and when he took a breath it seared his throat. Ash washed down, falling like grey snowflakes. He watched, bemused, as the flakes drifted in the air, almost beautiful.

'Tibo, come!'

'Yes.' He struggled to his feet and tried to think. Down, down – they had to get away from this summit – down was the way to go. Down to the sea. He imagined immersing himself in the sea's cool, clear saltiness, washing away this searing dust. And his father would be there, waiting with his boat. He would take Caxa to the sea.

But there was something missing. A gap in his head. Somebody else. *Medoc.*

He looked around. Further down the slope old Medoc was lying on his front like a beached dolphin, groaning with pain. Tibo grabbed Caxa's hand. 'Come on.'

Medoc had fallen over a shattered tree stump, and an ash-coated splinter had neatly run through the fleshy part of his upper thigh. Tibo could see the point sticking out. Blood dripped onto the ash-covered ground, brilliant red against the grey.

Medoc waved them away, wincing with pain. 'No! Get away. Leave me here. Look, you can see what I've done to my leg . . .'

Caxa knelt over him and inspected his injury. 'Not bad,' she said to Tibo.

'You know how to treat injuries?' he asked, surprised.

'Sculptors – always big rocks falling over, sharp flakes flying – injuries all the time. Father helped me learn.'

'So what do we do?'

Caxa slipped her hands under Medoc's injured thigh, to either side of the tree splinter. 'You get foot.' Tibo moved around and cupped his hands under Medoc's ankle. 'We lift together.'

Tibo nodded.

Medoc raged, his face a mask of grey ash streaked with blood. 'You don't owe me anything – I'm the fool who brought you up here, all the way to the gates of the underworld, and now look what's happening—'

'On three. One, two – three!'

They both lifted, jerking the leg up and away from the

splinter, with a rip of flesh as the leg caught on some barb, and Medoc screamed. But the leg was free, and he rolled on his back. Caxa took a stone blade from the belt at her waist, hacked a strip of ash-grimed linen from her tunic, and wrapped it around the wound. The cloth instantly stained dark crimson, but there was no life-threatening flow; this was not the wound that would kill Medoc. The bit of wood that had done so much damage stuck out of the ground, mute. As Tibo watched, swirling ash settled on it, covering it over, flake by grey flake, the ash sticking to the drying blood.

Somehow Caxa got Medoc up off the ground. He was leaning on her, his arm over her shoulders, his good leg planted firmly on the ground.

Tibo wrapped his arm around Medoc's waist. 'Down. We have to go down to the sea.'

Caxa grunted, nodded. Together they stumbled down the slope, helping Medoc.

The ash thickened, becoming a kind of blizzard of burning flakes. They wrapped their cloaks around their heads, leaving only slits for their eyes. Tibo's lungs strained at air that was hot and smoky and stinking of sulphur. He could barely see his footing.

And again the ground shuddered, and there was a deep rocky groan, as if the mountain itself were struggling to wake from some nightmare.

In the little community called The Black, Vala was in her house – or rather Okea's house. As the sister of Medoc's dead wife Bel, Okea was Medoc's oldest surviving female relative, and that was the way property was owned and inherited here, as in Northland. It was a warm day, midsummer's day, not long after noon. The house's hide door was thrown open to the southern light, and while everybody else was out at the Giving, Vala was taking the chance to get some work done. She used a mortar and pestle to grind up meat and boiled potato to make the soft stew that Puli liked, her second son with Medoc and her youngest child, two years old and a fussy eater since he'd been teething. It was a stew that old Okea sucked up by the bowlful too, cursing her broken teeth. Puli himself lay peacefully sleeping in his wrap on the floor at her side.

As the booms came from the fire mountain, Puli barely stirred, but Vala was increasingly uneasy.

Okea's house had been one of the first to be built in this little settlement, and so it was in a favoured position on a stretch of high ground just before the great platform of black rock that had given the place its name. Sitting cross-legged just inside the house's south-facing door, Vala could see a long way, over a swathe of landscape, with its clumps of birch forest and scattered farmsteads, the fires of the fisher folk smoking their catch down by the small harbour, and then the sea beyond, bright and blue and glittering. But today there was a haze over the sea, and a kind of orange tinge to the sky.

And now that big boom earlier, the more or less continuous rumbling since. What did it mean?

Mi and Liff came bustling up the slope. Mi held a rough rubber ball in her hand, a gift from the Jaguar people, a sacred token that always ended up in the hands of the kids. Liff was complaining noisily. 'Mother, she took it off me, she took the ball.'

'Well, you wouldn't come home otherwise—'

'We were playing round-the-houses! I was *winning*, and she just grabbed it and came in. Mother, tell her—' He grabbed at the ball. Mi held it up, out of his reach.

Liff, ten years old, was Vala's first child with Medoc. And Mi, twelve, was Vala's daughter by her dead husband back in Northland. She was nearly as tall as Vala herself now, on the cusp of womanhood, but she was still enough of a kid to play. Both of them looked hot, over-excited maybe by all the fun of midsummer day, with the Giving and the bladder feast to come. But Mi looked concerned, her small, pretty face pinched.

With a sigh Vala put down her mortar and pestle. 'So what's this all about?'

'She was cheating.'

'I wasn't. I had to make him come in. Vala, you should come out and see. Pithi and her family, and Adhao and all those nephews and nieces of his—'

'What about them?'

'They're going.'

'Going where? What do you mean, *going*?'

'They're just packing up their stuff and walking away. Down towards the coast. *That*'s why I stopped playing with you, stupid!'

'All right, Mi.'

'I thought we should come back here.'

'That sounds sensible,' came a voice from the gloomy house. Old Okea came shuffling forward, leaning heavily on the stick of Albian oak Medoc had carved for her. She looked oddly caved in, Vala thought, with her white-streaked hair around a weather-beaten face, her empty dugs, her knees and hips ruined by a life of hard labour. She was forty-eight years old. 'And *I'll* take the ball.' She took it in one claw of a hand and dropped it into one of the voluminous leather bags hanging from her waist. 'That way nobody's cheating, yes?'

Vala looked at the older woman. 'Everybody's leaving, she says.'

'Not everybody,' said Mi.

'Let's take a look for ourselves.' Okea shuffled towards the light. She glanced down at Puli as she passed, dismissive. 'He'll keep for a moment.'

Vala pushed down her resentment. It galled her to be sub-servient to an old woman who probably wouldn't be alive if not for the support Vala gave her. But she was her husband's sister, and this was Okea's house, and this was the Northland way. She checked on her child for herself, then stepped out of the house after the others.

Despite the smoke and ash in the air the day was brilliant, and she blinked in the light. The community of The Black was just a dozen houses around a hearthspace of trodden earth, characteristic Northland, though the farmers' small fields of potatoes and the penned cattle nearby were not. Today timber and turf had been heaped up at the centre of the hearthspace, in anticipation of the evening's bonfire. And, as Mi had said, people were moving, coming out of the houses carrying children and food and bundles of clothes and tools. One man was loading up a cart to be hauled by an ox. Others, evidently meaning to stay put, hung around outside their houses or in their doorways, watching the rest, and staring at the sky to the north.

Liff turned that way and pointed. '*Look*, mother.'

Vala turned and saw a pillar of smoke, rising to the sky. It was dark at its base, where it billowed and bubbled like the boiling mud of a hot spring. Further up, she had to tilt back her head to see, it became paler, fading almost to white, as it spread out across the sky like the branches of a tree. The cloud loomed over the mountain, the settlement, perhaps the whole island. It seemed much taller than before.

What did it mean?

'I can see fire,' Liff said. 'Bits of red and white shooting up.'

'I suppose *you* thought it was a thunderstorm,' Okea said to Vala.

Vala bit back a quick response. Okea never missed a chance to get in a dig at Medoc's new wife, a woman from what she saw as the soft country of Northland, which didn't have any mountains at all. 'No, Okea. I've been here eleven years, you know.' Since Medoc had met her, newly widowed, at an equinoctial gathering in Etxelur. 'And I've spent those years listening to that mountain grumble and burp. No, I knew it wasn't a storm. The question is what to do about it.' She didn't know the behaviour of fire mountains well enough to be sure. She looked again at the adults with bundles of goods, and the children and dogs running at their feet, excited in this break in the routine.

Should *they* leave? She thought about her little family, Mi and Liff, two squabbling, resentful children, her infant asleep in the house, an old woman who could barely walk. It was a typical family on Kirike's Land, or in Northland, widows and orphans, grandmothers and grandchildren, bits of broken families welded together as you might make a new sword from scraps of bronze. Now she was responsible for them all. She tried to make a mental list of all they'd have to carry for them to last two, three nights on foot or in a boat – the food, the clothes. And then there would be the walk itself, everybody weary, squabbling, the baby crying, the old lady hobbling . . . If only Medoc was here! But of course he was gone, off up the mountain itself, and Deri, Medoc's son, was out on his boat somewhere, no doubt chewing the fat with his fishing companions, and laying bets on how tall the cloud would grow.

Okea was gazing at her, waiting for a decision.

She swallowed her pride. 'Okea – I've never seen the mountain this bad. What do you think? Should we walk, or should we stay?'

There was a flash of triumph in Okea's rheumy eyes. But the old woman turned away, looked at the cloud, sniffed the air. 'Hard to say. I was only a little girl the last time it was really bad. Not much older than Puli in his swaddling. Such a fuss, walking. I would be a burden to you, I know that. The kids too. And Medoc wouldn't know where we were.' She started to shuffle back to the house. 'Maybe it will blow over. It always has before. Let's wait for Medoc. Besides, I've got my sewing to finish, and you have that cooking, you don't want it to spoil.'

'What about Xivu, the Jaguar man?'

'Oh, *he* went off with the first families to leave,' Mi said. 'He didn't wait to be asked!'

Vala glanced south again, at the calm sea, the litter of fishing boats. Everything seemed normal, if you looked away from the mountain. 'All right,' she said to Okea. 'Come on into the house, kids – you can keep Puli amused while I finish the stew.'

Mi came willingly enough, but Liff hung back. He was holding out his hands. Small flakes of grey were settling on his palms.

When she looked up, Vala saw ash raining down, thickening all the time.

*

125

From Deri's boat, the cloud rising from the Hood was an extra-ordinary sight. With the island itself a stripe of grey-brown on the horizon, you could easily see the sheer scale of the cloud, like an immense tree of steam and smoke that had taken root in Kirike's Land. And after the noon blast, which from here had sounded like drawn-out thunder, the cloud had grown bigger yet, and it had spread out sideways, feathering.

Deri and Nago were out on the ocean to the south of Kirike's Land, just the two of them in a hide boat big enough for eight rowers. They had set off at dawn, loaded up with nets and wicker baskets and bait for the fishing. It was midsummer, the weather was calm, the seas should have been jumping with cod, and Deri had been looking forward to a long, fruitful day, just him and Nago out on the boat. And as Nago, a distant cousin of Deri's, kept his mouth shut most of the time, it would be a quiet one too, a break from the noisy chaos of his father's household, the kids and dogs everywhere – not to mention the midsummer celebrations.

But the catch had been poor. Maybe it was because of the booms from the mountain, the faint whiff of sulphur you could smell even out here, the tremors that made the sea itself shiver and froth. Maybe the fish had been scared away. And now that cloud just grew and grew.

'So,' Deri said, at some point long after noon. 'Do you think we should go back in?'

Nago sat at his end of the boat. He was thin, with a cadaverous face with sunken cheeks and a nose like a crow's beak. His habit of staying motionless for long periods of time made you wonder if he was awake at all, or even still alive. Deri had never known such an incurious man. But Nago had lived all his days on the island, and he ought to know its mountains and their fiery moods better than Deri. At last, having thought hard about Deri's question, he shrugged. 'Why should we?'

Deri found it hard to say. Because the tide and winds might be wrong, on such a strange day as this. Because he had a vision of

126

Medoc and Okea and Vala and the kids, and Tibo, all watching the cloud, waiting for him.

Perhaps for once Nago understood Deri's mood. 'They'll be all right,' he said.

'Who?'

'The family. I mean, your father went up the mountain yesterday with Tibo and that Jaguar girl, didn't he? Medoc's older than you and me put together. If he thinks it's safe, then it's safe.' Nago glanced at their meagre catch in the bilge. 'Anyway we haven't got enough fish yet.' He slid back until he was lying on a heap of netting in the prow of the boat, and closed his eyes.

He was probably right. Deri determined to stop fretting.

But that cloud spread higher and wider across the sky. It was feathering to the west now. Soon it drifted across the face of the sun, which dimmed to a silvery disc. The whole sky began to take on a strange, glowing green tinge.

Then ash began to fall, a gentle rainfall of fine dust and a few heavier flakes. It settled on the boat and gathered in scummy swirls on the sea itself. This kept up until everything, the boat itself, the fish in the bilge, the bare skin of the sleeping Nago, was stained pale grey, the colour leaching out.

And then, in mid-afternoon, the mountain gave a second shout, even louder than the one at noon. Deri thought he felt a kind of concussion in his chest. An even greater volume of black smoke began pouring from the mouth of the tortured mountain, feeding the huge spreading cloud above. And it seemed to him that even as it mushroomed higher, its lower layers were beginning to descend, to fall back to the island.

Nago grumbled in his sleep, and spat ash out of his open mouth.

22

The mountain's second shout hit Tibo like a punch in the back. He was knocked sprawling, on his face this time, and went slithering down the ash-strewn slope.

He looked back over his shoulder at Caxa and Medoc. Somehow they had stayed on their feet, Medoc leaning heavily on the Jaguar girl, the two of them stumbling clumsily down the slope. Tibo saw this in glimmers of daylight under a sky that was turning black as night, with the ash falling all around. When they reached Tibo they both slumped to the ground.

Medoc cried out as his wounded leg was twisted again. Then he pulled his pack around his neck in search of a water sack. 'I remember the last time the Hood blew its top – I was a boy – the ash came down on the fields. We tried to keep the cattle off it, but you can't stop them eating the grass. They came down with a kind of murrain. Within a day they couldn't walk, and in a few days they died. Nothing we could do.'

Caxa, breathing hard, lay on her back, her arms and legs splayed. That seemed a good idea to Tibo. He sat down and lay on his back, his head swimming. He felt as if he had not properly woken up since the first shout at the summit had knocked him unconscious. As if the whole day was a nightmare.

'We said we'd always remember,' Medoc was saying now, in his droning old man's voice. 'The priests wrote it down. Remember what to do with the cattle when the ash falls . . . No! Get up!' Medoc limped over to Tibo and began shaking him. 'Tibo, son! Get up! You'll die if you lie there.'

Tibo pushed him away, annoyed. 'Get off me.'

'Help me with her. The girl.' Medoc crawled over, slithering over the ground like a slug, his bad leg leaving a trail of blood in the ash. 'Come on, Tibo!'

So Tibo sat up, and his chest ached, his head swam some more. He leaned over Caxa, dug his hands under her armpits, and with what was left of his strength hauled her to her feet. The girl coughed and shuddered, looking around blearily, her face drained of blood under her mask of ash.

'I saw it before,' Medoc said. 'The last time. Especially on the lower ground, in hollows. The cattle lie down in there and just die. Maybe something comes out of the ground.'

Tibo said, 'Well, we're not dead yet—'

There was a scream, coming out of the sky, like the cry of some bird of prey. They ducked instinctively. Tibo glimpsed something falling, trailing smoke. A rock smashed to the ground only a few paces away, shattering, spilling red-hot fragments.

Caxa stared, and said something in her own tongue.

More unearthly shrieks. Tibo looked up through layers of billowing smoke to see more glowing rocks flying in the air, each a red-hot mass within a black crust. They landed at random, making the ground shudder with each impact.

'We must go,' he said. He got his arm around Medoc's waist, and Caxa took his other side. They hurried on down the mountainside, slithering and stumbling.

'Faster,' Medoc urged them. 'Faster!'

As the afternoon wore on the column of smoke and ash climbed and broadened until it covered the sky over the village, blocking out the light altogether, and darkness closed in.

People came out of their houses, those who had remained. Some carried torches of burning reed and lamps. The sun itself was only faintly visible, dropping down the sky to the southwest, a pale disc intermittently visible through scudding clouds of smoke, but there was light around the horizon, an eerie yellow-green. It was an extraordinary sight, on what was the longest day of the year – it was oddly exciting, a world transformed. The big bonfire was lit early. The kids ran around in the ash fall, chased by the dogs. From Adhao's house, one man produced a flute of carved bone that he began to play, and the children danced around the bonfire. There was talk of starting the roast for the Giving. Half the village had fled, but there would be that much more for those who remained.

Then the pebbles started to fall from the sky.

At first it was a novelty. The little stones fell in a sparse rain, coming down through the ash, pattering to the ground. The children, amazed, ran around trying to catch them.

Vala picked one up, a disc shape the size of her palm. It was pale, full of broken bubbles, remarkably light.

'Fire-mountain rock,' Okea said, at her elbow. 'We collect it. It's the stuff you use for scraping dead skin off your heels.'

Vala had never known where that useful rock had come from. The sky!

The fall grew harder, and began to cover the ground. Soon the rock was ankle deep, and it fell with a steady hiss. Vala began to grow uncomfortable at the hail of impacts on her head and shoulders. The children, still excited, kicked and scooped the heaps of the stuff that started to gather. Then a child cried out as a heavier piece knocked her to the ground, leaving a splash of blood on her forehead. Her mother swept her up and hurried into her house.

Vala snapped, 'Mi. Puli. In the house, now.'

The children came running as best they could, pushing through the layer of warm pebbles.

Inside the house Vala picked up little Puli in his swaddling, and they gathered around the hearth, the fire not yet lit. Okea lit lamps, and handed out dried fish to the older children. She moved calmly, as if determined not to frighten the children. Vala felt a surge of gratitude. The woman had been a mother herself, after all.

And all the time the rock poured from the sky, hammering on the sloping thatch roof.

*

Out at sea the bits of rock fell all afternoon. Deri and Nago pulled their tunics over their heads, but the rock pounded their bare shoulders and legs, and it gathered on the water, rock floating like ice, forming floes that scraped against the boat's hull as they tried to row. The sun was hidden, the sky black save at the horizon. It was a nightmarish journey, without end.

They had to stop again to bail the boat, not of water, but of rock fragments that had gathered in the bilge. The larger ones were warm to the touch. As he shovelled, Deri looked over his shoulder. While they were rowing he had to turn his back on Kirike's Land. Now he was shocked by its transformation. The island was almost entirely obscured by the monstrous, blooming cloud. Deri thought he could see flame shooting up from the ground as if from a tremendous bonfire. And lightning flared in the cloud itself, sparking, filling it with a purplish light.

'Ouch.' Nago, his tunic wrapped neatly around his head, picked a bit of black rock from a crater burned into his skin, and regarded it between thumb and forefinger with curiosity, before flicking it over the side. 'That's new. That one burned me. If this rock fall continues we might end up walking all the way back.'

Deri laughed. 'You're one of the strangest men I ever met, cousin. But I think I could be stuck out here with worse companions.'

'I wish I could say the same about you.'

Another red-hot pellet fell, and embedded itself in the boat hull. Deri beat it out with his hand.

But another fell. And another. The men had to use bilge water cupped in their hands to douse the red-hot cinders before they could set fire to the boat, and shook scorching fragments off their bare skin.

Wood cracked. From outside the house came a crumpling noise, a cry of pain.

Liff rushed to the doorway, peering out through the continuing rock hail. 'It's Pithi's house! It's fallen down!'

Vala came to see. The disaster was only dimly visible through the rock fall, people pushing out of the debris with their arms over their heads, sheltering infants under their bodies.

Okea was at her side. 'We can't sit here until this house falls in too.'

'No.'

'We must go to the harbour. Maybe we can find a boat – Deri might be there.'

'But Medoc and the others—'

'There's nothing we can do for them,' Okea said.

'We could have done this half a day ago,' Vala said, anger and fear turning to resentment. 'When the mountain first shouted.'

Okea was not perturbed. 'We can argue about whose fault it was later. I will try to help you with the children. But you can see how it is with me. If you choose to go without me—'

'No,' Vala said. 'We all go. But the falling rock – we'll need some kind of cover.'

'My ox-hide,' said Okea. 'If we hold it over us – you, me, the girl – perhaps that will be enough.'

So they got ready. Vala had the children don their best leather leggings, and they all strapped water bottles to their waists. Mi took her favourite bow, made of good Kirike's Land ash, and slung it over her shoulder. Vala picked up a whining Puli, and tied him to her chest inside a spare tunic knotted behind her back.

Then they formed up into a tight group, Vala in the lead, Mi at the back, Okea and Liff between them, with the ox-hide spread over their heads, and they pushed out into the unnatural dark. The rock fell on the thick leather with a roar, and its weight made them stagger. But it was not the fresh-falling rock that was the worst problem but the layer of it on the ground. It was already over Vala's knees, almost up to poor Liff's waist. It was all they could do to wade forward through the heavy, rasping stuff, each step an exhausting shove. Okea seemed barely able to walk at all. They couldn't speak, the roar of the rock on their ox-hide was too great for that, and there was nobody around to help. Soon Liff was weeping steadily.

And from the north came yet another tremendous boom.

23

The three of them came stumbling into The Black, Caxa and Tibo to either side of Medoc, their tunics over their heads, battered, exhausted.

The village was scarcely recognisable. The thick rock fall and the grey ash had changed everything, the colours, the very shape of the land. The houses looked as if they had been stamped on by some tremendous booted heel, the thatch roofs imploded, the big support beams sticking up into the air like snapped bones through flesh. They found the wreck of Okea's house, smashed and flattened like the rest. Of the people there was not a sign.

They huddled together, like three ghosts, Tibo thought, grey from the ash, even their ears, their noses, even their lips around pink mouths.

'They aren't here,' Medoc shouted over the clatter of the falling rock.

Caxa pointed to the ruined house. 'We could search it.'

'No,' Medoc gasped. 'There's nothing for us here. Come, come.' He grabbed their shoulders, urging the two of them on.

They had no choice but to go on, stumbling through the heavy fallen rock along the trail that led from the village down to the sea. But Tibo saw Medoc's face, ash-covered, twisted with pain, and he saw how hard this choice had been for him. Surely his instinct had been to fall on the ruin of the house and dig, dig until he was sure that nobody lived. Medoc was saving them, Caxa and Tibo, or trying to. Was this how it was to be an adult?

They didn't try to speak. Tibo could see little in darkness

broken only by a faint glow from the horizon, the occasional glow of fire or a burning rock. As they struggled on he utterly lost track of time, of where he was.

And then they came upon the bodies.

The three of them stood together, wheezing for breath. At first Tibo thought they were just lumps on the path, shapeless mounds of ash or rock. Then he saw a hand, small and open, sticking up into the air, with a bracelet of broken shell around the wrist.

'Look,' Caxa said, pointing. 'Two adults. Children beneath. Cradled. Your family?'

'No,' Medoc said, grim. 'I recognise the little girl's bracelet. Okea made it for her. These are some of Adhao's family. People from the village. Come on.' The three of them stumbled on into the burning dark, heading downhill.

And they came on another group of people, sitting by the way, huddled under an ox-hide.

'I recognise that hide,' Tibo said, wondering. 'It is aunt Okea's.'

Medoc forced himself forward, bellowing, 'Okea! Vala! Is that you?'

Tibo saw faces peering from under the ox-hide: Vala, Okea, Mi, Liff, even little Puli strapped to his mother's chest. All of them. They all tried to huddle under the ox-hide. Medoc hugged Vala. Tibo grabbed Mi and Liff, and old Okea. Even Caxa joined in, submitting to hugs from the children.

'You haven't got very far,' Medoc admonished. 'Look at this!' He extended his wounded, blood-soaked leg. 'I climbed down off a mountain with this and I still caught you up.'

Vala shook her head, angry despite her tension, her fear. 'Even now you criticise me, husband. Even now! Will I ever do anything right?'

Okea held a bony finger to her lips. 'Enough. You can only move as fast as the slowest person in the group, and that's me.' She laid her hand on Liff's head. 'Vala, you go ahead. And you

135

young ones. Take the Jaguar girl. Get to the coast and find Deri, if he's there – get off the island. We will follow—'

'No,' Liff protested. 'We won't leave you.'

'You aren't leaving us. You're just going on ahead, to make things ready. Isn't that sensible?' And she looked them in the eye, Vala, twelve-year-old Mi, fifteen-year-old Tibo.

Tibo looked at his grandfather, and again he saw the pain of choosing in his face. He said briskly, 'If I know my father he'll be fretting like an oystercatcher over its nest. The sooner we get to the shore and let him get back to fishing the better.'

Medoc put his heavy hand on Tibo's shoulder and squeezed.

They began to stand. Okea stepped out from under the ox-hide, and winced as the rock pebbles battered her scalp. Medoc hobbled to join her. Okea waved her arms, as if chasing away ducks. 'Go, go!'

So they set off, gathered around Vala under the ox-hide. Without old Medoc and his wounded leg, without the hobbling Okea, they were able to move quickly, wading through the ash and rock. Tibo glanced back once. He saw Medoc and Okea together, clutching each other's arms, Medoc leaning to favour his bad leg, both bowed under the rock fall. Then, a few paces further on, they were lost in the gloom of ash and smoke.

The oars scraped over the crust of rock on the ocean. Still the rock fell around them, a thinning hail laced with burning cinders. The journey was a fight, an endless one. All the way in, a hot wind off the land had been blowing at their backs pushing them away. And now the sea itself was surging, huge waves pulsing away from the shore. Deri imagined the land itself trembling as the mountain shuddered and roared, rocky spasms that must be disturbing the vast weight of the ocean.

Deri wondered what time it was. Evening, maybe. It was a long time since he had seen the sun. And Deri thought he wasn't hearing right, after that last vast bang.

Nago grunted and fell forward over his oar. 'Oh, by the ice

136

giants' bones, I am exhausted.' He picked up a water flask, drained a last trickle into his mouth, and threw it over the side.

Deri gave up rowing in sympathy, though it didn't seem long since the last break, and he was desperate to get to the shore. But his body ached, his back and legs and shoulders, drained by the effort of fighting the elements for so long.

Nago twisted on his bench and looked back beyond Deri's shoulder. 'Take a look at that.'

Deri swivelled to see, and the wind off the shore hit him full in the face, hot, dry, laden with ash and smoke and stinking of sulphur. He narrowed his eyes, held a corner of his tunic over his mouth, and looked back at the island.

The mountain's ridged summit was now alight from end to end. It seemed to be spitting fire in great gobbets, balls white-hot that shot upwards into the great flat black cloud over the island, a chain of fire connecting the sky to the ground like the bucket chains they used in Northland to drain floods. And all along the length of the ridge he saw a heavier glow leaking out and flowing down to the lower land. Over the rest of the island he saw the more diffuse glare of fires burning – trees, probably, whole forests flaring and dying.

Somewhere in all that was his father, his son.

'I'll say this once,' Nago shouted back. 'Because one of us has got to.'

'Go on.'

'We're safer out here. We could row back out, beyond the falling rock and the smoke and the rest of it. Sleep it off, out on the open sea, where it's safe. And then come back in when the mountain's finished its tantrum.'

Deri nodded. 'You're right. One of us did have to say it. Not a family type, are you?'

'My mother died giving birth to me. My father, your uncle, cleared off quick. I don't have a family. I don't have a wife. But there are women I look after.'

Nago had told Deri more about himself in a few breaths than in all the years they'd worked together. 'How many women?'

'Two. The third died.'

'And kids?'

'Some. Of course they support themselves. But they like the fish I bring, and other stuff.'

'You don't want to stay out here any more than I do, do you?'

'No.' Nago hawked, spat out dusty phlegm, rubbed his hands and grabbed his oars. 'Let's get on with it. One thing. If I don't make it through this —'

'Don't talk like that.'

'If not now, when? I want you to find them. Just ask around, it won't be hard. Tell them about me. The kids, you know?'

'Yes. Of course. And you—'

'I'll do the same. Goes without saying.' He leaned over his oar. 'On my stroke. One, two—'

And on the word 'two' there was another fantastic bang. *Another* one. The sound was a physical thing, like a pulse of wind that hammered at Deri's chest as well as his ears.

Nago was shouting something. Deri could hear nothing but a kind of whining tone in his ears, and a dull roar from the island. He twisted again to look back.

The fire rising from the mountain ridge was a solid wall now, burning white. And a band of light, glowing red-white, had formed all along the mountain's face, below the summit ridge. It was descending, sweeping down the mountain's flank as Deri watched, much faster than before. As it progressed there were brilliant splashes of light, more forests flashing to flame. It was a wall of fire, sweeping down towards the lowlands.

Now Nago was pointing again, shouting something Deri couldn't hear. Deri turned. A wave was coming at them from the land, a big one, a muscular rise that lifted up the floating islands of rock scum.

Frantically they worked their oars, trying to turn the boat so its prow faced the wave.

*

The latest blast was another shove in the back for Tibo, a hot wind stinking of ash and sulphur that sucked the air out of his chest. He struggled to stand, to get a breath.

With Vala and Caxa and the rest, he was still huddled under the ox-hide. They were on a broad track now, crowded with people who forced their way through the rock drifts. This was a confluence of survivors from settlements all over the mountain's slopes, now funnelling down this main route to the harbour, miserable people shuffling along, laden with children and possessions, invalids being carried, old people leaning on sticks. Everybody was walking; it was impossible to get a cart through the knee-deep rock.

He turned to look back, ducking his head under the hide. The latest convulsion seemed to have cleared the air of smoke and rock, and he could see the mountain rising above the plain. And he saw a band of fire, glowing red-white and billowing, rolling down the slope. It looked almost beautiful, almost graceful. Then he remembered how far he had come that day, how far away the peak must be – and he realised how fast that wall of fire must be descending.

'Run!' he shouted.

Nobody moved.

He looked around at them, Vala's pinched, anxious face, Liff's wide eyes rimmed with dust. He realised that none of them could hear a word he said. He grabbed Vala's arms, shook her, pointed at the mountain. 'Fire. That cloud. We have to get to the beach, the sea. It's our only chance. We have to run!'

'Run.' He could see her mouth the word. She looked at the mountain dully. Suddenly she understood. 'Run!'

Tibo pulled the ox-hide away and dumped it on the rock drifts. They would have to live with the rock fall; the hide would slow them too much. He grabbed Caxa's hand and dragged her. Vala pushed Liff ahead, and wrapped an arm around Caxa and Mi, and pulled them forward.

They were among the first in the crowd to understand, to start running. At first they had to push past people still shuffling slowly towards the sea. But a few looked back at the descending cloud, and saw it as Tibo did. They started to run too, dumping bags and scooping up children, running along the track.

And then it was like a stampede, a great flow towards the water, people no longer helping each other but jostling and pushing and pressing. As he fought to keep his feet, his head aching, every muscle drained, his lungs dragging at the dense, smoky, sulphurous air, Tibo dared not look back.

Medoc knew the game was over when he saw the glowing cloud.

As it swept down the slope the band of light was resolving into a wall of grey smoke and ash. It was like a tremendous tide, Medoc thought. He saw it roll over a scrap of forest – it loomed high over the trees, you could see how tall it was – and the trees flashed and were gone, just like that.

Okea sensed it too. Or maybe she just felt like giving up. They held each other's arms, propping each other up, breathing hard, their faces grimed with ash and blood. Okea shouted, 'We can't outrun that.'

'No, Okea, my dear. Not even if we were sixteen years old.'

'The mountain has shouted many times before. In my life-time, and yours. And my mother and grandmothers told me of other incidents. There are records too. A priest showed me once. But I never heard of anything like *that*.'

'Tibo and Mi and the others can warn their grandchildren, if they survive.'

'Oh, they will,' Okea said. 'They are strong and brave. Vala is resourceful. You made a good choice there.'

He looked at her. The ash had worked deep into the crevices of her face, making her look even older. 'That's the first thing you ever said about Vala that wasn't an insult.'

'Bel was my sister.'

'Her dying wasn't Vala's fault. Or mine, come to that.'

A roaring noise swelled, like a gathering storm. A young deer ran out of nowhere at them, skidded to avoid them, and ran on downhill, eyes wide with fear.

'He might be lucky,' Okea said.

He felt her tremble. Tenderly, he wrapped his arms around her. 'Don't be afraid.'

She snorted. 'You're pissing your pants yourself.'

He laughed. 'I always liked you, Okea, you old stick, underneath it all.'

'Well, I never liked you.'

'Fair enough.' The roaring was so loud he doubted if she could hear him. 'I think—'

It was here, looming high over him, a mass of whirling dust and smoke and whole chunks of red-hot rock, a wall taller than the one that kept out the sea from Northland, a wall rushing down on him at impossible speed, faster than any horse or deer had ever run. When it hit, Okea was dragged from his arms. He was swept up. He was flying, in the light.

An instant of searing pain.

The little harbour was just a cleft in the rocky coast, a stretch of black sand. But it was the only half-decent landing spot across much of the south shore of Kirike's Land. And now it crawled with people, as if it were the greatest harbour in the world.

But no boats were leaving. The strand was littered with vessels crushed by rock falls, or buried by the ash, or overturned and smashed, as if driven ashore by great waves. Nothing seaworthy.

Tibo left the group and headed for the water, shoving his way through the throng on the beach, young and old, healthy and injured, all of them coated with ash and sweat and blood, white eyes glimpsed in chaotic semi-darkness. Their shouts were like the cries of gulls, against the background roar of the mountain, all jumbled up and muffled in his damaged hearing. At his feet the rock was piled up in drifts. You couldn't even see where the waterline was, so densely was the ground carpeted by the rock fall.

141

At last he found his ankles bathed in water, the rock scraping his shins. He took one stride, two, out into the water. Its cool was a huge relief for his scorched flesh.

There were boats on the water, he saw now, and people from the shore trying to get to the boats. But whoever sat in those boats wasn't necessarily welcoming, and Tibo saw oars and even knives wielded to keep people off. Any one of those boats could be his father's – or Deri could be far out to sea. He called, his hands cupped. 'Father! Deri! It's me! Father!' He could barely hear his own voice. He kept shouting.

Strong hands took his shoulders and he was whirled around. It was Deri, coated in ash, his tunic wrapped around his head. Tibo threw himself into his father's arms. Then they broke. They shouted into each other's faces, barely able to make out the words.

Deri pointed out to sea. 'The boat's out there. Nago. We must wade . . .'

'I have them. Vala and the kids. The Jaguar girl.'

They both hurried back to the family from The Black, who had come struggling down the beach after Tibo.

'Come, quickly,' Deri said. He took Puli from Vala, the little boy was an ash-coated bundle, and grabbed Vala's hand and pulled her down the beach. Tibo took Liff's hand and followed. Mi and Caxa came after, helping each other, holding onto each other's arms. After all this, Mi still had her precious bow over her shoulder.

Deri shouted at Vala, 'Okea? My father?'

Vala just shook her head, her lips tight. Deri turned away, and kept driving to the sea, through the crowd.

Soon they were in the water. It deepened quickly, and Tibo had to help Liff half-wade, half-swim. When they reached the boat it was surrounded by a loose crowd of people, a dozen or more, struggling to stand in the turbulent water. Nago, kneeling up in the boat, was wielding his oar, keeping them at bay. When he saw Deri and the others he leaned over and started hauling them out and into the boat, one by one. Vala flopped into the bilge like a landed cod, and she took her soaked child from Deri's arms.

Deri grabbed Tibo's shoulder, and hauled him in so he landed face down. 'Oars,' Deri said, taking his own place. 'Go, Nago! You, Tibo – Caxa, Mi – you too, Liff, if you can handle an oar – take one, they're in the bottom of the boat.'

Tibo quickly found a place between Vala and Mi. Nago, paddling furiously, had already got the boat turned so it faced away from the land. Tibo got his oar into the rowlock, and started pulling, with muscles already spent by the day's exertions. At first their rowing was uncoordinated and they splashed more than they pulled, but to frantic commands from Deri and Nago they soon worked into a rhythm, and the boat pushed through a surface skim of rock, out towards the open sea.

Tibo, rowing hard, looked back at the land. That glowing cloud, now a wall of churning red-hot dust and rubble that spanned the world, was scouring down the hillside to the beach. People ran, making for the sea in a final panic, but the cloud swallowed them. Erased them. And soon it was rolling over the water.

He rowed and rowed and rowed.

24

It did not grow dark that midsummer night in Northland, though the light sank to a deep grey-blue. A phenomenon of this strange northern place, Qirum supposed. Yet to the west there was a deeper darkness, a smear of black as if a pot of pitch had been spilled. Qirum fancied he could see a spark of fire at the heart of it, right on the horizon, or beyond it.

He saw all this from the Wall, its roof, a walkway studded with huge stone slabs and the tremendous carved heads of dead Annids. Tonight beacons burned bright, all along the Wall's length to left and right as far as he could see. Senior members of all Northland's great Houses were up here, from the Annids to the lowly Beetles, still in their Giving finery. All of them anxiously looked west, watching the sea. And on the breast of that ocean were more lights, sparks on blue-black infinity. Boats with lanterns and beacons of their own.

'You could not sleep.'

He turned. Kilushepa stood by him, dressed in a long, warm cloak, her hand on her belly. 'Nor you, it seems,' he said.

'Too much commotion. Shouting, running, all along the Wall.'

'It is the great event in the ocean.' He pointed to the spreading black cloud. 'The Annids think it is a mountain of fire, far off to the west. On an island called Kirike's Land.'

'If it is so far away, why are the Northlanders so alarmed?'

'Because great events on land can cause similarly great calamities at sea,' Qirum said. 'This is as Milaqa explained it to me. There will be a ripple, if you will. But a ripple that might

144

challenge all these people have built. *Great Seas*, they call them; there have been two, as far as I know. These events are embedded deep in their memories, their culture, their sense of who they are. And so they have their beacons, and the lightships out to sea. If the wave comes the distant ships will flash a warning back to the land.'

She frowned. 'Will their Wall not keep out the wave?'

'One would hope so. But even if not they have fallback plans. They open watercourses, abandon the lower ground – make ready to soak up the flood.'

'I suppose we would have to flee.'

'I imagine so.'

'Well, let's hope it doesn't come to that. I just found out I'm pregnant.'

He turned to her, astonished. For a heartbeat he wondered if it could be his – but no, they had always been careful about that, she had taken him in her mouth or her anus, or they had used her protective calfskin sheathes. A brat forced on her by some faceless Hatti soldier, then. And she was the Tawananna!

He laughed.

She glared out to sea.

The breeze shifted, coming from the west, and he thought he could smell burning.

TWO

25

The Year of the Fire Mountain: Late Summer

Every day at least one of the family went up to the Wall roof to watch for Deri. Even months after midsummer there were always others up there too, friends and strangers waiting, staring out into the Northern Ocean. And all through that cold, dismal summer the nestspills had come in a trickle, sometimes just a single boat, sometimes little flotillas, packed with men, women, hungry children, sometimes even a few animals, drifting across a listless ocean and then drawing cautiously into the docks cut into the seaward face of the Wall.

On the day her uncle Deri came home, it happened to be Milaqa who was on watch. She was sheltering from the sharp breeze coming off the sea, unseasonably cold, and was wrapped up in a thick cloak she would normally not have dug out until the autumn. But this was a particularly cold spot, for she stood in a gap between one monolith and the next: the space where the monumental sculpture of her mother's head would one day sit, Kuma Annid of Annids. Any boatload of her family would know to pull up to the small dock at this point.

When the boat came in, alone, a dark smudge against the grey sea, she recognised it long before it reached the Wall, its unusually slender form, the slight kink in the prow. No two boats were identical. Each boat in Northland was made by the people who would sail it, and their family and friends. The process of building itself was a happy event, shared. This was Deri's boat, built before Milaqa was born, and her uncle had always taken

149

her out to sea in it. The boat was like a memory from childhood, of sunlit days on the sea.

As she waited, her arms wrapped around her torso, the cloud seemed to grow thicker, the day a little colder. It had been this way all summer, since the fire mountain. When the haze of smoke and sulphur stink had cleared away the high cloud remained, a solid roof of grey over the world. Sometimes you could see the sun as a pale disc, silver-white, with shadowy wisps passing over its face, but more often than not even that was invisible. And in the night no star shone, and barely a glimmer of moonlight, though at full moon the queen of death made the sky glow silver-grey, as if in triumph. If the sunlight was shut out, so was its warmth. The first frost had come not a month after the midsummer. Everybody had stood about amazed at the sight, frost on thick summer grass, and on the green reeds in the marshlands. Milaqa thought she had never seen so many owls out in the twilight – and the swallows and swifts had already gone, fled south in search of warmth.

The boat came closer, resolving out of the mist that lay over the sea. Now she could see a handful of adults, one a woman with an infant strapped to her chest. Some of them worked at the oars, fairly coordinated but listlessly. She heard a man's calm voice calling the strokes: Deri himself.

Milaqa picked up the sack of water skins she had carried up here on every watch, and climbed down the narrow staircase cut into the Wall's sea face, down to the dock. The dock itself was just a notch in the growstone, crusted with barnacles and drying seaweed, but deep enough to take a boat like Deri's. The crew saw Milaqa coming. Deri waved, and forced a smile. They all looked thin, dressed in ragged clothes stained grey or black.

The rowers shipped their oars, and used them to guide the boat into the little dock, pushing at the growstone. Milaqa threw a rope from a growstone bollard, and Deri tied it to the prow. Milaqa recognised Nago, a cousin of Deri's who was his workmate out on the sea. The woman with the infant must be Vala, the younger woman who had married Medoc, her grandfather. There was one exotic-looking girl, dark. Perhaps this was the sculptor from the Land of the Jaguars, fetched at last by Deri from across the Western Ocean.

Deri himself was first off the boat. He staggered a little as he stood on dry land. He embraced Milaqa. 'Thanks for waiting for us.' His voice was a scratch, and he smelled of the sea.

'Here. Water.' She handed him her sack, and he pulled out a skin gratefully. She saw that his bare left lower arm had been burned badly, the skin wrinkled and livid.

Milaqa turned and helped the others off the boat. They moved cautiously, stiffly, even the children, their skin sallow, the bones prominent in their faces, as if they had been turned into little old people. One girl picked up a big, powerful-looking bow from the bilge. Vala followed the children, then the dark girl, and finally Nago, who managed a grin. 'Nice to see a friendly face, cousin.' Milaqa helped Deri tie up the boat. He introduced his son, Tibo, who was fixing knots clumsily. They had brought nothing with them save the clothes they wore, and a litter of water skins and fishing gear in the boat. From a debris of bones Milaqa saw they had been relying on fish to feed themselves on the journey, presumably eaten raw.

Deri bent to stroke the boat's scorched and patched hull, as if she were alive. 'She'll be fine here for now. No weather coming. I'll wait a day, then I'll fix her up. She deserves that.'

'And the journey?'

'As you'd expect.' He was thin, bearded, tense. 'We rowed out of there with nothing. We drifted, landed where we could. Begging for food, water.'

Milaqa thought about who wasn't here. 'Grandfather Medoc? And Okea—'

'Lost,' Deri said. 'Both of them. Come on. The sooner we get away from the sea the better.'

Vala was already leading the party up the staircase to the top of the Wall. They all moved slowly, carefully. But then, Milaqa thought, most of them had probably never climbed stairs before. 'You'll be safe here,' she said.

Deri shivered in the chill breeze, and glanced up at the grey lid of sky. 'I hope you're right.'

Medoc's family welcomed the latest nestspills. Deri went to the house of his wife's family, and he took Vala with him. The others were taken in by distant aunts, uncles, cousins. When they realised who Caxa was, a boy was sent running, and he brought back a woman in a great cape of owl feathers – an Annid, Tibo was told, one of those who made the decisions in this place. She greeted Caxa in what Tibo could by now recognise as a broken version of Caxa's own tongue. The Annid went off in search of the other Jaguar, Xivu, who had arrived on a much earlier boat. Caxa was reluctant; she had never wanted to come here at all. But in the end the fire mountain had taken away her choices, as it had for so many others.

Tibo himself was taken in by a cousin of Milaqa, called Hadhe, a kindly woman no older than Milaqa herself but with three children of her own. The kids were curious at first, and picked over his filthy clothes, before Hadhe got them off him and threw them on the fire. Hadhe's mother, whose house this was, loaned Tibo a cloak and took him to a freshwater stream where he bathed all over, cleaning off the salt and the blood and a crust of ash he'd carried all the way from Kirike's Land. They even got a priest to come out, a junior one, another cousin called Riban. The priest checked over his collection of burns, gave him salves made of herbs ground up in goose fat, and listened to his rattly breath. He was given more pungent herbs that made him cough, but Riban said it would clear the ash from his lungs.

Tibo, who hadn't come to Northland for years, was impressed by the family's houses, big sturdy constructions that sat on sculpted mounds of earth. And he was staggered by the Wall. It had looked impressive enough from the seaward side, a white line that terminated the ocean itself, topped with glaring human faces. But from the land side it loomed high over your head, even over the houses on their mounds, a smooth face like a cliff but scarred by ramps and ladders and chambers. People *lived* up there, on and in the Wall. If you looked up you could see them coming and going. And yet at the foot of this enormous structure grass grew and freshwater streams ran and wild birds gathered, and children ran and played with their dogs, as if it was perfectly natural to be living on the bed of the sea.

Hadhe took time to talk to Tibo. She said her own house was in a community called Sunflower to the south of here. The family had come up to live close to the Wall, like many others, to wait for loved ones from Kirike's Land. They were generous, Hadhe and her family. But when they woke him for the evening meal he saw how carefully they portioned out the dried fish and hazelnuts they offered him. Food was short here too, then, just as on the boat.

Tibo slept through much of the next day. Hadhe let him be, and he saw nobody from the boat.

Then, late in the afternoon, Milaqa called for him.

'We're having a gathering,' she said. 'The family.'

'What family?'

She spread her hands. 'The whole lot, all who have heard about you. Cousins, uncles, aunts.'

The thought appalled Tibo. 'What do I say to them?'

'You don't have to say anything. Just come and meet them. After all, you're going to be stuck here in Northland for a good while.'

So he pulled on boots and a cloak and followed her. The air outside Hadhe's house was sharp enough to make his breath steam.

Milaqa led him away from the houses and along the raised bank of a broad dyke, directly towards the foot of the Wall. There was nobody around. Smoke rose from some of the houses on their smoothly worked mounds, but many houses looked empty, dark, without smoke. The sun was starting to set, though the only way he could tell was by looking west to a patch of grey sky that was marginally brighter than the rest.

They came to the Wall itself. Milaqa led him up a staircase

153

cut into the face. As they climbed, Northland opened up to his right, looking south, a landscape of canals and house mounds and sparse smoke, spreading to a misty horizon. Not a single shadow was cast anywhere, so obscured was the sun.

They cut left, into the body of the Wall, and Tibo found himself following a narrow corridor lit only by oil lamps. Milaqa led him along a gallery, then up another staircase, then through a more enclosed corridor, then *down* more steps. At last she brought him to a broad chamber cut deep inside the body of the Wall. It was already crowded with people, who mostly sat or knelt on the floor, though there were a few wooden benches. By the light of oil lamps in notches and alcoves Tibo saw that the walls were covered in a kind of scrawl, the concentric circles and swooping lines of Etxelur writing. One man, dressed in the same owl-feather cloak as the Annid who had come to meet Caxa, sat on a raised chair by the back wall.

'That's your uncle Teel,' Milaqa murmured. 'Your father's brother. The only male Annid, of this generation anyway. And look, there's your father . . .'

Deri was sitting with Vala and her baby. Seeing Tibo, Deri patted the floor beside him.

Tibo joined him, and Milaqa squeezed in with them. There was a murmur of conversation, and the air was smoky from the lamps. Tibo wasn't comfortable here, with all these people jammed in. But at least the place didn't smell of ash. He leaned over to Milaqa. 'What's written on the walls?'

'Holy stuff. Praise for the little mothers who built the world. We're in a chamber on the border of the Holies, the temple District. Your cousin Riban arranged for us to have it for the day. Can't you read?'

Deri said, 'He can tally a cargo of fish faster than anybody I know. But there's not much call for reading scripture on Kirike's Land.'

'I read what I need to read,' Tibo said defensively.

Milaqa held up her hands. 'Fine by me.'

He saw Vala's other kids playing in a corner, some

154

complicated game to do with passing a bouncing ball. A part of him longed to run over and join in.

Now the man in the owl-feather cloak stood up. The conversation hushed.

'If you don't know me, my name's Teel. I must be your uncle or cousin, because otherwise you wouldn't be here. And I'm an Annid, as you can see from the cloak. The only Annid in the family, now that Kuma is dead.' He glanced around at the children. 'You should always remember that Kuma became the most senior Annid of all – the Annid of Annids, and she came from *our* family, a bunch of Beetles from Kirike's Land. I know how proud Medoc was of that. And Okea . . .' He listed more names of family members lost to the fire mountain, mostly old folk, and a sad litany of children's names. 'I think we'll miss Medoc most of all. If he was here, he'd be standing where I am, wouldn't he? In his smelly walrus skin, cracking his awful jokes. But we welcome Deri's party, who arrived just yesterday, and we thank the mothers for their deliverance.

'There are other nestspills here too, members of the family. Where are you, Barra?' A man stood up, short, stooped, smiling.

Tibo found he didn't like being called a 'nestspill', and lumped in with all these others.

'So here we are,' Teel said. 'We're family, we're here to help each other, in these hard times. We will find homes for you all. Ways for you to live. So – who has the first question?'

Deri stood up. 'Where is everybody? I never saw so few people on the land, working the waterways and wetlands. Even half the houses seem empty.'

Hadhe stood up in turn. 'It's the weather. We've had no sunlight.'

'Yes,' somebody said, a gruff man's voice. 'Not since your fire mountain spewed up all that cloud into the air.'

Your fire mountain. The phrase made Tibo flinch. It wasn't *his* mountain. It had killed his grandfather. But nobody else reacted, and the moment was lost.

Teel answered calmly, talking about the weather. After the

fire mountain it had been cold, bitterly so for the summer, and hail and rain had lashed the land. Plants had been battered flat, trees had lost their leaves early and had brought forth wizened nuts and fruit, and animals had become skinny or had starved altogether as they had nibbled at the sparse grass.

'This is why we came to Northland,' called the man, Barra. 'We had a farm on the north coast of Kirike's Land. We weren't badly affected by the fire mountain itself, but the early hail flattened our crops, which weren't growing anyhow. We could have starved over the winter.' He had a weather-beaten face, and looked like a practical man, a man of common sense. 'Crops must be failing all over, if the cloud extends right across the Continent, and I haven't heard anybody say that it doesn't. The Greeks, the Hatti, the Egyptians – what about them? They already had drought and famine, so I hear. I can't imagine what it will be like if their summer is as bad as ours.'

A priest stood up, in a loose cloak of wolfskin. It was Riban, the cousin who had treated Tibo's burns. 'He's right. The Swallows and Jackdaws have brought back reports to confirm it.'

'And you Wolves,' called out a man, 'ought to be in your houses smoking your strange weeds and praying to the little mother of the sky to spare us.'

'Believe me,' the priest said, 'we are.'

Teel stood. 'To answer your question, Deri, this is why there are so few people around in Etxelur. People are out in the country, fishing, hunting, trawling the rivers for eel, looking for decent stands of hazelnut and acorns . . .'

This was how people lived here. They didn't farm; they didn't raise crops or livestock. They lived off the land, off Northland itself, and there were few enough of them to be able to do that. And when hard times came they just journeyed a little further into their bountiful country, dug a little deeper into its wealth of resources. At least they had a chance to survive a few bad seasons, where farmers would have none when their reserves were gone.

Soon the discussion turned to the future of the nestspills. Listening, Tibo got the impression that everybody was saying: 'You are welcome *but* . . .' *But* we have to feed our own children first. *But* you can't have my job, as a Beaver or a Vole or a Swallow or a Jackdaw. *But* the fire mountain was on your island, on Kirike's Land, and maybe you should have stayed there and dealt with the consequences rather than come here and take up our space.

'Our grandmothers started out as Beetles, the whole lot of them,' one woman said earnestly. 'There's always work there. Scraping the canals . . .'

Tibo had had enough. He muttered an apology to Milaqa and Deri, stood, and walked out.

He found his way out through gloomy corridors to a gallery cut into the Wall's face, looking out on a fading day. Was this the gallery he'd been in before? Had they come from left or right? He wasn't used to this kind of vertical landscape. But he could surely find his way down – or, indeed, up. Impulsively he set off, picking a direction at random. He came to an up stair, then went along another gallery carved into the growstone and curtained over with skin door flaps, and then a down stair that he ignored, and another going up . . .

He emerged from the last stair onto the roof of the Wall itself. The western sky flared red, a sunset gathering despite the invisibility of the sun itself. This upper surface was empty save for a line of monuments – and one man some paces away, stocky, gesturing, exercising with a sword.

To the south, Tibo's left, Northland stretched away, the ground maybe fifty paces straight down. And to the north there was the restless ocean, its surface only a few paces beneath him. Standing on this Wall that divided two elements, the mass of the ocean looming over the peaceful land, the world seemed unbalanced to Tibo. Suddenly he felt as if the whole Wall was tipping, and he staggered.

'Careful.'

157

Tibo looked around. It was the man who had been exercising; his sword was a long blade of beaten bronze.

'What?'

'*Careful*. Is that word not right? My Etxelur-speak is still poor. Don't fall off the Wall. One way, you drown. Other way, you crack your skull like an egg.' He laughed.

He was older than Tibo, perhaps in his twenties. He wore a tunic under a bronze breastplate. His accent was thick, his words barely understandable. Tibo had never met anybody like this man in his life. 'What are you, a Greek?'

The man looked at him long and hard. Then he spat into the sea, over the rim of the Wall. 'I like you. That's why I won't cut off your ears for that insult. I am no ugly Greek. Can't you tell? I am Trojan. And you? Northlander?'

'I was born on Kirike's Land.'

'Where? Oh, the fire mountain island.' He eyed Tibo gravely. 'Was it bad?'

'I am alive. My name is Tibo. I have come to be with my family here.'

The Trojan nodded. 'I am Qirum. I have come to do business with the Annids. How is my Etxelur talk?'

'Better than my Trojan.'

Qirum boomed laughter. 'You don't seem happy to be with your family. Why?'

'They keep calling me a nestspill.' He had to explain the word to the Trojan.

'What's wrong with that? You *are* a nestspill.'

'In our Etxelur tongue the word is also used for a baby bird that has fallen from its nest.'

'Ah,' said Qirum. 'Something helpless that you would pity – or crush under your heel.'

'Yes. And I'm not helpless,' Tibo said.

Qirum looked him over. 'I can see that. So what do you want, nestspill?'

He said fiercely, 'Not to scrape the muck out of canals, that's for sure.'

'Ha! Nor would I. Good for you.' He returned to his exercising. He struck a pose, legs apart, worked the sword in a slash and vertical chop – then spun around and faced imaginary assailants coming from behind.

'So why are you here?' Tibo said.

'I told you. Business.'

'What business?'

'Not sure yet. Everybody's waiting. It's all been changed by the fire mountain.' He looked up at the grey sky. 'No sun, you see. If it's the same at home, then there will be trouble, even worse than before. Famine. People moving, whole populations. Towns emptying, cities being sacked. Maybe even Hattusa, Troy – what's left of it. Difficult times for trade. Northland will be affected too,' Qirum mused. 'But Northland was divided anyway.'

'Divided?'

'Somebody killed the Annid of Annids.'

'She was my relative. My aunt. I think.'

'Was she?' The Trojan shrugged. 'The man who got her killed was exposed. Now he's disgraced. Gone. But the woman *he* put in to replace your aunt – she's still there! And nothing's happening. No decisions being made. Everybody's just waiting under the cold sky. So I don't know what my business will be. But,' he said, eyeing Tibo, 'this is a time of opportunity, for a strong man, a clever man. When cities are falling at one end of the world, and the great power at the other end is locked in a struggle with itself.'

Tibo found these obscure words tremendously exciting. 'What kind of opportunity?'

Qirum grinned easily. Then the sunset flared brighter, and he turned west to face it.

The sky had cleared a little, and was full of colours. Above a yellowish band around the position of the sun itself, a green curtain smeared high into the sky, fluted and textured, like a tremendous swathe of dyed cloth. The green faded eventually into red, which towered ever further into the sky as the sun descended, deepening to a bruised purple.

'It changes as you watch it,' Qirum said, the exotic light glaring from his polished breastplate. 'Every night different. It's why I come up here at this time. The gods are angry, my friend, but even their anger is beautiful. Do you know, the other night I saw a moon, glimpsed through the clouds, that was as blue as a midsummer sky? Think of that.' He eyed Tibo. 'Have you ever fought?'

'Only with fists.'

'Maybe it's time you learned. Here.' He tossed him his sword, making it spin in the air, coming at Tibo hilt first.

Tibo astonished himself by grabbing the handle without slicing his fingers off.

'Come at me,' Qirum said. Tibo saw he was armed only with a short stabbing dagger. 'Come on. Don't be afraid.'

'I'll cut your head off.'

Qirum grinned again. 'I'll take the risk. Come. And when I've got the blade off you I'll teach you to wrestle. Always my favourite when I was your age, wrestling.'

Tibo considered, and raised the blade, and charged.

So it began.

26

The Year of the Fire Mountain: Midwinter

Everything had changed at Etxelur after the Hood's eruption, both for the Northlanders and for the dignitaries who had come from across continents and oceans for the Giving. As the cold clamped down and harvests faltered in the farming countries, travel became problematic – it was never wise to cross countrysides full of hungry, desperate people. Kilushepa and Qirum were not the only Giving guests to linger at the Wall, some of them keeping in touch with their homes by courier messages, talking, negotiating, as the world struggled to recover from the great shock it had suffered.

In the end, as an early autumn turned into a harsh winter, travel became impossible altogether.

Milaqa knew that Qirum, ever energetic and restless, had walked far, exploring Northland and the Wall and its Districts, sometimes in Milaqa's company and sometimes not. He showed no interest in the countryside below the Wall. But Kilushepa, during her pregnancy, was content to stay in the relative luxury of Great Etxelur. Here she had met and talked, hosted parties and attended them, endlessly weaving nets of contacts and alliances. But when her baby was delivered she changed. She seemed restless for escape, even though by now it was the heart of the winter.

Since midsummer Teel had told Milaqa to stay close to Kilushepa and Qirum, to find out what they were thinking, what they were up to. And that included volunteering as an escort when Kilushepa asked for a walk along the Wall.

So this cold morning Milaqa, bundled in her cloak, pushed her way out of Hadhe's house at the foot of the Wall. The door blanket crackled with frost, and the deep night cold had frozen over yesterday's snow so that her feet crunched through a fine crust and into the compressed dry, powdery stuff underneath. For once the sun was visible, low in the sky to the south-east, and she cast a shadow. In the pale sunlight the snow drew all the colour from the landscape save the occasional green splash of ivy, leaving only black and white and the blue of the long shadows, and it picked out details, crags on the hillsides and wrinkles and ridges on the uneven ground that were invisible in warmer times. By a watercourse she saw movement, fleet, furtive: an otter dragging the half-chewed carcass of a fish. The wintry land was beautiful, a consolation. But, only days away from the solstice itself, this was the coldest time of the hardest winter she could remember.

Cold or not the day's work had to be done. A party of adults and older children was gathering, bundled up in fur cloaks and hats and boots, their breath steaming around their heads. They carried knives and rope, and would soon be setting off inland to harvest the willow stands by the waterways. But Milaqa wouldn't be joining them. She hitched the pack on her back; laden with food and water for the Tawananna, it already felt heavy.

'They look busy.' Qirum came up to her. He was wrapped up in a heavy leather coat and leggings and bearskin hat, borrowed from Deri and cut and shaped to fit, and he slapped hands encased in huge mittens. He had his sword in its scabbard on his back.

'Willow,' she said.

'What?'

'They're off to cut willow trees. The people over there. This is the best time to do it, midwinter, to get the fine shoots we use to make baskets and backpacks.'

He grunted and turned away, bored already.

That was the reaction she'd expected. He irritated her as much as he fascinated her. 'At least they're doing something useful.'

'I thought you were the great rebel. The wild spirit who doesn't fit into this stuffy place. Now you're going on at me about *useful* work?'

'You've got absolutely no interest in people, have you? Nobody except the big folk, the decision-makers. You care nothing for people who actually *do* things.'

He considered that. 'Metal-workers, perhaps. I need to be able to rely on my sword. And bar-keeps, and brewers. And whores. Ha! *And you are the same.* Admit it, little Milaqa. You could go off and harvest willow twigs or whatever it is they are doing – but you do not choose that, do you? Instead you walk with me and the Queen of the Hatti. Of course you are blessed with freedom, here in Northland. In my country, no woman is free, no woman *owns property*, save for princesses. There are no princesses in this strange country, yet you are free to choose, aren't you? And because of that, like me, you too believe you are special, better than the rest. Perhaps it is simply having the courage to believe so, to think this way, that elevates our kind.'

'And if all the words you spouted were flakes of gold, Trojan,' said Kilushepa, walking stiffly towards them now, 'you would be rich indeed.'

Qirum laughed, admiring. 'There, Milaqa, what was I saying? As I believe I am better than your twig-cutting uncles over there, so this one believes she is better than me. Even though, strictly speaking, I *own* her.' He rubbed his mittened hands together. 'So – are we to make this walk?'

Kilushepa wore a hat of white winter-fox fur on her head, and was shrouded in a thick cloak of black-dyed fur, given her by Raka, the new Annid of Annids, in whose house she was staying. But she shivered, a long, drawn-out shudder that afflicted her whole body. 'By the Storm God's mercy, your land is cold, Milaqa. And to think I used to complain about draughty palaces in Hattusa!'

163

It was only a few days since she had given birth, after a short, difficult pregnancy. Under her naturally dark skin Milaqa thought she saw a bloodless pallor. Milaqa plucked up the courage to speak. 'Tawananna – you don't look strong.'

Kilushepa looked down at her, surprised, perhaps amused. 'Oh, you are an expert in medicine, are you, little girl?'

'No. But I've been there when my mother gave birth. And my cousins. I've seen how hard it is—'

'Lead us to the Wall, child, and hold your tongue,' Kilushepa said without emotion. She stalked away, heading north towards the looming face of the Wall.

Qirum's grin widened as he fell into step beside Milaqa. 'You got that about as wrong as you could.'

'I was speaking as one human being to another—'

'Kilushepa isn't a human being! Haven't you listened to anything I have said to you? Oh, she does have her frailties. Since the birth of the child she's been obsessively cleaning herself. Did you know that? Bathing and scrubbing, and douches and enemas. The Hatti are a funny lot who believe that any form of sexual contact leaves you unclean, and unfit to be in the presence of the gods. So you can imagine how it was for her to fall into the hands of the soldiers who used her – and into my hands, come to that. Now that the baby's out of her she's washing and washing and washing, trying to make herself pure again . . . But none of that matters. She's not weak, Milaqa. She's a queen! She's the Tawananna! Mark my words – we'll be the ones who will have to hurry to keep up.'

Milaqa led her party to one of the Wall's grander staircases. This was a sweeping flight cut into the growstone face, with broad treads and a facing wall inscribed with the names of Annids going back many generations.

Kilushepa and Qirum followed her up the stair. Kilushepa, lifting her robe to reveal booted feet, concentrated on each step. Qirum had been this way many times, but he looked around with interest as he always did, at the detail of the staircases, the

164

growstone surface, the small doorways that led off to chambers cut deeper into the Wall's fabric. Milaqa wondered what a warrior made of Northland and its Wall.

They climbed up a final set of shallow steps and emerged onto the Wall's roof: grey ocean to the left, the black-and-white snow-covered landscape of Northland to their right, the Wall itself arrowing to infinity ahead and behind. The Northern Ocean was flecked with ice floes, and the dark shadows of boats, all the way to the horizon. In this winter of privation the Northlanders had fallen back on the generosity of the little mother of the sea, but fishing in deep midwinter was always a hazard.

Milaqa stepped forward cautiously. The surface was swept clear of snow daily, and the central track was ridged, for better footing. She led them along the Wall, heading east. The air was mercifully still, but bitterly cold, and they all pulled their cloaks tighter.

Qirum studied the ridges as he walked, his eye caught by that small detail. 'It must have been the labour of years to carve all these fine lines in the stone, along the mighty length of this Wall.'

'Oh, no. You do it when the growstone is wet. You can just comb it in – literally, like combing your hair. When it's wet you can shape growstone with your bare hands. And the furrows stay when the growstone hardens.'

'Remarkable,' the Trojan said. He knelt, took off his mittens, and rapped the surface with his knuckles. 'A rock you can mould like clay!'

Soon they were over Old Etxelur itself. The circular ridges of the Mothers' Door, the grand old earthwork, were coated by snow, the profile of Flint Mountain and the densely populated Bay Land gleamed with frost, and the great watercourses were frozen solid. In the misty distance she saw huge herds move across the land, like the shadows of clouds. Deer, perhaps, maybe even aurochs, the wild cattle that the farmer folk found so fascinating.

Kilushepa looked down on the Door, contemptuous. 'How ugly. It reminds me of the palace of the Goddess of Death in the netherworld, which is surrounded by rings of walls in a desolate plain, just like this.'

'This is the very heart of Northland,' Milaqa said. 'Old Etxelur itself, where the Wall, or the first part of it, was built to expel the sea.'

'And all of this was sea bed, you claim,' Kilushepa murmured. 'I believe that's a stand of oak down there. Everybody knows oak takes centuries to grow.'

'But the Wall is more than centuries old, queen,' said Qirum gently. 'Older even than the most ancient cities of the east, older than Ur and Uruk. *This* was around when they were nothing but collections of shepherds' huts. You know the saying. "Everything comes from the west." And this is the heart of that west, Kilushepa.'

They moved on, walking past monoliths and monumental stone heads set up in their lines along the Wall roof. Milaqa tried to tell them something of the stories of the Annids commemorated here, but they weren't interested in Northland history, and she gave up. She said, 'We will walk until the middle of the afternoon, perhaps. We will arrive at a dock where my uncle Deri will meet us in his boat; we will be rowed back. We have food in the packs, and there are sheltered places. Or we can always duck down into the Wall; there are many places to eat.'

'And drink,' Qirum said loudly. 'We're walking due east. Aren't we heading towards the Scambles?' Kilushepa looked quizzical. 'A District within the Wall, Tawananna. It's rather interesting. You'd think the Wall is one great uniform mass. But it isn't. The character changes, quite markedly. I'll tell you one pattern I've observed. These Districts, their miniature towns-in-a-town – the centres tend to be a half-day's walk apart, or a little more. Just too far to walk there and back in day, you see. So a natural separation grows up.'

Milaqa, faintly disturbed, realised that she'd never seen that pattern for herself.

'As for the Scambles – well, it's quite unlike Etxelur, though often you'll find the grand folk in the taverns and music houses and brothels—'

'We won't be going there,' Milaqa said hastily.

'Then I hope you're carrying beer on that back of yours, girl!'

They came to a place where a tremendous scaffolding of long Albian oak trunks and cut planks had been built up against the landward face of the Wall. On its platforms stood huge wooden vats full of ground-up rock, dust, and frozen-over water. Up here on the roof, wooden panels had been set up to shelter those who supervised the work on the scaffolding below. Nobody was working today, though one man sat bundled up in furs, watchful, to ensure there were no accidental fires.

They paused in the lee of the supervisors' shelter. Milaqa opened her packs and passed around dried meat and fish with hazelnut paste, and water and beer.

Qirum was fascinated by the scaffolding. 'It is like a tremendous siege engine.'

'They are working on the Wall,' Milaqa replied. 'The Beavers and their assistants. They make growstone from crushed limestone, fire-mountain ash and other ingredients in those great vats. But you can see the water is frozen, and the growstone itself would be too cold to mix properly. So the work is abandoned for now. They work on a given section for years at a time. People come for the work, and others to support those who work. They live here. The site becomes a community, a village. Children may be born and grow up on the scaffolding, before the time comes to move on to another section of Wall.'

'Rather magnificent,' Qirum murmured to Kilushepa.

'The magnificence of the insane,' she said, chewing delicately on a piece of pickled cod. 'The same pointless task repeated over and over. The Wall is a monument of idiots.'

Qirum shrugged. 'I suppose I wouldn't want my children to

be growing up on a bit of scaffolding. Where is your daughter today, by the way? Little Puduhepa.'

'With her carer. A woman called . . .' She frowned, and glanced at Milaqa.

'The wet nurse is called Bela,' Milaqa said. 'You know her, Qirum. A friend of my cousin Hadhe.'

Kilushepa said, 'The woman is to be more than a wet nurse. I have given the baby over. And I have given instructions that a new name be found for the child. A Northlander name. I thoughtlessly gave the brat a Hatti name – a royal name, in fact. I was in pain, barely conscious, addled by the potions your priest doctors gave me, Milaqa. There is no purpose in the Hatti name, for she will be raised as a Northlander.'

'But she is your child!' Qirum said, aghast. 'How can you give her up? Is this because of your Hatti obsession with cleanliness, woman? Is the child just some impurity that has now been flushed out of you?'

'The child hardly matters. She is the product of a rape.'

'As I was!'

'And now she is abandoned. As you were.' She seemed amused by the observation.

Qirum stood stock-still. Milaqa could see the muscles clenched in his neck. For a heartbeat Milaqa thought he might strike Kilushepa. Then he pushed out of the shelter and strode back the way they had come, and ducked down a staircase, perhaps looking for a Scambles tavern.

Kilushepa had finished her fish. She wiped her fingers and mouth delicately on a small cloth. 'Well. That seems to be the end of the walk.' She stood and staggered.

Milaqa held her arm. 'Let me help you.'

The Tawananna snatched back her arm. 'Do not touch me.'

When they emerged from the shelter snow was falling. Her hood up, her head down, Milaqa led Kilushepa east along the Wall, towards the dock where Deri waited. They did not speak again.

168

27

The First Year After the Fire Mountain: Spring

Bren and Vala landed on Kirike's Land, stepping onto a shore of black sand. The rest of the boat's crew jumped out and hauled up the craft, its skin hull scraping.

Bren staggered up the beach to an outcrop of rock, and sat down. With his delicate-looking fingers the Jackdaw picked at his leather leggings, stained with salt and piss and puke, and pulled his cloak tighter around his body. He'd been ill throughout the journey and had been all but useless in the boat, and he seemed dizzy and disoriented now he was back on the land. He didn't even look around at their destination, after so many days on the breast of the sea.

Vala shivered in a breeze coming off a land choked by ice and snow. Home again, she thought. At first glance this bay, the Ice Giant's Cupped Palm, seemed unchanged from when she had last seen it – at least as it had been in the days before the Hood. There was the broad sweep of the water, there the ice-tipped mountains on the horizon. She made out houses at the head of the beach, beyond the waterline. Smoke rose up, so at least there were people here – people *alive*, when there were some in Northland who had doubted there would be a living soul left on Kirike's Land after the events of last summer.

But there were still scummy rafts of pale rock floating on the bay water, and washed up on the strand. On the land itself, which should have been turning green at this time of year, the ice still held sway. She thought she smelled ash in the cold air.

169

And the world was much too quiet. She listened for the braying of seals, the cries of the birds who should be nesting by now. There was only the lap of the sea, and the gruff voices of the men as they wearily hauled their gear from the boat.

And towering over it all was a pillar of grey-white smoke, still rising from whatever was left of the Hood, pluming high in the sky. It was hard to believe that she had lived only a day's walk from that monstrous mound, that she'd had a home almost on its slopes. Now, she supposed, there must be not a trace left of The Black.

A woman came out of one of the houses further up the beach. She waved warily, and Vala waved back. The woman ducked back into the house, emerged pulling a cloak around her shoulders, and walked down the beach towards the boat.

Bren sat listlessly.

Vala thumped his shoulder. 'On your feet.'

He looked up at her, his once handsome face weather-beaten under a ragged beard. 'Must I? I think I'll fall over if—'

'Somebody's coming. Look strong. We're here to help them, remember, not the other way around.'

He looked away, sullen. Vala got her hand under Bren's armpit and hauled him to his feet. He staggered, but stood.

She had no sympathy for him. She'd left her own children behind in Etxelur to make this journey, to see what had become of her home. After all they'd gone through it had been a huge wrench for her to let the kids out of her sight. But she had come, for she thought it was the right thing to do. And Bren had been ordered to come here by the Annids, after his disgrace when his part in Kuma's murder had been revealed, and his own House of Jackdaws had disowned him. If he could do some good here perhaps he could begin to redeem himself – that, anyhow, was how Raka had argued. But Bren had only complained about what he saw as a betrayal by his own niece, his protégé. He was nothing but a burden, Vala thought.

The woman came up. She had a shock of white hair loosely tied at the back of her head, and the dirt grimed in the lines on her face made her look old. She was thin, too, her cheeks sunken. Her tunic, under the cloak, was shabby, threadbare.

Vala knew her. 'Pithi?'

'Vala? I thought you were dead!'

Once this woman had been Vala's neighbour, in The Black. She was not yet thirty; she looked ten years older. When they embraced, Vala smelled ash on Pithi's hair.

Pithi said, 'You stayed in your house when we left.'

'In the end I ran to the sea, with my family. We got to a boat before the burning smoke came down.'

'We didn't reach the beach. We sheltered in a cave until it passed. The heat – we couldn't breathe. I lost one child. You remember little Gili? And my mother, her lungs weren't strong enough. And you? The boys, Mi?'

'They all made it. We were lucky. But Okea and Medoc . . .'

Pithi just nodded. Evidently news of death was commonplace. 'And now we live by the beach, for Stapi and Mura spend all day at sea.' Pithi's husband and older son. 'There's nothing left on the land. Even before the snow came, the ash covered everything, and the cattle got sick. We butchered them, but the meat is long gone . . .' She seemed to notice Bren for the first time. 'I know you. I was in Northland once. You were a Jackdaw. You traded us bronze knives for our seal furs. You were called Bren.'

He summoned a smile, ghastly in his snow-white face. 'Well, I still am called Bren, though I'm no longer a trader.'

'Why are you here?'

Bren glanced at Vala. 'To help you. The Annid of Annids herself ordered me to come here. To see what you need, what we in Northland can do to help you.'

'Kuma sent you?'

'Not Kuma,' Vala said gently. 'We have a new Annid of Annids now.'

Pithi stared at Bren, as if not really believing he was there. Then she turned and led them up the beach. 'You must come to the houses. There are quite a few of us, from all over. This bay is the best harbour on the island, and a natural place to gather.'

'How many?'

'Less than before the winter. But we are alive. Vala, there are people here who survived extraordinary things. In one place a glacier on the side of the fire mountain melted, all at once. A woman with her baby had to run from a torrent, she looked back and saw people drown – drown, on the side of a burning mountain! We found one village untouched by the fire save for the ash, but everybody lay as if asleep in their beds – all dead. Some say there is bad air that comes out of the ground. And one man, an old fellow with one leg called Balc – he tried to escape to the sea as you did, was missed by the boats, and lived by grabbing onto the corpse of a cow, which bloated with gas and floated to the surface. He lived for three days on that cow, drinking its blood, until a fishing boat spotted him . . . Is Bren all right?'

Bren was bent over, retching dry, his stomach long empty of food.

Vala rubbed his back. 'He'll be fine.'

Without straightening up he murmured to her, 'We can do nothing for these people. This blighted island. We can bring no food – we can't dispel the ice or the poisonous ash—'

'We can do small things. We can tell them of relatives and friends who live. We can take some of the sick, the very young children perhaps, away to Northland. We can give them hope. That's why we came. Now smile and do your job.'

He managed to stand straight, and with the help of the two women made it up the beach to the shabby houses.

28

Qirum came to the house as Milaqa was getting ready for the Annids' walk to the south. He just walked in, as he usually did.

Milaqa was alone in the house. Luckily she was dressed already, her tunic and leather belt over her loincloth and leather leggings, with her cloak set to one side. She wore her iron arrowhead on its thong around her neck, tucked into her tunic.

'You're late,' he said in his liquid Anatolian tongue.

'I'm always late.' She eyed him. 'Even when I'm not kept up until dawn in some dingy tavern in the Scambles, I'm late.'

He laughed, and belched heroically; she could smell the stale beer on his breath. 'There are no taverns where we're going, you told me. Best to get the blood running with the good stuff first.' As she packed up her kit, Qirum stalked around the house. He was always curious, always exploring. He tested the supporting structure of big old oak beams, poked a finger into the walls' weave of twigs coated with mud and plaster, sniffed the central hearth, brushed his hand over the children's pallets with their litter of toys, dolls, wooden swords. With his own sword in its scabbard on his back and his bronze breastplate on his chest, he looked as out of place in this domestic litter as if a wild aurochs had walked in. He watched her as she packed up her final bits: her bag, her tool belt with her sewing kit of bone needles and thread, her best bronze knife, dried meat, net for trapping birds, fire-making gear – flint, dried lichen and grass. He picked up a pad of sphagnum moss from the kit. 'For treating cuts?'

'Or wiping my backside.'

Scraps of fungus. 'And these?'

'From birch bark. For dressing wounds.' She took the stuff from him, packed it into her belt and picked up her cloak.

'You'll rattle as you walk,' he said.

'Sooner that than go short,' she snapped back. 'Whereas you don't need to carry anything but your sword, I suppose.'

'That and my air of command.' He laughed at his own joke, and pushed his way out into the light.

Raka gathered her party beneath the Wall, at the head of the great axial track called the Etxelur Way that ran dead south past Flint Island.

This was Raka's big idea for the spring, that as many of the senior folk as possible from Etxelur should go see for themselves what was becoming of the country, in what the priests were already calling 'the year betrayed by summer'. The sight of the Annids might reassure people, and would help inform the decision-making that had to follow. So, in this party, as well as other Annids there were senior members of most of the great Houses of Northland, the priests, the builders, the water workers. Many of the senior folk looked unhappy to be up and out on such a morning. It was near the equinox, but the sky was like a murky bowl, and there had been a sharp frost. Indeed, winter snow still lingered at the foot of the Wall, mounds of it hard as rock and covered with grime. Spring, but it felt like winter. Still, here they were, and even the highest of the high in Northland liked to keep her family close, and so the core of senior folk was surrounded by a gaggle of children, bundled up in their furs, who ran and played and chased yapping dogs, excited by the prospect of the walk ahead. Their noise lightened the mood.

Kilushepa was here, standing with the party around Raka. The regime of walks and other exercises she had undergone since the end of her pregnancy seemed to have done her good; she would always be tall, thin as a willow sapling, but she looked strong, determined. As Milaqa approached with Qirum, Trojan princeling and Hatti queen exchanged glances. Qirum and Kilushepa had barely spoken since that cold day with

174

Milaqa on the Wall, they were evidently not lovers at present, but they remained bound by common interests.

Voro was here too. He was gaining seniority among the Jackdaws now that Bren was gone. But he wouldn't meet Milaqa's eye. Ever since Bren's part in Kuma's death had been revealed Voro had seemed consumed by guilt, even though it had not been him who had drawn the bow, even though he had nothing to do with Bren's scheming. Milaqa treated this with contempt. Frosty relationships everywhere, she thought, on a frosty day.

A priest sounded a bronze trumpet.

Raka herself strode out along the track, and the rest followed, the seniors of the Houses murmuring gravely to each other, then a looser gang of family members, children and dogs. Their first destination would be a village by a marsh called the Houses of the Pine Martens.

In the lingering wintry weather, the world was struggling to come alive. There had been no swallows yet, and over the grasslands the male lapwings were still swooping and diving, desperately seeking the attention of mates. When the track cut through a patch of dense oak woodland Milaqa spotted the mouths of badger setts, littered with fresh spoil, as the animals cleaned out their underground homes and brought in fresh bedding in readiness for this year's cubs. And in the lee of a fallen trunk a carpet of bluebells was growing, glowing with a strange underwater light. Milaqa was entranced. She had no idea how the flowers had managed to blossom in the sunless cold.

Teel came to walk beside her. 'Quite a turn-out. All the great Houses represented.'

'Including us Crows,' she murmured.

He smiled. 'Don't try to fly out of the nest just yet, fledgling. It's a big day for Raka. This expedition was her idea. She's growing into the role. In the end the big loser of all Bren's manipulations was Bren himself. Banished to Kirike's Land . . . How he would long to be here!'

Growing into the role. Milaqa looked over at the new Annid of Annids. Bren's niece seemed very young, only a few years older than Milaqa herself. After the outrage about Bren, nobody had seemed to know quite what to do about Raka, his protégé. While the Annids dithered Raka had quietly started getting on with the job. And today, here were all the senior folk of Etxelur following Raka's lead. Milaqa felt oddly jealous. She seemed to be surrounded by people of her age doing far better in their chosen roles than she was – Raka, Voro, Riban – even Hadhe, she'd heard it said, was being groomed for a role as an Annid. Suppose she had been dropped into such a position. Would she have been able to handle it as well as Raka? Or would she have cracked on her first day, and gone running to a Scambles tavern?

The track emerged from the forest. Now they were approaching the marsh where the folk of the Pine Martens' Houses made their living. The oak and ash gave way to more water-tolerant trees like alders and willows, all bare in the grey sunless light, before they came to the grey gleam of open water.

Milaqa stopped at the water's edge. At this time of year the new growths of rushes, herbs and sedge should be showing, and in the deeper water white water lilies and bulrushes, all emerging to greet the coming summer. But today there was only detritus on the water, the litter of last year's life. Some of the children came to the edge of the water, searching fruitlessly for frog spawn or even tadpoles. Milaqa did see the round face and brown back of a water vole, peering from a clump of reeds. She thought it looked ragged, hungry.

She heard a grim muttering, and turned to see. The Annids and the other seniors were heading across the marsh along a raised walkway, to the scrap of higher land where the village itself stood. Milaqa hurried to follow.

And, from the causeway, she saw that the community's houses had been burned and smashed to the ground. Even the drying racks for fish and eel lay broken. There was nobody in sight.

The Northlanders stood on the edge of the hearthspace, shocked. But Qirum strode boldly forward. He used the tip of his sword to lift fallen thatch, splintered timbers. He exposed a small storage chamber dug into the floor of one house; even that had been broken open, the shellfish and snails stolen.

And he found a severed human head, a child's, apparently staring up at the sky, the skin of the face burned and blackened and shrunken.

They would not go on, or return to the Wall that night.

During what remained of the day, Raka showed quick and decisive leadership. She organised the men to construct lean-tos from the debris. The women and older children were set to gathering food from the marshland and the forest. The younger children were distracted by play.

Meanwhile the Annids and priests poked around the charred ruins of the settlement. The priests carefully gathered what human remains they could find; back at the Wall, they would be interred with the bones of their ancestors. Kilushepa and Qirum walked together, inspecting the grisly remains, talking quietly now in their own tongue, their enmity forgotten in the face of a worse disaster. Milaqa worked with the men, throwing herself into the heavy work, until she was hot and coated with ash. Confronted by such horror, she felt ashamed of her own earlier self-obsession.

The women returned with eel and shellfish. A fire was quickly built, and stones laid over it to heat; the gutted eel and shelled oysters would be fried on the hot rocks. In the lean-tos, some of the younger children were already being laid down for sleep.

While the meal was being prepared, and as the day's light began to fade, Raka gathered her advisers around her. They sat in a circle by the warmth of the fire and pulled their cloaks around them, like lumps of rock in the firelight. Milaqa sat near Kilushepa and Qirum so she could translate for them. After months in Northland the queen was deigning to learn a few words of her hosts' and prospective allies' language, but her grasp was weak.

Raka said now, 'We will speak low enough that the children are not alarmed.' There was a rumble of agreement. 'I wanted us to come into the country to see for ourselves how the long winter is affecting our people. I did not expect so stark a lesson as this. These people were robbed for their food – as simple as that. Evidently the disaster was so complete there was nobody left to bring the news to the Wall.'

'The raiders could have come from Gaira, or from Albia,' said Voro.

'Or,' said Noli, the stern elder Annid who had so vigorously opposed Raka's appointment, 'they could have been *us*. Northlanders, turning on their own.'

'Our kind would not do this!' snapped back a burly Vole.

'Our kind are human too,' Teel said. 'Our kind are starving too.'

'No,' Qirum said clearly. All eyes turned to him. He pushed back his cloak, so his breastplate shone in the firelight. He murmured to Milaqa, 'Translate for me. I was the first to inspect the ruined settlement. You saw me. The raiders were starving farmers. How do I know? Because of the way they tore these buildings apart. You saw the broken-open storage pits I found. In my country every city has a granary, a grain store, to feed the people in times of famine.' He snorted contempt. 'These petty raiders thought this was a farm, or a city. That there must be a grain store somewhere. That is why they dug into the very floors. They didn't know how you live. Hungry farmers did this – not you Northlanders.'

Raka nodded. 'All right. But for them to have come so deep into our country, to act so savagely, they must have been hungry indeed.'

Teel said, 'They will come again, or their kind. After such a winter, famine must rage across the Continent.'

Kilushepa spoke now, through Milaqa's translation. 'My country has suffered famine for years, because of drought.

Already, I believe, Hattusa – my capital – would have fallen, the empire itself crumbled, if not for your assistance, your potatoes and maize. I have spoken of this before. And now we have the burden of the fire mountain's clouds. If the empire of the Hatti were to fall now – if the other great states of the east were to collapse, Egypt and Assyria—'

'The Continent would swarm with raiders,' Teel said. 'So would the sea. Desperate, starving farmers, with their hungry children. And some will come dressed like this.' He reached over and rapped his knuckles on Qirum's breastplate; the Trojan grinned. 'Not just hungry farmers,' Teel said. 'Hungry warriors.'

Raka nodded. 'So what are we to do?'

Before any of the Northlanders could reply, Kilushepa took her chance. She stood, and pulled Milaqa to her feet. 'Speak my words well for me, child,' she murmured in Hatti. 'I will tell you what you must do, Annid. You must help me return to Hattusa.' She glanced around at the few Jackdaws in the company. 'Those of you who trade with us know my reputation. I was ousted by fools. Only I held that country together – only I can save it now. If you help me, I pledge that a saved and stabilised Hatti state will help contain the collapse of the countries around us. *We Hatti will protect you Northlanders*, and the legacy of your ancient civilisation. It is as simple as that.'

Milaqa was appalled by the way she used this massacre as an opportunity, and by the woman's hypocrisy. She remembered Kilushepa's contempt for Northland during the midwinter walk on the Wall. There had been no talk of the 'legacy of your ancient civilisation' then. But this, she supposed, was diplomacy, the business of the world, which left little room for truth.

Raka paused before she spoke again, evidently thinking through her response. 'And in return for this service, what reward would you want, Tawananna?'

'Only one thing,' Kilushepa said smoothly. 'I want the secret of the foods you give us. Potatoes. Maize. No more of your mash. Give us seeds. Let us grow these crops ourselves; let us feed ourselves, rather than rely on your hand-outs.'

There were shouts of outrage.

Noli protested, 'This was Bren's plan! This was what he had Kuma murdered for! Must we even discuss this grotesque entanglement?'

Raka, sitting quietly, held up her hand until there was calm. 'Tawananna, you will understand that we will have to consult. Such a grave step cannot be taken lightly.'

Kilushepa nodded gracefully, sat, and the group broke up into knots of discussion.

Teel tugged Milaqa's elbow. 'That's nice work by Raka. I mean, Kilushepa has taken her chance, but the Annid really isn't giving away much. The secret of our magic foods would be lost eventually anyhow through some spy or other, or another crooked trader like Bren – we've been lucky to keep it so long. Of course the Annids will take some convincing. But I think we can do a better deal than for some vague promise of friendship from Hattusa.'

'What do you mean?'

'Watch and learn, young Crow. Do you have the arrowhead?'

She slipped the thong over her head and handed the piece to him. 'What do you want with it this time?'

'To change the world. Translate for Kilushepa.' He stood easily, and spoke over the gathering conversations. 'Annid of Annids – forgive me. I have another concern to raise.' He held up the arrowhead, dangling from its thong. Everybody present knew its significance. '*This* killed Kuma. Even though she was wearing *this*.' Again he bent and rapped his knuckles on Qirum's breastplate. This time the Trojan laughed out loud. Teel turned to Kilushepa. 'And the only place in the world where such iron is made, madam, iron hard enough to use as a decent weapon, is Hattusa.'

Kilushepa smiled.

Teel said, 'Iron ore can be found anywhere. It's not like the copper or tin you need to find for bronze. We could arm ourselves quickly, with weapons that could fend off any warrior armed with bronze – *if* we could only make the iron to the right standard.

'I'm no Jackdaw but I think the terms of the bargaining are obvious. Tawananna, we have a secret you want – potatoes and maize. With that you could feed your people. You have a secret we need – your hardened iron. With that we could defend ourselves, even against hordes of farmer-warriors. Annids, Tawananna, I think you have some negotiating to do.'

There were murmurs of surprise, shock, anticipation. Kilush-epa stayed silent, apparently considering.

Qirum bent over and whispered to Milaqa in his own tongue, 'Your man Teel – what a deal-maker. I'm a good one too, so I know. Trading potatoes for iron! Just as in his youth he traded his balls for power. I wonder what history will make of this! But of course, if you want Hatti iron you're going to have to travel to Anatolia to get it. And I do mean *you*, Milaqa, you with your gift of tongues.'

29

The First Year After the Fire Mountain: Midsummer

'We think Caxa has run off to hide in the First Mother's Ribs,' Vala said to Voro.

Xivu, the Jaguar man, sat glaring at Voro from the shadows of Vala's house. 'Which, as I understand it, is your own strange name for the range of hills to the south of here.' His Etxelur-speak was uncertain, his tone dismissive. He had a warm blanket thrown over his shoulders as he sat close to the fire on this cold summer's day. With his very un-Northland dark eyes and strong nose and deep black hair, he looked out of place, Vala thought, sitting here in this wooden house loaned to her and her family of nestspills by a cousin, surrounded by cooking pots, racks of fish and scraps of meat, heaps of clothes for mending, and the children, Mi and Puli playing a complicated game of counters on a wooden board, while little Liff sat on Mi's lap, half asleep. Out of place and profoundly unhappy. And he looked on Voro with unconcealed contempt.

But Xivu was here because he needed Vala and Voro's help. Caxa was lost, Xivu's sculptor, his treasure. When he had begged the Annid of Annids for help, Raka had sent him to Vala to sort it out. In this sunless summer Raka had a lot more important issues to handle than the fate of a girl sculptor from across the ocean. After all, if Kuma's monumental image was not set on the Wall this year, it would be done next year, or the next, when they all had more time and energy; Raka was sure the little mothers would forgive them for the delay.

And Vala in turn had called in Voro.

'Why me?' Voro had asked. 'I'm a Jackdaw. A trader. Maybe you should send a priest.'

'The priests are too busy trying to persuade the little mothers to warm us all up. And besides – you're not doing much trading, are you?'

He looked away.

It was true. Everybody knew why. Voro was still being eaten up inside by a corrosive guilt from his association with the death of Milaqa's mother Kuma. Vala had said, 'You must put aside this shame.'

'Must I? How? It's like the clouds in the sky that won't go away.'

Vala touched his hand. 'Forget about Milaqa for now. Think about Caxa.' This was her bright idea, to solve two problems at once. 'Maybe you can help her. You're young, and so is she. You've both been through trials. You've got a lot in common.'

'Even though we were born an ocean apart.'

'Even so, yes. Go and find her. And if you do, maybe it will help you too. People will see you in a different light. You'll break up that cloud over you once and for all – even though, Voro, it looks a lot blacker to you than to the rest of us.'

He had agreed, and he had gone looking for Caxa, but he had returned – without her.

So here they all were. And Vala, sitting by the hearth, grinding herbs with mortar and pestle, was not impressed by Xivu's arrogance.

'Of course,' Xivu said now, 'this isn't the first time the sculptor has been endangered among you people. She nearly got broiled alive on Kirike's Land.'

'I know,' snapped Vala. 'I was there, remember?'

Voro studied Xivu. 'Why don't you go after her yourself?'

Vala laughed. 'Oh, she runs away from *him*. He's the main reason she's run off, I reckon.'

'Enough,' Xivu snapped. 'I told your Annid that this is not the way to handle the problem. In my country we would send a squad of soldiers to flush her out of the hills, like a hunted bird.'

'But this is not your country,' Vala said sternly.

'No, it isn't. This is Northland. Where this boy was manipulated into complicity in murder. Now you manipulate his guilt to make him do this task for you. And he will manipulate Caxa to bring her home. It is just as you build your country. You dig a ditch here, a dam there, *manipulate* a great river to run this way instead of that. *We* would cut through it. We would build a city of stone and make the river serve us!'

Vala ignored him. 'So, Voro, before you go out again, what would you like to eat?'

30

The First Year After the Fire Mountain: Late Summer

The long journey from Etxelur to Anatolia took all summer.

The party travelled the length of Northland, which was pretty much as far as Milaqa had ever journeyed before. Then they made an epic overland crossing south through Gaira, coming to the shore of the Middle Sea. And then they took to the sea, in Qirum's boat that had been waiting for him for a year, and they travelled east, the length of this calm ocean. For Milaqa it was numbing, a journey without end, and Qirum's bragging leadership had grown annoying; he of course had come this way before, as he constantly reminded the party. But in the end her mind opened up to the sheer scale and diversity of the world beyond Northland through which she travelled – and the effects of the long drought and of the fire mountain, which could be seen everywhere they stopped.

The last seagoing leg of the journey was to be a crossing from Greece to Troy. After this, Milaqa understood, they would travel by land eastward across Anatolia to Hattusa, capital of the Hatti empire – 'if the empire still exists,' Kilushepa said gloomily, 'if Hattusa itself stands.' And there Kilushepa would attempt the miracle of diplomacy and statecraft that would restore her to her throne.

But they had to get through Troy first.

Waiting for Qirum, the seven-strong party from Northland stood on a wooden jetty, their packs at their feet, wearing heavy tunics as protection against the unseasonal cold. The port was just another huddle of a dozen houses overlooking a small harbour, like so many on this Greek mainland, a place whose name Milaqa had forgotten as soon as she was told it, just another stopping point on this endless journey. There was some trade going on this cold morning, with seagoing ships and smaller coast-hoppers jostling for space in the harbour, and caravans forming up on land. Yet there was room for much more, Milaqa thought; you could see at a glance how trade had shrivelled with the long drought, and now this summerless year.

But Qirum's own ship stood proud in the water, its long, sleek hull black as night, waiting to serve them as it had all the way along the coastline of this Middle Ocean from the south Gaira coast. The carved bird's head peered from the stern, and the eyes painted on the hull glared, vivid. It was a formidable sight, even under a dismal grey sky.

Qirum walked up, leading three locals. 'So here's our latest crew,' he announced. The ill-smelling Greeks stood together by the jetty, their own packs on their backs, eyeing up the women. They looked hungry. Well, everybody was hungry. One of them seemed to have a bad leg, judging by the way he was standing.

And there were only three of them.

'A boat like this needs eight rowers and a pilot,' Kilushepa said. She stood with Noli, the Annid companion appointed by Raka for this mission of diplomacy. 'What are you playing at, Trojan?' She now spoke a heavily accented Northlander, practised with difficulty during the long journey, though she would lapse into her own tongue.

'This is all I could find. Times are hard. And nobody wants to sail to Troy across a pirate-ridden sea, it seems. So – no more passengers. *You* will each be taking an oar.' He pointed one by one to the men of the Northland party: Teel, Deri and his son Tibo, the young priest Riban, and Qirum himself. 'And you, Queen,' the Trojan said, 'will work the steering oar.'

'So it's come to this,' Kilushepa said with a sneer.

'Do you want to get to Hattusa or not?'

186

Deri shrugged, spat on his hands and rubbed his palms together. 'Let's get on with it.'

Tibo was the first to board the boat, intent, focused, eager, as he had been all summer. If Qirum told him he'd have to swim to Troy, Milaqa thought he'd try it. Riban looked wary, but he had toughened up on the journey, and he followed Tibo on board.

Teel, however, raised his eyebrows. 'I swear this Trojan is out to torture me. Do I *look* as if I was born to row a war-boat?'

Milaqa snorted. 'For a Crow you lack a sense of adventure, uncle.'

'And you do not, I suppose.'

'No, I don't,' she snapped back. 'Qirum! Get rid of one of these men. This one with the leg. He'll cause us more trouble than he's worth.'

'Not as much trouble as being one man short—'

'One *rower* short. I've watched you all summer. I can row as well as any of you.'

He laughed out loud. 'Typical of you, Milaqa. All right. But when you're hunched broken over your oar, remember this moment and don't blame me.' He walked up to the man she had chosen and told him in coarse Greek that he was not to be used. The man scowled at Milaqa, evidently sensing she had something to do with it, but he limped away.

Milaqa clambered aboard the boat and chose a bench on the right-hand side; Riban was opposite her, so close they were almost touching within the sleek hull. There was room under her bench to stow her gear. The bench itself was worn smooth with use, and its coating of black pitch was stained with rusty splashes – blood, probably.

Qirum briskly helped Noli to a seat in the stern, near the platform where Kilushepa would work as pilot. Here bread was stored in leather bags, and water and wine in clay jars. With an efficiency born of the long practice of the journey, Noli stowed away her own precious baggage, the little sacks of potatoes and maize seed. Kilushepa was helped aboard and stood at the stern, taking the steering oar in her right hand.

Qirum himself took the bench ahead of Milaqa, so Milaqa was looking at his broad back. As soon as he had stowed his sword, spear, bow and arrows under his bench he barked an order, and the rowers each took an oar. Milaqa fumbled with the rowlock, but she got her oar fitted.

They used their oars to push away from the jetty, and then it was time to row. Milaqa found a shelf on the floor against which she could brace her feet. She dipped her oar experimentally into the water, and pulled it back. It was heavy, and she could feel how the water dragged at the blade. But she had made her first stroke.

The man behind her tapped her on the shoulder. She looked back; it was one of the locals. 'Like this,' he said in strongly accented Greek. He held up his hands; he had wrapped the palms in thick leather bandages. 'Grip. No blisters.'

'Thank you.' She reached for her leather cloak, bundled up in a pack, and hastily cut strips from it with her bronze knife.

Qirum, settled over his own oar, waited with reasonable patience until his fledgling crew got settled. 'Ready, are we? On my count. One – pull! One – pull!'

At first it was a shambles. The boat wallowed, the oars clattered against each other with heavy wooden knocks, and bodies bumped as the rowers tried to find a rhythm. Qirum yelled obscenities in Greek, Trojan, Hatti and Northlander. Deri laughed out loud.

But gradually they settled down, the oars biting into the water more or less together, and the boat slid away into deeper water. Kilushepa hauled on her steering oar, and there was hard work to be done as the boat swung around. At last the prow was pointing out to the open ocean, and the shallow hull skimmed over the water. Qirum even stopped swearing.

Milaqa felt a deep exhilaration as she hauled on her oar. She could feel the way the big muscles of her back and legs made the boat pivot on her blade. The boat itself was an extraordinary craft, quite unlike the oak-frame-and-hide boats of the North-landers, which were designed for the rigours of the outer oceans. *This* was a black shadow on the water, sleek and menacing and startlingly fast when the rowers worked their oars properly. She had thrilled at her first sight of it, at the river mouth in southern Gaira. This boat was itself an instrument of war, as much a weapon as the bronze sword Qirum so cherished. And here she was, Milaqa of Etxelur, at its oar!

But as the day wore on, without a glimmer of sunlight, the rowing went on and on too, with only brief breaks for drinks and food and for pissing over the side. The energy in her muscles drained away to be replaced by a dull fatigue, and the joints in her back and neck ached. And still it went on, and she had to make another stroke, and another, and another.

Qirum glanced around, stripped to the waist, his brow beaded with sweat, his slab-like body tensed. 'Told you so!' he said. 'You could be up there peeling apples for the Tawananna. But no, you knew best, and here you are, with your feet in the bilge and your muscles on fire. Told you so!'

She forced a grin. 'Shame we aren't in separate boats so I could race you, Trojan.'

He laughed, shaking his head. But then he turned away, and she had still another stroke to pull, and another.

Heading roughly north and east, they crossed a sea quite unlike Northland's great oceans. *This* sea was a puddle, so crowded with small islands they were never out of sight of land. Smoke rose up from some of the islands, not from others. Following Qirum's curt commands, Kilushepa kept them clear of all the islands. Occasionally they would see ships, looming on the horizon. Kilushepa steered well clear of these too, hiding the boat behind the curve of the world.

They made one overnight stop, on a small island that Qirum said had always been uninhabited. By the light of whale-oil lanterns – no moon was visible – they hauled the boat up on a beach of gritty sand, and made a camp in the lee of a bluff of rocks. Further inland the island was thick with trees and bushes, their leaves pallid, oddly tired-looking. Qirum detailed some of his crew to go off into the interior to hunt for game, while others walked the strand looking for shellfish.

Released from the punishment of her oar, Milaqa wanted nothing but to curl up on the sand and sleep. But the kindly local man advised Milaqa to take care of her body first, or she would be as stiff as a plank by the morning. So she ducked around a rocky outcrop to a more secluded part of the beach, stripped down to her loincloth and plunged into the water. It seemed saltier than she remembered of Northland's seas, and more buoyant, and it was cold, but she swam back and forth, letting the sea replenish her drained body, and feeling her muscles recover as they stretched against the water's gentle resistance.

That night she slept a dreamless sleep. But the morning found her back at her oar, and the grim slog of completing the journey resumed.

31

The next day they got their first glimpse of the Anatolian shore. It was a thin brown stripe on the horizon, with low, worn hills, and long empty beaches against which waves broke in a skim of white, and not a splash of green anywhere. This was home for Qirum. He showed no pleasure in returning.

They turned, heading north, so they tracked the coast to their east, Milaqa's left. The rowing got harder. There was a current against them, and a wind blew steadily from the north. Milaqa and the rest laboured, but the landmarks on the shore seemed to crawl by. At last, on the northern horizon, Kilushepa pointed out a smudge of brown hanging over the land: smoke from the fires of Troy itself.

'There's a bay,' Qirum said, panting as he worked his oar. 'A headland . . . Once we round the headland and get into the bay we'll be out of this current, sheltered from the wind, and life will get a lot easier. Not long now, I promise—'

'Weapons!' Kilushepa's command was a harsh snap.

Milaqa looked up, confused. The men were already shipping their oars and scrambling for their spears and shields under their benches. Qirum looked over his shoulder, past Milaqa, and he swore, using his filthiest defamation of his Storm God.

And Milaqa looked back, along the length of the boat to the sea. There it was: a black scrap on the horizon that grew as she watched, a square of dark sail above a slim hull.

Qirum began barking instructions. 'Get ready. Use any weapons you have to hand. You too, ladies! I feared they would strike here, where every boat must round the headland to the bay. And see how they come upon us, riding down the summer winds as we labour against them, they have all the advantages. Of course anticipating trouble doesn't necessarily mean you can avoid it. They'll come alongside us, grapple us with hooks and ropes, maybe throw a net. Cut their ropes, slash their net. Don't let them board! Or you will be rowing another boat across a river of blood before the day is done.'

They quickly got organised, the men with their weapons and shields ready to defend either side of the boat, depending on how the pirates came down on them. Milaqa had no weapons of her own save her bronze dagger. She picked up her oar, and held it before her like a club. Teel looked terrified, Deri and Riban grim. Tibo had an expression of relish. The black ship closed on them silent as smoke over the water. Milaqa could see detail now, rents in that big sail, a glint of metal – bronze swords and spear points.

None of this seemed real. The scene was almost peaceful, as they waited; the sea lapped, the wind sighed in their faces.

'They're closing fast,' Deri said grimly. 'They'll pass by fast too. If they judge it wrong they'll miss us altogether.'

Qirum said, 'They're good seamen. Must be, or they wouldn't have survived. They *might* foul up. We won't gamble our lives on it. She's a big one. A fifty-seater. If she's fully manned we're outnumbered many times over.'

'This is not how it ends for you, Trojan,' Kilushepa said calmly. 'You, killed by a stranger for the scrap of food in your pack, the bit of gold in your pocket? You, who is destined to rule the world? You will survive this. So it's a fifty-seater. What's your plan?'

He stared at her. Then he laughed out loud. 'Gods, I am surrounded by monstrous women! But you are right, of course. We must not allow them close enough to use their advantage of numbers.' He rummaged under his bench for his bow and a leather quiver of arrows. 'Milaqa. Get me the lantern from Kilushepa at the stern.' Feverishly he used his knife to saw a bit

192

of cloth from his tunic, and tied it around an arrowhead. 'Move, girl!'

She worked her away along the boat, between the watchful men, and fetched the lantern. She had to shield it from the wind with her body as Qirum struck a flint to light it. 'Feed it,' he snapped at the man behind Milaqa's bench, the Greek. The man ripped bits of cloth off his own tunic to fuel the flames.

The pirate ship was closing now. Some of its crew dug oars in the water to slow the ship as it bore down. Milaqa thought she heard them chant, a rapid, ugly noise; they were pumped up to fight.

'Milaqa.' Qirum dipped one arrowhead, wrapped in cloth, into the flame; it came up burning. 'Help me. I'll fire the arrows. And when they close, *throw the lamp*. Try to hit the sail. Do you understand? You'll only get one chance.'

She picked up the lamp; it was a clay jug heavy with oil. 'I'm ready.'

'Good, because—'

Because they were here.

The pirate was another Greek boat, Milaqa saw, a sleek black hull with savage painted eyes. The hull itself was battered and showed signs of patching, a hardened fighting ship. And as Qirum had predicted it was about twice the length of theirs, and seemed to swarm with men.

The ropes started flying over, weighted with stones, with hooks of sharpened bone. Qirum's crew hacked at the ropes with their axes and blades. The pirates hauled with relish, laughing. Milaqa saw they were preparing to throw a weighted net over the boat, which would trap them all. One man looked directly at her. He wore a skull plate nailed to his shaven head, and his face was crowded with tattoos. He opened his mouth to reveal sharpened teeth, and a tongue that had been cleft like a snake's. He barely looked human at all. She clenched her oar, recoiling, shocked, suddenly flooded with fear. She was nothing to this man, she saw, her own self worthless. To him she was a

193

scrap of flesh to be robbed, used and discarded – and then forgotten, no doubt, before the night fell. What god would make a universe where such a horror could be inflicted on *her*?

But he hadn't got her yet.

Qirum fired off a flaming arrow – but it missed, and sailed harmlessly into the sea, where its flame died. He fired another and hit a man in the chest; he screamed and fell backward into the sea. A third thunked into the pirate's hull. And now, as the enemy ship closed, Qirum cried, 'Milaqa!'

For an instant she could not move. She couldn't take her eyes off the tattooed man, who grinned, and beckoned to her, an obscene gesture. Qirum called again.

With all her strength Milaqa hurled her lantern.

It smashed against the base of the pirate's mast, and flame blossomed. The men scrambled away from the sudden fire, trying to douse it using seawater scooped up with bilge buckets. The rowers managed to cut the last of the ropes, and the pirate ship drifted away, and Qirum loosed off more arrows, picking off the men. Tibo whooped, and hurled his spear uselessly after the pirate vessel.

'Now row!' Qirum shouted. 'Let's put some distance between us! Take your oars!'

The oarsmen, including Milaqa and Qirum, quickly settled. Soon they were in the familiar rhythm, chanting together now, a triumphant, 'One – pull! One – pull!' Milaqa, looking out over the stern as she rowed, saw the blazing pirate ship recede into the distance. The crew, abandoning their attempt to save the ship, leapt into the water.

'The gods spared us,' muttered Qirum as he rowed. 'If you had failed with your throw, Milaqa, even by a hand's breadth – and there's a great deal of luck involved in lobbing from one moving ship into another – we would all be dying, spilling our blood into the water by now. They toy with us, the gods, our little lives and deaths amuse them . . .'

Kilushepa put away her own knife. Throughout the incident

she had not moved from her bench at the stern, as expression-less as if nothing important had happened at all.

But Milaqa gave way to a deep shuddering. She couldn't get the image of the tattooed face out of her mind, that cleft tongue. He had come so close. She longed to be somewhere safe, to have the stout bulk of the Wall around her.

The kindly Greek behind her put his hand on her shoulder, squeezed.

32

They made landfall in Troy's harbour later the same day.

They left the boat with Qirum's Greek recruits, and made the short walk along a rutted road towards the city itself. They were all heavily laden with packs, save for Kilushepa and Noli, and they walked slowly, getting used to being on the land again, and in silence – exhausted, shocked, Milaqa thought. Teel had barely spoken since the pirate attack. Even Deri was subdued. Only Tibo, marching just behind Qirum, looked bright, curious.

Milaqa had had an air of unreality since the attack, as if the pirates had killed her, as if she was a ghost walking. She tried to concentrate on the landscape around her. What could she make of it? Well, this road from the harbour had once been paved. Now the stones were broken and scattered, the road long unrepaired. The land itself had been heavily farmed, as you could tell from the tight pattern of boundary walls – you could even see the scraped lines where the ground had been painfully prepared to take the seed. But on this summer day, when the fields should have been plump with green, only weeds grew, and ravens pecked at the hard, dry soil. In one field she saw a big skeleton, maybe a horse, picked clean, the eyes in its long skull gaping.

Qirum marched through this fallen landscape without comment.

The walls of Troy loomed before them, a band across the countryside. A pall of orange smoke rose up from a hundred fires, and within the walls the buildings were a jumble of scorched stone. It was like a vast tomb, Milaqa thought, like the mound-tombs built by the silent priests of Gaira, stone boxes where dusty men would rummage through the heaped-up bones of their ancestors. Troy would be the first large city Milaqa had actually entered. At Mycenae and other way stations, Qirum had always urged the party to stay hidden in the country outside. The cities now, he always said, swarming with the starving and desperate, were more dangerous than the lands beyond their walls. But they were going into Troy.

When the breeze shifted, subtly, Milaqa smelled death, the harsh, sour stink of it. She covered her mouth with the collar of her tunic.

As they neared the city the tracks branched out, heading for different gates. Qirum chose a track, and they came to a ditch that Qirum said was designed to keep out bandits on chariots. As they crossed by a light wooden bridge, Milaqa saw the ditch was full of corpses – many of them children – a rotting, angular mass. Here was the source of that stench, then. They hurried over the bridge, for they all knew that the gods of disease lingered around fresh corpses. Qirum clapped his hands, and carrion birds rose up in a squawking cloud.

'There has been a great massacre,' Tibo said.

'No, my would-be warrior,' Qirum said. 'Nothing so dramatic. The only battle being waged here is against hunger and thirst and disease, and these are the fallen foot soldiers of that battle. This is where they bring out the corpses each morning – the bodies of those who succumbed during the night.' He wrinkled his nose at the stink. 'They used to burn them. Looks like even that discipline has been abandoned.'

From close to, the wooden palisade around the city wasn't as formidable a barrier as it had seemed from further out. Its face was patched, the breaches jammed with rough agglomerations of timber and rubble, and it was scorched by fire. It had evidently suffered many attacks. Still, the wall clearly served to keep undesirables out. When they got to the gate they found people gathered around – crowds of them, sitting in an eerie

197

silence. There were even crude lean-tos, huddled up against the ramparts.

These people watched as Qirum's party passed. Their skin, their clothes, were the colour of the dust they sat in. Children, wide-eyed, listless and with swollen bellies, came forward to the travellers, hands out. Many of these wretches bore terrible wounds, Milaqa saw, hideous scars crossing little faces, severed limbs ending in fly-swarming stumps. Wounds that were memories in flesh of flashing bronze swords wielded by mighty heroes.

The gate itself was just another breach in the wall, through which ran a rutted track. Men lounged here, in armour of leather and with shields of wood, their kit poorer than Qirum's bronze breastplate, though their swords gleamed from polishing. The largest of them stood in front of Qirum as he tried to pass. 'No entry,' he said in rough Trojan. 'King's orders.'

'And who is king now? Never mind.'

The warrior looked briefly impressed by his accent. But he said, 'I'd walk on if I were you, brother. Troy's full. And no food to be had anyhow.'

'You look well fed enough,' snapped Kilushepa in her own tongue. 'But then palace guards always are, aren't they? Always the most privileged, until at last they betray their masters.'

Qirum raised his eyes to the heavens. 'Please – stay silent.'

The warrior looked at the Tawananna suspiciously. 'What did she say? Who is she?'

'Never mind,' Qirum said. 'Look . . .' He dug into a pouch at his belt, and produced a fleck of gold. 'Imagine how many whores you can buy with this. I am sure there are plenty of *those* still in Troy.'

But the man seemed doubtful about accepting the gold. 'You've been away a long time, brother. Things are bad in here. I'm telling you honestly, you seem a decent sort. Whatever you're seeking here has probably long gone.'

Qirum forced a grin. 'How bad can it be?' He produced another flake. 'This bad?'

The warrior hesitated. 'Make it two for me and each of my buddies here,' there were four in all, 'and you can go in and see for yourself.'

Milaqa saw Qirum's jaw work. This was obviously far more than he had expected to pay. But unless they got into Troy they couldn't achieve anything else. 'Very well.' He dug out more flakes.

The warrior counted them out, and handed their share to his companions. 'On you go, brother. I hope you find what you're looking for.'

So they approached the gate. At Qirum's brisk orders the men formed a loose ring around the women, weapons to hand.

And Milaqa entered Troy.

She easily spotted the palace mound. It was just as Qirum had described it, a hill at the northern end of the city surrounded by its own stout stone walls. But many of the buildings even within the citadel walls were burned out, their stones tumbled. Outside the central citadel Troy was a ruin – evidently destroyed long ago, for weeds had grown over broken walls and fallen roofs. People crowded in here even so, hollow adults, children peering apathetically from lean-tos. Smoke rose from dozens of fires, contributing to the brown fug above. More mutilated children crowded around the travellers, hands held out in supplication. Qirum touched his sword and snarled to keep them at bay. Milaqa remembered how she had once dreamed of the glories of the cities of the east, over cups of ale in the Scambles.

'There are no dogs here,' Noli said. 'Did you notice that? All long gone into the pot, I suppose.'

Qirum brought them along a path that ran beside a length of smashed-down wall. 'This was one of the city granaries, a big one. Never rebuilt since the Greek firestorm. There's no point coming here, to the city, yet the people come even so. For this is where the priests are, and the King, who promised to protect them and feed them.

'Well. To get to Hattusa we'll need transport, protection. We can find both here. I'll try to get us into the palace mound. We'll

199

be as safe there as anywhere, and that's where the food will be, believe me, and the clean water. In the morning I'll start looking for carts, and horses to pull them if they still exist, or slaves if not.'

'Northlanders don't use slaves,' snapped Riban, the priest.

Qirum stared at him for a long moment. 'Then you can pull the cart yourself —'

Screams pierced the air. Milaqa whirled around.

There was a crash of splintering wood, and a clang, strangely, of bells. From over the outer wall sparks arced in the air, torches or burning arrows, falling towards houses of wood and mud and straw.

A whole section of the wooden palisade came crashing down, and horses burst through the wall, rearing and neighing, pairs of them drawing chariots, from whose platforms huge men in armour roared and slashed with swords and axes. The chariots were jet-black, as were the men's garments. That strange, alarming sound of chiming came from bells tied around the horses' necks. It was chaos, suddenly spreading inwards from the wall.

People ran, screaming. Some got away, but mothers slowed to pick up their children, and many folk were so weakened by hunger or illness they could barely run at all, and the charioteers soon caught up with them. And where the flaming arrows fell houses were starting to burn.

Qirum glared. 'Raiders! Once the King's forces would have driven off such a mob long before they got to the city—'

'Never mind that,' snapped Kilushepa. 'What do we do, Trojan?'

'The citadel. They won't harm us if we can get there. Come.'

Kilushepa ran, dragging Noli by the hand. The rest of the party followed. Qirum, Deri, Riban, Tibo, even Teel, all drew swords and backed up, protecting the rest. Milaqa drew her own dagger.

For the raiders it was becoming a kind of sport. The charioteers ran down the people, the swordsmen hacking at the fleeing crowd as you would cut your way through dense undergrowth. And now Trojans were being grabbed and thrown back to be taken by the following foot troops – women and girls mostly, a few young men. This attack was for captives then, slaves and whores. Maybe the charioteers would ignore the Northlanders, Milaqa thought, if they were satisfied with the easier meat of the unarmed city dwellers, but she was ashamed of the thought even as it formed.

And suddenly, without warning, Tibo ran forward, sword raised, screaming, heading straight for the charging charioteers. Qirum tried to grab him, but Tibo was too fast. He was the only warrior running *towards* the invaders, Milaqa saw. He closed on the chariots and swung his sword, apparently aiming for a horse's neck. A charioteer easily parried it – the sword went flying out of the boy's hands – and with a single fist, a savage yank, the man hauled Tibo over the chariot, and he was lost.

'No!' Milaqa tried to run after him.

But she was held around the waist. It was Deri, Tibo's father. 'Not now,' he said, desperate, dragging her back towards the citadel. 'We'll get him back. But not now.'

More chariots came, a swarm of them pouring in a flood through the breached wall, and the death and the burning spread out across the city, to the screams of the people and the chiming of the horses' bells.

The Northlanders fled to the citadel.

33

Troy was a broken city. Even when the raiders had gone there was no sense of order, no authority beyond the petty gang lords who strutted through the rubble-strewn streets like emperors.

Still, Qirum seemed to find it easy to do his deals in the aftermath of the raid. He quickly secured the services of a handful of warriors, all former Hatti soldiers, or so they claimed. These men looked tough to Milaqa, but uncomfortably hungry, and she had no idea how to judge their loyalty. And Qirum turned up a couple of carts, hard to find in a city where even timber for the fires was growing scarce. He failed to locate any horses, but he did manage to get the Northlanders some food, fish and dried meat. He promised that none of it was rat flesh, or worse.

Hattusa was far to the east of here, many more days' travel, in the Land of the Hatti. But for now it was not Hattusa they sought but a boy from Northland.

'We will find him,' Qirum assured Deri. 'Find him and save him. Stick with me. You will see.' Tibo had made himself close to Qirum, Milaqa realised. Maybe Qirum had adopted him as a kind of pet, a half-tamed wolf cub. Just as he had adopted Milaqa, maybe, another impulsive affection that made no particular sense. Whatever the reason, Qirum seemed determined to see through his pledge.

His men meanwhile had been quietly extracting information from the survivors of the raid. The leader of the black charioteers was a man who called himself the Spider. It was said that he had been a military commander under the Hatti regime, before going rogue. Now he was one of the most feared of the bandit warlords who had sprouted like weeds in an increasingly lawless country. He was believed to have a base to the east. With that knowledge Kilushepa was prepared to allow a diversion to pursue Tibo.

'We are heading east anyhow,' Qirum told her.

'As long as the time we lose is not excessive.'

Teel growled, 'And as long as we don't get ourselves killed confronting this Spider.'

Milaqa hissed, 'Shame on you, uncle. Don't let Deri hear you say that. Tibo is your blood, as he is mine.'

Teel, as he often did, looked shifty, uncomfortable, priorities conflicting in his head. 'We didn't come here for this, for a rescue mission. He's probably dead already – you understand that, don't you? We're trying to save empires here. We can't save everybody, Milaqa.'

'But we can try,' she snapped back fiercely.

After three uncomfortable, uneasy nights in Troy, they left the city and set out east. They were the survivors of Qirum's party of Northlanders, and the dozen Trojan warriors he had hired. The Trojans took turns hauling the two carts on which Kilushepa and Noli rode, along with their baggage. The warriors grumbled or bragged every step of the way.

The road to the east was decaying, rutted. This was a country that Qirum called Wilusa – a shattered, starving place, and unseasonably cold when the wind picked up under the sunless sky. The fields were dry and unworked, the houses and barns looted and collapsed. Irrigation channels scored the land, but they were dry too, dust-filled and weed-choked. Teel pointed out the remains of stands of forest, long since cut to the ground for firewood.

From the beginning Qirum imposed a careful rationing system. It was just as well, Milaqa thought, for otherwise his hungry warriors would have finished the food they had brought from Troy in days, and then probably started in on the precious seed potatoes. And he allowed his warriors to hunt. Once they saw a herd of goats, running wild, and the men chased them, but the animals, hardy survivors themselves, were too quick.

They passed a stone watchtower. There was no sign of the soldiers who must once have manned it.

Kilushepa seemed dismayed by this abandonment. 'By such means as this tower we Hatti maintained security for generations,' she said to Noli and Milaqa. 'We were a great nation. Once we destroyed Babylon. Once we defeated the Egyptians, at Kadesh, in the greatest battle the world has ever known. But our empire was always under threat. The Hatti kingdom itself is a patchwork of many peoples, surrounded by a buffer of restless vassals and dependencies. So we built an empire like a fortress, with fortified towns connected by roads for the troops, marked out by watchtowers like this. Or at least that was how it used to be . . .'

They came to a river that flowed roughly south to north, towards the great northern sea that lay beyond the strait where Troy was situated. It was low and silty, the banks choked with reeds, but the water flowed and was fresh, and they refilled their skins and jugs.

They turned and headed south, working upstream. Kilushepa said they would find fords and bridges. Here, by the water, there were more houses, just shacks of reeds and bits of timber, hearths that looked recently used. But they never saw any signs of the people who must live here. The soldiers routinely robbed what they could find, pulling apart the little houses, emptying the traps and lines of any catches.

'They must see us coming,' Milaqa said. 'They run and hide.'

'Wouldn't you?' Teel murmured. 'We must look like bandits to them. Which of course we are, to all intents and purposes.'

Another day on from the watchtower they came to a small town, sprawling by a river bank studded with jetties. The party approached cautiously. The town was laid out a little like Troy, Milaqa could see, though on a much smaller scale, with a ditch and palisade surrounding an inhabited area within which a stone-walled citadel rose proud on a hillock. And just as at Troy shanties and lean-tos were pressed up against the outer rampart, a wrack of people washed up by a tide of hunger.

The road led them across the defensive ditch to an open gateway. There was a crowd gathered by the gate, pushing and shoving. Milaqa heard raised voices, shouting, and a man's agonised cry. Qirum's party slowed. The warriors touched the hilts of their swords.

Teel said nervously, 'We don't need any more trouble.'

Deri growled, 'We're not leaving until we're sure Tibo is not here.'

'If the Spider's black chariots are at work here,' Kilushepa said, 'I think we'd know it by the screams.'

'Perhaps they've been here,' Qirum said. He stepped forward, hands on hips, peering; the light under the unending cloud was uncertain. 'For I think that's one of the Spider's men who's doing the screaming.'

The mob surrounded a man dressed entirely in black, Milaqa saw now. They had him by the arms, and were dragging him under the gateway in the wall.

Qirum said, 'Left behind, I imagine. And now taking punishment on behalf of them all.'

Deri said urgently, 'He might know where Tibo has been taken.'

'Yes. Come with me – you, Deri, and Milaqa. You others wait, and keep your weapons hidden.' He set off immediately, with Deri and Milaqa hurrying behind.

And Kilushepa followed, striding boldly. Qirum just looked at her, and hurried on.

When they got to the gateway Milaqa saw immediately what the inflamed people were trying to do. The gate was a rough arch of stout wooden timbers. Ropes had been thrown over the arch, and were tied to the charioteer's chest, wrists and feet. Men started to haul at the ropes, and a baying cry went up. The captive was clearly to be dragged into the air by the big band around his chest. He was struggling, squirming. His face was a mask of blood, his eyes were pits of darkness, and his long black tunic was stained rust-brown. He was a big man physically, Milaqa saw, but there was no sense of violence about him.

Milaqa said to Qirum, 'They will haul him over the arch.'

'Yes. And bend him backwards until he snaps like a twig. A crude but effective punishment, I suppose . . . Kilushepa! Wait!'

But the queen, with an impressive burst of speed, was already striding towards the mob. 'Stop this!' Her voice, imperious, carried over the yelling of the mob. Even the captive was silenced.

Qirum hurried to her side and walked with her. 'Is this wise?'

'These are my people. I am still their Tawananna. Stop this, I say – stop it now!'

A woman approached her, ragged, limping. She led a little girl by the hand. 'Who are you to tell us what to do?'

'I am queen. I am Kilushepa. I am Tawananna.'

'Kilushepa's dead. That's what I heard.'

'Then you heard wrong. Here she is, here I am, in the flesh. Here I am, returning to Hattusa to take up the reins of power – and to ensure that people like you are protected once more.'

Milaqa was lost in admiration for this woman, who faced a murderous mob and held them spellbound with a few words, even if she must know she was making promises she could not keep.

And the captive, bound, blinded and bloodied, twisted and turned his head. 'Tawananna? Is it you? I heard you speak, just once. I would never forget that voice.' He spoke clear Nesili, his accent like Kilushepa's.

She walked up to him. The mob melted back, to Milaqa's continuing astonishment. 'What is your name, man?'

'I am Kurunta. You would not know me. There is no reason why . . . I was a scribe in the palace precinct. In great Hattusa! An archivist. I wrote, I read—'

The woman with the little girl pushed forward again. 'This man ran with the Spider. His men raped me. They killed my husband, and my son. And my little girl – look, Tawananna!'

She pulled the girl forward and exposed her face, and another ghastly injury inflicted by a hero's sword. Milaqa turned away.

But Kurunta twisted free of the grasping hands. 'Tawananna! Save me! I was a scribe before the world ended, and the Spider took me, and I woke in this nightmare of killing. Look what these people did to me!' He held up his arms. Milaqa saw that his hands had been cut off, his eyes put out. 'Look what they did!'

Kilushepa said to Qirum, 'We need this man. Pay off these people. Then let us leave this place.'

And she walked away, back towards the carts, leaving Qirum facing a surging, yelling mob.

34

After leaving the town the party continued to track the river, heading upstream, roughly south. This was the way to the Spider's main camp, according to Kurunta.

Kurunta rode with Kilushepa. Noli allowed the young priest Riban to tend to Kurunta's wounds, his ruined eyes, the crudely cauterised stumps of his arms, and to give him infusions of herbs to dull the pain. The drugs made Kurunta light-headed, and he talked and talked, like a lost child. Milaqa, curious, walked alongside the cart, following his stilted Hatti tongue as best she could.

'My father was a court scribe, and his father before him. We lived in a fine house within the walls of Hattusa. Once my father met the King himself, and took down his personal account of a battle. He was served food . . . little birds stuffed with olives . . . he said he never tasted the like. I married, I had a family. Two boys. Oh, we knew about the famine, the drought. How could you not, with the records we clerks kept and copied? But it always seemed remote. Not for us in Hattusa, fed on grain from Egypt.

'But then I was sent to the north coast, to a city called Lazawa.' A place Milaqa had never heard of. 'There had been a rebellion, raids by the Kaskans – a mess. I was one of a party sent to gather facts on how the country was recovering now that the rebellion was put down, or so the governor had told the King. This report would be brought back to the court.

'So we went out into the country. We had a corps of the

Standing Army of the Left to accompany us, under an overseer who reported to the King's own brother. I felt safe.

'We had a great deal of trouble on the way, but we reached Lazawa. And there we found that everything we had been told about the outcome of the rebellion was an utter lie. The town was a smoking ruin, the grain stores looted, the people driven off or enslaved by the Kaskans. There was not even food for us. Not even for our horses!

'And it was as we considered what we should do that the Spider fell on us . . .'

The Spider had been a regional governor, a 'Lord of the Watchtower' as the Hatti called it. As the years of drought wore on, the commands from the centre had grown sporadic and contradictory, and the cycle of supply and troop replenishment slowly broke down. Then the fire-mountain clouds closed in, and people started to starve, and the man had gone rogue altogether.

'I do not know his name,' Kurunta whispered. 'He wears the uniform of the army, the chariots are as the army ride, but he has painted or dyed everything black, so that all will know it is *he* who descends, *his* sword that flashes – *his* laugh you hear when you die . . .'

'And he descended on you,' Kilushepa prompted.

'Yes. Our troops fell, or fled, or defected on the spot. We scribes and our servants were playthings for the Spider and his soldiers. You can imagine what happened to the women, and the younger boys. Not one of them survived the first night. The rest of us were used for – amusement. One man was let loose, naked, and hunted like an animal. Practice for the archers, the charioteers. I knew him. He told good jokes. Another, who fought back, was tied to a post. They rode at him on their horses taking swipes with their swords, until nothing was left of him. And so on. I had never fought, but you can see I am a bulky man, Tawananna. They put me in a kind of arena of spears and ropes, with two others, and made us fight. Only one of the three would live to leave that ring. I had not struck another human being since I was a child.'

'Yet you survived,' Kilushepa murmured.

'I survived. The Spider told me that if I fought with him, with his troops, he would let me live. And I did,' he whispered. 'I did, Queen! And I have committed terrible crimes, or watched them. All to save my own skin.'

'It is nothing to be ashamed of. You see how it is,' she said to the others. 'The times we live in. And all this has come to pass under the nominal protection of the Hatti, still the greatest empire in the world. This is why we must work together, Annid. Lest the darkness fall over the whole world, for good.'

'I was educated,' said Kurunta. 'I was a scribe. The Spider has told me that that time has gone. That nobody will ever write or read again, as long as the world lasts, and that soon people will even forget that such a thing was possible. Even my sons, who I have not seen since I left Hattusa. Is it true, Tawananna? Is this the end of it all? Is it true?'

She took the bloody stumps of his arms in her hands. 'Not if I can help it.'

He subsided, muttering, turning his eyeless head as if looking for the light.

They came upon the camp of the Spider late the following day. It was visible from far off as a smudge of smoke on the southern horizon. It looked to Milaqa like the most substantial settlement they had seen since Troy itself.

Yet when they approached, it was not a town at all.

The centrepiece was another watchtower, guarding another road. On the plain around this tower bonfires burned, sending columns of smoke up to the sky, and there were tents and shacks of timber and reeds. Male laughter carried on the breeze, and a clang of metal, sword on sword.

'This is the place,' Kilushepa murmured, as she clambered down from her cart. Kurunta was sleeping now. 'Just as our mutilated clerk described it.'

'I will go in alone,' said Qirum. 'We mustn't challenge them.'

'That's foolish,' Deri snapped, in the broken Hatti he had learned. 'Let me go with you, at least. Tibo is my son.'

'No.' Qirum dug into the heap of stuff on the cart, found his bronze breastplate, and with quick fingers tied it in place. 'I know these people, remember – men like the Spider.'

'Because you are one yourself,' said Kilushepa with a faint sneer.

Qirum grinned coldly and said nothing. He set his ox-horn helmet on his head, fixed his sword in its scabbard on his back, and strode out towards the camp, heading straight for the watchtower at its heart.

Those left behind started to make a camp of their own. The men built a fire. Deri paced, as tense as a clenched fist. Kilushepa waited, silent and still. Milaqa thought it was quite likely the Spider already knew all about this petty force of Qirum's. She imagined some armed man's calculating gaze on her even now, and she tried not to shudder.

The light was fading by the time Qirum returned. He sat by the fire, and took a cup of wine from one of his warriors.

'He will talk to us,' he said. 'The Spider. I was only able to negotiate with him through his generals, his closest circle. The Spider is sharper than I imagined. I had to give away a lot.'

Deri frowned. 'A lot of what? Gold?'

'Information. I was getting nowhere. He was intrigued when I told him the Tawananna was here.' He smiled spitefully at Kilushepa. 'Although he asked, *which* Tawananna.'

'And the boy – what of him?'

'The Spider himself may not know. I got the impression he takes many prisoners, for many purposes. He will speak to us, however.'

Deri said, 'Us?'

'The Tawananna,' said Qirum. 'He was a governor, remember. I think it flatters his vanity to have one of the court come to his camp. And he will speak to a relative of the boy.'

'I will go,' said Deri.

'No,' Qirum said. 'No men. A woman. It must be a woman.'
And he looked at Milaqa.

Deri shook his head. 'It isn't safe.'

'He's right,' Teel said. Suddenly he and Deri were Milaqa's uncles, looking out for the safety of their niece.

But she said, 'I will go.'

Qirum nodded. 'He will not harm you. Well, I don't believe so. If he intended to, he could have set his warriors on us already. He is more curious than aggressive. I think he seeks – amusement.'

Kilushepa stood. 'More practically, this Spider is the only authority in the area just now, isn't he?'

Teel frowned. 'What exactly are you planning, Tawananna?'

She would not reply.

Qirum swilled another mouthful of wine, hurried behind a rocky outcrop to take a quick piss, and then returned, rubbing his hands. 'Are you ready?'

Qirum led them back the way he had come.

As the Trojan walked boldly through the camp, the Spider's warriors watched them pass. They were Hatti warriors, Milaqa saw, or a semblance of them. They were relaxing, and many had their boots off, their black-dyed tunics loosened, their long hair worn loose rather than plaited. They sat around the fires, worked at their weapons with sharpening stones, rubbed their feet with bits of rough rock. There were neat heaps of spears, leather helmets, shields of leather and wood. Subdued-looking women, many very young, prepared food and brought the men drink. Milaqa was selfishly glad they were here. She would not have liked to have been the only woman in the camp.

As they neared the watchtower they saw stranger sights. In a cage of wood and rope a group of women, girls and boys sat in the dirt, many naked, waiting in silence. A few warriors were gathered around another cage, laughing and shouting, gambling with bits of gold and precious stone, goading the cage's occupants with shouts and waved fists. Milaqa got close enough to glimpse what was going on inside the cage: two men, both naked, both *without feet*, their legs crudely wrapped in bloody cloth, were crawling in the dirt, dragging their bodies, trying to fight each other.

They came to the watchtower itself. Kilushepa pointed up at a standard of wood and bronze that had been fixed to its roof: an eagle, once apparently two-headed, now headless altogether. 'A sacred symbol,' Kilushepa murmured. 'Mutilated. How the world has fallen into decay . . .'

A hefty guard stood by a narrow doorway. He recognised Qirum, ushered him through. Milaqa and Kilushepa followed. The watchtower was half-wrecked, Milaqa saw, peering around in the reduced light. On the ground floor there was a space for a hearth, heaped up with wood, unlit. A set of steps carved into the stone wall led up to the remains of a platform where, in more orderly times, soldiers of the King at Hattusa would have watched over the roadway. Now a loose canvas had been stretched over the open roof.

'To keep out the rain,' came a voice from the shadows, speaking precise Hatti. 'Should it ever fall again . . . Come forward. You. The girl. I won't bite; I've already eaten today.'

Milaqa glanced at the others. Both Qirum and Kilushepa seemed utterly calm. She, however, was trembling. She took a step forward, then another. She had never felt so far from home. She kept seeing the pirate in her mind, his cleft tongue.

As her eyes adapted to the dark she saw a man sitting on a tall chair, his back to the stone wall. He was slim, not bulky, but she sensed he was strong, whip-like. He wore a black-dyed tunic like his soldiers, but embroidered with gold thread. His hair was long at his back, in the Hatti fashion. Clean-shaven, no older than his mid-thirties, he might have been called handsome. But one eye was a blackened ruin.

'What is your name?'

'Milaqa.'

'You are a Northlander, I am told. Yet you understand Hatti.'

'All Northlanders are educated.'

He laughed. 'I don't doubt it. I wonder if they are all as brave as you. Why have you come here?'

'You know why.'

'Tell me anyway.'

'I come for my cousin, Tibo. You took him from—'

'Yes, yes. And now you are here – now you see me – what is the one question you wish to ask me?'

She considered. 'What happened to your eye?'

'Ah. Good question.' He sat back. 'You understand I was governor here – we call it the Lord of the Watchtower – before the sky clouded over and the world ended? There was drought, famine, rebellion in my province.

'So a man was sent from the King's household in Hattusa to inspect the trouble. He had once been the Chief of the Wine Cellar, which is an old ceremonial title – very close to the King, an important man. He decided that all the trouble was my fault. His men jumped me before I could react. The punishment he ordained was blinding.' He smiled. 'A favourite of us Hatti. The men got as far as destroying one eye, before I got a hand free.

'This chair, by the way, belonged to that former Chief of the Wine Cellar. He had it carried all the way from Hattusa. Imagine that. Fine piece of furniture, isn't it? Even better now it is upholstered with the skin off the Chief's own back.'

Kilushepa stepped forward now. 'Are you done frightening children?'

The Spider hesitated. Then he stood, almost respectfully. 'You were the Tawananna.'

'I *am* the Tawananna. Tell me your true name.'

'I am the Spider.' He grinned, and spread his arms wide. 'A good name for the ruler of this land of the dead, don't you think? Where people live like flies off the carcasses of the dead, and I, the Spider, consume the flies—'

'Your true name.'

Again he seemed to hesitate. 'Telipinu,' he said at last. 'I call myself Telipinu.'

'You call yourself after a god?'

'I was born in Hattusa—'

'I can tell that much from your accent,' she said, dismissive. She turned away to inspect the tower, as if no longer interested in the man. There were piles of goods in the shadows here, gold artefacts, iron perhaps, amber, bronze. 'You take the last of everything. You loot cities already ruined. You make people turn on each other – you make children into whores, you make cripples fight. What is it you want?'

He grinned. 'I am Telipinu. The Vanishing God, whose absence causes the rain to fail and crops to wither. Whose rages cause the very earth to shake. Look around. This is a world of destruction and decay, Queen. After decades of drought, and now the desertion of the sun, there's nothing else left. What is a man to do but revel in it, while it lasts?'

Qirum murmured, 'We came here for a purpose.'

'The boy?' The Spider grinned. 'I had him found. Your description was enough. He was a good fighter, as it turned out.'

Milaqa wondered what that meant, what Tibo had gone through. She said, 'So we can take him away.'

'Well, I didn't say that. He belongs to me now. Why should I give him back to you? What have you in exchange?' His glare, though one-eyed, was probing.

It was Kilushepa who broke the moment. 'We have this.' She dug into the pouch at her belt, and produced something small and pebble-like that she handed to him.

He inspected it curiously. 'What is this?'

It was a potato.

'We have more,' Kilushepa said. 'It is a seed. It is simple to grow, and produces ample food. As soon as this weather relents—'

'I have eaten Northland food.'

'This is what Northland food is grown from. *This is their secret. Now I am giving it to you.*'

Milaqa turned on her. 'Tawananna, are you insane? You give our treasure to this man?'

Kilushepa deigned to look at her, and spoke in her broken

Northlander. 'I know exactly what I'm doing, child. First, I am trying to secure your cousin's release, for until that is done we will not be able to move on to matters of importance. And second, this crop is the secret to recovery for the Hatti empire. For the whole world, perhaps. But for the first year, the second, its distribution must be controlled. Rationed. Surely you see that, for otherwise the hungry will eat even the seed stock, and all will be lost.'

'But this man—'

'Is a monster. I know. But he is the only functioning authority of any kind we have encountered since Troy. And until I return to Hattusa, until the centre imposes its control again, this is how it will remain. This is the kind we must deal with, like it or not.' Kilushepa turned to the Spider and spoke in her own tongue. 'For your people – in a year or two, if not now – this represents survival. For you, it represents redemption. Will you take it?'

He stared at the root, holding it in both hands. Then he nodded, curtly. 'The boy will be brought to you outside.'

Kilushepa bowed. 'Then our business here is done. Good luck, Telipinu.' She turned away and made for the doorway.

Qirum and Milaqa followed the Tawananna out. Milaqa whispered to Qirum, 'That story about covering the chair with the skin of its owner. Was it true?'

'Try not to think about it.'

Tibo was brought from the back of the tower, his arm gripped by a burly warrior. His face was grimy, his clothes reduced to rags, his feet bare. He was struggling. 'Get off me . . . get off!' The warrior shoved him towards Qirum's party. He fell and sprawled in the dirt. Immediately he was on his feet, and would have launched himself straight back at the warrior if Qirum hadn't grabbed him around the waist. 'I'll kill you! I'll kill you all!' Wild with rage, Tibo had to be dragged every step of the way out of the camp.

And he told the story of his abduction, in enraged, tearful fragments.

How those who bundled him on the slave carts almost killed him, casually. And had just as casually spared him, on a whim.

How he had been thrown into a kind of pen with other boys, and women and girls. How a boy, another prisoner, had tried to rape him, and he fought.

How the guards thought this was amusing, and, drinking, laughing by the fire, they pulled him out of the cage and lined him up against one of their number. If he could throw the man to the floor first, before being thrown himself, he would be spared. He threw the man. But then there was another, and he threw him, and a third. The fourth man threw Tibo. And he was the one who raped him, at last.

He told this story over and over, until they had got him away from the Spider's camp, and into the arms of his father. And Deri wept. Milaqa had never seen her uncle weep in her whole life, because, he said, he had broken his promise to his dying wife that he would keep their only child safe.

35

Nago, ten years older than Voro and far more experienced a hunter, pointed to a poorly concealed hearth, a scrap of linen clinging to bracken.

Voro nodded, grinning.

Deep in the folded hill country of the First Mother's Ribs, Voro and Nago were tracking Caxa, as they would hunt a deer. Even after the clue Caxa herself had left them by etching her giant artwork on the hillside, it had taken them days to work their way up from the valley of the Brother River, following her trail. But now, at last, they had crossed a ridge coated with heather, and saw her smoke.

The men rested, snuggling into the heather and sipping water from their flasks, before closing in for what Nago insisted on calling 'the kill'. They were reasonably well hidden, Voro thought, though even the heather was sparse this year, and everybody doubted it would put on its usual autumn display of brilliant purple. But the thistles and poppies grew thickly. From this high vantage Voro looked south over the country. He could see the winding ribbon that was the Brother River, and the communities cut into the green along its banks, the character-istic hearthspaces connected by arrow-straight trackways. Further away, off to the south, he could just make out the shining water of the Sister, the two rivers curling towards their shared estuary off to the east. And beyond the rivers the tremendous plain of Northland itself stretched away. Despite the dismal summer, though it was so unseasonably cold, there was plenty of green in the clumps of forest, the reeds in the marshland. Given the landscape was so different from her own remote country, Voro thought, Caxa had done well to hide from them – indeed to have survived so long, more than a month, by living off the land, entirely alone. But she was here. No doubt about that. Voro only had to glance down at the hillside below him.

From up here the pattern she had designed was fore-shortened, but he had seen it from the villages of the valley of the Brother, from the lowland, as it had meant to be seen: a tremendous figure scrawled on the hill, a grotesque mashing together of a human baby with a fish's body and a wolf's head. It could only be Caxa, for, according to Xivu, this was character-istic of the art of her country. The markings had been made by scraping at the heather, by setting carefully controlled fires – it was a feat of ingenuity and persistence for one woman to have achieved all this alone. And she had completed it all in a single night. It had scared the life out of the people when they had woken the morning after to find this monstrosity glaring down from their hillside at them. But it had at last enabled Nago and Voro to track the girl down.

Nago glanced at the sky, and rubbed his beaky nose. 'So hard to tell the time of day. That's the worst of this god-baffling sunless sky.'

'That and the hunger.'

'And the cold.'

'Let's see if we can get this done today—'

'Yes, let's.'

The voice was a hiss from just behind them.

Voro rolled on his back. He saw a blur rising from the heather, lithe, dark, coming at him. A human figure, face blackened, hand raised with a stone knife like a claw.

Before Voro could move Nago rolled over and lashed out with one boot. The shadow fell away with a grunt, and Nago was on his knees before it, bronze knife in his hand. Nago could move remarkably quickly for such an old man, at thirty. 'Enough,' he snapped.

Now they were still, the elusive shadow resolved. It was a girl, naked save for scraps of soft leather around her chest and loins, skin smeared with soil and leaf matter. Barefoot, lithe, no wonder she had been able to sneak up on them so easily.

'Get away. Leave me alone.'

'Put down the knife,' Nago said. 'Come on, child. It's over. You don't want to harm us.'

Voro rummaged for the words in the Jaguar tongue Xivu had carefully coached into him. 'We come as friends. You remember Nago. In his boat he saved you from the Hood. My name is Voro. We only want you to come home.'

She hissed again, and crouched down. She had become more like an animal than a human, Voro thought. She replied in clumsy Etxelur tongue, 'This is not my home. My home is far away, across the sea.'

'Come back to *my* home, then,' Voro said. 'Please. You are welcome there.'

'With Xivu?'

'You don't have to see him if you don't want to. You can stay with Vala. You remember her—'

'I must carve the head.'

He spread his hands. 'Everybody is hungry this year. Nobody is thinking of carvings on the Wall.'

'But that is why I was *brought* here. I had no *choice*. I have had no choice since the day I was born.'

Nago sighed. He tucked away his knife, and dug a flask of water out of his pack, offered it to her. She ignored him. Nago said, 'If you put it like that, which of us has any choice, child? We just have to make the most of what we're given.'

But she scowled at him.

Voro touched Nago's shoulder. 'Let me talk to her alone for a moment. We're more the same age.'

Nago snorted. 'If it were up to me I'd just truss her up and bring her home. All right, do it your way. But I will only be a dagger's throw away if she gets those claws out again.' He walked a few paces away and settled down to a meal of dried meat from his pack.

'You say you have no choice,' Voro said carefully to the girl in her own tongue. 'Yet you have had choices that you have not taken. You could have just disappeared. Northland is huge, empty. You could have gone off to Albia or Gaira, or even further, and before long you'd have found people who had never heard of Northland at all – let alone of the Land of the Jaguar. You could have disappeared. Yet you did not. Instead you made this huge, terrifying mark on the hill. You *chose* to do that. Why?'

She looked at her hands. 'It is in my blood. As in my father's, and my grandfather's . . . It is what I do. I make art. Big art, to provoke awe in people. Or fear. Or longing . . . I had no choice. I could not walk away and – catch eels.'

He nodded. 'And you *have* to make the head of Kuma, for that is what you do.'

'And the head of the Jaguar king,' she said evenly, 'which will kill me.'

He grinned. 'I'll help you. I promise. I won't let this Xivu take you off to be killed.' He had talked this through with Raka and Vala, neither of whom had much sympathy for the Jaguar priest. They would surely offend no gods of Northland if they let this girl live – only the strange, savage gods from across the ocean who ordained her wasteful death, and Northlanders had no fear of *them*.

And for Voro, perhaps saving a life would recompense for his part in the taking of a life.

She stared at him, struggling to believe. 'Tibo said he would help me.'

'He saved your life on the fire mountain,' Voro said sternly. 'Now it's my turn. I'm a clever chap. I will find a way. Will you come?'

36

The last few days of the long journey to Hattusa were the hardest of all.

With increasing confidence Kilushepa led the party along rutted roads and trails that took them away from the coastal plain. The abandoned farms of the lower land petered out, and they entered a spectacular landscape of deep-cut gorges and sharp ridges. This upland was inhabited only by birds, scrubby grass and spindly trees, and the few farms crowded in the valleys. It was a landscape that made you work hard, for the Hatti roads cut through gorges and valleys and over ridges and summits without sympathy for mere human limbs, and the men hauling the carts grunted with the effort. And the lowland opened up as they rose, with sweeping views stretching far away, across an ocean of farms and scrubby forest patches, with glimpses of even mightier mountains on the horizon. Milaqa had grown up in Northland, a tremendous plain. She had never seen country like this.

Sometimes they saw herders, gaunt men tracking herds of gaunt cattle across the dusty plain. They glimpsed deer, wolves. Once they heard a deep rumble, like a groan in the earth itself, that Qirum said was probably a lion.

And still they climbed. Soon they were so high that the air was even colder than it had been at the level of the sea, a deep, bitter, dry cold that dug into your bones when the wind was up. Each morning they found their gear covered in frost, though it was still late summer, and on the shaded sides of the hills the men pointed wonderingly to patches of snow not melted since the winter.

This was the forbidding landscape within which the Hatti had set their capital city.

They came upon a patrol of foot soldiers. It was the first evidence they'd had that Hattusa was still functioning at all. Qirum called the party to a halt. The six soldiers were dressed in what Milaqa had come to recognise as standard Hatti kit, each with a long tunic, a thick leather belt, a conical helmet with a brilliant feathered plume, boots that curled up oddly at the toe, and their black hair grown long and thickly plaited at the back. The soldiers each carried sword, spear, pack. This was just as the Spider's troops had been equipped, save that their kit had been dyed black.

Their sergeant approached the travellers. Two of his men pointed spears, while the others headed for the carts.

'Take it easy,' Qirum murmured in Trojan. 'They're just inspecting us. Don't give them cause to get upset.' His men scowled, but kept their hands away from their weapons.

The sergeant, a weary-looking veteran, called in clear Nesili, 'Who leads you?'

'I do.' The Tawananna stepped forward.

The sergeant looked her up and down cautiously. 'And you are?'

She smiled easily. 'Do you not remember me? I was never very good at showing my face to the people. Always too busy with affairs of family and state. I am Kilushepa, Tawananna, aunt of Hattusili the Sixth – who I presume still occupies the throne?'

'He does.' The sergeant peered at her. 'If you are the Tawananna, they said you were dead. And that before you were dead you were a traitor.'

'Lies.'

'You tried to poison the King.'

Kilushepa was utterly fearless. 'Would I dare return if that was so? I was betrayed by my enemies at court, that much is true.'

'If those enemies still live, why have you returned? For revenge?'

'Not that. To help. For Hattusa, and all the Hatti realm, faces a terrible crisis. You must see that.'

'It's true, it's true,' he said grimly. 'My own wife and kids – well. You don't need to hear my little troubles.'

'The question is,' Kilushepa said, 'will you let us pass?'

He looked uncertain. 'I'm just a sergeant.'

Teel murmured to Milaqa, 'And yet what he decides now will shape all of history to come. What an extraordinary scene to witness. But he's not the first common soldier to be put in such a position, and he won't be the last. Every time there is a palace coup the decision of a lowly bodyguard can shape the destiny of a trembling empire.'

'You speak as if you're not here,' Milaqa whispered back. 'As if you're outside it all, looking in. Reading about it in some archive.'

'Maybe it helps me control my fear.'

Kilushepa simply smiled at the sergeant. 'What is your name?'

'Hunda, madam.'

'Hunda, then. Follow your heart.'

'Hmm. Well, you're impressive enough. And if it's true your family betrayed you, they deserve what's coming to them.' Milaqa had learned that to the Hatti family loyalty was the strongest bond – and to betray family was a powerful taboo, which even a king dared not break. 'On the other hand, if you're lying, you'll soon get what's coming to *you*. You may pass. No – I'll escort you the rest of the way. The country isn't as safe as it used to be.'

So the Hatti soldiers formed up around the party, and they moved on, with the sergeant leading, and Kilushepa on her cart. The Hatti soldiers and Qirum's hired Trojan thugs eyed each other with contempt and hostility. Tension crackled.

And soon they came over a final rise, and at last Hattusa was laid out before them.

A scribble of walls across the folded, mountainous landscape – that was Milaqa's first impression.

The great city, capped by a fug of smoke from its endless fires, was ringed around by a circuit of walls, mud brick over stone, painted brilliant white and topped by arrowhead crenellations, walls that strode up hillsides and over summits and ridges and along cliff edges, punctuated by huge blocky towers. In one place there was a tremendous structure, a square base tapering up to a flat summit, the sloping sides combed by steps. The outer wall simply rose up and over even this vast obstacle, although it was broken by an enormous gate. And the walls were not restricted to the outer curtain but extended inward in loops and folds, enclosing whole districts within the city itself. It was extraordinary – ghastly – a place of exclusion and control, as you could see at a glance.

But Milaqa could see that this monstrous fort-city had fallen on hard times, for the great walls were scorched and scarred, and the familiar mud-brown tide of a shanty town had washed up against the outer curtain.

They set off down a slope, following the track, heading for a gate in the south-west corner of the wall curtain.

'Of course we don't have your growstone,' Kilushepa said. 'Perhaps that's the next secret I should trade for, and we could build even higher. But even so, we've done rather well, haven't we? It would take you the best part of a day just to walk around the circuit of the outer walls.'

Riban just stared. 'I can't believe that you have built all this, *up here*. Most great cities are built on the lowland. That's what I've read. By the rivers, by the sea coast. Troy, Ur, Uruk, Memphis. They are placed for ease of access. Whereas Hattusa—'

'Whereas Hattusa,' Kilushepa said, 'is a fortress. Set in a country that is itself a natural wall of granite. We are five days' walk from the nearest river, much further from the sea. Most armies starve even before they get the chance to fall on Hattusa itself. And in the winter, when the snow comes, none can get through at all. Of course there are vulnerabilities. We have always depended on imports for almost every bit of food, every grain of wheat. But without our fortress capital, Northlander, we could never have won our wars against enemies within and without, never have established our dominion over the greatest empire the world has ever seen. All of which is utterly beyond your petty imagination.'

As they neared the wall they had to get through the shanty town. The people came rustling out of their shacks and lean-tos, as always, the children with cupped hands. The soldiers snarled to drive them back, but they came again, their hunger and need outweighing their fear. Kilushepa seemed perturbed by this, Milaqa thought, watching her. Not distressed at the plight of the children. Embarrassed by the spectacle they made.

Soon the wall towered over their heads, four or five times the height of Milaqa, and the gate was taller yet, wood with bronze panelling, guarded by two lions carved in stone. A huddle of soldiers at the gate, Kilushepa called them 'Golden Spearmen', had their own little shrine set up behind a sullen fire, with a small, crude statue of a god, dressed in Hatti warrior garb and carrying an axe and a spear that was jagged like lightning.

'Teshub,' Qirum murmured to Milaqa. 'Their Storm God, although actually they borrowed him from the Hurrians. Like everything else about this empire their pantheon is a patchwork.'

'Perhaps they're asking for his mercy,' Milaqa said. 'To blow away the endless clouds.'

'Then they need to ask harder.'

Their friendly sergeant was able to get them past the guards without any trouble. They had to abandon their carts, however. Qirum left a couple of his men to watch the carts, while the rest escorted the party through the gate.

Inside, the city was a warren of crowded alleys between tall, enclosing walls. Though the streets looked clean enough there

226

was a lingering stink of sewage, and Milaqa wondered if all cities smelled this way. There were many men wearing uniforms like the sergeant's; this was evidently an age when the military were to the fore. Near the gate the visitors passed through a district that appeared damaged, burned out, abandoned. Here there were beggars, and Milaqa glimpsed gangs – young men and women wearing garish colours, brightly dyed hair, staring from broken doorways. But then they walked on, just a short distance, to a more orderly area where well-dressed people hurried busily, both men and women, many carrying clay tablets; Milaqa imagined they must be clerks, scribes, palace and temple officials. This was a city with problems, but evidently still a functioning capital.

They came to a wide, straight track and followed it through a precinct crowded with temples, walls of white marble enclosing gods carved of some sea-green stone, dimly glimpsed. Officials hurried between the buildings, as did servants and slaves – cooks perhaps, cleaners, even these great houses of the gods must need the most basic kinds of maintenance. The track merged with others, evidently coming from other gates in the walls, and the crowd thickened. A baffling clamour of languages was spoken. Milaqa recognised fragments of Nesili, Trojan, Akkadian, Egyptian, Greek – even a few Northlander words here and there.

And now, to add to the confusion, a procession came down the great way, forcing people to stand aside. Around a cart which carried a roughly shaped monumental stone priests shouted blessings, musicians played drums and flutes and gongs, dancers whirled and acrobats and jugglers put on spectacular shows. People applauded, and formed up a loose spontaneous procession behind the cart. It was a display of energy, of vigour – of *fun*, Milaqa thought, surprising in what she sensed was a city of harsh discipline and fear.

But, bewildered by the rush, the noise, the crush, the looming walls, Milaqa felt turned around, lost. Even Troy had been nothing like this in scale. Hunda, sensing her disorientation, pointed out how you could always see the higher land within

227

the city walls – a big outcrop to the north of the temple district, and an even stouter-looking fortress within a fortress, the citadel that contained the palace of the King, and the great Sphinx Gate to the south that overlooked the whole city. As long as you could see palace or temple or guardian sphinxes looming against the sky you could find your direction, anywhere in this great stone tomb of a city.

When the procession had passed they walked on, heading steadily north.

They came to a modest dwelling, one of a short row of blocky buildings constructed of mud brick and plaster.

The sergeant turned to Kilushepa apologetically. 'This is my own home, queen. I can't think where else to take you that would be safe, for now. There is a man I know at the palace, he was the chief of the chariot-warriors and I got to know him when he reviewed our training. His name is Nuwanza—'

'I know him,' Kilushepa snapped. 'A second cousin of the King, and so a relative of mine.' In the Hatti empire all the senior army officers were relatives of the King. 'One of Hattusili's more sane appointments.'

'I will try to get a message to him. I'll find somewhere for your warriors too. Please . . . It is much less than you are used to, I know—'

Kilushepa smiled. 'I am very grateful to you, sergeant. Your loyalty and your wisdom will not go unrewarded.'

He seemed embarrassed. He pulled back the door curtain, and Kilushepa walked through into the little space within.

'By the Storm God's left nostril,' Qirum murmured to Milaqa as they followed Kilushepa, 'I suppose there have to be a few honest soldiers or the whole thing would break down. But Kilushepa's been very lucky in happening on this fellow – very lucky indeed, and not for the first time in her life.'

The house's single room was gloomy, the light a greyish glow from a window cut in the wall. A woman had been labouring at a grindstone. She stood nervously, wiping her hands. There was a low table, wooden shelves at the back of the room piled with clutter, a stack of cloth pallets and blankets. Children huddled over toys in a corner, staring wide-eyed at the strangers. The room was tiny, yet its floor of packed earth was clean, evidently recently swept.

Hunda spoke calmly to the woman, explaining who Kilush-epa was. The woman, called Gassulawiya, evidently Hunda's wife, only looked more nervous. Then Hunda disappeared, off to the palace.

Noli sat beside Kilushepa on the pile of pallets. Milaqa and Qirum settled on the floor. Riban helped Kurunta down, but he sat heavily, without hands unable to lower himself easily. The sergeant's wife bustled around with a tray of cups of wine and water, slabs of bread. Qirum drained a single cup of wine, and waved away the rest. 'Take sparingly,' he said to the rest in his own tongue. 'We should not eat up all that this poor woman has got.'

The woman took her tray to the children at the back of the room. The three of them chewed their bread, silent, staring at the newcomers.

Milaqa said in her clearest Hatti, 'Your children are charming.'

Gassulawiya smiled, still nervous. 'Not all mine.' She tapped the older girl on the shoulder; she was no more than eight or nine. 'Orphaned. A comrade of Hunda's, fell on patrol. Bandits. His wife already dead of the plague.'

'Ah,' breathed Kurunta, turning his sightless head to the voices. 'There are always lots of soldiers' orphans in such times.'

'And this one,' Gassulawiya said, pulling forward the young-est child, a boy about five with his left arm behind his back, 'not charming at all. Show the lady. Show her!'

The boy, holding his bread in his right hand, produced his left arm. The flesh was covered in weals, the result of a beating.

'Stealing meat,' said his mother. 'If he was seven he'd have been put to death. Stupid, bad boy. Stupid!' She cuffed the back of his head. The boy slumped back into the shadows.

'That is how these Hatti are,' Qirum murmured. 'Laws! The

severest penalties! Duty, discipline and sacrifice! You have seen their arid country. The farmers must work hard to feed the soldiers, who must fight hard to hold their sprawling empire together. Discipline is the only way to drive people to such unrelenting effort, and when times are hard they fall back on such barbarity.'

Kilushepa said quietly, 'And if you don't discipline that tongue of yours, Trojan, it will be sent back to your home city separately from the rest of you.'

They lapsed into silence, the tension palpable. Hunda seemed to be gone a long time. And until he returned, Milaqa thought, the day remained in the balance – and all their fates, not least Kilushepa's.

When Hunda did return he brought with him, not a set of guards to haul Kilushepa away, but a prince.

That was how the newcomer looked to Milaqa, anyhow. He glanced around the room, his eyes evidently adjusting to the gloom. He wore a long white tunic, spotlessly clean; he was clean-shaven with his hair worn long and braided. Bronze amulets hung at his neck, in the shape of crescent moons, animals. His fingers were crusted with rings, his wrists with bracelets. Despite all that he looked like a soldier, for he had a deep scar gouged into one cheek. He might have been forty. Gassulawiya cowered back with her children, as if hoping not to be noticed.

When he saw Kilushepa, the Hatti crossed the room in a stride and knelt before her. 'Tawananna.'

Kilushepa did not move a muscle. If she was relieved at this treatment, at obeisance rather than arrest, she did not show it in her face, not by the slightest twitch. 'You know me,' she said.

'Not by sight. I heard descriptions – they did not do you justice.' His accent was subtly different from Kilushepa's, to Milaqa's ears. 'You have returned.'

'Evidently. And who are you?'

'I am the Chief of Bodyguards. My name is Muwa. I am an ally of your cousin Nuwanza—'

She snapped her fingers. 'Muwa. I know that name. Your Kaskan accent gives it away – and *I* remember *your* description – that ugly chasm of a scar. You went rogue! You set yourself up as a warlord among the Kaskans, during their rebellion – oh, five years ago.'

'No warlord,' he murmured with an easy smile. 'I acted in the interests of the empire in stabilising a difficult situation.'

'By defying the King's orders?'

'I am Kaskan. They were my people. I knew how to manage them. These are challenging times, and we must all cope as best we can, and move on. Whoever I am, wherever I came from, I responded to your summons. I remember your work before your fall. You were competent.'

'Thank you,' she said drily.

'The Storm God knows it's competence we need now, and unless we get it Hattusa itself will fall, I am sure of it.'

Now she smiled. 'You are right. That is precisely why the gods have brought me back. We must talk. But first, sit.' There was only the earth floor; he sat down, good humoured. 'And wine!' Kilushepa called. Gassulawiya hurried forward with cups of wine for them both.

Muwa told the Tawananna the state of the Hatti empire.

'It's the drought,' he said. 'This endless, god-withering drought. The cold summer is only adding to our misery. It extends far from here, you know – beyond Assyria, even, and to the north and east, the great plains of Asia. We're suffering from huge movements of people, and raiding on land and sea. Then there's the disruption of trade. The King can't reward his subjects, he can't send tribute to his allies abroad. Luckily for King Hattusili the Pharaoh seems to understand this, and he continues to send his grain shipments to Hattusa, but only a fraction of them get past the bandits. This is all court gossip, you understand. It's said that it's the same elsewhere – Assyria – Mycenae has burned, I hear, the once rich valleys around it abandoned.'

Qirum said drily, 'That's a terrible thing if you care about Greeks.'

'You should care,' Kilushepa admonished him. 'For all the great states depend on each other, for precious goods, for food-stuffs, for mutual help against enemies. And if one state fails and dissolves into banditry and starvation, another may follow, and the system itself may collapse.'

'But you believe you have a solution,' Muwa said. He looked at the Tawananna with something like simple hope on his battered face.

'We will discuss all that,' Kilushepa said. 'But first you must get me into the palace.'

'Hmm. Frankly, the challenge is to ensure you don't get struck down as soon as you set foot within the citadel walls, for you can be sure your enemies' spies will already have reported you are back.' He stood easily, lithe, strong. 'A day, madam. Give me a day to set it up. Then I will come for you.'

'Be warned, Chief of Bodyguards.' Teel had spoken. He laid his arm over the sacks of seed. 'Betray us, and the treasure we bring will be destroyed. And all of you will continue to starve.'

Muwa's eyes narrowed. 'Your threats are unnecessary. I am a man of honour.'

Teel nodded. 'Then I look forward to seeing you tomorrow.'

With a bow to Kilushepa, Muwa left.

Kilushepa glared at Teel, shaking her head. Then she sat back on her pallet and closed her eyes. Suddenly she looked exhausted to Milaqa, all her strength gone. Her monumental bluff was evidently draining even her deep resources.

And it occurred to Milaqa that since returning to Hattusa, amid all the machinations and politics, she had not tried to find out about her own son – not even if he were alive or dead.

Qirum stretched, yawned, and blew out through pursed lips. 'Well, that's the day's business done. What now? Shall we go and see what Hattusa has to offer? They're not all stuffy and rule-bound here.' He dug Teel in the ribs; the Crow recoiled. 'Oh, I forgot. No whorehouse is any use to you. Although I could always find you a job. There's a certain kind of man who likes them plump and ball-less.' He turned on Tibo. 'What about you, brother? An older woman might be right for you – nice fat thighs, you can bury yourself up to the hip. You can pretend it's your mother if you like. Or we could find you a boy, I suppose. You could take a little revenge.'

Tibo was shut in on himself. He started rocking on his haunches.

Deri glared. 'Leave my son alone. Just be on your way, Trojan.'

Qirum shrugged, stood and gathered up his cloak. 'Suit yourself.'

When he had gone, Kurunta turned and reached out with a stump of an arm towards Milaqa. He whispered, 'I brought you to the Spider. There's nothing more I can do for you. Please. I'd like to go home.'

37

Milaqa took Kurunta's arm, and led him out to the crowded street. He claimed to be able to find the way, and he blundered through the high-walled alleys, dragging Milaqa behind him.

It turned out not to be far to the man's home – or what had been his home, one of another row of cramped houses. But there was nobody here who recognised Kurunta, and one woman threatened to stone them if this 'criminal' did not go away, and criminal he must be or else he would not have suffered such a terrible punishment.

'It's all different,' Kurunta wailed.

Milaqa said, 'You've been away a long time. I've seen it myself. You had children, yes?'

'Yes, two youngsters and an older boy who was almost grown—'

'Perhaps your wife moved away. Perhaps she went to live with family.' What she wasn't saying out loud was, perhaps she found another man. 'We can ask. Find out where she has gone.'

'No, no—'

'Or is there somebody else you can go to? A brother or sister – your parents, even—'

'Take me to the archive.'

'The what?'

'Where I worked. Please. Take me there.'

The archive was not far, and Kurunta was able to find his way from his home quite efficiently.

Under a small surface building, the bulk of the archive was kept underground, in a kind of cellar entered by a series of steps.

The store itself was an expansive room lit by smoky oil lamps and divided into three parallel corridors by wooden shelves supported by stone pillars. On the shelves were clay tablets heaped in stacks, or leaning against each other like drunks in a Scambles tavern. The air was dry and smelled of the dusty clay, and the tang of burning oil.

Kurunta walked in confidently. He seemed to know his way around with precision. He made straight for a shelf, but his mutilated arms made it impossible for him to handle a tablet. Milaqa picked out a tablet at random, and let him trap it between his forearms. He held it up before his face. It was roughly square, small enough to hold in one hand, and covered with angular pocks and scrapes. Kurunta breathed in deeply. 'Ah! The scent of dry clay. *Now* I'm home.'

Milaqa glanced around. 'There must be thousands of tablets here – the place is huge.'

'But this little archive would be lost in the great palace chambers. Five vast libraries – tens of thousands of tablets – all of them devoted to recording the feats of our great kings. A wonderful place. Can you read this, child?'

She took the tablet from him. She recognised the writing style, the speech of the Hatti rendered in the symbols of the old civilisations of the east. 'I'm afraid not—'

'Father?'

Milaqa turned. A young man in a plain tunic was coming down the stair.

Kurunta twisted his head blindly. '*Attalli?* My son? Is that you? What are you doing here?'

The boy, no older than sixteen, looked bewildered. 'Well, I work here now . . . I thought you were dead. We all did.'

'Not dead, not at all. And where else would I be but with my beloved tablets? Oh, come to me, boy, come to your father.' He held out his mutilated arms, and turned his eyeless face to the boy.

For a heartbeat it seemed Attalli, horrified at the sight, could not move. Then he rushed forward and embraced his father.

Kurunta turned, seeking Milaqa. 'Do you still have that tablet? Read to me, boy. Oh, please, just a little. Just to prove the Spider was *wrong* . . .'

The boy took the tablet from Milaqa, and began to read, hesitantly. ' "This is to record my great victory, my promotion to chief archivist." '

'Ha! Somebody is a boaster.'

' "I achieved this with the support of the gods Ashur, Enlil, and Shamash, and the Goddess Ishtar. With their divine aid I smashed my enemies as did the Great King Tudhaliya . . ." '

38

Voro was astonished when the Annid of Annids herself came to the village.

In this little place called Sunflower, by the bow of the Brother River, it was already dark, the late summer evening closing in. The sky, as ever this year, was moonless, starless. But the big public hearth was piled high with burning peat blocks, lamplight shone from the open doors of the houses, and food smells wafted across the open space. The adults worked at the day's catch or cooked. Children ran, playing, burning off the last of their energy, dogs yapping at their heels. Voro himself was gutting an eel with a flint blade, one of many useful skills he had learned in his time here with Caxa.

And on the slopes of the foothills of the First Mother's Ribs, which loomed to the north, you could see people working at the figure on the hillside, the lights of their torches flickering, and children's laughter carried on the breeze.

Now the Annid of Annids walked into the hearthspace. Her party broke up, dropping their packs. Raka herself doffed her cloak to reveal her bronze breastplate, shining in the firelight. She walked over to Voro. 'Jackdaw.'

Voro wiped his hands on an apron smeared with blood and eel guts. 'Raka – Annid – I wasn't expecting you.'

She raised her eyebrows. 'Really? But you asked me to come. You even asked me to arrive when it was dark, and so I have. I trusted you, but I admit I was puzzled. And I'm even more puzzled to see a bit of happiness in this dismal year. The laughter of children has been a rare sound.'

'It's best you see it all at once.'

'See what? Never mind. Something to do with Caxa, I presume? I was comforted to know she was found. Though Xivu would have been much happier to have her back in Etxelur, and safely in his care.'

'She's safer here,' Novo said defensively.

'I know, I know.'

She looked so like her uncle Bren, he thought, and she seemed to have grown much older in the months since she had taken on her heavy responsibilities. But she had nothing of the man's arrogance, his contempt for those around him, his mockery. And she had shown mercy to Caxa, responding to the girl's human plight, regardless of the demands of states and gods. It was a strange trick of the gods to have delivered such a great Annid of Annids into the role through Bren's machinations. He smiled at her. 'It will all wait until morning, Annid. And in the meantime, you're a guest here. Have some eel.'

She laughed. 'You're kind. Yes, I'm sure we'll have a good night.' And she walked away, back to her party, loosing the ties of her armour plate.

In the morning the children, too excited to sleep, got started early, and their laughter as they ran around the hearthspace woke everybody else.

Voro emerged from Hadhe's house, where his cousin had been putting him up since he had arrived here with Caxa. He wore his cloak, for frost lay thick on the ground. Raka, the Annid, stood with her party in the middle of the hearthspace, all wrapped in cloaks. And they were looking up at the hillside, where the dawn light illuminated the heather-covered slope, and the figure cut into the hill was already visible.

Voro padded over to the Annid. 'What do you think?'

She turned to him, her eyes wide with wonder in the gathering light.

For days the people had been trampling the heather on the hill, under Caxa's direction, until they had turned the slope into

238

a tremendous panel of writing. Now, on the hillside, the carefully laid out pattern of concentric circles, swirls and loops was vivid in the daylight, the brown of the cleared ground a sharp contrast with the fading purple of the heather. And its message was clear.

'"My Sun,"' breathed Raka. '"My Sun." That's what the Hatti kings call themselves.'

'It was all Caxa's idea. She created a design up there, a hideous god, that scared the people to death. When they took her in she got rid of it, and came up with the idea of creating something much bigger – an appeal for the sun to return, big enough to be seen by the gods. She got the young folk to work on it with her, help her work out how it would be laid out on the hill. And, you can see, she recruited them to make it with her.

'Once they knew what they wanted to say, it only took them a few days to make the sign. The villagers here say they will maintain it for ever as a sign of thanks, once the sun comes back. This is what Caxa does, Annid. Works of art on a huge scale. It's in her blood. Something new in our world.'

'Good work, Jackdaw. Good work indeed. You make sure she doesn't worry about Xivu. Leave him to me; as soon as the spring comes we'll ship him off home – and let the next generation deal with the Jaguar folk.'

The young folk were still up on the hillside. Their younger siblings went running up to meet them, while the adults returned to their houses to begin the day's chores.

39

When they did it for the third time that night, Kilushepa rode Qirum. It was just as well she did, for he had no energy left after the hasty passion of their first two couplings. And now this, the third time, her lithe body writhing over him like a whip, her skin shining from the unguents her ladies had applied – he had thought he had nothing left to give, and yet he felt the familiar pressure gathering in his loins. And at the peak of it she withdrew, and swivelled over him, and took him in her mouth.

When he was done, he flopped back, panting, sweating.

She sat easily on the bed, cross-legged. The serving girl, herself naked, who had stood by the door through the whole performance, came forward with scented cloths for Kilushepa to wipe her mouth and crotch. She had a glass of wine too for Qirum, the good stuff from the King's own cellars, for that was what the girl had found the Trojan liked after he had performed, that and maybe a quick tit-grab.

'You exhaust me,' he said to Kilushepa now. 'You draw me up like water from a well. You mine me—'

She held up her hand. 'You have many gifts, Trojan, but poetry isn't one of them.'

'Well, and you are a gift of the gods, to me . . . Who is your own god, Kilushepa? The Storm God, who rules the heavens?'

She smiled. 'I pray to his spouse, the Sun Goddess of Arinna. The protector of the state, of kings and queens.'

'You are my Ishtar, I think. Goddess of sex and war. What a combination! That's you, Kilushepa. Fire through and through. And yet . . .' He touched her thighs. There were scars there, inflicted by some soldier's raking nails, that ran up into her pubic hair. 'Given what you have been through – how you were used, and then you gave birth, by the gods' mercy – it's a miracle your body works so well.'

She grunted. '"Works so well." Like a well-oiled chariot wheel, perhaps? *That's* a soldier's poetry. But it's no miracle, Qirum. Remember, I kept a king for many years against the competition of the junior wives, some of the most beautiful, and generally younger, women in Hattusa, who all eyed my position. I learned to use my body and to maintain it. There are arts the ladies have here, ideas and techniques brought in from the Egyptians and from the people beyond the Indus. Even in my captivity I was able to use some of this to mitigate the worst of the damage that was being done to my body. But you were used too, as a child.'

It was as if a shadow passed over him. He glanced at the serving girl, oddly embarrassed; he didn't want even this trivial girl to know of his past. 'I don't think about that.'

'But you must think of it. As I think of my own trials. How can you not? I sometimes imagine the anger that must rage in you. Like a fire mountain. An anger that longs for expression.'

'It is gone, it is done, look at me now!'

'Yet you bear the scars, inside and out. As I do. I know I will never be as I was.' She grinned, slyly. 'You should have known me at sixteen, seventeen, eighteen—'

'I'd have been left an empty bag, like my ball sack feels now.' He massaged his cock, which ached pleasantly. 'Do you remember the first time? After I saved you from the booty people – we were in that ruined house in Troy—'

'I'll not forget it.'

'This is something of a contrast, isn't it? It's good to see you in your natural home. Like a bird back in its silver cage.'

'Oh, this is nothing. We're in the palace precinct, the King could hardly keep me out given the support Nuwanza has mobilised for me – and given that my son still lives, and embodies

241

a strand of inheritance. But all this is far from the true luxury that the Hatti court is capable of.'

He surprised himself by taking her hand. He knew that his privileged cock was doing the thinking for him, but he found he felt surprisingly tender towards her. 'We have been cold to one another. We have let events drive us apart. Other people.'

'Yes.' Her delicate fingers squeezed his palm, rough with the calluses of sword fighting. 'And, let's be honest, we both enjoy the sparring, for that's the sort we are. But there has always been something between us, Trojan. Something more than self-interest. As to the future, I intend to *win*.' She said this firmly, flatly. 'But regarding my position in the new court – well, there are many possibilities. It may be I will be able to resume my position as Tawananna, with Hattusili still on the throne.'

He grunted. 'The existing Tawananna may have something to say about that.'

She waved a hand, dismissive. 'The King's mother-in-law is a greedy crone. She will be no obstacle. The King himself is more of a challenge. A cunning man, and a circumspect one, or he wouldn't have survived the complicated family politics of our court to get to where he is now, and he wouldn't have lasted once he got there. But still, he can be removed, or controlled.' She eyed him. 'I may have to marry him.'

He laughed. 'But you're his aunt!'

'*That's* no obstacle, not here. We are all one vast family, centuries old; every marriage you make is to a cousin of some kind, unless you're farmed out to a pharaoh or an Assyrian king. My ultimate goal is the next generation – to get my own son installed as *tukhanti*, the crown prince, heir to the throne. There are always plenty of princes and princesses running around the city, and out in the country there are whole mobs of disinherited descendants. I told you we are a very old family. One must fight for one's position.

'What I'm telling you is that I must either be a royal widow, or a royal wife. I cannot be with *you*. Not openly. You can't be my husband. Yet I want you at my side. My partner. My ally.' She

242

took his hand again. 'For you will help me make all this come to pass.'

Absurdly, he felt his eyes prickle. 'Of course. Anything.' His life had been turned on its head since he had met her. He had never known such heights of passion, or such depths of rage, when she had casually insulted him before others. For all his ambition and his dreams, he knew he could never have risen to *this* without her. In his heart there had always been a grain of doubt, the derisive voice of Praxo at the back of his head, perhaps, reminding him that she was driven by self-interest, that she was using him. But seeing her now, his vision of her face softened by his tears, that last grain of doubt washed away, and he saw nothing but glory for himself in the future: a king in all but name, here in the capital of the Hatti, the power and wealth of an empire his to command, and a queen to warm his bed – and, perhaps, his heart too.

She pressed gently, 'You will do anything that is needed, to make this come about?'

'Anything,' he said gruffly.

She touched his cheek. 'Now go. Get cleaned up. I would dine; the gods know I need to keep up my strength.'

He rolled off the bed, landed on his feet with a jump, and took a robe from the serving girl. 'Good idea. Though you've so used up my cock I probably won't be able to piss straight!'

When Qirum had gone, Muwa Chief of Bodyguards emerged from his hiding place, behind billows of soft fabric in a corner of the room.

Kilushepa was fixing her hair, using a mirror of polished bronze the girl was holding. She turned. 'You heard it all.'

'Yes.' He glanced over his shoulder; the spy-hole in the wall was well concealed.

'What a coarse man he is. All that bragging. He turns my stomach. Well, I led him to confess his intentions. It wasn't hard. I, of course, am entirely loyal, while wishing to offer my service in this year of famine. *He* would murder the King, if that's what it would take to further his own ambition.'

'It was clear from what he said.'

'And his rage – his desire for revenge against the world, for the abuse that was inflicted on him as a child – that was there for all to see. He is like a bull, loose in the palace. Who knows what the man is capable of?'

'I have a feeling we are soon going to find out, Tawananna.'

'Oh, do hold the mirror properly, you idiot child . . .'

His business done, Muwa withdrew from the chamber.

40

Hunda led Teel, Milaqa and Riban through the city to the Mound of Lelwani, Goddess of the underworld. This was the huge structure of sloped walls and steps which Milaqa had spotted from outside the city itself, a great flat-topped heap of stone over which the city wall strode. Hunda said it was a 'pyramid', and was the envy of every Egyptian who came to Hattusa, a boast that only made the Northlanders shrug and roll their eyes.

But it was beneath the Mound that the lair of the Hatti iron-makers was to be found.

Hunda was extremely wary, for, he said, the mystery of the Hatti's hardened iron was kept secret from the ordinary population, and even from most of the court. 'Some say only the King himself is supposed to know about it. On his accession each successor to the throne is led to this place by his Chief of Bodyguards to meet the Master of the Iron, and to be shown his secrets. I've never been this way myself before. I wouldn't want to now, but Chief Muwa ordered me, as he was ordered by the Tawananna herself.'

'You needn't worry, man,' Teel said. 'We know how precious this secret is. After all, if not, we wouldn't have come so far for it, would we? Or paid so high a price.'

Hunda glanced at him as he hurried them down yet another alley. 'I am putting my life in the hands of you people. And my family's, I suppose. But if it must be done, let's get it over.'

He brought them to the base of the pyramid. A flight of steps led up to a raised platform – dozens of steps, perhaps a hundred, Milaqa thought – and on the platform itself a tremendous gate had been cut through the towering city wall. There was nobody around save a few supplicants to Lelwani, scattered on the steps, kneeling, nodding and praying.

Hunda grunted. 'You're supposed to climb the steps on your knees, and then climb down again the same way. This is to have Lelwani intervene on behalf of the spirits of your loved ones, down in the underworld. And there's a tithe to be paid to the priests at the top. A few years of that and you end up praying to other gods for relief of the pain of your wrecked knees. But we're not going up there today. Come on – this way.'

Keeping an eye on the pilgrims so they didn't spy where they went, Hunda led the Northlanders around the side of the mound to where it butted against the city wall. This neglected corner was shabby and filled with litter, a few rags, smashed clay tablets, the bones of some small animal roasted and consumed. Checking again to be sure nobody saw, Hunda kicked this debris out of the way, bent down, and pressed a stone near the base of the mound wall. A section of the wall slid back, revealing a doorway. 'There's a counterweight, ropes and stone blocks, a clever little mechanism—' The receding stone stopped halfway. 'Jammed,' growled Hunda. 'Like all things clever, it trips up all the time. Help me.' Teel stood back while Milaqa, Riban and Hunda got their shoulders against the polished surface of the stone slab. It gave with a jerk, scraping back and out of sight, revealing a darkened passageway. Hunda reached inside, fumbled in the dark for a shelf, and pulled out a clay lantern. He had a fire-making kit in a pouch on his soldier's belt, a bit of flint and pyrite, and he soon sparked a flame.

'Follow me into the underworld, then. And just remember – I've never been down here before either, and I'm even more afraid than you are. After all, Lelwani is my goddess . . .' He led the way through, then hauled on a rope.

The doorway slabs slid back into position, and the last bit of daylight was shut out.

*

Hunda's lantern revealed a stone-walled passageway, dank and cold. 'Muwa didn't give me directions past this point. Only one way to go, it seems.' He led the way along the dimly lit passage.

Milaqa didn't feel all that nervous; she had grown up exploring the Wall, which had its own tunnels and passageways and buried chambers. But she glanced up at the heavy stone slabs that spanned the roof, and hoped the Hatti engineers were as competent as Northland's Beavers.

They had only walked a couple of dozen paces before the way was blocked by a curtain of thick, stitched leather. Hunda dragged this aside, revealing an eerie red glow, and hot, dry air rolled out over the Northlanders. Hunda beckoned them forward once more.

And so Milaqa entered the lair of Hattusa's Master of the Iron.

It was a wide box of a chamber, with stone for its walls and roof, and with massive pillars of granite blocks regularly spaced. Evidently this was a workshop. The heart of it was a great pit within which a fire burned. The fuel was not wood, but lumps of what looked like some kind of glowing rock. Frames of wood and metal were suspended over the pit. Around the room were scattered benches and slabs of stone with tongs, hammers and pincers. There were mounds of rock in one corner, rust-red, and peculiar heaps of what looked like metal, but misshapen and almost frothy, pocked by frozen bubbles. Milaqa was reminded of the lumps of floating rock Deri had brought back as curiosities from Kirike's Land.

One corner of the chamber was domestic. There was a kitchen with joints of meat hanging from hooks, heaps of clothing, jugs for drinking water or wine or piss, and a couple of pallets. And on one of the pallets a man was stretched out on his back, snoring with a deep rumble. He had a tremendous belly that strained the scorched tunic he wore, and massively strong arms, like a farmer's, Milaqa thought, but his bare, hairy skin was pocked by scars and little black craters.

A boy came forward from the shadows, skinny, pale, with thick, unruly black hair. He wore a stiff body-length leather apron, and he was wiping his hands on a rag. 'Muwa told me you were coming,' he said.

His voice was oddly cracked, Milaqa thought, and his manner was ungainly, shy, but he looked too old for the way he was behaving – he was eighteen, nineteen maybe. Perhaps he just wasn't used to company. Like the sleeping man his arms were pocked with scars and burn marks. There seemed to be a little crater burned into the point of his chin, but when Milaqa looked more closely she saw it was a mole, not a burn mark at all.

As Milaqa studied him, the boy blushed and dropped his gaze. She struggled not to laugh at him. He was worse than Voro.

Hunda said, 'You aren't Partahulla?'

'No. That's him.' He gestured at the sleeping heap on the pallet. 'That's the Master of the Iron. I'm his apprentice. My name's Zidanza. Should I wake him?'

Hunda regarded the Master of the Iron. He was sleeping soundly, an empty wine flask his side. 'He's drunk.'

'And old. Very old,' said Zidanza. 'Older than you'd think. Spends most of his time asleep. And the rest kicking my backside.'

'Then you must do most of the work around here,' said Teel.

'Well, yes. But he is the Master, not me.' Zidanza studied them doubtfully. Milaqa supposed the Northlanders must look very strange to him, as he looked strange to her, a pale creature like a worm, a creature of the underground, toiling in this gloom. He laughed, a kind of giggle. 'You can imagine we don't get many visitors down here.'

'And I imagine you're good at keeping secrets, Zidanza,' Teel said.

'Well, I have to be. Not that I'm let out much.'

'What about your family?' Milaqa asked.

'They think I'm serving with the army. Off fighting Hurrians or Kaskans. Sometimes I think I rather would be. Look, I'm not sure what you want. Muwa just said you would come.'

Milaqa dug the iron arrowhead out of her tunic and held it out on its thong. 'I'm here because of this.'

He took the arrow in his hand, turned it over. He wouldn't look her in the eye, but he let his gaze stray from the bit of iron so he got peeks of her chest. 'Ah, yes.'

'What do you mean, *ah, yes*? This thing killed my mother.'

He looked directly at her, startled. 'Well, it would. This is our iron – though we meant the arrowhead to be ornamental, not functional. That's what our iron is for, you know. Ornaments. The old man,' he nodded at the dozing Master, 'says his grandfather made gifts for the King to give to the Pharaoh Tutankhamun. Two armlets and a dagger. Or it may have been his grandfather's grandfather. That's what we make here, luxury stuff, mostly for the King to give as gifts. But of course they're functional too. The Pharaoh's dagger could have killed a man. And this arrowhead, if shot properly, would penetrate bronze armour.'

'It did,' Milaqa snapped, and she pulled the arrowhead back.

'That's the secret, you see,' the boy said. 'Our iron isn't brittle, like the common stuff you'll find bandied about in the market. Ours is hard and resilient. It's all to do with the way we make it. That's why Hatti gifts of iron are so precious – because nobody else in the world knows how to make iron the way we do here. The secrets are all in the head of the Master of the Iron, one man in each generation, who answers only to the King.'

Teel asked, 'And will you be the next Master?'

The boy looked shocked to be asked. 'Me? No. Of course not. I'm not nearly high-born enough. No, my job is to assist the current Master, and to help train his replacement, when he is selected.'

Riban walked around the workshop, curious, peering into the pit. 'How do you make your iron, apprentice?'

Zidanza looked doubtfully at Hunda. 'We don't talk about this. Let alone to foreigners. No offence. Maybe I should wake the Master—'

The sergeant shook his head. 'These aren't normal times, Zidanza. Answer their questions.'

Zidanza grinned. And, with an audience for perhaps the first time in his life, he opened up.

He took them around the secret stages of the processing. In the pit of fire, twice-burned coal was consumed to give a high temperature, much higher than you needed for the smelting of mere bronze – which, by comparison, Zidanza made sound like a game for children. This twice-burned coal was what Milaqa had taken for rocks on the fire. Iron ore subject to such heat resulted in the porous, floating-rock-like product he called a bloom. But this was not yet the finished product. You had to heat it again, and beat it, and quench it with water to cool it – but not too rapidly or you would crack it – and then heat and beat and cool it again, over and over. This got rid of 'slag' that you removed from the melt, until you were left with ingots of iron – he showed them samples, small finger-sized bars – that you could work up into finished objects like Milaqa's arrowhead.

Teel smiled at Milaqa. 'Following all this?'

'Very little. But I see how complex it is. I wonder who first worked all this out.'

'Who knows? Probably not one person. A whole chain of people, trying this and then that, over generations perhaps, trying to make this hard, *useful* iron, out of humble rock.'

Hunda joined Milaqa and Teel. 'So what do you think? What do you need to take away, if you're to have a gift of Hatti iron-making?'

'Nothing,' Teel said, 'save the wisdom in the head of the Master. Everything else we can build in Northland.'

Hunda looked doubtful. 'I can't imagine the King allowing you to steal away his Master of the Iron.'

Partahulla stirred and snorted, choked briefly, then chewed a lump of phlegm in his sleep. Zidanza, eagerly showing a lump of bloom to Riban, didn't notice.

Milaqa said to Teel, 'But it's not the Master who's doing all the work down here. Not him, but his apprentice. Perhaps *his* is the head we need.'

Teel frowned. He seemed startled by the idea. 'Well, let's test him.' He walked over to Zidanza and Riban. 'Apprentice. I'll share one of our secrets with you now. We don't want iron-making so we can make gifts for kings. We want it so we can fight wars. Not just one arrowhead, not just one dagger – we want to equip an army, as now they are equipped with bronze.'

Zidanza looked astounded. 'A whole *army*. Why, the first army with decent iron weapons would be unbeatable.'

'We know,' Teel said. 'That's why we want to be the first. But don't worry, we are allies of the Hatti kings. If, in theory, I asked you to turn out, not one arrowhead, but hundreds – thousands – and daggers, swords, even armour – could you do it?'

He looked around the workshop, thought about it, and scratched his head. 'I'm going to need a bigger pit.'

Teel grinned at Milaqa. 'Good answer. I think you're right, niece. Now all we need is for Kilushepa to persuade the King to let him go . . .'

41

Two days later the Northlanders were summoned to a session before the *panku*, the King's council.

Muwa came to collect them from Hunda's house. Hunda himself was here waiting. Nobody knew where Tibo was, he had left before dawn, and a faintly concerned Deri was out searching for him. But Noli, Teel, Milaqa, Riban were all ready. Teel and Riban carried the precious sacks of seed stock. They had all put on their smartest, cleanest clothes. Teel and Noli wore their Annids' cloaks, and Riban the priest had looped around his neck a very ancient ceremonial axe of Etxelur flint, finely shaped and polished until it shone.

They set out through the city, flanked by Hunda and Muwa with an escort of palace guards, and climbed the sloping streets. Heading north, they passed out of the temple district and came to a rocky outcrop, itself crowded with grand buildings and mausoleums, from where they had a good view of the 'lower city', separated from the rest by its own walls and split up into precincts by more walls within – and the citadel itself, behind even stouter walls, which contained the apartments of the King. To their left, the west, Milaqa could see an astounding temple, dedicated to the Storm God, a box of stone set on a mighty plinth surrounded by lesser buildings, workshops, breweries, bakehouses, residential houses – a temple so huge it was like a city within a city, complete unto itself.

From the outcrop on which they stood a pair of spectacular stone bridges led directly to the King's own house. But Qirum's party was not to be so honoured as to go this way today. They had to make their way down from the outcrop, and through a gateway in the western side of the citadel wall.

At this gate Qirum waited in his polished armour. 'So today's the day. A day on which all history will hinge . . . Iron for the Northland! I have the scent of victory in my nostrils – my blood is on fire, as before a battle.'

'Maybe,' Muwa said drily. 'But you're not invited in, Trojan. The Tawananna specifically said you were to wait outside the citadel.'

Qirum looked baffled, then grew quickly angry, as was his way. 'But Kilushepa told me—'

'Just wait, Trojan. Get something to eat. Do a bit of whoring. You'll learn the outcome soon enough.'

Qirum was smouldering. But to Milaqa's relief he didn't try to force his way past Muwa; he just stalked away.

When he had gone Muwa produced a clay tablet from a pouch at his belt, which he gave to Hunda. 'A message from Kilushepa. She says you are to go to this address. You'll understand what to do when you get there.'

Hunda looked as confused as Qirum had, but he obeyed, and slipped away.

Muwa beckoned. 'The rest of you, follow me.'

And he led them into the citadel of the Hatti king.

Within the citadel's walls they passed through wide courts lined with columns, each with its own guarded gateways. The citadel was a jumble of distinct buildings, and yet there was a cohesion to the design, Milaqa thought, all these grand structures serving a single purpose, unified by courtyards and colonnades. It was not like the rest of the city here. The courtyards were swept clean, the buildings well maintained, there was no crush, there were no hungry children with their palms out – indeed nobody they saw, finely dressed and evidently busy, looked hungry at all.

They were brought to a house of stone and mud brick that looked imposing to Milaqa, but she could see it was dwarfed by the grander buildings on the very top of this hill, the highest ground of all, where the King in his apartments could view his capital city at his leisure. Inside this house was a single vast room, the walls adorned with tapestries and filmy curtains. Soldiers, bodyguards, lined the walls of the room, their faces blank, their weapons visible.

And Kilushepa was already here, waiting patiently. In full Hattusa finery at last, she looked impossibly glamorous to Milaqa, with her hair piled high and her figure draped in a robe of soft, brightly coloured fabric; her eyes were lined by kohl, her lips stained a deep plum-red. Milaqa thought it was astonishing how far she had risen since her lowest moment, when Qirum had rescued her from a column of booty people, a whore of her own soldiers. And if she still felt begrimed inside, and Milaqa understood the deep Hatti taboo about cleanliness, she showed no sign of it.

Muwa guided the Northlanders in, and settled them on benches on one side of the room. It was only when the North-landers had taken their places, and after serving children had come among them with plates of delicate foodstuffs and cups of wine, that the members of the *panku* arrived. Of course, Milaqa thought, they would not be kept waiting by mere foreigners. There were a dozen of them, nine men and three women. They all wore clothes at least as gorgeous as Kilushepa's; all wore their hair elaborately plaited or braided, and the men were clean-shaven. They were all so heavily coated with creams and other cosmetics that Milaqa could not tell how old any of them were. And, unlike Kilushepa, they were all festooned with jewellery, pendants around their necks, rings on their fingers, bangles on their wrists and ankles, gorgeous wares from Crete and Egypt, and they tinkled and clattered as they moved.

None of them deigned to so much as glance at the North-landers. They took their places on benches opposite, and pecked at the foodstuffs brought before them, chatting in low tones to each other.

Muwa hastily told them about Hatti politics. 'The *panku* is a

254

council called for specific purposes – to consider the rights and wrongs of a particular issue, and to advise the King. You see, it doesn't have a formal constitution. And it doesn't have a fixed membership. Anybody can serve – the palace servants, the bodyguards, the Men of the Golden Spear, the Captains of the Thousand – even cooks, heralds, stable-boys. Anybody who has the King's ear at a particular time, or who just happens to be around when the *panku* is called.'

'It sounds a mess,' said Teel. 'Our Annids are much more proper about deliberations and decision-making.'

'Well, this is our way,' Kilushepa said. 'This is a rather ancient institution, fallen by the wayside in recent times, but revived by the current King who likes its flexibility in these times of change and stress. You shouldn't underestimate its power. There have been times when the *panku* has even challenged the King, over the conduct of a war for example. So don't think that if it goes badly for us at the *panku* we can appeal to the King. This is where we need to make your case well, and win it.' She glanced at the members of the *panku*. 'I can see, however, that the crone who calls herself the current Tawananna has not dared to show her face. The most important people here are the two men in the centre. The one on the right is Nuwanza. My second cousin, and the man who has supported me so far in my quest for rehabilitation. The other is called Tushratta. He is a closer relative of the king – ours is a complicated family – and one of his senior advisers. The rest are not important, nobodies come to show their pretty faces, and have a bit of fun, and maybe to make a name for themselves. I, by the way, will do the talking.'

Noli nodded silent agreement.

But Teel was tense. 'If we leave without the secrets of the iron—'

Kilushepa held up a silencing finger. 'You will get what you want – and I will get what *I* want – although things might not work out quite the way you expect.'

Now Nuwanza, Kilushepa's cousin, rose to his feet. The hubbub of conversation among the *panku* members died away.

*

Nuwanza smiled at Kilushepa, and extended outstretched arms to the Northlanders. He was a portly man of about forty, and he struck Milaqa as sane, competent. 'All children of the little mothers of sea, sky and earth are always welcome here in our magnificent capital, which bathes in the light of My Sun, our King. And we are aware that you have journeyed far and have braved many perils to bring us your gifts. Please, cousin – proceed.'

So Kilushepa began. Sitting calmly, her voice carrying through the large room, she outlined again the journey they had undertaken – and the promise of potatoes and maize.

She showed a sample seed potato from the sacks. 'It will grow where no other useful crop survives, in the uplands, in poor soil, anywhere, given water. A given field will produce more raw food in the form of potatoes than any other crop. Potatoes can even be grown *between* grain crops, thus multiplying the value of a piece of cultivated land. As a root, the crop is difficult to steal, for it remains underground until it is dug up, and few raiding armies will pause to do that . . .'

Milaqa marvelled as she spoke on, making a humble root crop seem almost glamorous. But so it was, she supposed, if your concern was the destiny of an empire, and how it was to be fed.

'Finally – one can survive on *nothing but* this root, and cow's milk . . . I am sure you can see how this will transform the potential of our farmland, and all our fortunes.' Kilushepa handed the root to Nuwanza.

'Such a humble thing,' Nuwanza said, turning the potato over in his hands. 'Yet each mouthful of food I put into my mouth is a humble thing.' He glanced at the few sacks. 'You cannot feed a city of fifty thousand on a handful of these roots, no matter how vigorously they grow, queen.'

'No. It will take years – crop after crop must be planted, and protected, and harvested, and the seed dug in again. Nuwanza, what we must do, you and I and our allies in the palace, is to work for stability – frankly, to hold the empire together for the three or four or five years it will take for these new crops to start producing on a massive scale. With these crops, these gifts from the gods, as soon as the sky clears, the famine will be banished and a new generation will grow up fat and healthy. And then new Hatti armies will march out to subdue the rebellious dependencies, and once more impose the will of My Sun the King on surrounding nations.

'But without this gift – and let us speak honestly, councillors, for if we do not acknowledge the magnitude of our debt we cannot begin to repay it – without it our empire might crumble. *Hattusa itself might fall.* Just as, indeed, we might already have fallen if not for the gift of the Northlanders' mash, which filled the bellies of our troops when we had nothing else to give them.'

Tushratta leaned forward grandly. He was a thin, older, more sinister-looking man than Nuwanza, Milaqa thought. 'I do not deny the magnitude of your achievement in bringing us this treasure, fair Kilushepa. And this from a position of desolation, of false banishment.'

Milaqa saw Kilushepa sit straighter at his use of that word 'false', an indication of how far her rehabilitation had already come.

'But,' went on Tushratta, 'you ask too much in return. We cannot give up our Master of the Iron! For centuries our gifts of iron have awed the other Great Kings, of Egypt and Assyria . . . How can you expect us to sacrifice that?'

Then followed a long and complicated sequence of negotiations, which Milaqa found hard to follow. Kilushepa argued that the Northlanders lived far away, and would pledge not to divulge the secret of iron-making to any of the Hatti's local rivals. And they wanted the iron only for tools and weapons, not for gifts; they would not try to compete with the Hatti kings on that level. Noli confirmed this, speaking quietly. The Hatti seemed to think war-making was a rather vulgar and wasteful use of such a precious substance. 'Like stopping up your enemy's mouth with gold,' said Tushratta.

But the Master of the Iron had been in his post since the King himself was a small boy. How could such a venerable gentleman be taken away? Perhaps the Northlanders would be willing to leave an apprentice or two to learn the craft at the feet of the Master himself, and then take the secrets of the process home. But that could take years; the Northlanders insisted they needed the iron now.

The argument seemed to be stuck in stalemate.

Then Kilushepa rather grandly stood – the first time she had been on her feet in the whole session, Milaqa noted. 'I have the solution,' she announced. 'It has just struck me – of course – you are right, good Tushratta, it is unreasonable to expect the King to give up his Master of the Iron. But the Master has an apprentice, and he seems an able lad, from what I've heard. I doubt if the King even knows he exists. And if *he* were to leave, no harm would be done to the iron-making tradition here, for the Master would soon find another assistant to train up.' She turned to the Northlanders. 'Annid Noli – would you consider this?'

Teel grinned, and murmured to Milaqa. 'Now we see Kilushepa's tactics. We told her about the apprentice we wanted. Did you imagine the queen would ask for him from the beginning? No, for it would never have been granted. But by arguing so hard for the Master, Kilushepa makes the loss of the apprentice seem a trivial price to pay.'

Advised by Teel, Noli agreed to the deal.

But Milaqa was shocked when the *panku*, led by Tushratta, again refused, with bland smiles and apologies. Even the apprentice was too precious to be given up.

Suddenly Teel's smugness was gone; he was furious. He growled in their own tongue, 'I'm starting to think these slimy creatures never meant to give us anything at all. This isn't negotiation, not bargaining – this is robbery!'

But Kilushepa, as calm as ever, continued to press her case. She at least did not seem downcast.

Then a runner summoned Muwa. He went to the chamber

door. When he returned, he looked grave. 'Members of the council – honoured guests – I am afraid your discussion is moot. For Zidanza the apprentice won't be going anywhere.' He stood aside.

Hunda walked in, heavily bloodstained. He bore a body, limp – a tall man, but lightly built, and dressed in a scarred leather apron. He put the body on the floor. The stink of blood was shocking in these fragrant surroundings.

Kilushepa shrieked. Coming from such a calm woman, the sudden noise was doubly shocking. 'Zidanza! Dead!' She rushed to the body, and pulled back his apron. The hilt of a dagger protruded from the lower belly, which was a torn, bloody mass. Kilushepa grabbed the knife and hauled it out of the body, and the courtiers gasped and turned away.

And while everybody else was distracted by Kilushepa's performance, Milaqa stared at the body. At the young man's face. At his chin.

Hunda said, 'The body was found not far from the citadel walls. He had been raped, I am sorry to say. There is bruising around his mouth, his thighs. Abused, raped, then killed.'

Kilushepa held the knife resting on her palms, and showed it to Muwa, Noli, Teel, Milaqa. 'Look at this! Do you know whose this is? Do you?'

'It is the Trojan's,' Teel said. 'There is no doubt.'

Hunda nodded, as if reluctant to admit it. 'But none saw Qirum do this.'

Kilushepa pointed dramatically at Muwa. 'But you heard him, Chief of Bodyguards. You were there in my apartment when I goaded him to make his threats. He said he would do anything he could to advance his own ambitions against the King. How better than to slaughter this apprentice, and then his Master of the Iron – for surely he will be the next victim? And the sexual frenzy that has been visited on the boy – is this not some kind of twisted revenge for Qirum's past, when in the ruins of Troy he was forced to prostitute his own young body to survive?'

Muwa looked grim. 'I'm afraid you are right, madam.' He

259

turned to his men. 'Send the orders. Find this Trojan. Kill him if you have to. Make sure he gets nowhere near the Master of the Iron.'

The meeting of the *panku* began to break up. The council members flooded out into the street, looking back with horror at the corpse, or with disdain, Milaqa thought, as if the boy were somehow ill-mannered to be bloody and dead in such surroundings.

Over the hubbub, Nuwanza called across to the Northlanders, 'I am afraid the Chief of Bodyguards was right. Our discussion has no further purpose; clearly we cannot give you what you want. Let us meet again tomorrow and consider some other recompense. You will leave Hattusa laden with treasures for the service you have performed for the King, believe me.' He spread his hands. 'But not the iron you sought.'

Kilushepa nodded, and Teel bowed gracefully, and thanked him.

Milaqa plucked Teel's sleeve, and whispered urgently in her own tongue, 'That's not Zidanza.'

'Hush,' he said mildly.

'But it isn't! Zidanza has a mole on his chin. I noticed it; it looked like a burn, but wasn't. *This man, whoever he is, has no mole.*'

'Well, he wouldn't, would he?'

'What?'

'He's not the apprentice.'

She was utterly confused. 'Then who is he?'

'That doesn't matter, does it? I see it now. The real Zidanza is in hiding. Soon we will smuggle him out of the city, and we will bring him back to Northland.

'What a strategist the woman is! Kilushepa knew the *panku* would not give up the Master, or even his apprentice. But she wanted to fulfil the agreement she made with us; she sees the value of our friendship in the long term, where these fools cannot. So she arranged for this – subterfuge. We get the apprentice. *They* believe he's dead, and will not miss him. In the meantime they have their Master, who will soon train another junior, once they stir him from his bed. And all the time the councillors think that Kilushepa has won them the secret of our foods for nothing! What a victory she has won.'

'This is insane,' Milaqa said. 'And what of Qirum? Did he kill this stranger?'

'Oh, of course not. Why would he?'

'Then who did?'

'That doesn't matter either, does it?'

'But why would Kilushepa falsely accuse Qirum? He saved her life – he was her lover.'

'She's said it herself. He was a stepping stone. Useful to her once, but he had become an irritant. Evidently she used this opportunity to resolve that problem too.'

Anger burned; all she could think of was Qirum. 'Is that how you see people too, uncle? As problems to be solved?'

'This is how the world works, Milaqa. And if you want to be a Crow you need to learn to think more like Kilushepa. What a woman!'

She turned on her heel, leaving him behind.

At the door the sergeant was still waiting, his tunic stained by the blood of the stranger.

'Please – Hunda . . .'

'Yes?'

'Get me out of here. Out of the citadel. Now.'

He hesitated for one heartbeat. Then he led her out into streets bubbling with agitation and rumour after the exit of the *panku* members. People flinched back from the bloodstained soldier. Hunda led Milaqa towards the gate of the citadel, but when she got the chance she turned a corner faster than he did, and disappeared from his sight. She felt tremendously guilty; Hunda was a good man, and today he was obviously bewildered by the events he was suddenly caught up in, and here she was using him unscrupulously. But she had to get to the gate before the palace bodyguards.

When she arrived at the gate Qirum was still standing there, where she had last seen him. For once, it seemed, his own sense of self-preservation had deserted him. And, she noticed, there was no blood on him, no sign of a desperate struggle with an iron-maker. He asked, 'How did it go? Did my Kilushepa—'

'Your Kilushepa betrayed you. Run, Qirum.'

His face clouded. 'She would not.'

'She claims you killed a man. An iron-maker.'

'She would not – I did not!'

'Where is your dagger?'

He checked his belt. He drew a dagger, but it was not his – a clumsier design, good enough to mimic his own weapon's weight and size. '*She* took it when I slept. After our love. She betrayed me. And the Northlanders? That snake Teel—'

'He knew nothing of it. But now the deed is done, he relishes it—'

'I am betrayed by all but you, Milaqa.'

'Run. Hide. Get out of the city. You have only heartbeats before they come for you.'

He hesitated. Then he kissed her, once, on the cheek, just as he had on the first day they had met. 'I won't forget this.'

There was shouting behind her, from the citadel. She glanced back, saw men running, swords drawn – Hunda coming, yelling at her.

When she looked again, Qirum was gone.

And much later, when she got back to Hunda's home – and she found Deri there, cradling a weeping, bloodstained Tibo – she discovered who it was who had killed the innocent man, whose rage and inchoate desire for revenge had been unleashed in so useful a fashion. They began to talk urgently about how to get the boy out of Hattusa before he suffered the dread judgement of a Hatti court.

42

Qirum walked into the camp of the Spider, alone this time, unarmed.

The warlord sat alone in the dark, in his shack of pointless treasures. Outside, the din of the camp continued, the animal noises of rutting and fighting. The Spider considered the Trojan. The new wounds he bore, from the hard journey he'd made to get back here. The obvious rage inside.

'We need to talk,' said Qirum.

'What about?'

'Northland. And the Tawananna. And . . .'

'Yes?'

'Revenge.'

THREE

43

The Second Year After the Fire Mountain: Late Spring

'Hit me,' Hunda said. 'I mean it. Come on. Hit me.' He grinned.

Tibo just stood before the Hatti sergeant. A few soldiers watched idly, with Milaqa and Voro standing by uncomfortably. Before Hunda, Tibo was a boy-man before a man-boy, Milaqa thought. On a patch of Northland ground trampled to lifeless dust by Hatti soldiers' boots, the two of them stood naked save for grimy loincloths, barefoot, without weapons, the dirt clinging to their legs.

Kilushepa had loaned the Northlanders a thousand or so warriors, and here they were, with many more followers – servants and slaves of the officers, weapon-makers and cooks and cobblers, dentists and doctors, and women, some of them wives, many of them booty-women with exotic looks and strange tongues, brought from places far from here. There were children running around, even infants, some of them conceived and born during this army's long journey here by sea and land. One man, bizarrely, had a young piglet on a long rope. Meant for that evening's meal, its snout twitched at the piles of filthy clothes, the boots, the smoking hearth.

Around the Hatti camp the ground was scored by sewage gullies and the ruts of chariot wheels, with further out an elaborate defensive earthwork of ditches and ramparts. It was a place of filth and stench, like a pen of animals, where disease had already run through the ranks like fire.

But Northland had to accept this great unnatural scab in its heart, because the reports were persistent and ominous. Qirum was building an army. The Trojans were coming to Northland.

The moment stretched, the challenge hanging in the air between the two fighters. Hunda was actually shorter than Tibo. Many of the Hatti struck the Northland folk as short – *cattle-folk*, they called them, stunted after growing up on a diet of rotten meat and teeth-grinding bread. And Tibo had bulked up; still just seventeen years old, he had pushed his body hard in the months since he had been freed from the camp of the warlord called the Spider. Yet it was obvious that size didn't matter, even the mass of Tibo's muscles didn't matter. Even stripped to his loincloth, even with that thick braid of hair at his back hanging loose, Hunda looked like a soldier, a warrior. For all his size Tibo still looked like a frightened boy.

'Come on, hit me,' Hunda said again. He sounded almost gentle. 'Or are you afraid? After what that Wilusan savage did to you, you've got a lot to be afraid of, haven't you, pretty boy? '

Tibo roared and lashed out, a bunched fist at the end of a massive arm swinging towards Hunda's head. But Hunda ducked underneath the swing and jabbed with a hand held flat like a blade, hitting Tibo just under his ribcage. Tibo folded, the air gushing out of him in a great sigh. Hunda slammed his fist into the boy's temple, and Tibo was sent sprawling in the dirt.

Around them the watching men laughed.

'We should leave,' Voro said. 'I can't watch this.'

'Well, you can't leave,' Milaqa said. 'You've got to talk to Muwa about the warning beacons.'

'The Hatti won't listen. You know what they're like. They treat us with contempt.'

She looked at him, exasperated. 'What will your pricked pride matter when the Trojans come? You're a Jackdaw. A trader. You're supposed to make deals with strangers. If you can't talk to some Hatti sergeant about a set of beacons that might save all our lives, then what's the point of you?'

'Look, Milaqa—'

'Oh, just sort it out, Voro.' She turned away from him.

Tibo's trial was not yet over. Hunda walked casually around the fallen Northlander, who lay on his belly, down on the dusty ground. 'You're a strong boy,' Hunda said. 'Nobody would deny that. That's good. You want to fight. That's good too. But you are a blunt blade. You *hesitate*. Maybe you *feel* how it would be to receive the punch you deliver. That slows you down, just for a fraction of a breath. But that's enough to get you killed, because I can guarantee you that the animals Qirum has been recruiting from the ruins of the palace kingdoms are not going to be stopped by fretting how much they're going to hurt *you*.' On impulse he gestured to the soldier with the piglet. 'Give me that.'

The man brought the animal over. Hunda snapped a finger and beckoned to another of his men, who tossed over a bronze dagger, which Hunda stabbed down through the rope and into the earth, tethering the pig. The piglet walked around, snuffling at the ground around the dagger. It did not seem to be frightened; like most young animals it was too busy being curious about the newness of the world.

The boy struggled to his feet.

'Kill it,' Hunda said.

'What?' Tibo looked at the piglet, his own empty hands.

'Kill it. Right now. Prove to me that you can. Or you'll drink nothing for the next day but your own piss. Now!'

Tibo gathered both fists into a club. Staggering slightly, he stood over the pig, legs splayed, and flexed his body, preparing to use all his core strength, Milaqa saw. The piglet looked up, still apparently unafraid. Tibo hesitated, for one more heartbeat.

Then he swung his fists down, smashing the animal's skull with a crunch like a walnut under a heel. The men whooped and applauded, catcalling in a dozen tongues. Tibo struck again. There was a stickier impact as his fists drove into the grey mass within the skull, and blood fountained and splashed. The piglet's body twitched, its legs scrabbling as if it was trying to run. Tibo brought down his fists over and over, reducing the animal's head to a bloody pulp of flesh and splintered bone.

Voro looked as if he might vomit. Hunda grinned, arms folded.

44

The war trumpets pierced the Gairan night air. Urhi knew what that meant. At last, the Spartans were coming, to join Qirum's ragged army.

Urhi couldn't sleep after that.

The snores of his whore irritated him. He was a scribe, and scribes got whores who snored. He slapped her rump until she stopped. But still sleep didn't return. Spartans! The very name terrified him. Urhi rolled off his bed, pulled on his clothes and boots, shook out a cloak.

He emerged from his house into pre-dawn gloom. This was late spring, but this far west, much closer to the Western Ocean than the dry Anatolian plain where Urhi had been born, there was damp in the gusty wind, and you could feel the chill even on a good spring day, even at noon. Everyone feared a second year without a summer, and it was looking as if it would turn out that way.

The men on guard were dozing, sitting cross-legged by the big common fire, huddled in their cloaks. But Urhi was not surprised to see Erishum awake, squatting on his haunches, idly polishing the blade of a spear. The sergeant looked east, where the Spartans were coming from. He glanced at Urhi. 'You heard the trumpets too.'

'I did.'

'Are you up for a little expedition, scribe? I would prefer to meet the Spartans before they come to us.' Erishum stood and brushed back loose hair with his hands. He wore his hair in the Hatti style, thick at the back of his neck, and as he tied it up he murmured commands to his men in the Trojan that was the common language of Qirum's camp. One man brought him cloak, boots, conical felt helmet, and others prepared to form up a party to travel.

Erishum had once been part of the palace guard in Hattusa. He had been among a handful of Hatti soldiers who had no liking for Kilushepa for one reason or another, and had thrown in their lot with the Trojan. He had quickly grown to be one of Qirum's most trusted men. Urhi despised Erishum as a traitor to his king, while Erishum despised Urhi as a weak-wristed scratcher of clay. But they each recognised a certain strength in the other, Urhi thought. Or a sanity, perhaps. They were uncertain allies in the dangerous instability of Qirum's household.

A groom brought them horses. The animals stamped and snuffled in the dark, confused to be awake and moving so early. Urhi refused a mount; he hated horses, and they hated him. But soldiers rode whenever they could.

Erishum mounted, wrapped his fist around his horse's mane, kicked its sides gently, and led the way. Urhi walked after the party, which maintained a slow and steady pace. By the light of torches, they followed a trail through scrubby dune grass beaten flat by the passage of Qirum's army. They passed a couple of sentries, and Erishum exchanged murmured words.

They came to higher ground, a bluff. From here the ocean opened up to the south, and Urhi heard waves softly breaking. This was the southern coast of Gaira, and the Middle Sea stretched to the horizon. But Urhi knew that not very far west of here the land closed in from north and south to form the strait beyond which extended the Western Ocean, which, it was said, could swallow up the whole of this inner sea like a raindrop in a wine cup. Even so, for Urhi who had been born and raised in the heart of the Anatolian plain, to be so close to this huge, restless body of water was deeply disturbing. But Qirum was making plans on a scale that matched the grandeur of this panorama. Through the winter he had brought this force – *his* army now, not the Spider's, though that was the core on which he had built – all the way from Anatolia, the length of the Middle Sea, to this western country. And he intended to go much further. With this army he intended to mount the Trojan invasion of Northland.

Urhi heard that trumpet call again, and a wider noise, a murmur like the growl of the sea itself, ragged, chaotic. He had been around armies long enough now to recognise the sound. It was the merged din of thousands of voices, of boots tramping the earth, of the rattle of wheels, of the crying of women and the laughing of men: the sound of an army on the march. Urhi walked further up the bluff, pulling his cloak around him. Erishum walked beside him, silent, strong. And in the pre-dawn light they saw the torches of the approaching army, sparkling in a line along the coast, the men marching, the wagons, a few horses being ridden alongside the column.

Erishum pointed. 'The elite warriors in front, the officers and the fore-fighters. Then the specialists, the archers and the charioteers and the slingers, and the common men – barefoot half of them, probably, judging by the volume of their complaints. Then at the rear there is the train, with an escort to fend off raids. Scouts riding out around the column – see them? Competently commanded, and a formidable force.' Erishum's eyes were sharper than Urhi's; he was more than a decade younger than the scribe, a mere twenty-five, though battle had left him looking older.

Urhi said, 'And there. Between the common soldiers and the train, that mass of people shuffling along – booty people?'

'Yes. The hobbles slow them down.'

Urhi had once been lost in such a crowd. He suppressed a shudder.

Erishum said, 'Come then, scribe, let's face the Spartan, and hope we survive the encounter.'

Erishum ordered one of his men to dismount and run back to the camp to rouse Qirum. He held onto the mane of the man's abandoned horse, and looked meaningfully at Urhi. The scribe sighed. You had to ride to meet a warlord, of course. Of all the

273

symbols of status and power a horse was the ultimate; you were half a man without one. So he found a boulder to stand on and briskly mounted the nag. Luckily for him it seemed docile enough, and responded to his nervous prompting.

The party rode down a shallow bank towards the Spartans.

They soon encountered scouts. Erishum and his men kept their swords in their scabbards. Erishum murmured greetings in Greek, Trojan and Hatti; there was a good chance in these fragmented times, with ancient states collapsing like puffball mushrooms, that this so-called Spartan army, led by a Spartan prince, would be a coalition every bit as polyglot as the ragtag force Qirum had assembled around the Spider's original pack of murderers, thieves and rapists.

The scouts let them pass, and Erishum led the way boldly towards the elite cohorts at the head of the army. It wasn't hard to distinguish the best soldiers. They were taller than the mass of men following them, thanks to a decent diet, and they wore good-quality armour and weaponry. They were clean too, or comparatively, and their skin glowed with oils. Their hair was prepared in a variety of styles, some long and loose like a Greek's, some even plaited at their necks like a Hatti's. As they marched they were trailed by a gaggle of servants and by lavish-looking carriages, from some of which the nervous, painted faces of women and boys looked out. Some of Erishum's men bristled at the glares they got from these hard men, their wordless challenges. But Erishum was calm, even smiling.

Urhi kept his head down and avoided looking any of the Spartans in the eye. Urhi had met their sort before, too many times. These heroes from the citadel-nations of the east had been born into wealth and power, bred with war in their hearts, trained for it from boyhood. They were men who knew how to fight, how to storm cities and raid beaches – how to kill men like Urhi with bare hands, snuffing out a man's life and mind and essence for the sake of a momentary advantage, or a bit of treasure.

At length they were brought before Protis himself. They dismounted, wordless.

Protis walked among the visitors, peering closely into their faces. He was a prince of Sparta, driven off when that city was sacked and burned by raiders, and now seeking fresh opportunities. He wore a linen tunic, fringed kilt and boots with turned-up toes in the Anatolian style, and a cloak of wool pinned by silver brooches the size of Urhi's fists. His black hair was cut short at his forehead but was long at the back, and his upper lip was clean shaven, but he wore a neatly cut beard. He was not as bulky as some of those who surrounded him, though Urhi had a sense of a kind of lean strength, like a whip. He looked young, surprisingly so, perhaps even as young as twenty, his features soft and symmetrical – almost like a woman's, Urhi thought, fascinated. He had none of the battle scars that so disfigured men like the one-eyed Spider. He was almost pretty. Yet this man was reputed to be one of the most savage killers roaming this fallen world.

When it was Urhi's turn, the scribe forced himself not to flinch from his gaze. The man's eyes were a pale, washed-out blue, as beautiful as the rest of his face. There was a scent of perfumed water and oils. And as the Spartan leaned close to him Urhi saw those fine nostrils flare. The man was *smelling* him.

The Spartan stepped back. Urhi bent forward, his arms spread, all but prostrating himself, and spoke in clear Greek. 'Lord Protis, your fame echoes around the known world. My name is Urhi. I am a clerk, a scribe. I serve the great Qirum. I am unimportant, only a mouthpiece. My lord Qirum awaits eagerly in his tent. He has gifts, and has prepared a feast which—'

'Oh, straighten up,' the Spartan snapped. 'I prefer to look at a man's face, not his shoulder blades. I know nothing of this Qirum. I had heard nothing of him before rumours of the force he was gathering – and his invitation to me to fight alongside him. A nobody from Troy, who dared summon a prince of Sparta!' He won a rumbling laugh from his men.

'An invitation, Lord,' Urhi stammered, 'not a summons—'

Protis said softly, 'Tell him that if he keeps his promises, all will be well. By which I mean, he will continue to live. If not . . .' From a fold in his cloak he produced a dagger of bronze, and in a single fluid movement had the point at Erishum's throat.

Erishum did not so much as flinch. He spread his empty hands, a wordless command to his men not to react.

Urhi bowed again. 'I will take the lord Qirum your message at once.'

The Spartan laughed. Then he removed the blade and walked away.

Erishum touched Urhi's arm. 'Straighten up and walk. Better he gets this posturing out of his system before he meets Qirum himself. Walk, scribe! The blade was at my throat, not yours.'

Urhi forced himself to walk away, to take one step after another back to his horse, surrounded by the grins of Protis's huge warriors.

45

Qirum clambered down from his high throne and hauled back the layers of rugs that covered the bare earth floor of his house, sending servants and slaves hurrying out of his way. Then he took a dagger and began to scratch a map in the dirt with the blade's tip.

Protis and Telipinu, the Spider, watched from their couches of stuffed sheep hide, while they consumed the feast Qirum had prepared for them, of honey and lamb, kid and boar. Protis looked faintly amused at Qirum's antics. The Spider just looked on, cold, scarred, as ever emotionless. Urhi wondered if Qirum would have been better advised to have somebody else shift his rugs for him. The Hatti kings were remote figures, whom only the most senior ever even saw, let alone touched. Even a king's shoes would be made only from the hide of cattle slaughtered in the palace precinct. Qirum, in his ignorance, had none of that aloofness, and in the eyes of the Hatti at least was much less impressive for it.

Qirum pointed at his scrawled map. 'Here, you see. The Middle Sea, that stretches from Gaira in the west to Greece and Anatolia in the east.' He stabbed the dirt with his blade. 'We are *here*. Far to the west, on the southern coast of Gaira. My plan is that we will strike north-west over this great neck of land. I have made this journey myself before. You see there are two rivers here, whose courses all but meet at their headwaters, *here*.' Another stab. 'On the other side of the watershed we'll need to find ships. We will sail down the course of this great river, which the people call the God's Dream. We will reach this tremendous estuary, called the Cut, and travel north and east to its far shore, which is the southern coast of Northland itself.'

The house, a tent of canvas draped on poles, was crowded, right to the billowing walls. Behind the three principals gathered advisers, guards and warriors, including Urhi and Erishum for Qirum, men sitting or standing, watching each other with a hostility barely sublimated into rivalry. There was a stink from these men of sweat, of blood, of stale wine, of horses. And they *were* all men, though in a Hatti gathering, even a Trojan one, a few women would likely have been present: royalty like the Tawananna, a few priestesses. Since his catastrophic clash with Kilushepa, Qirum would allow no woman near him, save for whores ordered not to speak when he tupped them, on pain of death.

A disparate bunch they might be, but they seemed eager enough to follow Qirum's plan, Urhi thought. The Hatti and other Anatolians were comfortable with the overland sections of the journey. And the Greeks, used to their own island-strewn seas, would not baulk at journeys by ocean or river. If these warriors could work together Qirum would find himself at the head of a formidable force indeed.

'We will land with much of the campaigning season left.' Qirum swept his knife again, sketching arrows and advances. 'The country is big, perhaps fifty days' march north to south from the Northern Ocean to the Cut, and as much east to west, from the estuary country *here* to the forested peninsula of Albia *here*. But the people are few . . .'

Protis leaned forward. 'And what of this Northland? What treasures are there? Are there great cities? Masses of people to slaughter and enslave?'

'No,' Qirum said bluntly. 'Northland is not like any land you've seen before, Prince. Not a land of farms and cities, not like Greece or Anatolia or Egypt. There are great works there, canals and dykes and tremendous walls that span the horizon. But not cities. The people are wily, but there are not great swarms of them. *They do not farm.* They have a patina of

278

civilisation, but in truth they are like the savages of the northern forests, or even the beasts that prey on them, for they live solely by what they can gather and hunt. And they are not experienced fighters, for they do not engage in war, as we do.'

The Spider nodded. When he spoke his speech was slurred from the heroic quantity he had already drunk. 'I have heard your arguments before, Trojan. Yet I am still not sure I understand. If there are no slaves to take, no cities to sack—'

'Not even goats to screw,' a man called coarsely, and there was laughter.

'Then what am I fighting for?'

'For a kingdom,' Qirum said, and he fixed his gaze on Protis and the Spider and the senior men, his expression intent. 'A new kingdom. The land is the thing. The people are worthless. But we can bring in our own slaves, like your booty people, Protis, gathered from the collapsing polities of the east. The Hatti have always done this. With our slaves we will farm the rich land until we are fat on wheat and grain, and our cattle run as numberless as raindrops. And we will build our own cities, where none have sprouted before. Northland is an empty space, a hole in the world. We will fill it with a new realm not seen in the world before.'

The Spider grinned, showing his sharpened teeth. 'New cities! I like that. Let mine be called Telipinu City.'

'Yes!' Qirum stood and paced. 'You!' He pointed at Urhi, who scrambled for a slate and stylus. 'Write this down. Telipinu City. Protis City. Qirum City! New Troy, New Mycenae, New Hattusa! Write it down lest we forget.'

Protis watched Urhi, amused. 'You are not yet a king, but you have a king's scribe.'

'I found him in Abydos, a city in the Troad, near Troy itself, which I besieged with the Spider at my side. I say I found Urhi. We burned his city, and he watched his family die, and as he was marched away with chains around his neck with a thousand others he loudly begged to be allowed to use his skills. My soft heart let him live a while longer. But he knows that I could

279

cast him down once more in a moment, don't you, good Urhi? Make sure you write that down too. Go on! Write it down!'

Urhi forced himself to smile as, with laughter raining around him, he worked his clay slate, his stylus pecking like a bird's beak as he made the wedge-shaped characters.

Protis laughed. 'A new kingdom, then. With you installed as king, and us as your companions, I suppose.'

He used a Greek word, *basileis*, which Urhi understood as meaning more than companions – it meant lords, with power and holdings of their own. And Protis and the Spider exchanged a glance which every man in the room could read, a glance that said that in the end these two would not be content to remain *basileis* of any man.

But Qirum said only, 'You know my circumstances, Prince. I have lifted myself up from the ruin of my home city as a heavy stone is lifted from a pool of water, and now I address you as an equal.' Qirum waved a hand. 'Look at us, all survivors of the great smash-up of the states to the east – you Greeks, you Anatolians. You men of the Troad, my own country, from Troy and Abydos and Zeleia, and from the wider Anatolia, from Phrygia to Lycia. Even you Hatti, like the Spider here, who knew when to run from a burning house!'

The Spider said to Protis, 'He has a particular distaste for the Hatti – don't you, Trojan? For he was bested by a woman in Hattusa. Not just any woman, mind – the Tawananna herself.'

'Yes! But one day I will return, at the head of a formidable army – an army raised in my own kingdom – and I will do to that dismal country what I should have done to Kilushepa when I first slept with her, and split it wide open from breast to pubis.'

That raised a coarse cheer.

'We will be a great people,' he went on, shouting, waving his arms, stalking back and forth. 'And a *new* people. Not Greek or Trojan or Hatti any more. As tin and copper come together to make bronze, so our blood will mix to create a new people in a new kingdom – and all men will know our names, for ever, as we remember the Great King Sargon of Akkad. Tomorrow we will start, we will form up our forces for a great journey – and then a war!' He won a louder cheer for that.

'And now we will set out our case before our gods.' He clapped his hands, and nodded to a senior slave. To a rumble of approval from the men a new feast was brought in, more wine, the meat of ritually slaughtered sheep. Priests brought bowls of entrails of birds and snakes, regarded as key sources of divination by Trojans.

And then the holiest relics were produced. A small statue was set up beside Qirum's throne, a plaster representation of a human figure with a bull's head, its arms upraised. Qirum made his obeisance, muttering prayers. 'The Storm God. You Greeks know him as Zeus, and the Hatti as Teshub. Closer to Troy than any city in the world, the god who has always fought at our side—'

Protis said, 'He wasn't fighting too well on the day my father joined in your city's sack.'

Qirum snapped, 'That is a quarrel for our fathers in the underworld. Troy's most sacred statue of the Storm God was lost later, and not to the Greeks, but when Hatti raiders came to feast on the decaying corpse of their own supposed protectorate. This, though, this has been purified and blessed; this has seen endless sacrifices – in this, the Storm God is present.' He bowed again, muttering prayers.

Then he straightened up, and clapped his hands again. To a howl of appreciation from the increasingly drunken men three girls were brought in, chained together at neck and feet, all pale, all naked. One, Urhi saw, had been smeared by mud, the second, shivering, had been shaven bare from head to crotch, and the third appeared to be glistening wet – Urhi imagined that was the result of some viscous oil smeared on her skin rather than water, which would run off and dry. The girls stood before the leering, shouting men, huddling together for protection. Urhi wondered if they had been drugged.

Qirum stalked before the girls, waving his wine cup so that droplets splashed the girls, red as blood on their pale flesh. 'Here you are, you men – meet your first Northlanders. Healthy stock, aren't they? All that wild meat they consume, I suppose. Snatched in raids by my most trusted men. Not a one over sixteen years old, and every one of them a virgin.

'It is the Trojan way, the Anatolian way, to interrogate the gods of our enemies before going into battle. After all, what is war but a trial before the gods? And he who pleases the gods the most is permitted to win – and live. And so here they are, the goddesses of Northland, made incarnate before you. The little mothers, they call them, the little mothers of the earth and of the sea and of the sky, of dirt and damp and cold.

'What have you to say for yourselves, mothers? What have you done with your people? Why have you kept the fire of war from their bellies, the genius of farming from their hearts? Why are your children so *few*, you mothers, ten where there could be a hundred, a hundred where there could be ten thousand? Are your wombs so barren?' He lifted the heads of the bewildered girls with fingers under their chins, and he squeezed their breasts and grabbed their backsides, making them flinch.

At length the Spider stood up and lifted his kilt. 'I'll tell you how I'd like to interrogate them.'

Qirum laughed, waved Protis forward, and began to remove his own kilt. 'Just as I planned – come, friends, my *basileis*!'

The men roared, their faces greasy from meat, their chins stained by wine. The chains were removed from the girls.

Qirum arranged it so that each of the three leaders deflowered one virgin each. Then they each moved on to another girl, and then the third. The Spider went at it enthusiastically. Protis, though, was more fussy. He preferred to use the anus of his second girl and the mouth of the third, as if they were still virginal.

When the leaders were done the girls were taken out, but more whores were brought in for the crowd of leering men. The women disappeared in knots of bodies, like slabs of meat thrown to dogs.

Urhi forced himself to watch it all, and he tried not to think of what he had seen done to his wife and his daughter in their last hours.

The feasting continued to the dawn. Then Qirum called them all outside, for he had arranged another stunt. Once more he had his priests produce the three Northlander girls, naked and done out in their guises as the little mothers, their bruises treated, the blood washed from their thighs.

And Qirum had his soldiers hang the little mother of the sky from a scaffold by her wrists, so she turned in the wind; and the little mother of the sea was forced into a barrel of seawater that was nailed shut; and the little mother of the earth was buried alive. The men, still drunk, gambled on which of them would die the first, and the last.

46

The Second Year After the Fire Mountain: Midsummer Solstice

On the morning of the Giving, Milaqa found her uncle Teel waiting in the shade of his house in Old Etxelur. In his heavy, dark tunic, he was a lump of darkness on a bright if sunless day.

Together, saying little, they walked across the rich earth of the Bay Land towards the Wall. On this midsummer day the face of the Wall gleamed a brilliant bone-white, incised with galleries and adorned with banners celebrating the Giving. In crevices high in the face sea birds gathered in rustling swarms, terns and gulls, their guano striping the walls, and on the roof the great heads of long-dead Annids stared stoutly out to the excluded sea.

As always, people had come from afar for the ancient festival, and Giving celebrations were already under way all along the foot of the Wall. Milaqa heard laughter, saw running figures, glimpsed smoke rising from a dozen fires. As they walked along the track towards the Wall, Milaqa and Teel passed people sitting in little groups, blankets on the ground, fires blazing, while children ran and played. Milaqa smelled food, smoked fish, broiling meat. But many of these people looked thin, pale, gaunt after another hard season in the shadow of the fire mountain. Milaqa suspected many of them had come this year, not for the joy of the Giving, but for the dole of potato mash and salted fish they could expect from the Annids.

'Everything's odd,' she said to Teel.

'Is it?'

'This is always such a special day. I'll swear I remember Givings when I was only four or three or two. And yet even today we are all preoccupied.'

'I don't think the Trojan will be taking a day off.'

'Oh, do you have to be so morbid? He's still in Gaira, according to the spies and the spotters on the south coast. And it's midsummer! Can't we forget about Qirum just for one day?'

He glanced at her. 'Because, you think, even if he does come, it would never be today? But it might be on just such a day as this that Qirum *would* choose to move. Think about it. Every culture knows the solstice; every culture marks it in some way, just as we do. And Qirum has a coalition of warlords to pull together, from a dozen shattered nations. Today would be an easy rallying point in time, if he needed one . . . It's my job, and yours, to think of the worst possibility, while others hope for the best. Or maybe it's just my personality. But I agree. It does no good to frighten the children.'

They walked on past the families, like dark clouds crossing. Teel was grim, morbid, obsessive, all the cares of Northland weighing him down. But he was also the uncle who had played elaborate games with Milaqa on other Giving days, long ago. She slipped her hand into his.

The Water Council was already in session by the time Teel and Milaqa arrived. Despite its archaic title, the Council was a general-purpose quarterly convocation of Annids and other senior folk. The meeting was taking place in a dedicated chamber deep within the body of the Wall, lit by oil lamps. The Annids were sitting or standing in little groups, arguing and complaining, as servants hurried between them bearing trays of food and drink. The air was thick with greasy smoke and laden with heat, and Milaqa felt as if she was being buried alive. But the Annids never went short of their treats, she noted sourly, whatever the weather.

Riban came to meet them, bearing drinks: beer for Milaqa, clear water for Teel. After having travelled across the Continent with them the young priest knew their taste. He led them to a small group centred on Raka, the still-new Annid of Annids. She had got herself stuck in a raging argument with Noli, the stern old Annid who had so opposed her own original appointment.

'We must deal with the Trojans, one way or another,' Raka insisted. 'As well as the other powers. It is pointless and distracting to pretend that the great tide of warriors which is likely to break over us is not real!'

Noli said, 'But it is not a tide that faces us, not a mindless thing, a force driven by the will of the gods. Not a Great Sea. It is an army, a mob of humanity. *They need not be here*; there were other choices that could have been made.'

Teel put in, 'You went to Hattusa, Annid.'

She turned on him. 'Where I stood helpless as you made your deals. It is you and your kind, Teel, who have brought disaster down upon us in your endless game-playing.'

'Not game-playing,' Teel said sternly. 'Politics.' He used a Greek word: *politikos*.

'Even the word for what you do is foreign to us!' she snapped at him. 'To manipulate farmer-kings, to play off one against another. And now you plan to head off one lot of cattle-folk by planting another lot in the heart of Northland. How can you be sure we can rely on these Hatti?'

'I think we can trust Kilushepa,' Teel said. 'She has as much reason to deal with the Trojan as we have. More, perhaps. If anybody is to blame for creating the monster it is Kilushepa. Without her he would still be a petty bandit screwing teenage whores in the wreck of his home city. She never imagined, I think, that after she cast him down he would rise up as he has.'

'But Kilushepa herself is not secure in Hattusa,' Raka said anxiously.

'As long as she lasts she will support us. After all, she has sent a close ally in Muwa to serve as the general of her force here.'

'What "force"?' Noli sneered. 'A thousand men? The rumours are that the Trojan has many times that number. The farmers will always outnumber us.'

Teel would have spoken again, but Raka raised a hand to

silence him. 'We can come through this trial. We *will* come through it. And we will do it with the blessing of the little mothers, without losing the essence of what we are, of what our country is, even though we are so few compared to the farmers. This is what we must tell the people.' She was deeply impressive, and her words stirred Milaqa's heart.

But then a cry went up, echoing through the galleries of the Wall. 'The beacons! They are lit! Oh, they are lit!'

The Annid of Annids led the way, hurrying to the Wall roof. Noon was approaching, and the sky was brighter.

And all across the tremendous plain of Northland, on earthen mounds raised ages ago against the threat of flood, the beacon fires burned, pinpoints of brilliance. Teel touched Milaqa's arm and pointed. She turned to see the fires coming alight all along the Wall's upper parapet too.

'I hate to say it,' Teel said. 'I was right, wasn't I? About Qirum, and the midsummer day.'

The beacons were a wave of prearranged signals that had washed across Northland all the way from its southern coast. Now that wave of light had broken against the Wall itself, bringing with it a simple message. The Trojan was coming.

47

Qirum's fleet had hauled anchor before dawn.

As the long midsummer day wore on the ships pushed steadily west, tracking the shore of the great estuary the natives of this place called the Cut, following the southern coast of Northland. It was high tide, and the dark waters washed over stony beaches.

Qirum himself was at the steering oar at the stern of his own ship, a big bristling pentecoster that would have dwarfed his old eight-man scow. His Greek pilot had given it a name, the *Lion*, after the Greek custom. Erishum, Qirum's trusted sergeant, stood at the prow, weapons to hand. This ship was the lead in a motley fleet of over a hundred vessels scattered across the swelling water, ships stolen from kings and pirates, some even rightfully purchased, many of them heroically sailed out of the strait and north along Gaira's coast with the Western Ocean. Ships that bore an army, its warriors and followers and their horses, even chariots and siege engines packed into their hulls.

It was good to be back at sea. Qirum could hear men calling across the water, pilots passing bits of information, the crews mocking each other as fighting men always would. He could hear the horses too, their frightened whinnies carrying over the water. He relished the smell of pitch and resin, of the men's wine and salted meat, even their earthy stink of piss and vomit, and above all the sharp salt scent of the air that lay over the ocean. Even to bring his army so far, to assemble such a fleet, was a huge achievement. And at this key moment, with the first landing on Northland soil imminent, it was Qirum's ship that led, Qirum himself who guided it, he who would be the first to spring onto Northland soil, the first to fight, the first to kill.

But that landing had yet to be made, that moment of glory yet to come. For now Qirum and his force were still at the mercy of the sea. Huge oceanic waves forced their way into this great throat of an estuary, and the boat creaked as it rose and fell. The men, most of them warriors from the eastern countries, looked uneasy, queasy, and more than one had emptied his guts over the side. At least the wind was strong enough for them to use their sails, but it blew too hard, driving the ships too fast for the comfort of the pilots, and it brought a bite of cold too on this unseasonably chill midsummer day.

It was just as well, Qirum thought, that few of the men knew of the invisible traps that the Northlanders had planted all along the shore.

Now the traitor came back the length of the ship to speak to him. He had to step carefully past the twin ranks of rowers, twenty-five men in each, their gear stowed beneath their benches, their weapons to hand, their oars shipped. The man, arrogantly dressed in the Jackdaw-feather cloak of his cere-monial office in Northland society, himself looked unsteady; he was no sailor. But he smiled at the Trojan's discomfort. 'You're doing well, Qirum. Just hold your course.'

Qirum snarled, 'I don't need pats on the head from the likes of you, Bren.'

'Of course you don't. But nevertheless—' He glanced up at a sunless sky. 'A midsummer day, a clear still morning. The weather is kind, believe it or not. You should see the storms that ram their way up this estuary in the winter.'

Qirum glanced to the shore to the north. It was a strand of empty shingle beach, with a blur of forest in the distance. To the south, nothing could be seen but water. This estuary was so wide that you could not see one bank from the other. 'I see no walls. Where are the mighty Northland walls, as I saw in the north?'

'There are some on the south coast, but nothing to match the structures in the north, like the great Wall that shelters Etxelur itself. Here the issue is the management of the great rivers, and the tidal washes, whose flow is diverted and channelled to keep them from tearing at the land. Look over there.' He pointed to a section of coast that looked as if it had been undercut and slumped into the water. The exposed landscape, under a sward of green, was chalk, white as bone. 'Without conscious management this very land would be cut away by the sea, as you see over there. You must understand that Northland is not just a question of walls. It is a system of water engineering that spans a whole country, a system designed and evolved to—'

'So this precious land has been saved from the sea. I've heard all this before. To what end?' He peered at the empty shoreline. 'I see no people here.'

'But there are signs of them. See the ruined boat?' An oval shape on the strand. 'And there is a fish rack, abandoned. And there, that black scar is an old hearth. They know you're coming, Trojan. And they have laid their traps.'

Bren had revealed the Northlanders' hidden defences to their enemy, underwater, concealed in the sand and shingle, and had no doubt already saved the fleet from disaster. The problem was Qirum could *see* none of it, and nor could his men. Qirum was a fighter by nature, not a thinker. He longed to be on those beaches, splashing through the last of the surf, wielding his sword against the foe – but there was no foe to be seen here, nothing but empty beaches, and air.

Best not to think about the enemy and his cunning. Best not to let his mind get addled by twisted words from manipulative scum like Bren. Best to think of his own strengths, and purposes. He was already thinking ahead, as a great king should. When he had built his kingdom in Northland, when the time came to strike at the Hatti and their lizard-queen in high Hattusa, it would be an overland expedition, by river valley and mountain pass, the like of which the world had never seen . . .

There was a cry of alarm, floating over the water. The crew craned to see, and Qirum turned, holding the steering oar steady. One of the ships, a big pentecoster laden with horses, had broken from the loose column and was driving for the shore, its sail flapping. Qirum bellowed for the pilot to right his course, but he was surely too far away to be heard.

Beside him, Bren plucked his sleeve. 'That's the *Gryphon*.'

'I can see that.'

'There's no point shouting. The man hasn't forgotten the course he's supposed to keep. He's lost control of the craft altogether. Look at him.'

And indeed, Qirum could see the pilot of the rogue ship hauling at his steering oar to no effect. As the ship listed horses bucked and neighed pitifully. The men scrambled to bring down their sail and tried to ship their oars, but their movements were an uncoordinated tangle in the heaving bilge and they got in each other's way. Still, for a moment hope flickered in Qirum's heart. The beach here was shallow, and Greek ships were designed to be driven far up the shore. If the *Gryphon* encountered no obstruction perhaps most of the crew could survive the landing – and the horses, which were more valuable than the men.

But long before the ship reached the shore something seemed to reach up out of the water, a blackened claw that pierced the hull and dragged at the vessel as it passed. The *Gryphon* tipped over onto its right-hand side, its mast dipping to the water almost elegantly. Men and horses tumbled into the water screaming, their oars and weapons and bales of clothing and food falling with them.

And then a swarm of arrows flew into the air from the shore, like bees. They seemed to come out of nowhere. They fell on the men and animals struggling in the water, and the screaming intensified. There were shouts of anger from the other ships. Shields were raised, and a few arrows were loosed in return, to fall uselessly in the water.

'So there are defenders,' Qirum snarled.

'A tree stump,' Bren murmured.

'What?'

'A tree stump. That's all it was – all that was needed. Upended, stuck in the beach, the roots sharpened. Covered over by the sea at high tide, they knew we would have to come in on the high tide, and it would rip open the hull of any ship trying to land. Simple but effective. And then the defenders on the land just pick off any survivors. I told you it would be like this. All the way along the coast.'

Qirum snarled, 'Except for the one weak point you will guide us to.'

'Not far now.' Bren smiled, utterly confident.

And Qirum's eye was caught by a spark of light, rising into the air from the green coast. It was like a firefly, but he had seen no such insects in this part of the world.

Erishum called from the prow. 'Fire! Lord Qirum, it is a fire arrow!'

Qirum could do nothing. The arrow fell, swooping straight down towards the *Lion*, and hit the sail. The woven fabric began to burn immediately. The men yelled and scrambled.

'Cut it down!' Erishum, fast to react as ever, strode forward, yelling. 'Cut the sail down! Get it over the side!' He slashed at the rigging with his own sword. It was a chaotic scene for a few heartbeats as the men hauled at the burning cloth and kicked it into the river. At last the sail was overboard, still burning, drifting on the water's surface.

Qirum, breathing hard, stood amidships and surveyed his crew. None had been lost, and only one seemed badly burned. And there were no more arrows coming; there was no need for the shields. 'Back to your stations. To your oars! No more sails. Who needs the strength of the wind? From now on we drive ourselves hard and strong all the way to our landing on the Northland shore!'

He was rewarded with a roar of anger and determination. The men moved to their places, scrambling for their oars in the bilge. The drummer took his place in the prow, and, facing the men, began a steady one-two beat. It took only a few strokes for the men to settle into their rhythm. Soon the oars were cutting into the water, and the *Lion* surged forward.

Erishum came back to speak to Qirum. 'We were lucky.'

'We shouldn't have been in range. I blame myself for that.'

'We were at the limit of an archer's reach. It was a good shot. And aimed to pick us out.'

Qirum considered. 'They recognised me.'

'Or perhaps *him*.' Erishum gestured at the traitor. 'You could recognise that ludicrous feather cloak half a day's walk away.'

Bren looked up, huddled in his cloak. 'You may take this as a warning of the campaign your opponents will wage. With cunning and stealth and intelligence.'

'Cunning they may be, but we've no obligation to help them. Be done with this ludicrous thing.' Qirum bent down, grabbed the man's cloak by the scruff, hauled it off his back and cast it away into the water. Loose black feathers fluttered in the air. Dressed only in tunic and kilt, Bren looked diminished – fragile, old. He wrapped his arms around his chest.

Qirum looked back at his fleet. More drums were sounding now; more oars were being lowered into the water, more sails furled, as the crews followed his lead. The ships surged through the water, energetic, as if angered themselves by the loss of their fellow. 'How much longer to this landing place, traitor? How long?'

Deri lay with Nago and Mi in the long grass. They were with a party of two dozen, some Northlanders, some Hatti scouts and warriors. Looking out over the ocean, they watched Qirum's flagship recover from the burning of its sail, and its renewed surge through the water. It was at the head of a navy that had been barely touched by the Northlanders' defence measures so far.

Deri clapped Mi on the back. The girl still had her bow on the grass beside her. 'Good shooting, kid.'

'I'm not a kid, uncle.' Mi spoke with a thick Kirike's Land accent. She was fourteen years old now, but looked younger.

'Well, whatever you are, you did your job well. I've never seen an arrow fly so far!'

'Medoc taught me.'

Deri nodded. 'My father was a good man, and I could use him at my side right now. If we'd had any luck we'd have sunk that ship and taken out fifty men, Qirum himself, and that worm Bren in the process.'

'It was him, wasn't it?' Nago asked.

'You could hardly mistake that Jackdaw cloak. The arrogance of the man in wearing it is beyond belief. Yet he thought he was safe, out on the water, I suppose.'

'So he told them about our beach defences,' Nago said ruefully. 'They knew to avoid the shore. We only got the one ship. All that work wasted. And all because of one man, because of Bren.'

Deri rubbed his face. 'He hasn't won yet. Nor has Qirum.'

'But he must have told them about—'

'About Shark Bay. I know. The one place the Trojans can land.' Deri was determined not to look downcast; he forced a grin. 'But every setback brings an opportunity. At least we know where they will land. And we can be ready to face them.

'There's nothing more we can do here.' He stood and turned to the wider party, and snapped out orders in their own tongue to the Hatti scouts; the men ran to their horses and galloped off. 'The tracks are good along this coast. If we make good time we can be ready to give these Trojans a warm welcome. And don't forget your bow, Mi. I have a feeling you will be very useful in what's to come.'

48

The inlet Bren called Shark Bay was the outflow of a minor river. A narrow valley with walls of eroded chalk led inland from the beach.

As the ship turned to face the shore, as the landing at last approached, Qirum gave up his place at the steering oar to his pilot, grabbed his weapons and armour, and made for the prow, Erishum at his side. The two boats following were commanded by Protis and the Spider, his two *basileis*, and were filled with their best fighters. These three boats, the hardened spear-point of the entire force, would make the first landings, and the heroes they carried were ready to win the day for the Trojan force.

Bren pointed out the features of the shore. 'The Annids decided that the whole coast could not be rendered impassable. We Northlanders do rely on trade. This place was chosen as a safe landing. It was thought well enough defended naturally, by its sandbanks. Can you see?' The sandbanks were visible as a maze of pale brown shadows under the water. 'If you don't know this coast, any experienced sailor would avoid this inlet.'

'But if you do know it, there is a way through.'

'Yes, as I told your pilot—'

'Then get back to the stern and tell him anew. I don't want any mistakes now we're so close.'

The traitor hurried back.

The rowers worked more gingerly now as the pilots carefully guided the ships through the banks. As they passed the men threw out markers, pigs' bladders weighted with rocks, to guide the ships following.

Erishum pointed to the shore. 'They're ready for us.'

Qirum peered that way, and saw the glint of metal, a fence of spears, just inland from the water's edge. The enemy at last, silently waiting. He grinned. 'Good. We need a fight to sharpen our wits. It's too many days since I killed a man—'

An arrow hissed through the air; it fell short of the ship, but not by much.

'Shields!' Qirum snapped.

Behind him the rowers, without missing a beat, manhandled their shields over their heads. The first arrows clattered down into the boat.

'Somebody has a good arm,' Erishum said.

'Maybe the same freak of nature who set fire to our sail. He will pay for that, in time.' More arrows fell now as they came within range of the shore, and Qirum and Erishum raised their own shields. But Qirum stood proud in the prow of his ship, defying the Northlanders' lethal hail.

The landing itself was only moments away. Qirum felt his heart race, his blood surge. Of the whole operation the landing required the most skill. If you got your run at the shore just right, if you timed the very strokes, then you could drive your ship half a length up the shore before it came to rest, and that alone could punch a hole in any defence. But the rowers had to work precisely to the rhythm of the drummers, even though they kept having to duck behind their shields, for all the time the enemy bombardment continued, the fall of arrows thickening. Mostly the arrows clattered harmlessly against shields or armour, or hit the wooden deck, but some, as always, found a way through to flesh, and a man would scream, and the ship juddered as a rower was lost.

And now the first answering wave of arrows from the ships behind the lead flew over Qirum's head, falling on the shore, and the first Northlanders, surely, began to die. Encouraged, the men rowed faster, their discipline growing tighter. Qirum felt the salt wind in his face as the boat leapt forward, and the hail of arrows from both sides thickened in the air.

The hull struck the sea bottom with a shuddering crunch, and slid over the shingle, and the last of the water surged around the prow. Qirum raised his sword with a roar. Even before the boat came to rest he leapt out into the surf.

Nago, with Deri at his side, stood firm at the centre of the Northlander line. They both wore armour borrowed from the Hatti. The plan was to strike at the Trojans just as they landed, when they were most vulnerable, with the bulk of their force still trapped at sea. Nobody expected this small force defending the beach to hold for long, but the more damage it could do the better.

But here came the ships! Somehow, whenever he had imagined this moment, Nago had never thought of the ships themselves. Now here they were, three of them rearing up out of the beach, sliding on their wooden bellies over the rough stones of the beach, with painted eyes glowering as if they meant to devour the defending warriors themselves. They were monsters, an aquatic nightmare. It was hard not to flee in superstitious terror.

And the first man was already out of the still-moving lead boat, short, stocky, his face livid with a kind of rage. Nago knew this man. It was Qirum himself, first to set foot in the country he meant to make his own. The Northlanders held their line – all save one man who broke and ran forward, yelling, waving a sword. Qirum ducked inside the man's clumsy slice and slashed his own short, heavy sword across the man's midriff, cutting through cloth and flesh and stomach wall. The man fell forward into the seawater, and blood spilled red. Qirum laughed, exultant.

A Hatti officer roared, 'Scrape these bastards off the beach!'

The defenders charged, bellowing, in their line, and Nago and Deri ran with them. Nago pumped air into his lungs and clenched his muscles, a fisherman trying to become a fighter, trying to remember the training the Hatti corporals had given him.

And he saw the first Trojan he was going to close with, a huge fellow from the lead boat. He carried a sword in his scabbard and a spear in his hands, but he had no shield. Rather he was kitted out with full armour, bronze sheets on his breast and over his thighs, jointed extensions to protect his neck and shoulders, and his face was shielded by a grill of bronze under a boar-tusk helmet. It chilled Nago that he could not see the man's face, this stranger determined to kill him. The man came at Nago with a muscular roar.

Don't hesitate: that was the one message the Hatti corporals had rammed into the heads and hearts of the Northlander fishermen and canal-dredgers. Don't hesitate to strike, to kill, or you will be killed.

Nago ducked under the Trojan's sword thrust and swung his own weapon, hoping to cut the man down at his legs, only to have the blade clatter against shaped armour plates on the shins. A spear stabbed down, and Nago rolled on his back on damp sand to avoid the thrust. He struggled to his feet, but while he was still off-balance the warrior raised his spear again. Nago, almost falling, lunged at the man with his sword point-first, probing, finding a joint in the armour – and he drove his sword up under the man's right shoulder plate, sliding it beneath the metal and into soft flesh. The warrior collapsed, gurgling behind his mask. He would have pulled Nago down, but Nago stayed upright, stepping back, holding onto the hilt of his sword, feeling how it tore through the man's body as he fell. The Trojan landed on his back, like an upended crab in the shallow seawater. Nago dragged out his sword, positioned the blade again, and thrust down into the man's mouth, driving through soft tissue until the blade ground on bone. The man coughed frothy blood, and subsided.

Nago pulled back the sword, breathing hard. For a heartbeat he could not hear the battle rage around him, could not see the grounded ships or the bloody froth. Just him and the man who he had killed, that was all that populated his world. He longed to be in his boat. Just him and the ocean.

Then a sword blade flashed past his face, and the severed hand of a Greek warrior, still clutching the dagger that would have killed Nago, fell in the spray. The man dropped back screaming, blood pumping from his arm.

Deri reached over Nago to finish the man off with a sharp thrust through the ribs. He straightened up, bleeding from a cut to his shoulder, breathing hard, his leggings soaked with spray. 'Don't make me save you again, cousin.' And then he twisted away, to take on another massive Trojan.

Nago raised his sword and looked around. More ships were landing. Eager to get into the fray, men were splashing out into deep water, struggling with heavy shields or armour. There were horses scrambling in the surf too, Nago saw. And the Hatti and Northlanders were wading out to meet the invaders. Arrows and stones hailed onto the struggling mass from the boats further out, and from defenders deeper inland. The whole of the littoral was becoming a shapeless melee, with a thrashing of blades and spears, and blood ran everywhere, bright crimson among the fallen; even the sea ran red. Nago already felt exhausted, as if his fight with the huge armoured man had used up his energy for the day. Yet it was barely begun.

He charged forward, back into the tangle of fighting.

The first man he met had no armour, no weapons; he floundered in the surf, having apparently fallen out of his ship. Nago swiped at his throat with his sword blade and left the man dying on his knees. Next came a formidable man with a long plaited queue like a Hatti. The two exchanged three heavy blows with their swords, each parrying the other, before the man slipped in the water and Nago drove his sword through his quilted tunic and into his belly, and thrust and dragged.

And the third man was Qirum. Nago's last vision was of the Trojan's open mouth, laughing, his flashing bloodstained sword.

Pain, bright as sunlight off the sea.

*

To Mi, watching from the long grass above the beach, the battle was a press of squirming meat and blood and metal that filled the bay.

She saw Nago fall. In an instant the fighting closed over him like a bloody tide, and his body was lost. One of her own family, cut down by Qirum. Something congealed deep inside Mi, hard and sharp, an arrowhead of determination.

Still the ships further out crowded in, trying to land. Mi took her quiver of arrows, and her finely made Kirike's Land bow, and she fired off her arrows one by one, sending them high into the air so they fell among the incoming ships and so were sure to kill only the enemy.

She would not pull back from the beach until all her arrows were gone.

49

The Second Year After the Fire Mountain: Autumn

After the landing that became known as Midsummer Invasion, Qirum quickly broke through the crust of defences on the south coast. Hopes that the invaders would be hampered by the marshy country and the relative scarcity of food stores proved unfounded; scouts and nestspills fleeing his advance reported that he marched north with shocking speed. The Trojan knew Northland, and was well prepared.

And soon Qirum was building what was rumoured to be a city in the very heart of Northland: 'New Troy', only days to the south of the Wall itself.

All this came in the course of another difficult summer without sunlight, another summer of hard scavenging on land and sea – a summer soon terminated by early frosts. The Trojan was feared by all, understood by nobody. Many believed he was the embodiment of the little mothers' abandonment of the world. Nobody but a few hotheads wanted to fight him.

Then Qirum offered to talk.

The emissary from New Troy was a tough-looking Hatti soldier called Erishum. In a smoky chamber deep within the Wall, he and his two companions addressed the Annids in their conclave. Milaqa was summoned to attend, with Deri and Teel.

Milaqa thought the three men from New Troy looked utterly out of place here. Fully armoured, bristling with weapons, heavily muscled, they were like lions among young deer. Yet

Raka faced the men bravely, though she was dwarfed by them, and spoke well and clearly.

Teel murmured, 'An embassy from a king! The newest king in the whole world, I imagine.'

Deri was disgusted. 'Just another brute from a pack of brutes – but a tough one.'

'Yet he appears to have come here offering peace between us.'

'Peace, brother! There can no more be peace between us and the cattle-folk than between fire and water.'

'But he is not talking of peace,' Milaqa murmured. 'Maybe my Trojan is better than yours, uncle . . .' The priest who was translating Erishum's Trojan and Raka's Etxelur tongue spoke clearly enough for all to hear. 'I think the word the priest gave as "peace" was not quite that. Not "treaty" either.'

Teel eyed her. 'You spent more time than any of us with Qirum; you should know what he means to say if anybody does. Then what is the man offering?'

'The word is more like "challenge".'

The Annids who surrounded Raka didn't really know what the warriors wanted. None of them understood a warrior-prince like Qirum, Milaqa realised. But any opportunity to avoid further bloodshed should be taken.

An agreement was reached. A party would be sent to New Troy to hear Qirum out. And as Raka pondered who would travel, Teel wormed his way forward and whispered urgently in her ear, pointing back at Deri and Milaqa.

It was quickly decided that the elder Annid Noli, representing Raka, would lead just three people back to New Troy, with Qirum's warriors, drawn from the group who had earlier travelled to Hattusa: Teel himself, Deri who since his defiant fighting on the day of the Midsummer Invasion had proven himself a symbol of Northland's robust defiance – and Milaqa. Milaqa who had been able to translate Erishum's phrasing more accurately than Raka's own translator. Milaqa who, as everybody seemed to have heard by now, knew Qirum himself more closely than anyone in Northland. She wasn't given the chance to refuse.

As the meeting broke up Milaqa felt a swirl of emotions. She was still just eighteen years old. Here she was about to walk into the very heart of an epochal conflict. And once again she would be dealing with Qirum, the most exciting, terrifying, disturbing element in her life.

Mostly she was resentful. 'You're using me,' she accused Teel. 'Again. Because you think I have a connection to Qirum.'

'Well, you do.' He grinned at her anger. 'You always did. *And* you helped him escape in Hattusa. I could say this is all your fault.'

She flared. 'I'll never apologise for saving a life. Kilushepa plotted to have him killed – his reputation destroyed – it was all lies, and you know it.'

'Fine. But what did you *think* would follow?' He laid a hand on her shoulder. 'Oh, it's not your fault, little Crow. You're right, an impulse to save a friend can never be wrong, whatever that friend chooses to do with the life you give him back. And, yes, I'm using you. I have no choice. In such times one must use every available resource. But I haven't forgotten I'm your uncle. I know I'm supposed to protect you, not lead you into danger. Forgive me.'

'Forgive you for what?'

'For the next time I do it. You should get ready; Erishum wants to leave tomorrow.'

Milaqa went straight to the Scambles and got comprehensively drunk.

50

The party would walk to New Troy, Noli ordained. Traditionally Northland folk did not ride – horses were beasts of the cattle-folk – though many had started to learn since acquiring horses from New Troy, or the Hatti. So it would be now.

As the four of them gathered before the Wall, Noli, Teel, Deri, Milaqa, in stout walking boots with light packs on their backs, Erishum laughed at their stubbornness. But he sent his two warriors ahead on horseback, taking his own mount with them, while he walked with the Northlanders. He would be one man, alone among four. Milaqa imagined the minds of both Deri and Erishum turning back to the bloody day of the Midsummer Invasion. But with Noli sternly watching both men as if they were wilful children, no words were spoken, and their swords stayed sheathed.

New Troy was two days' ride south of the Wall. The journey on foot, down the ancient Etxelur Way, would probably take four or five days. Erishum claimed that Qirum, King of New Troy, had purposely planted his city no closer to the Wall as evidence of good intentions, Erishum said, a peaceful gesture. If he was ever minded to do it, it would take more than a day for him to march on Etxelur, by which time the Wall folk would have plenty of warning. He had deliberately left a thick barrier of space and time between them, hoping for peace, said Erishum.

Noli merely grunted. 'If he were so eager for peace, the Trojan would not have come to our country at all.'

To begin with the walk south was easy, even pleasant, if

Milaqa didn't pay too much attention to the company she was keeping. It was close to the autumn equinox now, and though there had been precocious frosts the weather was fine, a watery sun for once showing through the usual high cloud. For all she liked to bury herself in smoky Scambles taverns deep within the carcass of the Wall, Milaqa was enough of a Northlander to feel her spirit expanding as they crossed the tremendous flat expanse of the country, the green land crossed by the dead-straight lines of tracks and dykes, the communities like knots in a weave. But the poor summer had left its mark in marshland choked with dead reeds, trees already shedding stunted leaves, a land that was strangely quiet in the absence of many familiar birds. The fungi were flourishing this cold autumn, especially colonising the dead tree trunks, from little bright white dots to huge powdery puffballs, and the most common sort, bright red caps flecked with white. Deri, only half-joking, urged Erishum to sample these Northland fruits. The Hatti was wary enough to refuse the poisonous gifts.

Erishum, in fact, barely noticed the country at all. Milaqa knew that to the Hatti and the Trojans and Greeks this landscape was unbuilt, unmade, unfarmed, an un-world. To them, Northland was worse than incomprehensible. It was invisible.

They spoke little during the walk. And Milaqa had too much time to think about the Trojan.

Qirum! He had long been the most vivid character in Milaqa's own life. Now, three months after his Midsummer Invasion and his planting of a city in the very heart of Northland, he was by far the most vivid personality in the country, perhaps the whole world. But to Milaqa he was not Qirum the warrior, Qirum the ruler – he was not King Qirum. To her he was Qirum the man, savage, magnificent, murderous, laughing, and when she thought of him she felt hot inside, as if her heart was melting like a bit of Zidanza's iron in the forge, ready to be hammered into some new shape.

Did she love him? Did she lust for him? She could not tell. You might as well lust after the sun. She had always sensed that if she got too close to him she would be burned up. Yet he shone so much more brightly than other men! Maybe that was why, at the comparatively elderly age of eighteen, though she was no virgin and had had a string of brief, furtive relationships, most of them forged and finished in the Scambles, she was still effectively alone, still had no children – unlike cousin Hadhe, say, with her new husband and growing children, and pregnant again too. Qirum was distorting Milaqa's life with his powerful enigmatic fascination, just as he was distorting everything about the way life was lived in Northland. But his actions had already caused people to die – including a member of her own family, Nago. And now Milaqa had to deal with him again.

After a couple of days they started to see evidence of Qirum's presence. The country looked abandoned. The ancient track ran through empty settlements, past broken houses and cold hearths, empty fish racks, eel traps left unset. The managed country itself showed signs of a lack of maintenance, reeds clogging weirs, dykes choked by weeds. In one settlement they disturbed deer grazing on wild flowers that carpeted a hearth-space evidently untrodden by human feet for months.

'This can't go on,' Noli muttered. 'Leave it too long and things will start to break down, and once that starts it will be difficult to recover. Northland needs constant tending.'

A half-day further on they came to a wall. It was just a low rampart crudely dug out of the ground, backed up by the ditch from which the dirt had been taken. But it cut right across the venerable Northland track.

Noli paced before the barrier, fuming at this latest insult to her land's tradition. Speaking through Milaqa she challenged Erishum. 'I suppose this land is now "owned" by Qirum.'

Erishum grinned easily. 'Oh, no. This is one of the estates the King has granted to the Lord Protis. We've yet to come to the King's own lands.'

He led them west, following a rough track along the line of the rampart. Beyond the rampart, looking south, Milaqa glimpsed horses, cattle, sheep: farmers' livestock brought to

Northland. They soon came to a gate, and a track that led south into the estate, running off to the flat horizon. Like the rampart itself, the track had nothing to do with the older layout of Northland. Two warriors waited by the gate, huddled in cloaks against the cold, a small fire burning before a crude shelter of poles and deerskin. They were wary as the party approached, but relaxed when they recognised Erishum. The Hatti spoke to them softly in an Anatolian language Milaqa did not recognise. In response, one of them took to his horse and galloped off south.

'We can wait here in the warm,' Erishum said, indicating the shelter, the fire. 'Qirum will send a chariot—'

'We will walk,' Noli said through Milaqa.

Erishum shrugged. He said something in his own tongue to the remaining soldier, who looked Noli up and down and laughed.

The party walked on through the scruffy gate, and Milaqa felt an odd shiver that she had suddenly walked into a land where, perhaps, the will of the little mothers of sky, sea and land no longer held sway. They came to more ramparts and low walls, some little more than scratches in the ground. These were not defensive but markers, field boundaries. People were working with spades and picks, and oxen dragged ards to turn the soil. In some places, crops were already growing.

'Farmers in Northland,' Teel said. 'We're seeing history, Milaqa. And all because of Qirum, the waif from the ruins of Troy – a king!'

'A king,' Deri said drily, 'who approaches even as you speak, brother.'

Milaqa turned to see, her heart pounding. Noli stood firm and tall, an Annid of Etxelur, her travelling cloak drawn around her, her face expressionless.

The party came along the rough track through the farmland, a handful of men riding horses, an empty chariot, a few troopers jogging alongside. Qirum jumped extravagantly from his horse before it had even pulled up. His warriors, in the garb of Hatti soldiers, watched the Northlanders more warily.

Qirum made straight for Noli and bowed deeply. 'Annid! I was happy when the runner brought news of your coming. You honour me by accepting my invitation.' He spoke in the Etxelur tongue, better than he had been able to manage last time Milaqa had seen him, though it was still heavily accented. He moved among the group. He nodded to Teel and Deri, stiffly. Deri just glared back. The Trojan clapped Erishum on the shoulder, a gesture of easy friendship.

Then he stood before Milaqa. 'We meet again,' he said in his own tongue.

'The mothers draw us together.'

'Who? Oh, those goddesses of yours? I think they have very little to do with any of *this*.' He indicated the wide farmland. 'You grow more beautiful.'

'Liar.'

He laughed out loud. 'You speak this way to a king? Well. You are evidently still a truth-teller, Milaqa. I remember that about you above all – that and the fact that you once saved my life. And what of me – am I unchanged?'

She considered him. He was dressed simply, at first glance, in a tunic and kilt of some white, woven cloth. His head was bare and he was clean-shaven, but his hair was worn longer than she remembered, and it was plaited, a little like a Hatti queue. But that tunic cloth looked very fine quality, with gold thread sewn into the hem. Over the tunic he wore a single piece of armour, his familiar chestplate of shining bronze, and in the hilt of the sword in its scabbard she saw a jewel gleam. She could smell the oils on his hair and skin.

'Why,' she said, 'I think you're wearing kohl around your eyes.'

He laughed again. 'You have to put on a show. But it makes me value those who knew me before, Milaqa – like you. For who else would have the courage to tell me the truth? And I need that, you know. I always will. Come.' He took her arm, and led her and the rest of the party back to the horses and the chariot. The chariot was a big machine with six-spoked wheels, a Hatti design. 'Speak for me, Milaqa. Annid Noli, please ride with me. I will drive the chariot myself.'

'Tell him I prefer to walk on the honest earth.'

Teel stepped up to Noli urgently. 'He does you a great honour, to come out to meet you like this. Remember, in his eyes, he is a king. We are here to negotiate – to blend our spirits with his. We must respect his gesture. I urge you, Annid . . .'

As Noli hesitated, Milaqa said in the Trojan tongue, 'The Annid is honoured and is delighted to accept.'

Qirum held out his hand to Noli, and the Annid had no choice. She stepped forward stiffly, and let Qirum help her up onto the platform of the chariot. Qirum winked broadly at Milaqa. Deri and Teel, looking even more uncomfortable, were loaded onto horses behind their Trojan riders' backs.

The little party rattled off to the south, following a rutted track.

'Look around.' Qirum waved at the fields, the crops that grew around abandoned Northlander flood mounds. 'Only months since we first set foot here. Already this empty, barren land is bearing fruit.'

'Stop being so provocative,' said Milaqa. 'The land was neither empty nor barren before you came. And slow down. I think the Annid might throw up.'

Qirum laughed. But he dragged at the stallions' harness until the chariot slowed a little. 'But still, see how much we've done. We have brought wheat and barley, as well as sheep and goats and cattle. The crops are not native to this land, and the colder air, the heavier soils, inhibit their growth. But we have been joined by others from the Continent, from Gaira and beyond, who have brought the crops they grow there. Lentils. Peas. Beans. Flax. Poppies. Even the poorer soils can be made to bear a crop, millet or rye if you handle them right . . .'

'Farmers from Gaira, here?'

'Most of those you will see are booty people, brought over

after we landed. I don't know where half of them came from originally. Probably they don't either by now! But as news of my new kingdom has spread through the Continent, people have flocked here of their own accord – strong, ambitious people eager to carve their names in the blank face of this empty country. You should thank me. These nestspills from the sunless summers might have come here anyway. At least by coming to me they have a choice other than raiding.

'*And there are Northlanders here*, Milaqa. Your own people, able to see at last what madness it is to live the way you do. Look around; you will probably recognise some of our old drinking partners from those long nights in the Scambles taverns!'

For all his boasting, it did not take long before they approached the centre of his new realm. Another, stouter wall surrounded tightly packed fields, and a mound rose up over the flat horizon, an old flood mound now crested by a ring of stone wall. Milaqa recognised the plan of the place. The mound was now Qirum's citadel, the heart of his new walled town, like the Pergamos at the heart of long-ruined Troy, like the citadel of the Hatti kings at Hattusa.

In the centre of Northland, this was a city. This was New Troy.

51

The outer wall was earth topped with heaped stones, fronted by a ditch with sharpened stakes stuck in the ground. The only crossings were wooden bridges over the ditch, leading to gates manned by more soldiers.

Once they were within the wall they passed people working the fields, while others looked on from houses, some substantial with turf walls and thatch roofs, others just lean-tos. They all looked exhausted. And all stepped aside when the King passed.

Qirum, evidently proud of his city, boasted of its features. 'Now we are on my own estate. You see, within the ring of this outer wall, I am creating factories to make weapons to fight war, and precious goods to buy peace. The other estates are mostly given over to farming. Each of my *basileis*, my senior generals, Protis and the Spider, has been granted extensive estates, as have some of the senior men under them. I have borrowed many ideas from Protis, who is from Sparta. All the powerful Spartans own land, you know, and the people who work on it. But in return all male Spartans are expected to serve in the army. They have assemblies where the citizen-warriors can make their views known to the King. And the King organises the education of the boys centrally, so they are all raised as warriors, as citizens. It is a healthy and productive system.'

Milaqa said, 'So you are surrounding yourself with other powerful men, many of whom are no doubt every bit as ambitious and energetic as you. Isn't that dangerous?'

He winked at her again. 'I make sure to keep a healthy rivalry bubbling. Let them simmer with resentment. Let them fight each other! That way no one of them can gather the strength to challenge me.'

They came to the inner stone wall around the citadel, where they clambered down from the chariot and the horses. More guards, heavily armoured and wearing plumed boar-tusk helmets, came out to meet Qirum.

Noli stepped up to the wall itself and stroked its surface. It was two or three times her height, and roughly finished. 'This is facing stone from the Wall,' she said. '*Our* Wall. There have been raids – I never understood why they needed such stone. Now I know. And for this folly they risk compromising the integrity of the Wall itself, which keeps the sea from overwhelming us all.' She turned to Teel. 'Are we among the mad, Annid?'

'Have patience,' Teel counselled.

The soldiers opened a tall wooden gate, and Qirum led the party into the citadel. Paved steps cut into the mound led up to the ornate door of the King's house. This was a square construction with a flat roof, of the kind Milaqa recognised from her travels in the east, but it was much cruder than those ancient palaces, a wooden frame clad with stone, and roofed over by long timbers and a thatch of river reeds. Servants or slaves, many of them women younger than Milaqa, mostly barefoot, came running out. Bearing towels, jugs of hot water, trays of fruit, they fawned around Qirum and his guests. None of the servants would look Milaqa in the eye. She wondered how many of them were Northlanders.

Qirum led them into the single large room that dominated the house. There were rugs and mats thrown over the floor, and a clutter of couches, cushions and low tables. Guards stood in the corners with hands on scabbarded swords, watching the newcomers. Cut into one wall was a kind of shrine, shelves with little statuettes of gods; priests intoned steadily, their backs to the visitors. Qirum crossed the room to speak to the priests.

The Northlanders stood together in the middle of the room, uncertain, ill at ease.

Milaqa wandered over to the single south-facing window that

looked out over the rest of the citadel. Standing by the window, breathing air laden with smoke and the stink of cattle dung, she saw this place through the eyes of Qirum, saw it as it might become. This prospect would one day look out on a palace complex of workshops, kitchens and granaries, and beyond a crowded city bustling with people. But for now the new fields and farms were no more than a scratch on the ancient ground of Northland, and in the undeveloped lands beyond she saw water spreading from clogged weirs, a field flooded by a collapsed dyke.

Qirum returned to the Northlanders. 'I apologise for keeping you. I have always believed in keeping the gods happy first and foremost.'

Noli asked, 'To whom do your priests pray?'

'To the Storm God who sends us to war – he is represented by the bull. And to the god we Trojans know as Iyarri, and the Greeks call Apollo. In one of his aspects, Smintheus, he is the god of plagues, and of mice.'

'You pray to be saved from plagues?'

'We have had a number of problems during our first summer in this country. A number of deaths. But thankfully now—'

'I can see why.' Noli pointed grandly out of the window. 'You let the weirs clog, the dykes crumble. Because of your brutish ignorance the land is returning to the marsh from which my ancestors saved it, and from such marshes rise the diseases that deservedly afflict you. You can tell that traitor Bren, if he is in this pile somewhere, that I hope the plagues carry him off too, if they haven't already.'

'I will take your views into consideration,' he said with dry humour. 'In the meantime you are my guests—'

'I intend to spend as little time here as I can, Trojan,' Noli snapped. 'Here I am, here we are, as you requested. Let us hear whatever it is you have to say.'

Milaqa saw anger behind Qirum's facade of good humour. Milaqa suspected he wanted to lavish hospitality on them, to put on a show – to demonstrate he was a king. Noli wasn't playing the game. Qirum said carefully, 'Despite your curtness, madam, I guarantee your safety here. And I promise you safe passage back to Etxelur, bearing news of this meeting. I hope you appreciate that much.'

'We do,' Deri said gruffly.

'Then let's get on, if you're in such a rush.' He turned to Erishum. 'Bring the tablets.'

The man left the room, and in a moment returned with two clay tablets, each small enough to hold in the hand. Erishum handed them to Noli, who glanced over them and passed them in turn to Milaqa. 'Can you read these?'

The tablets were marked with the angular writing used by the Hatti and their allies and satellites. 'With time—'

'Let me save you the effort, Milaqa,' Qirum said evenly. 'This is our custom. In times gone by a war could be settled by sending out a single champion from one side to challenge a man from the other. You would try to resolve it that way, you see, before committing men in their hundreds to die. Well – perhaps it will still come to that. But in these more civilised times we go one step further, and first send out words to be our champions.'

The talk of war chilled the room. But Noli kept her composure. 'Words? These little blocks of clay?'

'The block in your left hand, Milaqa, is a tablet of peace. The one in your right, a tablet of war.'

'Peace? On what terms?'

'There will be no more Northland,' Qirum said simply. 'Well, this is already true. All of Northland is now the Kingdom of New Troy – my kingdom. Mine to use as I please. In fact I have already parcelled up much of it; I will show you the maps, if you like. All that remains is to mark the boundaries. But you of Etxelur can live in peace. Your Annid of Annids will serve as one of my *basileis* if she likes, but I, and my heirs, will remain the overking. You can even keep your Wall; you can live as you like, in the strip of land bordering it. After all there are few enough of you. The tribute I will exact will be modest. Food, wealth, a levy of soldiers—'

314

'A tribute that will pay for what, exactly?'

'For protection,' he said smoothly.

Noli smiled thinly. 'Let me be clear. Perhaps you should translate for me, Milaqa, to be sure he understands. This is what you call a settlement. This is our reward for *peace*.'

'It is.'

'And you see it as just? Very well. And the terms of your tablet of war—'

'When your resistance is crushed, you, your children, and your grandchildren unto eternity, will work on the farms of my estate. The Spartans have this system. They call the owned ones helots.' He said this as if imparting an interesting fact, rather than making brutal threats. Not for the first time Milaqa wondered how much she really understood this man.

Noli was expressionless. 'And what of the canals, the dykes – what of the Wall? What will become of the works of Northland?'

He laughed. 'Oh, I care nothing for your Wall! Let it fall or stand, I don't care. No, wait – I always rather liked those big stone heads that adorn it. What was the name of your Jaguar-girl sculptor, Milaqa? Perhaps I will have her chip off the old faces and replace them with my own handsome smile – looking down on Northland, for ever!'

Noli seemed to consider. Then she took back the tablets from Milaqa and raised them both, as if she was going to smash them to the floor.

'Annid – wait.' Teel took her arm, and guided her a few paces away. Deri joined them, and Milaqa. They spoke softly, but Milaqa was sure that there were ears to hear every word. Teel said, 'We must consider his offer.'

'What offer? To be a vassal or a slave?'

'You see how strong he is already. At least we can buy time, find ways to deal with this threat—'

'No,' Deri said sternly. 'This place, this "kingdom" of warriors and farmers, is like a growth in the body that kills you if you don't cut it out.'

315

'Sometimes such a thing will kill you *because* you cut it out,' Teel replied.

Noli shook her head. 'In another generation it will be impossible to shift them, and all will be lost. You heard how he spoke of the Wall. This fool understands nothing of how Northland is maintained, how we have preserved it in the hundreds of generations since the days of Ana and Prokyid. This is a day that has long been threatened. The records of the Annids show how we have kept the cattle-folk at bay, and their warriors and weapons and war-making, through ingenuity and determination. But a final conflict was inevitable, I suppose. Has it has fallen to our generation to face that conflict? Then face it we will. We must resist this man, this monster. And if we fail – well, at least our children would not have long to suffer servitude, for soon the sea will rise up and drown all of us, warriors, slaves and all.'

'All right,' Teel said hastily, hushing her. 'Save the speeches for the Water Council. But do we have to *tell* him we will resist? As I said, if we can only buy some time—'

'By lying?' Noli looked at him with utter contempt. Teel rolled his eyes.

Qirum faced them, hands on hips, growing impatient. 'Well?'

Noli looked down on him, stern, rather magnificent, Milaqa thought. She quietly handed the tablets back to him. 'We reject your terms, Trojan. We will not rest until we have driven you from this land, and burned down this palace of shit you have built. Is that reply clear enough for you?'

Qirum was ominously still. For all his promises of safe conduct Milaqa felt their peril building with each heartbeat. At length he said, 'I bring civilisation to this place. Civilisation, to replace your antique savagery. Do you think I grab power for its own sake? And your tone – do you Annids imagine you are superior to the cultures I represent? You may have no armies, but do you not control the water that feeds this land? Is it not just as the way the kings of Egypt and Hattusa control their great irrigation

316

networks, and so control the people? Are we not images of each other?' He was smouldering now. 'Do you imagine you are superior to me, woman? Do you imagine you are *better*?' And Milaqa knew the deepest levels of his personality were being exposed, the shameful memory of his boyhood.

'This conversation serves no purpose.' Noli turned on her heel and stalked from the room.

Qirum, furious now, lunged after her. But Milaqa grabbed his arm, despite the glares she got from Erishum and the guards. 'Don't, Qirum. She's going to have to convince the Annids to fight you. If you send back her head in a basket you'll make the argument for her.' She tried not to flinch from the anger that burned in his eyes.

Then he calmed, apparently through sheer effort of will. 'You're right. Of course. You always were a wise one, as well as a truth-teller. I must be patient. After all, the next time I meet that woman she will be dancing on the end of my cock.'

She pulled away from him, repelled. 'Is this why we must fight, Qirum? Because yet another woman has wronged you?'

He looked her full in the face, and she felt that strange, liquid, hot-metal sensation inside. 'Milaqa – come to me. Fight by my side.'

'You ask me such a thing, at a moment like this? Why?'

'Because we must stand together, the likes of you and me. We who are outside. We who have no place. We have more in common with each other than with those who' – he waved a hand at the others – 'weigh us down.'

'You'd have me fight my people, my family?'

He smiled. 'I listened to you complain about them long enough in the Wall taverns.'

'Perhaps. But I could not betray them.'

'No.' He sighed. 'I suppose I would expect nothing less. Ah, Milaqa – even though the world has separated us, I pledge that I will never harm you.'

Teel plucked at her sleeve. 'We must go. I think Noli is out of the building already. It would not do to become separated.'

Milaqa let herself be led away. Qirum stood alone, briefly, in this great room, in his palace of wood and mud and stone. He smiled at her, then turned away.

52

The Second Year After the Fire Mountain: Late Autumn

Mi came running into the hearthspace of My Sun, her big
Kirike's Land bow slung over her shoulder. She was breathing
hard, sweating despite the chill of the day. 'They are coming,'
she said. 'The Trojans! They are coming!'

Hadhe and Vala were sitting with the other women at the
open-air fire in the hearthspace. They were working on the
fruits of the autumn forests: acorns from the oaks being readied
for the winter storage pit, and leaves, bark, flowers from the
horse chestnuts, all of which could be used in cooking and in
medicine.

For a heartbeat nobody moved. Somehow Hadhe couldn't
hear what Mi was saying, couldn't take it in. Here was her
village, her home, the neat houses around the central hearth-
place, the big communal house standing proud on its flood
mound, the hopeful symbols carved by Caxa into the high
hillside that had become so popular that everybody called this
place 'My Sun' now, rather than its old name of Sunflower.
Even the bare earth of the new defensive rampart they had had
to build did not spoil the beauty of the prospect. She took a deep
breath, of air that was tinged with the smoke of the quietly
crackling fire, and with a deeper, burning scent of the turning
leaves. And the child inside her, five months into its term,
turned in its contented sleep.

She looked at Mi, this urgent fourteen-year-old with her bad
news. It had been five months since the Trojans had landed,

319

three since Noli's showdown with Qirum. The summer was long gone, the season when the soldiers liked to fight. They were safe, for this year at least. Weren't they?

'I saw purple hairstreaks today,' she said.

'What?' Mi snapped. 'What?'

'Near the oaks, when we were gathering the acorns. What pretty butterflies they are. The sun was shining right through their wings. It's been a funny year for butterflies and moths, but—'

'Butterflies? Didn't you hear what I said?'

Vala got up and put an arm around her daughter's shoulder. 'Mi? Are you sure?'

Mi pointed to the south, in the direction of New Troy. 'I saw their fires, mother. Smoke. I crept closer.'

'That was foolish—'

'I took care!' Mi snapped, defiant. 'They would not see me! But I saw them. Men. Horses. Chariots. Weapons everywhere.'

'They were hunting,' Hadhe said. 'That is what they do. They eat the bread from their farms, but they hunt for sport.'

'These were too many for hunting. There were a hundred men – maybe more. I counted! And they had breastplates, plumes in their helmets, shields. I have seen this before. I have watched them train. It is a *phalanx*.' Another Greek word that had entered the Northlanders' vocabulary since the coming of King Qirum. 'They are marching. They will be here tomorrow at the latest.'

Hadhe might be hesitating, but the alarm was spreading. The circle at the fire was breaking up, and the men emerged from the houses. One woman was calling for her children. Caxa came out of the shade of a house. Hadhe saw that the slender Jaguar girl had been sketching designs on a clay tablet.

'What's going on?' Hesh came walking over from the house, pulling a rope belt around his tunic. Hadhe's second husband was a heavy-looking man with an odd little ring of beard around his mouth. His first wife had died in childbirth, and he had no children of his own. He leaned over Hadhe and hugged his wife,

320

his breath rich with stale Trojan beer. 'You woke me up,' he said, grinning at Mi. 'All I could hear was your voice.' He flapped his fingers like a duck's beak. 'Quack, quack.'

Mi was furious. Hadhe recalled she had already fought against the Midsummer Invasion, had already killed Trojans. She had a right to be furious, Hadhe supposed. 'You're a fool,' Mi snapped at Hesh. 'If my father was here—'

'But he's not,' Vala said sternly. 'And as Hadhe's husband he is your uncle, girl. Show some respect.'

'Respect?' Mi stamped her foot in frustration. 'Why won't any of you listen to me?'

Hadhe, still sitting, said, 'I believe you saw what you say, Mi. But – well, we must be sure. Maybe it's just another show of force.' And there had been plenty of those, including spectacular chariot drives along the wide straight avenues of Northland. All meant to intimidate. 'And besides, we should be safe.' The new defensive rampart that circled the community's central hearth-place was a bank of earth taller than the tallest warrior, and out of sight beyond it was the ditch from which the earth for the bank had been dug, implanted with broken spears, arrowheads and thorns laced with various exotic poisons. All this had been set up at Raka's order. 'None of us wanted to build such a thing. You know I argued against it as a waste of effort.'

Vala knelt by Hadhe and took her hand. 'Listen, Hadhe. I heard the fire mountain's shout, but did not believe its warnings. Just as we did not believe Qirum would raise an army, but he did. We did not believe he would land in Northland, but he did. Now we don't want to believe he will start a war. And yet—'

'And yet his soldiers are coming,' Mi insisted.

And Hadhe was sitting here as if trying to make it all go away. She pushed herself to her feet, laying her hand on her belly. I'm sorry, she told the child within. Maybe I have been lost in your dreams of the womb. She faced Mi. 'You say a hundred. How long would it take them to get here?'

'Less than a day.'

'We cannot fight a hundred,' Hesh muttered.

'But we must,' Mi insisted, young, earnest, defiant.

He nodded. 'Yes. I will gather the men and older boys.' Of whom there were about forty in the settlement. 'We should check the rampart, man it. Burn the bridges over the ditch. Ready our bows and spears . . .' These were all actions they had planned under the tutelage of the Hatti warriors Raka had brought, actions they had never really imagined would need to be taken.

'Use the women too, and the older girls,' Vala snapped. 'I can throw a spear. Remember what that Hatti corporal said. The Trojans will need more attackers than defenders, two to one, three to one. The more of us we can muster the better chance we will have.'

Hadhe glanced around, trying to think, to contribute. What else? 'What about the children? The infants should be taken to the flood mound, with their mothers. If the Trojans do break through the rampart, at least we can fall back there and make a stand. As for the older children, Mi—'

Mi stood with Hesh. 'I'll fight.'

'Oh, no, you won't,' Vala snapped.

Mi flared, 'Mother, I'm old enough to choose.'

Vala held her shoulders. 'Oh, child, but you're not old enough to die!'

Hadhe stepped forward. 'Mi – listen. We need someone to evacuate the older children. Those old enough to walk, not old enough to fight. Your brother Puli, he's only four. And my kids, Keli, Blane . . . There are plenty of others. Round them up and get them out of here before the Trojans come – if they come. Take them to the Wall, where they will be safe. Please, Mi. Find a couple of others to help you.'

'They won't leave their mothers.'

Hadhe squeezed her arm. 'That's why it must be you. Tell them it's a treat, a hunt for eels or grass snakes. They'll believe you. Go.' She pushed her away, gently. 'Take blankets, water flasks, fire-making gear, mashed food for the little ones. Oh, and

322

take Caxa. I think the Annids would want her to be kept safe. She can help with the children. And, Mi. This is most important.'

'Yes?'

'When you get to the Wall, tell them what's happening here. Tell them we need help.'

Vala hugged Mi. 'Maybe you'll be back here in a few days and the sun will be shining and everybody will be fine, and nothing will have happened.'

'I'll have been wrong,' Mi pointed out. 'But I could live with that.'

'Good girl,' Vala said. 'Go now. Go!' She turned away quickly, and Hadhe saw how she was fighting back a sudden tear.

As Mi ran off to find the children, the adults huddled, talking urgently. Through his wooden teeth the priest began muttering prayers to the little mothers, while checking that his bronze knife was in its sheath at his waist.

The Trojans had marched through the night, behind their king.

The hundred or so warriors were mostly Anatolian, equipped in the Hatti fashion, and some even sported thick Hatti queues. But in the months since the landing Protis the Spartan had trained them up as infantry in the disciplined Greek style. So they marched as quietly as a hundred such men could be expected to, though there were always muffled coughs, muttering voices, the creak of leather shields and the clank of bronze weapons and armour. Further back came the chariots, and the neighing of horses carried in the moist night air. The soldiers had grumbled about being woken for the march, but soldiers always grumbled, and the promise of the first real action since the landing was enough to stir most of them. And there would be women, and boys for those who preferred that kind of thing. The women of Northland had proven to be big healthy animals, a much better ride than the dead-eyed forced whores of the booty people brought over from the Continent, or the dusty, worn-out, slack-uddered farmers' wives you would find on a raid in Anatolia or Greece. They were ready. Qirum was sure of it.

And at last, only a little before the dawn, Qirum stood before a Northland community, a king with his army at his back, and Protis and the Spider at his side, his *basileis*. They were here in force, for Qirum was determined to make this first serious assault a statement of intent.

Not that the prize they had come so far to take looked like much in the blue-grey dawn light. Just a rough earth rampart and ditch around a huddle of houses, with that one big dwelling up on its mound. But you could only fight what the enemy put in front of you; you could only take what he had to lose.

First they had to cross that ditch. Qirum turned and murmured a command to Erishum. The sergeant gathered half a dozen engineers. They moved forward, dragging logs and sections of a wooden platform.

In response a gate in the rampart opened, and men came filing out. It was too dark to see clearly, but Qirum thought there could be no more than fifty of them. All seemed armed, though, and some were armoured, in leather or bronze. They lined up on the far side of the ditch, and shouted threats and launched the odd arrow at the engineers. But the Trojans were already in the ditch; they raised their shields and kept working. Soon the bridge would be ready.

'So here we are,' murmured Protis, standing by Qirum. He had learned to speak a coarsely accented Trojan, as an honour to his new king. But his voice was as expressionless as his eyes, even as they were about to give battle. The man made Qirum shudder. 'We have no element of surprise. We came walking in by the most obvious route, straight up the road from the south that runs through the heart of this country. We could split our forces and come in from the back, the sides . . .'

'Or the chariots,' murmured the Spider. 'Get them across that ditch and let them run at the defences.'

Qirum snorted. 'You Hatti love your chariots. Look at this place. We don't need chariots, or subtlety of tactics. Do you really think we need more than a frontal assault to finish off this lot?'

Erishum hurried back and reported that the engineers had completed their work.

'No more talk.' Qirum pulled his sword from its scabbard with a ringing sound, and he raised his voice so the men could hear. 'Let's get this done. Are you ready to live like men, or die like heroes?' In response Erishum slammed the shaft of his spear against his leather shield, over and over. Soon all the men were banging their shields, stamping their feet, yelling. Qirum raised his sword. 'Onwards!' And he marched forward, closely flanked by the Spider and Protis, with the best of their men following. The heroes always led the charge.

Immediately there was a whoosh and clatter, and the blue-grey sky above the settlement darkened. Arrows and stones, hurled from within the settlement. The defenders weren't entirely unprepared, then. Good – it would make for a better fight, and the men needed it.

Protis roared, 'Shields!' He raised his own shield, as did Qirum, as they marched. The order was repeated up and down the line, but Protis's bellow had been so loud there was scarcely a need; like most successful commanders he had lungs like an iron smelter's leather bellows.

The arrows and heavy stones clanged against the bronze face of Qirum's shield, making him stagger. But he kept advancing. And javelins were thrown from the ranks behind him; they fell on Northlander flesh, and there were screams and cries.

Now there was a roar ahead. The Northlanders outside the rampart were coming forward. Evidently they meant to meet the Trojans as they reached the bottleneck of the engineers' bridge. Better not to have let the bridge be built in the first place, Qirum thought; it showed the typical indecisiveness of the untrained, the inexperienced. No matter.

Suddenly the Northlanders were only paces away. Qirum saw their strange red hair, their faces pale with anger or fear.

The two sides closed in a hail of slingshot and arrows. At first it was just the three of them, Qirum, Protis and the Spider, side by side on the bridge's rough panels. The first man Qirum faced was tall, young, healthy-looking, with an odd little beard around his mouth. He looked astonished when Qirum thrust the tip of his own sword into his throat, almost delicately, as a surgeon would lance a wound. Here was the benefit of training, which beat the hesitancy out of a man; it was easier to die than to kill for the first time, as the man was no doubt already explaining to the little mothers, his feeble goddesses. Qirum got his boot on the man's chest and shoved him back, thus retrieving his sword, and he surged forward once more, laying into the next man, and the next. Beside him, Protis swung his sword and the Spider stabbed with his spear, flesh was broken and blood spurted. Protis especially was extraordinary in such a situation, a whirl of slashing blades.

Surrounded by roars, in a mist of blood, the three companions slew and maimed, driving on as the defenders fell back before them. Soon the three of them, just three against fifty or so, had driven a deep hole into the ranks of the defenders. Behind them, Erishum led more men over the bridge to pour into the attack, hacking, screaming, driving the foe back.

A cry went up from the defenders, in their own strange tongue. *Fall back!* At the rear, men streamed back through the rampart gate. Those at the front had to scramble backwards, fighting as they went. Erishum and the other sergeants yelled encouragement at the Trojan forces, to keep pushing, keep killing.

It didn't take long for the Trojan surge to reach the gate. There was a final brave stand by a handful of Northlanders, who held the Trojans back long enough for the gate to be slammed shut, before they died in their turn. The commanders would not allow any pause, any falling back, any break in the assault now it had begun. Protis called, 'Shields up! Bring the ladders! Come on, you lazy slugs, do I have to do it myself?'

Handfuls of men carried the stubby siege ladders forward from the little army's short train, protected from the arrows by the raised shields of others who ran alongside. Good training paying off again, Qirum thought, watching from under his shield.

The Spider turned his own shield over and pulled out an arrow with some difficulty. It had penetrated bronze plate. 'Iron,' he said, turning the arrow's head before his king's eyes. 'Good stuff too.'

'Well, we knew they had it,' Qirum said. 'From what they stole in Hattusa.'

The Spider glanced at the rough rampart. 'It will make no difference. Iron or not, these savages don't know how civilised men fight.'

'Well, they know now.'

Soon the first ladder, rough steps hacked into a halved tree trunk, was up against the wall. This time Protis was the first to charge. 'Let's get this over.' He took the ladder at a run, not using his hands, sword in one hand and shield strap in the other, relying on sheer momentum to keep from falling as he climbed. He slammed the shield into the face of a defender at the top, who fell back screaming, his face a bloody mass. Then Protis was up and over the rampart, sword swinging, and he dropped out of sight on the far side. His men followed in his wake.

All along the wall more ladders had been propped up, more Trojans were pouring over. The defenders were already falling back.

Qirum roared, 'Let me at them!' But he had to push his way through the men to get to the ladder, and clamber his way to the top.

Standing near the central hearth – there were still piles of acorns beside a half-filled pit, from the work abandoned yesterday – Vala saw the Trojans break over the rampart, and the men of My Sun falling back, only to be cut down as they fled. One man – she knew him well, a fatherly fellow of about forty called Maos – slithered screaming down a rampart wall that was already slick with bright blood. At the bottom of the wall he rolled over, and from a great gaping slash in his belly snake-like entrails spilled and dragged on the ground.

It seemed only heartbeats since the assault had started. It was not yet fully dawn. But already everything was lost.

'Mother!'

Vala whirled around. Liff, her twelve-year-old warrior, came staggering towards her, trailing his sword on the ground, his tunic front soaked with blood. Yet his sword seemed unbloodied; he probably hadn't inflicted a single wound.

The first Trojans had dropped down into the hearthplace and were running forward, yelling, swords in hand. Huge men with weapons running at her, only paces away, and nobody left to stop them.

She shoved Liff so he fell backwards into the acorn pit. He looked up, shocked. She screamed, 'Cover yourself! '

The blade, coming from over her shoulder, slashed down the right side of her face.

There was an instant of shock; she staggered. Then blood spurted, filling her right eye. On the ground she saw a lank of her hair, bloody flesh that might have been her cheek – her *ear*, on the ground. And then the pain hit her, as if a fire mountain was bursting inside her head. Bright with agony, she tried to run, staggered.

A heavy mass slammed into her legs, and she was driven face down into the dust. Her cut-open head scraped over the ground, and more pain came, brilliant, blinding. A hand grabbed her shoulder and she was rolled onto her back, in the grip of overwhelming strength. She could see the man over her, though blood was pooling in both her eyes now. She tried to scream, and a fist drove into her mouth, hard and filthy. She felt teeth crack, she tasted blood and dirt, and there was more agony, shocking, sudden. A rough hand dragged up her tunic, and her legs were pulled apart, other hands, other men. And then the man over her thrust and he was inside her, tearing at her dryness. She tried to call for her husband, for Medoc, but he was long dead, and her throat was full of blood.

53

Hiding in the communal house on the flood mound, the women and children could hear the fighting outside, the screams of the men, their husbands and brothers and sons in the battle, brief as it was. And the worse screams when the fighting was done, punctuated with laughter, as the injured were put to death.

Then the Trojans came pushing into the house. Blinking in the dark, they laughed when they discovered the women here. One girl, too young, too pretty, was immediately raped by a brute of a Trojan, there in the middle of the floor, before being returned weeping to her mother and her little brother. The rest cheered the man on. Then they searched the house for food and water, shoving cowering children aside to find it. The women were ordered to strip and their clothes were taken away. The men worked through the crowd, groping and punching, but there were no more rapes, for now.

All this before dawn had fully broken.

The day wore on, horribly slowly. More women were shoved in by the Trojans. All these were injured, all had been raped. Vala had to be carried in, swung by her hands and feet between two men. Her head was a mass of blood, the skin sheared off, her ear gone, the flesh scraped and full of grit where it looked as if she had been dragged across the ground. Part of Hadhe's extended family, Hadhe thought of Vala as an aunt. Now, her body used and broken, Hadhe could only cradle her. She did not even have water to wash away the grit.

The women and children huddled, shivering from the cold, naked, bloodied, hungry, thirsty. Nobody spoke. Hadhe longed to know what had become of her own children. She wondered if she would ever find out.

Later in the day, as the evening drew in, Hadhe heard gruff voices, a clink of metal, leather sliding, sighs of relief, and she smelled meat cooking. She imagined men loosening their armour, taking their boots off after the day's work of killing – just another day for them, the end of a unique existence for each of their victims.

The light was dying when men came to the house again. Two of them this time, more grandly dressed, heavy in bronze armour and with elaborate conical helmets. One carried a sword in his hand. Hadhe thought the other might have been Qirum himself, but his face was obscured by his armour.

The man with the sword walked among the women, inspecting them. The women, naked, their legs up to their chests, quailed back against the wooden walls. He handled them roughly, lifting faces, pulling back hair, pinching breasts. At length he selected one, a young mother called Sila, and another, Sila's younger cousin Leb – and, at last, Hadhe. He chose these three by tapping their shoulders, and beckoned them to stand. The others looked away.

Hadhe felt numb. This was unreal. Why me? Why not her, or her? She stood tall, hoping her pregnant belly would show, and put them off. But then Qirum looked at her more closely – yes, it was him – and yes, he recognised her. He said a couple of words to the other man, who shrugged, and drove Sila and Leb out of the house. Qirum himself grabbed Hadhe by her wrist.

Once outside, Hadhe wrapped her free arm around her body in the chill as Qirum dragged her down the mound. My Sun was all but unrecognisable from the home it had been just that morning. Only three houses still stood; the rest had been burned, the storage pits broken open and robbed. Even the rampart had been smashed down in a dozen places. In one corner men and boys huddled, Hadhe saw, naked too, roped together at hands and feet. And a stack of corpses had been heaped up, all stripped.

The soldiers in the hearthspace seemed oblivious to all this. They tended their feet and inspected damage to shields and armour. The ground was scuffed and littered with their armour and boots, with their turds and pools of their piss, with splashes of drying blood. Some men were wounded, with cuts and burns salved with potions, honey, grease, mashed-up roots. A surgeon with a kit of bronze tools – forceps, chisels, a saw – prepared to set a broken arm. The man was held down by his companions, a bit of wood between his teeth.

There were some Trojan dead. They had been set out respectfully near the gate through the rampart, and covered with blankets stolen from the houses. Hadhe found no joy in seeing that some Trojans, at least, had fallen today.

Sila was dragged off to one of the surviving houses, and Leb to the next, and Qirum took Hadhe to the third. A skein of geese crossed the sky. Greylags, perhaps.

Qirum pushed her inside the house. The floor was littered with furs, there was a heavy wooden couch, and a serving girl, barefoot, stood by a low table laden with food, water and wine. As it happened this had been the house of Sila's family. Qirum clapped his hands to send the girl away. He kicked off his boots, threw himself back on the couch, and considered Hadhe.

Hadhe stood in the middle of the floor. She was tempted to cover her body with her arms, but she stood tall, still hoping she might be spared because of her pregnancy.

'Speak to me,' he said, in heavily accented Etxelur-speak. 'You hear me? I know Milaqa.'

'She . . .' Hadhe hadn't said a word since the morning, and her throat was dry as dust. She tried again. 'She is my cousin.'

'You want water?' He threw over a sack.

She grabbed it and gulped it down.

'What's your name?'

'Hadhe.'

'*Haa-thee.* I saw your face before.'

'I'm Milaqa's cousin,' she repeated.

That word baffled him, but he seemed to get the idea. 'The

battle. What did you think?' He sought for the words. 'Frightening? Like wild animals, were we?' He growled and made mock-claws with his fingers. 'I want to make your Annids frightened. That way they won't fight. That way people won't have to die. They have to learn. I offered peace; they rejected it. This is what happens when you reject peace.'

'I have children,' she blurted.

He pointed at her belly. 'In there? I don't care.'

'No . . .' She saw no point in telling him other than the truth. 'Three. Three other children. Two have been taken away to the Wall . . . The third. A boy. He fought.'

He shrugged. 'If he lives, he is with the slaves. You will never see him again.'

'Only yesterday I did not believe you would come. Not like this.'

'You were wrong.'

'I even argued against preparing, defending ourselves.'

'Wrong.'

'What will happen to us?'

He shrugged. 'The men will be slaves. But we are a long way from those who buy slaves. We may have no use for them. The women will be sold as slaves too. Or, if you are not sold, you will cook, clean, spin, draw water for my soldiers. Or' – he patted the couch – 'you may keep my bed warm.'

Anger flared. She took a step forward, almost stumbled. 'You slaughter our children. Murder our husbands. And you expect us to sleep with their killers? What horror is this?'

He laughed at her. 'It is our way. All across Greece, Anatolia, Egypt, the whole of the east. Women are booty.' His face hardened. 'If you don't stay with me, I will give you to the Spider. You'll be dead by morning. With me, maybe you'll live. Your baby inside you will live.'

'Why? Why do you want me?'

'For your cousin. For Milaqa.' He lifted his tunic, revealing an erection. 'I'm being kind to you.'

She hesitated. Then she knelt beside the couch.

*

In the morning, it did not take long to organise the march back to New Troy. A few carts were laden with what loot there was to be had. The booty people, all naked, those who could walk, were roped together and hobbled, and shoved into rough columns. Those who could not make the march, including most of those used as the night's camp whores, were swiftly dispatched, and added to the pile of corpses. The pyre was then set alight and burned with a greasy stink.

Torches were applied to the surviving houses, and dirt was kicked on the big central hearth. Then the column formed up, and Protis led the march south, out of the smashed community.

But Qirum lingered, along with the Spider, and a handful of picked men. The Spider, in his days before joining Qirum, had developed a particular trick in these situations that Qirum never tired of watching.

The men stayed just out of sight of the ruined village, as the sounds of the marching column slowly receded, and waited. The sunless sky brightened slowly. From the forest, a wild pig came rooting in the ruined hearthspace, looking for scraps. Qirum noticed a strange sign in the Etxelur script, loops and lines, cut into the hillside. Idly, he considered sending a man up there to break it up. Something to be done later. He began to feel sleepy, after the hard work of yesterday.

And then the Spider grinned and pointed at the acorn pit, beside the ruined fire. Qirum saw one hand emerge, then a blond head, and a slim body. Soon a boy climbed out of the pit, bloodstained, bewildered.

For a while the watching men allowed the boy to wander around the ruined village. Nobody else came out. Then the Spider unsheathed his sword. This was his speciality – to return to devastated farms and villages and cities, to wait until those who had hidden away came stumbling out into the ruins, and then to slaughter them in turn. It was the exquisite shock on the victims' faces that seemed to thrill the Spider, the sudden horror of one who had thought he was saved.

333

But not today, Qirum suddenly decided.

'No.' He held back the Spider's arm. 'Sorry to disappoint you, man. I have a better idea. The rest of you stay back. You!' he called in Etxelur-speak.

The boy turned. He actually had a sword in a scabbard at his side. His hand went to the hilt.

'Don't dare!' Qirum roared, striding across the churned-up ground. 'And don't run!'

The boy stood stock-still, snared by the command. He took his hand from the sword.

Qirum stood over him. The boy's tunic was encrusted with blood. Piss trickled down one leg. Comically, he had crushed acorns stuck in his hair. He was no older than twelve, thirteen. Yet he looked back at a warrior-king with a trace of defiance. On impulse Qirum reached out and ruffled his hair. 'Name?'

'I am Liff. Liff, son of Medoc, son of —'

'I don't care whose spawn you are. Do you want to live, warrior Liff?'

'All men die.'

'True. But not today.' Qirum pointed. 'You go that way, north. You find the Wall. The Annids. You understand? You tell them what you saw. You tell what King Qirum did here. Yes?'

The boy just looked at him, baffled.

'Go.' He shoved the boy's shoulders with his fingertips. The boy stumbled. 'Go, go!'

The boy couldn't seem to turn his back. But at last the spell broke, and he turned and ran, heading for the great Northland track that headed north.

Qirum turned away and walked back to his men.

54

The Third Year After the Fire Mountain: Early Spring

Four months after the attack on My Sun, after a desolating winter of hunger and want, of raid and counter-raid, of a slow bleed of deaths on either side, a woman came to the Wall.

She had escaped from New Troy. Once she had been a young mother of My Sun, the first community to be attacked. She had seen her children killed, and for months had been used as a warrior's servant and whore. She had bided her time, killed a man, got away. She brought news that there was growing discontent in the Trojan camp, because the easy victories had stopped coming. The Northlanders had learned how to resist; every flood mound south of Etxelur had been turned into a citadel, a tough nut to crack.

And the woman said that Hadhe was still alive, and living in New Troy with Qirum.

Raka, acting quickly, summoned Noli, Deri, Teel, Milaqa, the party who had gone to New Troy before. Perhaps this was a chance to get through to Qirum, by sending Milaqa and others of Hadhe's family. And maybe the Trojan would be in a mood to listen this time, if his campaign of brutality wasn't working.

Milaqa sensed the tensions that lay behind this decision. Not everybody had Raka's flexibility of thought. To *talk* again, talk to the pack of rapists and murderers Qirum's men had proven themselves to be? But the longing for the killing to end drove the Annids to contemplate this course.

And, she wondered, maybe Qirum had taken Hadhe as a lure

for just this kind of approach. Was Qirum wily enough to think that way?

But this time only Deri and Milaqa would go, Raka quickly decided. Deri the warrior who had already faced the Trojans, Milaqa his drinking companion from the old days, figures Qirum knew and could understand. Their job was to get through to the Trojan before more people died – and before Kilushepa in far Hattusa, alarmed by the news of the Trojan's long-term plans against her, fulfilled her own threats to bring a stronger Hatti force to Northland and nip his ambitions in the bud. Nobody in Etxelur wanted to see more Hatti troops in Northland.

The travellers packed their kit.

Once more they began the journey of a few days to New Troy, walking steadily south down the Etxelur Way, Deri and Milaqa side by side. It was early spring, but the day was dismal and would be short, the air damp and cold. The year was still too young to show if the fire mountain's shadow would be cast over the world for a third year, but the sun was ominously invisible today.

Away from the Wall the way soon deteriorated, overgrown with weeds. Deri stumbled on an ash sapling growing out of the road surface, his heavy winter cloak flapping. Milaqa suppressed a laugh. Deri snapped, 'May the mothers curse those Trojans! Once this road was as clean and unspoiled as a baby's skin. And why? Because we spent our time fixing it, pulling up the weeds, rather than building walls to keep out Trojans.' They came to a flood, a swamp, thick with rotting matter, which the road, half submerged, crossed like a causeway. Milaqa pressed a cloth to her face. 'And this,' Deri said. '*I* did this. I led a party to block the main dyke that once drained this swamp, a straight cut down to the valley of the Brother. What heartbreaking work that was! To ruin the labour of centuries. And all to make a bog to trap the boot of a Trojan.'

Maybe it was a symptom of Milaqa's own detachment from the disaster unfolding over Northland, but she didn't feel like shedding tears over a bit of muddy ground. 'It's not ruined. It can be fixed, when we get the time. It will dry out again. In the meantime, no chariot could ever pass through here. Isn't that the idea? This is the grand strategy. Flood the land. Let the Trojans sink in the mud if they try to march, and in the meantime let the diseases that rise from the swamps pick them off one by one.'

'But this is a perversion of what Northland *is*, Milaqa. It's a place where people preserve life – not create death, like this. Ask a priest if you don't believe me. I'm with Noli; I'm worried that if this goes too far we won't be able to put it back together again. And it's not just the land. You know, back at the Wall I met a little boy, one of a family of nestspills, who got caught up in a raid. He said he found an arrow, and stuck it in the eye of the man who was raping his mother. An arrow in the eye! Even if every Trojan in Northland left tomorrow, that incident will have left a scar in the heart of that boy that will last a lifetime. That's the legacy of Qirum, the monster you have a "special bond" with, as Teel always says.'

She scowled. 'That bond is what we're relying on to keep us alive.'

'Let's hope that Qirum remembers that. And let's hope all his half-tamed killers remember it too.'

Thus, bickering, stumbling, avoiding flooded ground and traps, they continued their way south.

They stopped a night in a little community called Mother's Fingernail, after a distinctively shaped arc of sandstone that dominated its hearthspace. Deri had a friend here called Boucca, widow of an old companion from the fishing boats. The place was not far from My Sun, and had suffered from Trojan raids. Now the people lived in shacks amid the ruins of their houses, rings of burned-out stumps in the ground. But it was surviving, and the travellers were shown hospitality. That night Deri and Milaqa huddled under borrowed blankets in Boucca's lean-to, windproof and warm.

As they walked on, the next day they began to spot traces of

Trojans: the prints of heavy boots pressed into mud on the track surface, the occasional turd deposited at the side of the road, the skin and gnawed bones of a hare discarded by a hasty fire whose embers were still warm.

They spent one more night on the road, huddled together in a lean-to of branches and brush. They had brought fire-making gear, kindling, dried meat, and there was a stream nearby for water. Milaqa slept well, despite the situation. She felt safe to be with her uncle, as she had when she was a little girl.

The next day, before noon, they saw the fires of New Troy rising from the plain ahead, gathering in a pall on a windless day.

Deri said they needed to be ready to meet scouts or foraging parties. So they walked with their cloaks thrown back, their weapons visible, their hands open. Milaqa began to call out in the Trojan tongue, and in Greek and Hatti: 'We mean no harm. We come from the Wall. We were sent by the Annid of Annids. We are here to talk to your king. I am Milaqa daughter of Kuma, and your King Qirum has promised me his protection. We are from the Wall, from Etxelur. We come here in peace . . .'

A boy emerged from a copse, walking out of the trees right into their path. The three of them stood stock-still, Milaqa, Deri, the boy. He was no more than twelve. He carried a basket of mushrooms. He was skinny, his face grimy, he went barefoot, and his ragged cloak did not look sufficient to keep him warm.

Milaqa smiled and stepped forward.

Deri touched her arm. 'Careful.'

'The Trojans brought no boys here. He has red hair. This is one of ours, even if he is working for the Trojans now.' She spoke clearly in her own tongue. 'Where are you from? Was it My Sun?'

The boy dropped the basket and ran, straight down the track towards the smoke of New Troy.

Milaqa cupped her hands around her mouth. 'Tell them Milaqa has come. Milaqa, daughter of Kuma. I have come for my cousin Hadhe, who lives in the King's house. Tell King Qirum that Milaqa has come to see him!'

Deri shrugged, and they walked on.

A little later a party approached, soldiers on horseback, and a cart pulled by oxen led by another Northlander boy. The party was commanded by a stocky man in the garb of a Hatti officer: Erishum, Milaqa recognised with relief, Qirum's sergeant. Her chances of living through the day had increased markedly.

Erishum got down from his horse and peered at her. 'Just as the boy said. You are Milaqa.'

'I know,' she replied in his tongue.

'Mouthy little whore, aren't you? I'll take you to the King. But I warn you, he is in a foul mood today. As most days. Whatever you have to say, say it well. Get in the cart.'

It was a farm vehicle, or it had been, smelling of earth and dung. Two more soldiers climbed up beside them, their hands on their swords. Erishum kicked his horse's flanks, the cart jolted away, and the party followed the road to New Troy.

They were taken briskly through the outer rampart. Within, Qirum's estate seemed much changed to Milaqa since she had last seen it in the autumn. Of course the cold hand of winter lay on it now, but even so many of the newly walled-off fields looked abandoned. She saw few people – scarcely a wisp of smoke rose from the crude houses – and fewer animals, dogs, goats picking at the boggy ground. In one place she saw a gang of children, ill-clad, shivering, digging holes in the earth. They were watched over by a bored-looking Trojan who idly studied the bobbing rumps of the little girls.

As they neared the stone walls of Qirum's citadel they climbed off the cart. The town was much changed too, shabbier, meaner, but much more crowded than in the autumn, though the country outside the walls was empty. Milaqa remarked on this to Deri. He murmured, 'Perhaps they have all come here for food.' As they followed Erishum through the town Milaqa saw children peering from the doors of the rough houses, while scared-looking women cowered indoors, and babies cried. These were not homes, not families, Milaqa thought; they were parodies of families, Qirum's warriors with the bed-warmers they had taken from raids in Northland, or booty women driven in from the Continent. Some of these women must have been allowed to keep their kids, and others had babies inflicted on them by the endless rapes of their new 'husbands'.

Once inside the citadel they were taken straight to Qirum in his house with the big central room. A big fire blazed in a hearth, and a linen screen covered the window, obscuring the view over the town. The priests were here, murmuring prayers to Apollo god of fevers and disease. Qirum himself lounged on his couch, a flagon of ale on the floor beside him. He wore a loose robe of some fine fabric, not a warrior's garment, more like something you would wear to sleep. There was a sharp stink in the room, a cess-pit stench. There was no sign of Hadhe.

When he saw Milaqa and Deri, Qirum lurched to his feet. 'Milaqa! So here we are again, two rejects from humanity reunited.'

Milaqa began to murmur a translation for Deri.

But Qirum waved that way. 'Oh, get him out of here,' he snapped at Erishum. 'Feed him, bathe him, give him a whore, whatever he wants. Oh, no, better not, after all his mother's probably one of the whores. Ha! Don't harm him though. Just get him out of my sight.'

Deri glanced at Milaqa.

'Go,' she said, in her own tongue. 'I'm more at risk with you standing here silently provoking him. This is why we came, uncle.'

Reluctantly Deri nodded. He bowed sharply to Qirum, then let Erishum lead him out.

'So we're alone,' Qirum said. 'Beer?'

'Why not?'

He snapped a finger. In a heartbeat a barefoot serving girl came running with a brimming pot. Milaqa drank it gratefully. Qirum sat on his couch and patted it. She sat beside him, though at the couch's far end.

'Just like old times in the Scambles,' Qirum said. 'Save for a few gibbering priests and the guards in the corners.'

She wrinkled her nose. 'And what smells like a bucket of shit.'

'It is a bucket of shit. Taken from a dead man, his last gift to this world. Ha!' He drank his beer. 'It's all because of some poison or other your uncle and his irritating friends like to smear on their arrows. My physician is trying to work out what it is from a dead man's turds. Listen. What causes sneezing and blisters, and then vomiting and shitting, and then muscle cramps, convulsions, choking, a heart attack?'

'I'm no priest. Our priests give out the poisons.'

'My surgeon thinks it might be hellebore. Some of the symptoms are similar. They use hellebore in Gaira, I know that. Is it hellebore?'

'I really don't know.'

'Well, if it is, our antidotes don't work, or so my useless clown of a head physician tells me.'

She grinned. 'Things aren't going as you expected, are they, King Qirum?'

'No, they aren't, by the Storm God's left testicle. If it isn't the poison it's the sickness rising up from the soggy ground, and I have the priests chanting to Iyarri about that from morning to night. And then there are these wretched winter days of yours – if you can call them days at all!' He gestured at the window. 'Look – the light's going already, and I've barely woken up. A man needs the sun, as does a field of wheat. We are men from countries of light and heat – decent places to live, not like this gloomy bog of yours.'

'Then go back there.'

'And then there's the hunger. Our crops struggle to grow in these drowning fields. Some of your warriors and their Hatti scum allies have been mounting raids on the granaries. Takes a lot of courage, I'm sure, to sneak up on a grain of wheat. You know, I have people out there *foraging*. Like rooting pigs! They bring back mushrooms. Birds. Even crows, toppled from their nests! They dig up hibernating animals, dormice . . . Pah! Yet it is all we have.'

You are hungry because you do not know how to live here, Milaqa thought. Northlanders live off the land; they can easily melt away into the country for a few days. While you Trojans and the Greeks, used to your great stone cities crowded with people and loot and food, are left baffled. You cannot see the riches all around you, even at this time of year, in the rivers, the seas. And evidently those you use as slaves will not tell you.

She said sharply, 'I thought you were feeding yourselves by raiding our communities. Like your raid on My Sun.'

'Where? Oh, that was the first one, wasn't it? Ah, yes – Hadhe, your cousin. That's why you've come, isn't it?' He called to a servant, and briskly ordered her to summon Hadhe. 'What were we saying – My Sun?'

'That was easy pickings for you. And my own family suffered.'

He scowled, as if she was being unfair. 'I saved Hadhe, didn't I? And I didn't wield every sword personally.'

'Well, we've learned to fight back since then.'

He grunted. 'If you can call it fighting. You flood the ground – you cut your own roads, to stop us advancing. Sometimes when I attack a settlement, which is all but lost in the green in the first place, I find it empty! Abandoned! It is like fighting fog – like fighting the diseases that strike down my warriors. You won't stand and fight like men!'

Because we would lose if we did, Milaqa thought. That was the prevailing wisdom of the Annids and the Hatti who advised them. She leaned forward. 'This is why I am here – Deri and I – as well as for Hadhe. To make you see sense, Qirum. Your great adventure has not worked. You cannot defeat Northland, it is too big and ancient for that. Even the Wall is too big for you. And besides, we are prepared now. But nor can we defeat you, for we are too few. So this stalemate goes on, with pointless cruelty and suffering on both sides. Let us end this now.'

He laughed hollowly. 'And then what? Shall I withdraw from Northland? My *basileis* would butcher me if I tried.'

'Let's just stop the fighting. That's all the Annids want, for now.'

'Ah, but I can't, you see. There is a question of honour. And surely you know, little Milaqa, that all of this is only a step on the road to a greater goal.'

'The day when you mould an army out of Northland clay, and march on Hattusa? This is all so you can get your revenge on Kilushepa, isn't it?'

He grinned, and drank more beer. 'More or less. We are all driven by personal goals, Milaqa. What else is there in life? And my goal is to destroy that bitch, and the country that spawned her.'

Yet there was more he did not know. 'Qirum. I probably shouldn't tell you this. Your plans against Kilushepa. She knows.'

'Of course she does. She probably has spies in this very room.' He glanced at his priests, who seemed to shiver slightly, no doubt hearing every word. 'What of it?'

'She is no fool. We have had a new embassy from Hattusa. Her position there is strong once more. She does not intend to let you become a significant threat. Not significant enough to damage her, in any case.'

He sat up. 'What does that mean? Is she coming herself?'

'She is sending more troops. Soon there will be a Hatti force here strong enough to—'

'Is she coming herself? She is, isn't she? Well, well. My show-down with the bitch queen might not be as remote as I have feared.' His eyes were alight with passion; he no longer seemed drunk at all.

'I shouldn't have told you.'

'Your Annids will say you shouldn't. But you and I know you have done the right thing, Milaqa, don't we? You came here to bring forward the ending of this war. Well, I believe you have. Just not the way those dried-up old sticks on the Wall intended you to. Ha!'

'Milaqa?'

343

Hadhe stood in the doorway. Her hair was tied up, her skin looked oiled, and she wore an expensive-looking gown that did not conceal the swelling of her pregnancy, now eight months advanced.

Milaqa ran forward, and the cousins embraced. 'Your children are fine,' Milaqa said quickly. 'Keli and Blane. After My Sun, they both reached the safety of the Wall, and they live there still, with the family.'

Hadhe was trembling. Milaqa imagined having to wait so many months for such brief, vital pieces of news. 'Thank you. And Jaro—'

'There was no sign of him. He may have died in the fighting. The bodies were burned, we could not tell. And Hesh – lost too.'

She nodded. 'But Hesh lives on through his unborn child. I will mourn them later. Thank you, Milaqa.'

Qirum was pacing now. 'How touching. Say what you have to say to each other and get out. I have much thinking to do. You, guard – send for the *basileis*.'

Hadhe murmured in the Etxelur tongue, 'I haven't seen him as animated as this since winter closed in.'

'I gave him some news – I fear I have made a terrible mistake.'

Hadhe shook her head. 'Nothing we do or say is right or wrong in the presence of such men as this; all we can do is survive.' Under the expensive facial oils she looked old, Milaqa thought, old and worn out, and there was something elusive in her eyes. She was not yet eighteen years old. 'Things could have been worse for me, in My Sun, on that terrible day. I was lucky, comparatively. Your poor aunt Vala—'

'I know. They found her body in the ruins of the mound house.'

'She survived the fire mountain, but she could not survive the Trojans. *I* survived. I did not deserve to, for I had argued against defending ourselves against the Trojans. I could not believe it was true, that it could ever happen. If I had not, perhaps we would have been better prepared.'

'I have some sway over Qirum. In some ways he's so like a

child, you know. Maybe I can persuade him to let you go. Deri is here. We could get you home.'

Hadhe patted her bump. 'No. I cannot travel – not now. As I said, I am surviving here. More than that. I am trying to be a wife to Qirum. A companion at least. I think he needs that.'

That baffled Milaqa. It didn't sound like Hadhe at all. What was going on in her mind?

But there was no time to discuss it further, for the generals were arriving for their council, and Qirum was impatient for them to be gone. After a hasty goodbye to Hadhe, Milaqa was hurried out of the palace.

It was only later, when Erishum and his guards had escorted Deri and Milaqa far from New Troy and set them walking north again, that Milaqa discovered that the bronze dagger she kept at her waist had gone.

Qirum's response to Milaqa's mission came a month later. The Trojan army left their city and marched on the Wall.

The bulk of Qirum's army followed the great central track of the Etxelur Way. As they advanced, Northlanders fled or hid.

Qirum established his main camp just off Etxelur Way on the south bank of the Milk River, an easy march from the Wall's central District of Great Etxelur. Even as he dug in, he began a cycle of patrols and raids far along the face of the Wall to east and west, cutting tracks and smashing dykes and weirs, seeking to cut off Etxelur from the country that sustained it. For their part the Annids ordered the digging of great ramparts and ditches before the line of the Wall. As the weather eased the fishing fleets went out; the oceans would provision the Wall even if the country could not.

So the siege was set. Both sides dug in, and on both sides the dying continued.

55

The Third Year After the Fire Mountain: Late Spring.

After midnight the party came out to repair the Words on the Wall. It was pitch dark, under a sky choked with cloud.

Tibo stood with his father at the balcony, in a gentle, cold rain. They were high on the Wall here, high over Old Etxelur. The night was cold, and the day under a sunless sky hadn't been much warmer. Looking down, Tibo saw that the latest bonfires the Trojans had built at the base of the Wall had died back, thanks to the heavy rain earlier in the day; only a sullen red glow came from the huge heapings of wood. Further out, nothing could be seen of the enemy save the diffuse lights of the Trojans' fires. Some of the fires cast reflections in standing water. Northland under siege had become a soggy landscape, all the way to the face of the Wall itself.

And beyond that was only darkness. Any Northlanders between here and the horizon were in hiding. If the land was dark it was silent too – almost, anyhow. You rarely heard the sounds of the night any more, the cries of wolves, the calls of owls. Even the animals and birds fled from the Trojans.

But tonight Tibo thought he heard something coming out of the gloom, a murmur of voices, a deep creaking like the swaying of a gigantic tree. The Trojans often worked at night, launching their pinprick raids on the Wall under cover of the dark. Were they up to something this night?

The rain fell harder. Tibo lifted his face, letting the droplets prickle on his skin. It felt oddly soothing, cooling. Briefly he closed his eyes, and concentrated on the feeling of the moisture on his face. He had continued his military training, but his anger kept getting him into trouble, and he had been working with cousin Riban the priest on mastering his rage. Caxa had tried to help him too, as, she said, he had once helped her. But sometimes it felt as if his head was too full, of the hours on the fire mountain when he thought he would die, the days in the camp of the Spider when he wished he had. Now he faced these Trojans, who ripped up the very country his ancestors had made. In a world full of such huge destructive forces, he needed his strength, and he needed his anger to fuel that strength. But he had to learn to put aside that anger until he was in a position to unleash its lethal energies usefully. At least he had found a way to treasure moments of stillness, like this, whenever he could. He had even begun to sleep properly, some nights anyhow.

His father clapped his shoulder. 'You all right? Here comes Mi with the lantern bearers. We'll be moving soon.'

The bearers were coming forward now, carefully carrying a wide-mesh net to which small oil lamps were attached, already lit. The bearers stood at the balcony in a line, and let the net down the face of the Wall, gently, gently, making sure the lanterns were not spilled. The watching Trojans would see this, of course, and they would know what the Northlanders were up to, but there was nothing they could do about it. The bearers were mostly older folk and children, too old or young to fight. As Raka kept saying, in this war for survival every Northlander was a warrior, and could find some role to play.

Mi murmured quiet commands to make sure her team worked as one. Fifteen years old, focused, intense, Mi always seemed capable, always in control, despite her youth. Some people were flourishing in this protracted war, and Mi was one of them, people said, one of the brighter of the young generation. She was using the hideous death of her stepmother Vala to fuel her determination. She was coping. That was what people said. Nobody said such things of Tibo. He didn't care, as long as he got the chance to kill a few more Trojans, before, inevitably, one of them killed him.

Again he heard that deep creaking from the landscape below, a crack like a root breaking. 'Father, I think the Trojans are doing something out there.'

Deri grunted. 'Whatever it is we'll see it in the morning, and we'll deal with it then. As we have everything else they've thrown at us.' He stretched and yawned hugely, and Tibo smelled the fish on his breath. Everybody's breath smelled of fish, as did their farts. There was plenty of fish to eat on the besieged Wall, delivered to the growstone harbours facing the Northern Ocean that the Trojan ships couldn't reach, but little else.

At last Mi whispered to Deri, 'Ready.'

Deri nodded, and beckoned to his team. The other sign-makers came forward now, all along the balcony, picking up their paint even as Mi's team finished anchoring the net securely. Tibo lifted a jar of paint and fixed it to his leather belt with a bit of rope. The wooden jar was heavy, and would make climbing awkward. There were brushes too, simple tools of split willow; Tibo took a couple and stuck them in his belt. He also had his sword in its scabbard, strapped to his back, out of the way.

Deri led the way. He sat up on the low balcony parapet, swung his legs over, and then began to climb one-handed down the net.

Tibo followed his father. Soon he was clambering down the net, down the outer face of the Wall. The climb was easy save for the awkward bulk of the jar, and the scabbard digging into his back. But the Wall was covered by greasy rain-soaked soot from the Trojans' fires, and soon his hands, his bare legs, the front of his tunic were all stained black. Of course the soot stains were the reason they were here.

To left and right, in the light of the lamps, the others climbed down in a rough line, all along this part of the Wall's face. These workers were all fighters, men and women, all seasoned in combat. A couple of times the Trojans had hastily erected long ladders and come swarming up to the painters' nets, trying to use them to gain access to the Wall galleries. If the Trojans tried that again it would be the job of Deri and Tibo and the others to hold them off. There was no sign of Trojan activity tonight, not here. But Tibo was wearing no armour, and he had his back to a plain occupied by the enemy, and the space between his shoulder blades itched as if inviting the kiss of an arrowhead.

Around halfway down the net he came to grooves cut into the growstone face, visible in the light of the torches, swooping circles and lines, with splashes of red and orange paint under the obscuring film of the soot. This was the Word he was to work on. He anchored himself, braced against the net with his booted feet on the face of the Wall, and tied a loop of rope from his belt to the net. Then he got out a brush, dipped the frayed end in the paint bucket, and started smearing the sticky stuff on the Wall. Soon the orange stain of the paint added to the black muck on his tunic. He just had to paint the grooves as far as he could reach, and then move on, down or sideways. After the first few trials nobody had bothered trying to clean off the Trojan soot; it was found that from a distance, across the landscape, the repainted Words stood out even more strongly against the soot's dark background than the white face of the Wall itself. All the better if you could use the Trojans' own efforts against them.

The Words had been an inspiration of Caxa, the Jaguar-girl sculptor who had memorably carved a sign to the gods outside My Sun – a sign now desecrated by the Trojans who had smashed the place up, but the Annids had promised that some day it would be restored. The Trojans' advance on the Wall had cut off Etxelur, the Wall and the Annids from the rest of Northland. So Caxa, inspired by the colourful banners that were draped over the Wall's face on festival days like the midsummer Giving, had suggested painting slogans on the Wall itself: tremendously tall designs, Words that could be seen many days' travel away. The idea had been accepted with enthusiasm.

349

Soon sections of the Wall's white face were covered with the ancient ring-and-groove lettering of Etxelur, messages shouting out to all who could see, and read them:

THE WALL STANDS!
THE LOVE OF THE MOTHERS PROTECTS US ALL!
THE TROJANS CANNOT PREVAIL!

Of course the Trojans responded. Even if they couldn't read such signs they could guess their purpose. So in their assaults on the Wall the Trojans defaced the signs, and built bonfires to smear them with soot. In response the Northlanders had cut the signs deeper into the Wall's sheer face and painted over the soot. It had become a strange side-battle in this war, a battle over words, symbols, ideas, one side writing, the other side erasing, over and over. And it was a uniquely Northlander battle too. Most Northlanders could read and write, whereas in Troy and Greece and the land of the Hatti, literacy was the province of the scribes – not even the kings could read the proclamations they applied their seals to. Regardless of what the Words said, their very existence were a reminder of the uniqueness of Northland civilisation.

Tibo worked steadily, shifting his position, balancing the weight of his bucket. The work was easy, if repetitive. It seemed to satisfy some corner of his soul to complete such a simple task, just filling a groove with paint. Another way to achieve the calmness Riban had urged him to find within himself. And as he worked on he became aware of the dawn approaching. He worked with his back to the landscape, but gradually he made out the face of the Wall before him in the gathering daylight, a blue-grey wash that picked out the pocks and flaws in the Wall's growstone surface.

Then there was another wooden creak, louder, and voices calling from the plain.

Tibo turned to see, hanging one-armed from the net. Northland had emerged from the dark, flat to the horizon under a cloudy blue-grey sky. The land was scarred by the Annids' huge new defensive earthworks, ramparts and ditches, running for long stretches along the face of the Wall. At the base of the Wall itself water stood in hollows, building up against the growstone. Trojan raiders had long ago torched the windmills on the Wall's roof, so now, in chambers safely tucked deep within the Wall, work gangs were turning great wheels to keep the pumps working – gangs manned by volunteers, it was said. But it was impossible to keep the flooding down completely. Looking along the face of the Wall itself Tibo could see more relics of the Trojans' many assaults: broken ladders, the wreck of a battering ram that had smashed itself to pieces against the Wall's growstone face, earthen ramps, even pits where Qirum's men had tried tunnelling under the Wall.

But this morning, Tibo saw, astonished, Qirum was trying something new.

At first he thought the thing silhouetted against the dawn light was a huge man, a terrifying figure. Then he saw that it was no creature but a man-made thing, a tower of wood and rope roughly nailed and bound together. Platforms stuck out of it like great tongues, protruding towards the Wall. Some of them were surely high enough to be able to reach the galleries, like the one from which he dangled.

And the tower was moving. It was mounted on wheels, thick and solid, that looked as if they had been cut from the trunks of huge, ancient oaks. Teams of oxen dragged this thing over the muddy ground, and it cut deep ruts as it passed. There were so many of the animals that they combined in his view into black slabs of heaving muscle, their breath steaming in a cloud. Men drove the oxen with sticks and whips, and warriors jogged alongside the tower, their bronze armour bright in the gathering light. Chariots followed, perhaps bearing commanders. There were men in the tower itself, dwarfed by its scale. They looked like toys, Tibo thought, toy soldiers that Puli or Blane would play with.

This was the source of the tremendous wooden groans he had heard through the night. It was a siege engine.

'Father!'

'I see it.' Deri was hanging on the net, staring. 'I heard of such things in Hattusa, but I never saw one before – and I never heard of one so big. But then I imagine no siege in history has ever faced such a barrier as the Wall.'

'Where did it come from? It wasn't here yesterday.'

'They must have brought it up overnight, in pieces, on carts. Then they put it together in the dark, and here it is.' He shook his head. 'We must never underestimate the Trojans, son.'

Now the Wall community was waking in the dawn, and cries of alarm echoed in the galleries. Soon the first resistance began. Arrows and stones flew from the galleries above Tibo's head, some of the arrows burning. Tibo glanced up, and saw Mi with her lethal Kirike's Land bow firing off shot after shot, one glowing spark sent flying through the air after another.

The first fire arrows fell on the tower. Some sank home in the engine's wooden frame, but they burned only slowly, per-haps the wood was wet, and there were men with blankets and buckets of water and earth to douse any fires that did catch. Meanwhile, down on the plain, the Trojan warriors raised their shields and fired back in response, but being so far below their arrows fell well short, thumping back into the muddy ground.

And all the while the great engine lumbered ever closer to the Wall. Now it approached the band of ditches and ramparts that had been dug out before the Wall itself. Trojan engineers rushed forward to break the ramparts and lay boards over the ditches. The few defenders stationed there put up some resistance, but when the Trojans arrived, when the swords glittered and the blood splashed, they fell back.

'We aren't going to stop it,' Tibo murmured.

'There's a way to go yet. But you and I might have some fighting to do today, son. Come on.' Deri dumped his jug and brush, letting the paint splash down the Wall's face, and began scrambling back up the net. 'Words will have to wait.'

Tibo followed his father up the face of the Wall, staring over his shoulder at the engine's lumbering advance.

On the balcony, even as she fired her own bow, Mi called out commands, redirecting the arrow fire. Now the defenders began to target the oxen that dragged the tower. Unless you had a lucky shot it would take more than a single arrow to bring down a mature ox, but it was all but impossible to miss an animal in that compressed mass, and the wounded animals writhed and bellowed in distress, disturbing those around them. The drivers had to work hard to keep the beasts moving in formation, with oaths and blows.

And now Mi heard a roar, coming from somewhere below and to her left. A mass of warriors had run out from a concealed entrance in the face of the Wall. They formed up into a rough block and headed straight for the Trojan force, their weapons held aloft, yelling defiance. The units were commanded by officers from Hattusa, but by now Northland's army contained men from Etxelur and the other Wall Districts, the rest of Northland, and from allies in Albia and Gaira. They sprinted over boards hastily thrown over the ditches, and made for the engine, coming at it from the side. The Trojans formed up in response.

But before that battle was joined there was another tremendous wooden groan, like a huge cry of pain. Mi saw that *the engine was leaning*. Its front left corner was tipping into a hole that had opened up in the ground beneath its wheels. Faces everywhere turned to the siege engine, the defenders on the Wall, the warriors on the ground, the engineers at their work breaching the ramparts.

'Ha!' a man called, leaning over the balcony. 'I did that! I helped dig that trap! Just brush and a dusting of earth over a hole in the ground. One of Raka's bright ideas, meant to trap a chariot, but if it catches that monster it will do for me!'

The engine tipped further still. Mi was surprised by how easily it was going over. For all its bulk it had to be tall to reach the

Wall's galleries, and so it must be top-heavy, and once it started to fall it was doomed. The drivers beat the broad backs of their oxen, but the panicking animals could do nothing now. Indeed, Mi saw, some of the bellowing oxen were being dragged backwards as the tower tilted. When their traces broke the animals stampeded, causing more panic among the increasingly disorganised Trojans. Men trapped in the tower itself ran, yelling. Some of them jumped to the ground, arms flailing. The commanders' chariots turned away sharply, fleeing the disaster.

The end was near. As the engine tipped further and further panels fell away from the tower's sides, falling to the ground in a hail of wood shards, and Mi heard the pop and crack of big structural beams breaking, like bones snapping. At last the tower's huge flank hit the ground, and the engine collapsed into the dirt, whole tree trunks wheeling out of a cloud of wood shards that flew into the air.

Mi heard whoops of triumph all around her. It looked as if the whole population of the Wall, swollen with nestspills, had come out onto the galleries to see.

And from below there came the raucous shouting of fighting men. The Northland defenders were closing now, encouraged by the catastrophe of the tower to finish off the raiders. The surviving Trojans got themselves organised, but they faced a fighting retreat along the road to the south.

Mi yelled encouragement, releasing the grief and anger that always lingered inside.

56

'We must be patient, King.'

'Patient? Patient, you say, man? Patient! Pah!'

Qirum raged around the principal room of his palace. He snatched another cup of wine from a terrified serving girl, who quailed and ran off barefoot. He stalked past the table full of the gold drinking cups his generals had learned to bring him as gifts, past the rich tapestries hanging on the walls. He drew his sword from its jewelled scabbard and held it up before a tapestry. He could have slashed it to ribbons in a heartbeat. Yet he stayed his hand.

The Spider stood, silently watching him, hands behind his back. Hadhe sat on a low couch with her baby, just two months old. The child was having trouble feeding, and whimpered, not loudly, just enough to be distracting. The only other people in the room were the four guards standing like statues in the corners, and another serving girl who stood by the door. All of them waiting on Qirum's next word, his next reaction – all of them save the Northlander baby, who was obsessed with his own empty stomach.

Qirum threw his sword to the carpet. 'Pah! I can't even trouble to destroy this garbage, this offal, this shit. Why are we here, Telipinu? Why do we waste our spirits and our soldiers' lives on this soggy plain of a country?' He picked up a golden cup, crusted with gems. 'It doesn't even have treasures worth looting. Even this trinket came from Gaira, didn't it?' Qirum threw the cup against the wall; it collided softly with a tapestry and fell to the floor, undamaged. 'These Northlanders treasure duck eggs and hazelnuts more than gold!'

Hadhe smiled. 'Well, you can't eat gold.' Her Trojan had become passable in the months she had lived in this citadel. She was not outwardly defiant, but she never used the proper honorifics, not even for the King himself.

The Spider ignored her. 'You know why we're here, King. It is your own strategy, your grand plan. You are building a kingdom here – a country, with farmers and warriors, a new city, a temple fit for the Storm God one day – all from nothing. It takes time.'

Qirum nodded. 'Time, good Telipinu. But how much time? How many more days in this soggy marsh? And on the Wall, those smug Northlanders are pissing all over the ruins of my engine – laughing at it, laughing at me! And Kilushepa, come to that, if the spies are right that she has returned to Northland. Why shouldn't they laugh? The engine was another abject failure.'

The Spider shook his head. 'No. Not a failure. Another lesson learned. We tried a ram; this growstone of theirs is too thick, too resistant. We tried ladders, dirt ramps; the Wall is too high, too easily defended. We tried burrowing, only to find the Wall's roots are too deep—'

'I was convinced my engine was the answer.' It had been born from Qirum's own sketches, his own imagination.

'And it so nearly did succeed!'

'It fell over, man.'

'So we build another, better. We make it like those great tombs of the Egyptians. Broader at the base, narrower above, with longer platforms for the warriors. Impossible to topple.'

Qirum eyed him. 'You've been thinking about this.'

'And some of my men. Such a device would need a lot of wood to build. Well, the lands of Albia and Gaira are full of wood . . . Lord, no man has ever laid siege to such a mighty wall as this, in all history. And when you bring it down your name will be celebrated from Gaira to Egypt and beyond. But we must learn how to do it.' Hadhe's baby whimpered more loudly. The Spider glared at her.

Qirum protested, 'But all this will take another season, at least.'

'This is a siege, Lord. Sieges last years, not months.'

'A lot of years if those Northlanders on the Wall continue to grow fat on fish from the northern sea, which we cannot reach.'

Still the baby cried, wailing in discomfort.

'But you know we have sent ships north, which – oh, will you stop that foul racket!' The Spider strode over to Hadhe, reaching to grab the baby. She quailed back.

Qirum stepped between the Spider and Hadhe. 'Leave them, Telipinu.'

Just for a heartbeat the Spider did not back down. Qirum was aware of the four guards tensing, quietly reaching for their weapons. Then the Spider stepped back deliberately. 'Lord, your weakness for this bed-warming whore and her bastard brat is . . .'

Qirum put his arm around Hadhe. 'All part of my complicated charm, Telipinu. Which is why I am king and you are not.'

Hadhe murmured, 'And I know you will always treat the child well, King. Despite what I do now.'

He stared at her. 'What's that? What do you mean?'

There was an odd moment of stillness. The Spider had turned away, disgusted. The guards had melted back into their corners, putting away their weapons. There were no eyes on Qirum and Hadhe. She whispered in his ear, 'It was my fault. That My Sun fell, that my children were lost. Perhaps this makes up for that terrible failure.'

And he saw the knife flash in her hand. He flinched back, but the blade dug through his tunic and scraped his belly, and he felt warm blood flow. She drew back her arm, but before she could strike again he grabbed her wrist and forced it back. Her eyes met his; her face was expressionless.

Immediately the Spider was at her back. He slit her throat with a single swipe of his own blade; the blood, bright and gushing, flowed down her white tunic. She had been holding the child; he rolled to the floor, screaming, as she fell back.

The guards ran to Qirum's side, their own blades drawn. He could smell their fear at this failure to protect him.

The Spider stood before the King. 'Fetch the surgeon,' he snapped, and a guard ran.

Qirum lifted his tunic and inspected his belly. 'She only scraped me . . . Not much in exchange for her life. Well, she was no soldier.'

The Spider looked down on Hadhe's corpse. 'Why did she do it? You were good to her. You protected her from me only a heartbeat ago.'

Qirum breathed hard, his heart pumping, his body belatedly reacting to the sudden threat. 'But she lost one child and saw the banishment of others, and the death of her husband, and the rape, murder or enslavement of everybody she knew. She did have a grudge to bear, I suppose. Though it was not me who wielded the sword.' He looked down on the knife, which was on the floor. 'That looks like an Etxelur blade. I wonder if it was smuggled in by Milaqa and that uncle of hers. Or maybe Hadhe just swiped it.'

The surgeon came bustling in, looking anxious, as well he might, for if he failed to treat the King properly the cost would likely be his own life.

The Spider pointed his dagger at the child on the floor. 'Shall I finish off that thing?'

'What? No, no. Surgeon, find it a wet nurse when you're done here.' He considered. 'Ensure that it grows up never knowing who it is, where it is from, who its mother was. That's sufficient punishment for the mother's shade to bear in the underworld, I think. But don't harm the child.'

The surgeon nodded, gingerly cutting away the King's bloody tunic.

'All the time she's held that knife, over months and months, waiting for the one moment when the guards were distracted enough to give her a chance. And I thought she was growing fond of me. People always surprise you, don't they, Telipinu? Oww, man, be careful with that salve! Now, where were we?'

The Spider grinned, and knelt down to wipe the blood off his knife on Hadhe's tunic. 'Talking about siege tactics.'

57

'We must be patient,' Teel said.

'And I agree,' Raka said.

In this crowded room deep within the Wall, an annex to the great Hall of Annids, the air was thick with the smoke from the lamps on the walls, with stale aromas from cloaks of elderly feathers and fur, and with a sharper stink of fear, Milaqa thought.

Now Noli, her hunger-gaunt making her seem more stern than ever, held up a hand. 'I do not question the vigour of our fighters, or their bravery, or the hard work and ingenuity that has been put into our defences. But the fact is the Trojan bear cub continues to find ways to test those defences. We were lucky that his absurd tower stumbled into a trap.'

Deri said, 'The trap was meant for chariots, granted, rather than siege towers. But it worked. A simple hole in the ground defeated all the ingenuity and labour that went into that monstrosity.'

'And the lesson you draw from that?'

'Why, to dig more holes!' Deri cried. 'To be still more vigilant.'

'And to wait?' Noli asked. 'Is that all you have? To wait, and wait, until Qirum gets bored and goes away?'

'Yes,' said Kilushepa sharply, in Northlander.

Milaqa turned with the rest. The Hatti queen swept into the room, with Muwa her Chief of Bodyguards and Hunda her sergeant at her side. Milaqa hurried forward to translate for her. The Tawananna's hair was cropped short these days, she had only a touch of kohl at her eyes and rouge on her cheeks, and she wore a simple white robe, less grand than the Northlanders'

House cloaks. Yet she instantly commanded attention, Milaqa saw, even from the Annid of Annids.

'Yes, you must wait,' Kilushepa said. 'It is how a siege must be withstood, and believe me, I have witnessed several, and studied many more from history.' She waved a hand. 'If you are improvising your defences, well, so is Qirum improvising his assaults. All this is as novel to him as it is to you. Let him waste warriors and wood on his ridiculous siege engines.

'Meanwhile you people are safe, here in your Wall. I have seen it for myself. You have fresh water, from the streams that flow to the Wall. You are cut off from the country, but you have your ingenious harbours on the Wall's ocean face; your fishing fleets come and go with impunity. You have tribute brought to you from the lands all along the northern coast, from the World River estuary to Albia – why, I believe there are even boats plying from Kirike's Land. Meanwhile your people in the country have simply faded away into the marshes and forests, the wild land where Qirum's troops cannot follow. They are safe too. You may be growing tired of the taste of fish – frankly, so am I, and I only just arrived. But that's a small price to pay for survival. *You are safe.* Sit in your Wall. Wait it out.'

Milaqa thought she was hugely impressive. But since her return to Northland, and Milaqa had shadowed her closely ever since to aid with translations, the Tawananna had not asked about the fate of the child she had borne and left behind here. Not once, not a word. Any more than she had asked after the fate of her son in Hattusa.

'But,' Noli said, stressing her words with blows of fist into palm, *'for – how – long*? Kilushepa, you have seen the flooding at the base of the Wall. The Beavers tell me that they have no record of a full year when they have been able to perform *no* significant maintenance on the Wall and its systems. In the end the flooding will eat away at the growstone. And out in the country the drainage and diversion systems are either neglected or purposefully wrecked – purposefully, *we wrecked some of them ourselves*, to make the land difficult for Qirum! How long do you believe the siege will last – years? There may not be a Northland left to recover by the end of it.'

Teel murmured, 'Come, Noli. The Wall has lasted hundreds of generations. It is not likely to fail tomorrow.'

Raka said, 'And we have our fallbacks. The wheels, the manually driven pumps.'

'"Manually,"' Noli said with disgust. *'That's* a milkwater word for what's going on in those chambers. Trojan prisoners strapped to the wheels and whipped into the work by Hatti thugs!'

Milaqa was shocked. She'd believed the official story that the wheels were manned by volunteers.

'It is necessary,' Raka said unhappily.

Noli snapped, 'Necessary! To keep slaves? Northland has never kept slaves, not since Ana's time.'

'They are not slaves—'

'Slaves, I insist, who we beat and work to death. This is hypocrisy, Annids! Lies we tell ourselves, and our people. This may destroy Northland more thoroughly than any flooded lowland or blocked dyke.'

Deri said, 'But, respectfully, what choice is there? If you are advocating going out to meet Qirum in open battle – I have seen his troops. I have fought them. I would not recommend it.' He nodded at Kilushepa. 'Even with your fine troops at my side, queen, and I mean no disrespect.'

Kilushepa said evenly, 'I agree with you completely. It is easy to lose patience – but if you lose that, you lose everything. This is in fact the mistake that Qirum's own people made at Troy, when that city was besieged by the Greeks. If only they had kept their patience they could be starving the Greeks out even now, still safe and rich and strong. Instead of which—'

There was a commotion in the corridor outside. People turned to look, and Milaqa peered to see over their cloaked shoulders, in the dim light of the flickering oil lamps.

Tibo stood there, panting, uncertain. 'There is a man,' he said.

'He says he sailed from Kirike's Land. He had a cargo of their dried fish . . .'

'Yes, boy,' Raka snapped. 'What of it?'

'He was attacked. His ship. *Attacked on the Northern Ocean.*' He looked around, searching for Deri. 'Father – it's Adhao.' A neighbour of Vala's and Medoc's on Kirike's Land, before the fire mountain. 'May I bring him in?'

Soaked by seawater, his tunic drenched in blood, Adhao had to be carried in by Tibo and the other men. He was badly wounded, a deep gouge in his belly. A priest hovered at his side, helplessly pressing moss into the wound as he was carried.

Muwa, watching, murmured to his queen, 'That's the mark of a sea pike.'

Raka frowned at Milaqa's translation. 'A what?'

'A spear. Fifteen paces long. Bound at the joints with iron bands . . . A weapon, lady, used when one ship attacks another. As the Greek galleys have for centuries assaulted ships along our own coasts.'

'It's true,' Adhao said, gasping, his Kirike's Land accent thick. 'They came at us, big ships with painted eyes. We could not fight back. We did not know how. All of us died – all save me, and they did *this* to me before dumping me in the harbour on the Wall. They said I was to serve as a message.'

Deri sucked his teeth. 'Then they have found a way to get their ships to the seaward face of the Wall. They must have sailed all the way around Albia, to the west and north. Quite a feat, for sailors from the gentle waters of the Middle Sea.'

Raka asked, 'What does this mean?'

Kilushepa said, 'It means Qirum has worked out how reliant you have become on supplies from the northern sea. And it means that he has found a way to cut off that supply, or impede it at least, by blockading it with his ships.'

Noli drew herself to her full height. 'And do you still say we should do nothing, Tawananna?'

'Yes,' Kilushepa said sharply. 'Even with this setback, you have reserves. Perhaps we can find a way to fight back. Greek galleys on your northern seas must be vulnerable. Yes, I still counsel patience.'

But Noli pointed at poor Adhao, who writhed with the pain as the priest tried to treat him. 'Patience, until Qirum does to all of us what he has done to this man? Patience, while that monster from the barbaric east raises generation after generation of his cattle-folk warriors, right here in Northland? Patience, until the Wall itself crumbles and we are all lost, and our land, and even the memory of it, erased by the sea? I will not have it.' She glared around at the Annids. 'Will you? And you, and you?'

She was greeted by a swelling growl of approval.

And, before long, the decision became clear. Northland would fight.

As the meeting broke up Milaqa murmured to Teel, 'It feels like everything's changed.'

'Yes,' he said grimly. 'Just as Qirum, or his wily *basileis*, probably intended when they sent us this "message". For an open fight will suit them better than it suits us, believe me.

'Maybe this day was inevitable, however. There's much they couldn't talk about in an open session. Such as the rebellion of the Districts, or the threat of it. Qirum, wily little brute that he is, has been making moon eyes at the leaders in the Market, the Manufactory – even the Scambles, it's said. Not everybody in this great linear city of ours cares much for the Annids, who tax remotely and hand down their laws, and ask for young men and women to come lie down and die for Etxelur, while scarcely ever bothering to show a face beyond the Scambles. If even a few Districts broke away and threw in their lot with him—'

'Once Qirum was inside the Wall—'

'All would be lost. So maybe we have to act now while we still can. And – ah, Deri.' He touched his brother's arm as he passed.

Deri paused and looked at him. 'Any bright ideas?' he asked blackly.

The moment was tense. Though they had always tried to keep it from her, Milaqa had often glimpsed the rivalry between them, these brothers so different, the sturdy fisherman, the wily politician.

Teel sighed. 'I don't want this any more than you do. But if we must fight, let us fight to win. Let's put our heads together, brother, for once. We must speed up the training for a start. Use more Hatti veterans to train more Northlanders. And we should call in favours, from Albia, Gaira, the World River.'

Deri nodded. 'And we must put pressure on the iron-makers. What a bunch of fusspots they are! We must make them understand that a dozen flawed arrowheads are better than a single perfect specimen.'

Teel glanced at Milaqa. 'Though we give battle, we must continue to *think*. For I continue to believe that it is through intelligence we will ultimately prevail.'

She wondered what he meant by this latest oblique remark; Milaqa had been used by Teel more than once.

Adhao cried out again. The Annids clustered around him, and Raka called for the priests with their medicine kits.

As it turned out they had only months to make their preparations. Before the end of the latest summer without the sun, the third since the fire mountain, the Trojan brought his army to the Wall.

58

The Third Year After the Fire Mountain: Late Summer

On the night before the battle the Northlanders emerged from the crevices of their great Wall, marched south, and formed up into units. They almost looked like an army, the Trojan scouts said, dismissive. And at last they were offering battle.

Despite the urgings of his *basileis* to strike before dawn, Qirum was prepared to wait until the sun was risen before responding. He had laid siege to the Wall for half a year already, it had been months since his spies had reported the Annids were preparing for battle, and there was plenty of the campaigning season left to get this done. Waiting a few more hours would do no harm.

The day was well advanced when Qirum at last emerged from his tent and walked out into the field, before his lines, alone. Qirum wore no armour, nor did he carry weapons or a shield. He wanted the men to see him, and his enemies, if they could peer that far. He caused a stir among the men as he walked along the lines, and there were ragged cheers from the still-loose formations.

The land was flat to the horizon. The dew was heavy in the marshy grass; his boots left footprints in the soft earth. The sky was a milky blue, the sun pale, but at least you could see the sun this morning. The dew would soon burn off, but the day would never get overwhelmingly hot, for it never did here. A good day for fighting, then. In the air he saw a bird of prey, a kestrel perhaps, eerily stationary above the ground, watching some hapless prey. And at his feet there was a patch of some ragged pink-headed flower about which butterflies and bees fluttered. He wished the busy creatures well; soon this little stage of life would be trampled and blood-soaked. He breathed deeply of the fresh, slightly chill air. This was not home, and never would be, and yet it had its riches, in its own way, on such a day as this.

In the north the Wall was a faint bone-pale line. Before it he saw the enemy lines, a mass of men in the mist, with smoke from their fires rising into the still air.

He turned to survey his army. Facing the enemy, they were drawn up in units of fifty or a hundred each, in three rough blocks: Protis and his Greeks in the centre, with Qirum's own Trojans to the left and the Spider with his mostly Hatti exiles to the right. The men were strapping on armour if they had it, sharpening blades with whetstones they would dump before the charge, boasting and joshing, gathering their energies – summoning up the will to fight. Behind the main blocks there were units of archers and slingers, and further back the charioteers were readying their vehicles, harnessing up the horses. The animals skittered and neighed.

And as the King walked before his men the songs began. The Trojans thumped spears on shields and chanted battle cries. The Anatolians sang hymns to their Storm God; Qirum recognised one mournful lament, a soldier's prayer to be buried at home beside his mother. The Greeks were different; they preferred to stay silent, watchful, ready – ominous. Qirum briefly wondered how it would have been for the generation before his in Troy to have faced a siege by thousands upon thousands of such silent, competent warriors.

He could hear similar music wafting across the field from the Northlander lines. He recognised more doleful Hatti elegies – hymns to the Sun Goddess of Arinna, perhaps. They had all come so far from home, he thought, to kill and be killed on this distant plain.

The Spider walked out to him, laden with the King's armour, which he set respectfully on the ground. Qirum put on his breastplate, and shields for his shoulders and thighs, and shin guards, and shaped pieces for his forearms, tying each leather strap tight. The Spider was already fully armoured himself, with sword and spear at his back, his helmet under his arm. As Qirum dressed the Spider sniffed the air, peered around with his one good eye, stepped forward and dug his heel into the ground. 'This bog will cut up.'

'The same for both sides.' Qirum glanced towards the enemy. 'Just as the scouts said, they advanced across the river they call the Milk to face us. They seem to have sought no advantage from the terrain, as I would have done. But then, I would never have sallied out from the Wall and its defences.'

The Spider shrugged. 'There's no high ground advantage to be had on this tabletop of a country. Do you want to speak to the men?'

'Enough speeches, I think.'

The Spider nodded. 'Then if you will permit me to be your champion—'

Qirum clapped him on the shoulder. 'Let's see if you can finish this before it's started.'

The Spider strapped on his helmet and strode forward across the plain between the armies. He began to bellow insults, in his own tongue and the locals'. 'Northlanders! Savages! Women, dogs, children all! Is there a man among you, just one man, who will face me and settle this?'

Seeing him advance, the men roared.

Deri stood with Muwa before the Northlander lines. He could clearly see the lone warrior approaching, his stride purposeful, even eager. Behind him the Trojans were yelling, cheering, slamming weapons against their spears, thousands of them; it was a noise like a thunderstorm.

Hunda came out of the block of Hatti at the centre of the Northlander line and walked before the men, lifting his arms. 'Answer them!' he yelled in his own tongue. 'Are you going to let them make all the noise today? Show them how Hatti can sing!' And in the Etxelur tongue, 'Show them how Northlanders can yell!'

Soon the whole line was roaring back at the Trojans, the Hatti and the Northlanders at the centre, and the more exotic blocks of warriors from Albia and Gaira to right and left, the dark wolf-men of the forest, the white-robed priest-warriors from their country of skies and open spaces and stone circles.

Milaqa ran at Hunda's side, without armour or weapons, shouting translations of his Hatti words. Her voice could not match Hunda's battle-trained bellow, but her thin voice got the message across. Deri would have preferred her to be far from this field, but he had no control over his niece. He could only pray that her own sense would see her survive the day.

'He comes to issue a challenge,' Muwa said to Deri, raising his voice over the din. His Northlander tongue was clear if heavily accented. 'The Trojan. You understand that if we send out a champion to meet him, the issue may be resolved without further loss of blood, whoever lives, whoever dies, if honour is served on both sides.'

Deri grunted. He began to tighten up his armour, borrowed from the Hatti. 'I have learned more of your bloodstained customs than I ever wanted to know.'

'I will go, if you wish.'

'Thank you, my friend. But Northland's champion must be a Northlander. And as you said, I don't even have to win.' He spoke evenly, and yet he felt fear and a kind of deep regret in his heart. He was not by nature a warrior; he was a fisherman, forced into this role by circumstance. He glimpsed a scrap of blue in the sky above, a rare sight these days. Was this to be the day he died?

And then a roar went up from the Northland lines. Startled, Deri looked round. A single man was already walking out to meet the Trojan challenger. Armoured, bristling with weapons, it was Tibo.

Deri ran after him.

Muwa followed. He warned Deri, 'If you drag him back you

will make a fool of him, and of yourself. This is all about honour, remember.'

'But I cannot let him die.'

They caught up with Tibo. He marched forward, his pace steady, unrelenting. He said, 'Leave me alone, father. I have no intention of dying.'

'It is not your place to do this.'

'You speak of honour. I know that man. *That is the Spider.* Who has been more dishonoured by this man than me?'

Despite Muwa's urging, Deri grabbed his son's arm and forced him to stop. 'Please. I'm begging you. In your mother's memory – let me take your place.'

Tibo, his face hidden by bronze armour plates, would not look at his father, and would not speak further. All the efforts by Riban and others to calm Tibo had come to nothing, Deri saw, gone now there was a scent of vengeance. There was little left of the son he had raised in that twisted face, only the rage that had always threatened to consume him. And Deri, who had failed to protect his son from the death of his mother, or from the fire mountain, or from the brutalising at the hands of the Spider, could now not save him from himself.

He let him go. The boy continued his steady march towards the Spider, who waited for him, hands on hips.

Muwa touched Deri's shoulder. 'We can accompany him. We can carry his weapons—'

'And carry his broken body back from the field.'

'If necessary. But you must not fight for him.'

Deri nodded curtly.

Tibo faced the Spider.

They stood a dozen paces apart on a patch of unremarkable green sward, in a flat, featureless landscape. Yet the world pivoted on the two of them.

The Spider grinned. He pushed his helmet off his head, and dropped it. 'No armour. Come on, boy, I remember you, I know you picked up some Hatti-speak in the camp.'

'No armour,' said Tibo thickly, and he began to work at his own straps.

Soon heaps of discarded armour plate lay at the feet of the two men.

Muwa and Deri stood back, some paces behind Tibo. 'This might help the boy,' Muwa murmured. 'He may be quicker than the older man, more agile.'

'Only the mothers can help him now.'

'Now the weapon,' the Spider said. He hefted sword and long spear, one in each hand. 'What's your choice, little boy? The sword? No, not for you—'

Tibo hurled himself forward, spear held aloft. The Spider easily sidestepped, nimble in tunic and boots, his legs bare, and he swept the shaft of his own spear so it caught Tibo's legs, tripping him, and he went sprawling in the grass. The Spider pivoted and prepared to lunge, but Tibo rolled and was on his feet in a heartbeat.

The Spider could have struck again, perhaps even ended it. But he backed away, applauding ironically.

Muwa had hold of Deri's arm. 'You must *not* intervene.'

Deri raged, 'You call that honourable? To goad the boy? If the red mist closes in his head—'

'It is his fight. He must learn to master himself, and his own flaws.'

But Deri feared his son had little time left in which to learn anything.

The Spider walked before Tibo and made a lascivious curled-tongue gesture. 'As I was saying. The spear's the weapon for you. Look at my spear, boy, the shaft of ash, the bronze head. Lovely piece of work. I remember those nights in the camp. Your warm little arse. It was the long spear for you then, wasn't it?'

Tibo charged again.

Again the Spider sidestepped easily. This time he swung the blade of his spear across the back of Tibo's legs as he stumbled by, and the boy went down screaming, blood pouring from a wound on the back of his right calf, shockingly bright. He tried to get to his feet, but his injured leg gave under him and he went down again.

'Hamstrung,' Muwa murmured.

The Spider stood before Tibo, his arms spread wide. 'Come then. Finish me. Finish me as you longed to, all those nights when you warmed my bed, and the beds of my men.'

At last Tibo made it to his feet, using his spear as a crutch. Even now, thought Deri, even now the boy might have had a chance if he only thought clearly, if he used the Spider's arrogance against him, if he looked for a gap in the man's sloppy defence. Or he could throw down his weapon and admit he was beaten – he would be dishonoured, maimed, but he would live.

None of this came to pass. Tibo raised his spear, steadied himself on his one good leg, and hurled himself forward. It was less a run than a controlled lunge.

The Spider knelt, jammed the butt of his spear into the soft ground before Tibo, held it firm. Tibo could not stop, could not turn aside. He fell onto the spearhead. The watching Trojans roared. As the metal cut through cloth and flesh, sliding deep into the stomach cavity just below the ribs, Tibo made a gurgling, choking sound. Blood and darker fluids poured down the shaft and over the Spider's hands as he held the spear firm. Then he twisted the shaft, Deri heard a ripping sound, and Tibo gave an animal cry.

Deri would have gone forward, but Muwa grabbed him, arms around his torso. 'You must not,' he murmured. 'You must not.'

The Spider cautiously let go of the spear. It remained jammed in the ground, and propped up Tibo's body, precariously balanced. Still the boy lived; his arms moved, his fingers twitching. The Spider, soaked by Tibo's blood, walked around the pinned boy, like an artist before his creation. 'What fond memories this brings back.' He ran his finger delicately down Tibo's back. Then he pulled up Tibo's tunic, and ripped down his loincloth, exposing his buttocks. Deri could see the boy had soiled himself. The Spider pulled his face elaborately. 'Oh, how unfortunate. But still – once more, shall I give you something to remember me by as you sink into the underworld?' And he lifted his tunic up.

Deri raged against Muwa's strong grip. 'You will get your chance,' Muwa murmured. 'Another place, another day, the man will die at your hands. But not here—'

An arrow slammed into the Spider's back, knocking him to the ground. He lay still, dead immediately. There was an angry roar from the Trojans.

Deri looked back at the Northlander forces. Mi had come out of the lines. She screamed abuse, brandishing her bow. Others from her unit of archers came to drag her back. Another damaged child, Deri thought.

To gruff shouts of anger, outrage, dishonour, Trojans started to advance, all along the line, spontaneously, raggedly. Their sergeants had to follow the events; they ran forward, bellowing to the rest to follow and form up.

And Tibo slumped and fell at last, the spear twisting out of the ground.

'So,' Muwa said. 'Dishonour on both sides, and we must fight after all. But at least we got rid of the Spider.'

Deri spat, 'And that's worth the life of my son, is it? My own life ends with him, whatever happens today. Come – help me with him. I won't leave him here.'

They hurried forward to the body before the Trojan line reached it.

59

The commanders stalked before the Northlander lines. 'Hold
your places! Let them come at you! Let the archers do their
work!' The words were repeated by bellowing translators in the
tongues of the Northlanders, Albians and Gairans, and in the
several dialects spoken by the Hatti warriors.

Milaqa was at the rear of the lines now, in the ruins of an
abandoned, oft-raided settlement, standing on an old flood
mound with Raka, Kilushepa and other leaders. From here
they got a clear view of the field, of the units of the Northlanders
and their allies, of the scuffed little arena in the middle of the
field from which Deri and Muwa hurried back with the body
of Tibo – and of the Trojan horde closing like an approaching
storm.

It was happening, she realised. The battle that had been
anticipated all summer, if not since the Midsummer Invasion
last year. It was here, it was now. But the scale of the armies
drawn up on the plain below the Wall, the thousands of men
and their glittering weapons, the rigid discipline of their phalanx
blocks, the sheer determination to kill they represented – nothing had prepared her for the reality of it. And already blood had
been spilled, her own cousin's.

But battle had yet to be joined. In this still, oddly luminous
moment, Milaqa looked around, at Kilushepa surrounded by a
handful of Hatti soldiers, the Tawananna sleek and determined
in a grand, colourful, highly visible robe that swept to the
ground. Raka, Noli and the other Annids also wore their robes
of office, their faces pinched after the hunger of the blockaded

summer. There was Teel, her uncle, standing in his owl cloak with the others, all his manipulations and stratagems now ending in this day of blood and bronze and iron. And the soldiers, yelling, waving their weapons, holding the line as the Trojans advanced, their commanders whipping up their lust for the fight. There were a few Hatti veterans among them, and foreign units from Gaira and Albia, but most were Northlanders, from across the Wall and the lowland, here to defend their homeland from the greatest threat it had faced since it had been saved from the sea itself.

But, Milaqa thought, looking across the battlefield, they must be outnumbered two to one by Qirum's forces. Only their wits and their courage would enable them to see out the day.

The Trojans passed some predetermined mark, and the Northlanders' planned response began. First, to shouted commands, the Northlander archers raised their bows and began their lethal work. Soon the single arrow fired by Mi with such devastating consequences was followed by a hundred others, a thousand, a flock that seemed to blacken the sky as they rose. The slingers too hurled their lumps of sandstone. As the volleys fell Milaqa heard distant cries, and gaps appeared briefly in the lines of the advancing Trojans. Yet the fall of arrows was not even. This was a stratagem of Kilushepa's; she had suggested targeting the Trojans on Qirum's left flank but sparing the Greeks at the centre, in the hope of causing rifts among the allies.

The advance was not stopped. Those who survived just stepped over the fallen, although Milaqa saw little knots of squabbling men form over the dead, like carrion birds, fighting for armour and weapons.

And now Milaqa saw arrows arcing up from the Trojan lines in a response. In half a dozen languages, there were cries of 'Shields, shields!' The men before her in their blocks and rows raised their shields, overlapping them with a clatter of wood on wood, and the Hatti troopers standing with Kilushepa on the exposed mound raised their own shields to make a kind of shell to protect their queen and the Annids. The first arrows fell, most clattering into leather shields, or falling away harmlessly, but some found a way through to soft flesh, and men fell screaming, some only paces from Milaqa, blood splashing bright. Yet still the lines held.

Next, to guttural commands, the units of Albians on the right of the Northland line formed up for their counter-charge. They were huge men, with good bronze weaponry but with shields only of wood, and no armour save for heavy skins of bear and wolf. These Pretani warriors, come to honour an ancient alliance between their country and Northland, were men of the thick forest that still coated the peninsula. Some said that as the farmers had advanced, clearing the forest that had once covered the Continent, the old gods had fled to Albia, and today they were ready to unleash their fury on the sons of the men who had burned them out. Whatever the truth of that, the Albians lacked the discipline of the others, despite months of training under Hatti officers, and it was thought they were best used as shock troops before the battle proper was joined.

Now, at their leaders' barked commands, they roared, picked up the pace, and ran directly at the Trojan lines, apparently oblivious to arrow-fire. Milaqa saw how their bear-like aggression alarmed the Trojans, who closed up in their compact blocks.

Albians slammed into Trojans, and the fighting began at last, a collision of blades, blood and flesh.

And now, from the left of the Northland line, Milaqa saw the final surprise element planned by the military men: units of archers running right out onto the field, wielding their bows even as they ran into the closing gap between the armies.

Mi, beside commander Piseni himself, ran with the other archers through a narrowing corridor between the armies. She was dressed for speed, armed only with her bow and her quiver of special iron-tipped arrows, with no more protection than a light tunic and the boots on her feet. The Trojan infantry was close, only heartbeats from meeting the Northlander army.

Piseni, the Hatti who had trained the Northlanders' archers, was a warrior of the bodyguard of the Hatti king in Hattusa. He was the best archer Mi had ever seen – better than her, better than Medoc, better by far than anybody she had practised with back on Kirike's Land. And as they had trained through the summer he had picked out Mi and fifty others, the fastest runners, the best shots, for a special assignment. A task to be completed at a specific moment in the battle, he said – one moment that could determine the outcome of the war.

Now that moment had come, and here she was running between the closing lines. Nothing in her training had prepared her for this reality. The charging phalanxes didn't seem human; they were like huge animals, bristling with armour and weapons, that would roll over her and obliterate her in an instant. The air was thick with arrows, slingshot and javelins, some of them lanced into the ground close to Mi, and the noise was tremendous, thousands of male voices yelling as one.

But she was here, with a chance to kill a few Trojans and avenge her adopted mother. What else was life for? She screamed with aggression and exhilaration.

Close to the centre of the facing lines, Piseni stopped dead. 'Make ready!' he yelled. He took his own bow, notched it with a grey-tipped arrow, and aimed it at a running Trojan. 'Make your formation! Hold your fire!'

Mi stood beside him, readying her own shot. Others stood at her sides and behind her back as the formation gathered. There was a moment of stillness, of waiting.

She watched them coming, over the length of her arrow, the men leading the Trojan charge, and her archer's eyes made out every detail. The fore-fighters, Piseni had called them, the elite warriors, those who would lead the charge for glory. They were bigger physically than the men who followed, and the best equipped. They wore armour of varying designs, bronze breast-plates with extensions to cover the neck and shoulder and thighs, leather kilts, shin guards. Some wore conical helmets like the Hatti, some elaborate helmets with horsehair plumes or savage-looking boars' tusks. They had shields of different types too, some shaped like towers, some with big indentations so they were like two shields in one. They all carried weapons, spears and swords in hand or in scabbards. Many had armour plates or masks or grills over their faces. Closer and closer they came, and still the archers held their positions.

Piseni called, 'Hold your fire! Don't waste a shot!' – and an axe caught him in the chest, a lucky shot by some brute in the Trojan lines, and he was thrown back, landing with his chest cavity splayed open, splinters of broken bone sticking out of his frothy flesh.

Mi looked down with horror. She had never been so close to violent death before, even though she herself had killed. The rest of the archers stood in their rows as Piseni had taught them, their bows notched, as shocked as she was.

And still the Trojans advanced.

Mi screamed, 'Fire!' She released her own bow.

The arrows sang through the air, taking only a heartbeat to reach their targets. The hardened iron tips punched through softer bronze breastplates and faceplates. Fore-fighters went down, shocked and screaming, to be trampled by those who followed. Mi knelt, notching her bow again, as the row behind her fired in turn. And then she stood and fired again. You had to make every shot count, it had been impressed on her in training over and over. Though Zidanza and his apprentices had toiled at their foundries deep within the Wall all winter, there had been no time to make as much iron as they hoped, and not enough ore either, once the shipments arriving over the Northern Ocean had been stopped, and some of the arrowheads, hastily manu-factured, would inevitably be brittle or otherwise flawed. You had to make every decent shot take a life. So she picked her targets, one after another, that man's visored face, the next's shining breastplate. She loosed each arrow without thinking, imagining its flight, where it would strike, and then immediately launching another, over and over.

But now the Trojan lines were nearly on her, and the North-land lines too were breaking, running forward to meet the

Trojans. Both sides carried spears two, three, four paces long. Too late Mi tried to run.

The two lines came crashing together all around her, the long spears clattering and stabbing, and men cried out and blood spurted. A Trojan shield slammed into Mi, and she was on the ground. She had lost her bow, her quiver. She was surrounded by a forest of legs, of kilts and bronze armour plate, and over her head swords flashed and the long spears thrust, and the screaming intensified. A booted foot stamped on her back – no, she was being *walked over*. Then a hand grabbed the scruff of her tunic and hauled her back along the crowded ground, through the Northlander lines. It was Deri, she saw, yelling at her.

The hilt of a sword slammed into her temple and the world fell away.

60

Deri had scarcely hauled Mi to safety when a huge Trojan ran straight at him, spinning a sword over his head. Deri raised his shield to fend off the first blow, taking an impact that felt as if it drove his arm back into its socket. But he and the Trojan were shoved together as the lines closed, shields clashing with a slam. Deri was face to face with his man, their faces a hand's length apart. His breath smelled of strange spices, and he wore an elaborate helmet with a horsehair plume. Arms pinned by the struggling crowd, it was difficult for either of them even to move, let alone make an effective strike. But the Trojan was stronger. With a single hand in Deri's chest he shoved him back, and raised the wicked blade of a bronze dagger. Deri twisted so the descending weapon landed on his breastplate. All the air was knocked out of him by the punch, but the bronze blade only scratched Deri's heavy armour of hardened iron. And in that instant Deri swung his own sword across the man's throat, cutting through flesh and gristle until the blade lodged in bone. *No hesitation.* The man gurgled and choked. Deri yanked at the sword to get it free of the bone; it came away with a scrape. The sword was a new kind sent from allies on the Continent, to the east beyond Gaira, bronze but with less propensity to snap at the hilt when you used it to slash than others. Well, it had already proven its worth. The Trojan, bleeding out, had no room to fall. Deri pushed him down by brute force and stepped over the body to get at the next man following.

This man had no armour save a leather helmet, a small round shield, leather kilt and shin guards over a tunic. Already the

Northlanders were cutting through the Trojan elite; Piseni's archers had done the job that was asked of them in thinning out the fore-fighters. But the man was muscular and determined, Deri could see from the blood smeared on his tunic that he had already killed today, and he raised a stubby spear. But Deri was faster; he swung the flat of the sword to chop at the man's belly, twisted the weapon and hauled it backwards, dragging out a loop of grey entrails. The man looked down, as if astonished. Then Deri slammed the hilt of his spear into the man's forehead with a satisfying crunch of bone, and the man fell back.

His falling created a space, and Deri had a heartbeat free of the fight. He was already breathing hard, already his arms and chest ached from the heavy blows he had taken. Neither of the men who had stood by him at the start of the fighting was still there; both of them had been replaced by those pushing from behind. Yet the battle was only moments old.

And here came the next man, as lightly equipped as the last. Deri managed to get his spear in play this time, and impaled the man before he got within arm's length. But before he could get the spear loose another came, and he had to swing his sword again, this time a lucky strike that cut the man's face open so that he fell back, jaw dangling, screaming in a strange, liquid way. And then the pressure from behind shoved him forward almost into the arms of his next opponent, and he lunged and stabbed again.

So it went on, the great blocks crashing into each other in a band of bloody friction, where men screamed and lunged and slashed and stabbed in a compressed, struggling mass. There was a stink of piss and shit from emptied bowels, and the blood was everywhere. Deri had to fight just to stay upright, let alone to give himself room to swing a blade. He had barely moved from the position where he had started, the lines were collapsing in on the front where they met, and soon he found himself slipping on a heap of corpses underfoot. Yet he remembered Tibo, and Nago, and Vala, and all the others who had fallen because of the

Trojan, and let the anger fuel his muscles as he slew and maimed, again and again.

And then above the screams and battle cries he heard a new sound, like thunder, rolling across the field. Some of the more experienced men recognised it. 'Chariots!'

Standing on the flood mound with the commanders, supporting a battered and dizzy Mi, Milaqa saw the Trojan chariots coming from behind the enemy's right flank. There were dozens of the charging vehicles, pulled by swiftly running horses, the sound of their hooves loud even over the battle's din, and bells clanged noisily. They were a shocking sight, a mass of spinning wheels and rearing animals driving at the Northlanders' left flank where the Spider's advancing Hatti units had been met by Gairan priest-warriors, strange silent men who fought ferociously. Now the fighting men were distracted by the noise, and the sergeants bellowed for them to hold their shape, to keep fighting.

Kilushepa pointed. 'A mix of Greek and Hatti types. Look, can you see, Raka? The fleeter ones are Greek, lighter, with two men – four-spoked wheels. The Hatti are the big ones with three men, and their six-spoked wheels . . .'

Milaqa murmured hasty translations.

'They are running better than we supposed they would,' Raka said. 'We had hoped the ground would be too soft.'

Teel said, 'Qirum had the initiative. The weather has been dry, the groundwater low, the ground reasonably firm. He knew that. This was a good day to fight, for his purposes.' He let the criticism hang in the air, unspoken. We should not be fighting the man at all. And if we must fight, not today.

And Milaqa watched, astonished, as the chariots slammed into the Gairan lines, huge masses of hurtling wood and straining animals that cut a bloody swathe through the ranks of men, like blunt blades passing through flesh. The big three-man Hatti chariots were the most effective, each with a driver and shield-bearer accompanying an armoured warrior who shot arrows

382

from a distance, and stabbed and slashed when his chariot closed. As the chariots spread chaos and panic through the Northlander lines, the Trojan infantry pressed with renewed vigour. The fighting became even more intense and chaotic.

Now the surviving chariots emerged from the crush, having passed right through the Northlander phalanx, and they drew up, preparing for a fresh strike. Hasty cries went up from the commanders for the archers to reform and take on the chariots. 'Aim for the horses!'

Hunda clambered up the mound. He was bloodied and panting; he had been in the thick of the fight, but Milaqa knew that Muwa had sternly ordered him to make sure the person of the Tawananna was safe. 'Madam. This position may be threatened. Please fall back.'

Kilushepa knew better than to argue. She began to help Hunda lead the Annids down off the mound.

Mi lunged forward, as if trying to get off the mound and back into the fray. But she staggered, still dizzy from the blow to the head she had taken on the field.

Milaqa grabbed her arm. 'No, you don't. Besides, you lost your bow.'

'We must do something . . .'

One more chariot, a big Hatti three-man vehicle, belatedly broke out of the crush. The crew looked around for a fresh target. They spotted the commanders on the flood mound, pointed up. The driver hauled on his reins and the chariot veered that way.

Heading straight for Milaqa on the mound.

'We can take it,' Mi said suddenly. 'That chariot coming.'

'What? How?'

For answer Mi slithered down the slope, to the edge of the tide of battle, where broken corpses lay unmoving. She grabbed a sword and spear – but as she straightened up she staggered again, the bruise on her head purpling.

'You are insane.' But Milaqa saw there was no other choice than to follow her. She scrambled off the mound, found a spear, and stood by her cousin.

And the chariot charged towards them. The driver was dragging at his reins, trying to control the horses, and the warrior and shield man were looking up at the notables on the flood mound. None of them seemed to notice the young women standing before them.

Mi began running before the chariot reached them. Milaqa joined her, spear in hand. Mi jumped first, grabbed the chariot driver by the neck and fell back, pulling the astonished man off the chariot with her. Milaqa managed to leap up on the platform itself. Without thinking, she swung her spear and caught the warrior with its shaft. He fell from the chariot before he even saw her. But now the plummeting chariot, out of control, was tipping over. The last man, the shield bearer, yelling in fear and anger, swung his shield at Milaqa. She ducked, but the shield caught her on the back of the head, and she fell out of the chariot onto a mound of bodies, warm and slippery. She heard a splintering crash as the chariot went over – and then a huge weight fell on her back, knocking the air out of her.

She sank into a dream of stone and bronze and iron.

61

'You idiot.'

The words were in Hatti. That was the first thing Milaqa was aware of, that the language was Hatti.

And then, that she was still alive. She opened her eyes. The daylight was fading from a clouded-over sky. Smoke billowed. She smelled grease, like meat burning. She tried to sit up, and pain banged in her skull.

An arm around her shoulder lifted her to a sitting position. She turned her head cautiously. Kilushepa sat with her. They were back on the flood mound, she saw, sitting on a blanket spread on the bare earth.

And on the plain before her, bodies lay strewn. People moved among them, some stripping the bodies of armour, clothes, boots, others hauling naked and broken corpses onto carts. Occasionally a wounded man would be found, and surgeons would be called. Many of the surgeons were Egyptian, brought in from that country by the Annids for their expertise, especially in the kinds of injuries to be expected in battle.

Away from the battlefield pyres burned. And to the south, far off, more pyres.

'That's the Trojans,' Kilushepa said. 'Honouring their own dead. Since the fighting stopped for the day, behaviour has been civilised. The living have been returned on either side; the dead are not being dishonoured. Not that I've seen anyhow, despite the precedent set by that animal the Spider, and may he rot in the underworld for it.' She glanced at Milaqa. 'I take it you can understand me. That you remember your Nesili. The knock on the head—'

'I'm fine.' Although she wasn't. Her body was a mass of bruises, and her aching head wasn't even the most painful spot. Yet she wasn't bleeding anywhere, at least not much, nor was any bone broken. She stretched, gingerly. 'I've been lucky.'

'You have.' Kilushepa pointed to the wreck of a chariot, just below the mound. 'Only heroes take on chariots on foot. Heroes and idiots, like you.'

The memory returned sharply to Milaqa. 'What about Mi?'

'Worse off than you. She is back behind the lines. Your uncle Teel is caring for her. She will recover. She is with the rest of the soldiers, who are tending their wounds, eating their soldier-bread and drinking their wine, consuming the barley and goats' cheese that they believe kills pain and restores strength. And you were left to my care.'

'I'm grateful.'

The queen stroked Milaqa's hair. 'I do marvel at you, child. What a mixture of rebel, hero and genius you are! I never saw the like. But you only did it because your cousin went first, didn't you? I understand, you know. There have always been plenty of people like you in the Hatti court. You don't really know what other people are feeling. You can only *guess*. So you do what they do without ever quite understanding why. It's a flaw in your heart, child. And your uncle Teel shares the same flaw, I sense – or it's a strength, depending on how you look at it. Depending on how it is *used*.'

Milaqa, deeply disturbed, wasn't sure she understood. 'And the battle – is it over?'

'No. The fighting just stopped, because of exhaustion. It may resume tomorrow. I have urged Raka to send an embassy to Qirum, to negotiate a truce.'

'Our weapons. The iron arrows—'

'They helped. The Trojan has the advantage in numbers, and without the iron, and without some good strategy from Muwa and his generals, the day would have been lost. But even with the iron we can never win a battle like this. Just as I have been telling Raka and any of your Annids who will listen. The trick is to pick a battle we *can* win.'

'What kind of battle?'

Kilushepa hugged her close, an unexpectedly human gesture. 'That will wait for tomorrow. You must wash away the dried blood, change your clothes. Look, they are lighting another pyre . . .'

The men lowered their torches to the dark tangle of bodies, and they threw on whale oil, and soon the flames were rising high in the gathering night. Out on the field, Milaqa saw birds coming down to feed, rooks and buzzards, and dogs loped. When the men gathered up another corpse, Milaqa watched, astonished, as a cloud of butterflies rose up from the disturbed body, flying into the fading daylight.

62

The Third Year After the Fire Mountain: Autumn Equinox

After three days of fighting the Battle of the Wall finished inconclusively. The Trojans withdrew to their siege lines.

Two months later the priests were still busy at their pits all along the roof of the Wall, and in the interment chambers deep within, storing the bones of the war dead within the growstone, readying them for the longer war against the sea.

And yet again Milaqa was to be sent to face the Trojan in his lair.

She was to be accompanied this time by her uncle Teel, Annid of Annids Raka, a gaggle of other Annids, priests and advisers – and by Kilushepa herself, with a squad of Hatti troops under the command of Muwa. Once again the bewildered, bloodied Northlanders were going to try to come to an accommodation with the monster in their midst.

Milaqa had her own special mission once more. Again she was to be used to try to reach Qirum, who had retired to New Troy once the campaigning season was done – to speak to his heart, and to put an end to the war.

She thought she understood what was really going on here, why such a formidable expedition had been formed around her. Milaqa knew enough of Qirum's culture, she had seen it in Anatolia, to understand that marriages to seal unions between nations were common. Was that what was being planned here, with herself used as bait? After all as a daughter of an Annid of Annids she was the nearest Northland had to a princess, though it galled her to admit it. Well, Milaqa was now nineteen years old; she was nobody's gift, nobody's whore. Besides, every time she had been pushed at Qirum in this way before it had ended in disaster.

Or maybe there was some deeper scheme here, she wondered, which she had yet to glimpse. If there was, Teel was giving her no hint. She had found all the high-ups increasingly obscure recently, Teel even more enigmatic than usual. She had no choice but to go along with their schemes, whatever they were, and wait for the chance to make her own decisions, take her own chances.

When the procession formed up at the foot of the Wall, people stopped what they were doing to come and stare. Children leaned over soot-stained galleries, adults labouring to rebuild defensive ditches and ramparts stopped their work and leaned on heavy shovels, the priests looked down from the roof of the Wall. Even now Milaqa felt distanced from it all. It was as if she was the only real person in a world of puppets. Save, perhaps, for Qirum.

Following the great Etxelur Way south, they were passed without trouble through the Trojan lines, the desultory besieging force left in place for the winter. Most of the Northlanders walked. Kilushepa, however, preferred to ride with her ladies in a horse-drawn carriage. She had gifts for Qirum and his *basileis*, a custom in the countries they all came from, she said. The queen herself took special care of these items, which were wrapped securely in linen blankets and ox-hide and stored in her carriage and other carts.

Milaqa, like most people in the Wall, had seen little of the country since Qirum had begun his siege, and she was shocked at its state, the canals and weirs blocked, the dams broken, the hearthspaces weed-choked or flooded, the houses burned. But the people had survived, mostly. After the first Trojan attacks they had melted into the countryside and lived as their ancestors had, supported by the land's natural bounty. And now they too came out to stare as the procession passed, strange, wild-looking people.

'The land itself is flourishing,' Raka observed at one rest stop, as they sat by a broad marsh. She watched a family of harvest mice busy in a nest woven in the tall grass. 'Perhaps there's a lesson in that. The land, you know, that's what's important in the end, not our petty human squabbles. Perhaps we have lost sight of the will of the mothers.'

Teel nodded. 'Those who are to follow us will listen to the mothers' wisdom, I am sure.'

More of his enigmatic obliquity. *Those who are to follow?* Would Raka not be leading the recovery when peace came, Teel not still be gliding among the Annids with his hints and tricks?

One of Muwa's men, bored, pulled his sword from its scabbard and began slashing at the long grass, where the harvest mice had made their nest. Kilushepa stopped him with a sharp word in the Hatti tongue. That surprised Milaqa. She would not have thought the Tawananna, who had refused even to acknowledge the existence of her own daughter in Etxelur, would care anything for mice.

They were still a long way out from New Troy when they were met by a patrol. And as they passed through deep layers of earthworks Teel looked quietly pleased. All this defensive effort was a response to the campaign of petty retaliatory raids he and others had been organising ever since Qirum had begun his own assaults on Northland communities.

Their reception at the gate in the wall around the lower town was prickly at first. Highly trained soldiers on both sides, some of whom must have met in battle only months before, faced each other down. But there was no trouble, both sides kept their discipline.

Qirum's man Erishum came out to meet the Northlander party, and escorted them through the gate. The city inside the wall seemed emptied out to Milaqa, depopulated, with none of those hungry crowds she had seen last time. She wondered if the Northlanders held here had found a way to slip away from

390

this kingdom of mud and hunger and gone back to the country, quietly abandoning Qirum's dream.

They were shown to a house of mud brick and thatch, in the shadow of the walls of the citadel itself, evidently the house of some warlord evicted for the purpose. Carpeted inside and with tapestries on the walls, it seemed grand to Milaqa. Kilushepa said it was small and poky, but it would do. Erishum waited with them until a runner brought a message that Qirum would be prepared to meet Milaqa at sundown.

This sent Kilushepa into a kind of regal panic. 'And it is already mid-afternoon! There is barely time to make this wild woman anything less than grotesque – oh! How I hate to rush these things.'

Milaqa glared at her, suspicious. 'What "things"?'

Kilushepa chased out everybody but her serving women, Raka, and Teel – the only man, 'but, ball-less, you will cause no offence,' she said dismissively. Then she turned on Milaqa. 'Strip.'

'What? I will not.'

'Do it, child, or I will have the soldiers do it for you, I don't have time to waste.' She clapped her hands. Her ladies, barefoot on the carpeted floor, hurried in with trunks of clothes and cosmetics brought from the carts.

Milaqa turned to Teel and Raka in outrage. 'What is this? Is she to dress me up? Am I a doll, a toy?'

'No,' Raka said. 'You are our ambassador. You must make an immediate impression on the Trojan, and the right one. Put yourself in Kilushepa's hands. Look – Qirum calls himself a king. Kilushepa is a queen. How such people behave towards each other is a mystery to us, and with the mothers' blessing it always will be. But she knows how you should present yourself to him.'

Teel lay back on a couch, sipping water and wine. 'Don't argue for once, Milaqa. Trust the judgement of others.'

'If I didn't trust you I wouldn't be here at all.'

Teel shrugged. He would not look her in the eye, which was unlike him.

And Kilushepa was waiting, arms folded, glaring.

Milaqa shrugged, and began to peel off her travelling clothes.

'We will burn those,' said Kilushepa.

'We will not,' replied Milaqa.

As soon as she was naked the serving women closed in on her. They scrubbed her from head to toe with water and soaps, and washed her hair and dried it vigorously with towels. They even shaved her armpits, but she baulked when they tried to shave her pubic hair. Then they began to rub scented oils into her skin and hair.

She sneezed. 'There's something getting up my nose.'

'Stop complaining, child,' Kilushepa snapped.

'Try to enjoy it,' Teel advised. 'This is called being pampered.'

'Give me the life of a soldier any day.'

Now they dressed her in a robe of thick, colourfully striped wool. It looked beautiful, Milaqa had to admit. It seemed to shine in the light, and felt greasy to the touch; the wool was thick with oil. But the robe was cut so low in the front that her breasts were bare.

She tried walking around. 'Are you sure you've put it on the right way round? I feel ridiculous walking around with my udders hanging out. And it's so heavy and clumsy I keep tripping up.'

'No,' Kilushepa all but snarled. 'It's you who are heavy and clumsy, you great she-aurochs. Lift your feet when you walk. *Lift!*'

Now she was sat on a stool with a mirror of polished bronze held up before her face, and the cosmetics were applied. These came from tiny boxes of glass and silver and gold, themselves ancient and exquisite, the travelling kit of a queen. Milaqa's oiled hair was teased into curls and glossy tumbles down her neck. A white power was applied heavily to her face, so she turned pale as a ghost, then bright red starbursts were carefully painted on her cheeks, chin, forehead. Black kohl was delicately applied around her eyes, by a girl younger than she was, who came so close Milaqa could smell the spiced meat on her breath. Perfume was dabbed at her neck, her breasts, a scent of rich flowers.

Then she was made to stand, and the finishing touches were applied. A bodice and golden belt were tied around her waist – the belt was heavy, she was astonished to find, it was not plate, it was *solid gold*, from Kilushepa's personal collection. A brooch was fixed to each side of her bare chest, and bangles, more gold and silver, were slipped over her arms. Kilushepa herself set a headband in her hair, richly jewelled.

When Milaqa stood to face Raka and Teel, she rattled.

'You are beautiful,' Raka said.

'I'm ridiculous.'

'Not in Qirum's eyes,' Kilushepa said. 'To him you will be the embodiment of royalty, of a Trojan princess. The fulfilment of a dream – a woman fit for the king he imagines he has become. And within this beautiful shell is you, Milaqa, the mate of his soul. To him, you will be perfect.'

'And irresistible,' said Teel, grinning sourly.

There was a murmuring outside the house. A lady came running in.

'It is time,' the Tawananna said. 'You have been summoned. Already! I told you, we did not have a breath to spare.' She faced Milaqa one last time, critically, her mouth pursed. 'It's been like putting rouge on the cheeks of an ox. But the results are moderately acceptable, for which I take full credit.'

'Of course.'

'Erishum will escort you to the citadel, to meet Qirum. He has a carriage.'

'I'll walk.'

'You will use the carriage. Once you're in the King's presence – well, of course, you've no idea how to behave, but neither does that brutish Trojan, so I suppose it will not matter. Don't trip over. Don't drink too much. Try not to hit anybody.'

'Yes, yes.'

'One more thing.' Kilushepa snapped a finger, and a girl came running with a package still sealed in ox-hide from the journey. As the servant began hastily picking at knots, Teel and Raka watched intently. Suddenly the atmosphere was tense, but Milaqa could not imagine why. The girl unwrapped the hide and an inner linen cover to reveal a box. Shallow, about the length of Milaqa's forearm, it was elaborately carved with images of oak leaves and mice, and inset with gold. Kilushepa took this, and handed it to Milaqa. It was not heavy.

'A gift,' Kilushepa said. 'We have sent tokens for Protis and the other savages. But this is for Qirum himself.'

'What is it?'

'A gift fit for the king Qirum imagines he is. A treasure from old Troy, looted when the Greeks sacked the city, and acquired by me at great expense. The Greeks called it the Palladium. Qirum will know what it is.' She glared at Milaqa. 'Do you understand? This must be opened by Qirum himself. This gift is for him and him alone.'

Milaqa nodded, not much interested in one more bit of manipulation. She took the ox-hide from the girl and wrapped up the box again, to keep it safe while she carried it.

Raka stood, came to Milaqa, and unexpectedly hugged her, leaning over the box. 'I must not smudge your face. Even in my eyes you look beautiful. Thank you, Milaqa. The mothers will reward you for this. And I—' She broke away, and Milaqa was startled to see tears in her eyes.

Teel stepped up now. 'Don't mind her. She always was sentimental, that one. She's got worse since she's had to send soldiers out to die. Well. Good luck, Milaqa. You made a good Crow, in the end, even if your training was a little unusual. As was your career. But then we live in unusual times.' He patted her arm.

She stared into his face. His skin was slack, a plump man's face emptied by years of privation. A face that hid secrets. He seemed to want to say more, but now, in this last moment, the flow of words on which he had built his career failed him. 'What are you keeping from me this time, uncle?'

Teel just smiled.

Kilushepa plucked at her sleeve. 'Come. A king awaits.'

Clutching the box, she turned and walked out through the door. Erishum gravely stood in the evening light. She tried to focus on the challenges that lay ahead, and put aside a growing unease.

63

When she walked into Qirum's crowded inner chamber, carrying Kilushepa's gift, at first the King simply stared.

He had been lying on a couch by the window, where a filmy drape lifted in a soft breeze. Lamps burned in alcoves cut into the wall. The usual guards stood in the corners, and a single priest bowed before the small shrine at the back of the room. Bear-like military men, officers in elaborate tunics and leather kilts, were gathered on low stools, arguing over clay blocks scattered on a low table, apparently records of troop movements or provision shortfalls, the business of an army. A boy in a plain tunic stood by, nervously translating the languages of Qirum's officers for those who needed it. Serving girls flitted around the men, bearing trays of drink and food, under the watchful eye of an older woman who stood by one door.

And Qirum gazed at Milaqa, transformed by Kilushepa's arts. At last he jumped up from his couch. 'Out, all of you.' The servants filed out immediately. The military men got up reluctantly, glaring at Milaqa. 'Oh, leave the tablets, Asius, you fool. Out, out. You, priest. And you.' He waved to his guards. They looked uncertainly at Erishum, who nodded, and they left their places. 'Go on, all of you. You too, Erishum!'

Erishum was the last to leave, evidently reluctant. When he had ushered the rest out, he pulled a heavy cover over the doorway.

The two of them stood at opposite ends of the room, Qirum barefoot in a wine-stained robe, Milaqa still holding her box, from which the ox-hide wrap had once more been removed.

'So we're alone,' Milaqa said. 'For the first time since—'

'Since I became the King.' He laughed. 'But really we're never alone. Even now we'll be watched. Even if I ordered it not to be so, my men know the consequences if anything should befall me through their negligence. But we are as alone as I will ever be until the time comes for me to venture into the underworld. By the Storm God's teeth, Milaqa. Suddenly you are beautiful.'

'You're blushing.'

'So are you. Right down to your—'

'Stop looking.'

He laughed. 'Well, I can scarcely promise you that! Kilush-epa's doing, this, is it? That woman always did know how to twist my heart. And now she's doing it even from afar – even though she knows that if I ever lay eyes on her again I will kill her with my bare hands.'

She felt an absurd prickle of jealousy. 'I'm standing here flapping in the wind. Must we talk of her?'

'No. I'm sorry.' He took big clumsy steps towards her, reaching out. But he stopped short, and dropped his arms. 'Milaqa, you occupy a special place in my spirit. I'll never forget that you saved my life when Kilushepa betrayed me in Hattusa. It is a cruel fate that has separated us, a game of the gods that has put us on opposing sides in a war. And now, to see you like this – I am overwhelmed.'

'As I will be soon,' she said practically. 'My robe is heavy, and this box is getting heavier. Could I sit down?'

'Of course – I apologise. Sit with me.' He went to the table, brushed the clay tablets and wine cups onto the floor with his arm, took the box and placed it on the table. He sat on the couch, patted it.

She sat beside him cautiously; she didn't entirely trust her dress. 'The box is a gift from Kilushepa, and all of Northland. As from one great king to another, the Tawananna said. In this box, she said you'd know it, is something the Greeks took from Troy. She called it the Palladium.'

His eyes widened. Then, eagerly, he took the box, turned it

around, found a catch. The box's lid slid open, pushed by some hidden spring. Within, on a bed of purple cloth, lay a small statue. To Milaqa's eyes the stone figure of a woman with her arms upraised, worn almost to featurelessness and stained with smoke, was unimpressive. But Qirum was astonished. '*It is true.* Milaqa, no Trojan has seen this since the Greeks sacked my city before I was born, and took away our most precious treasures, our most sacred relics. This is the mother goddess. She is the one the Greeks call Athena, in some of her aspects.'

'I can't make out her face.'

'She is old, and much loved – or was. Some of us believed that she had been smashed, not just stolen. What must Kilushepa have paid some Greek warlord for this? How did she find her in the first place? Well – now I have her.' He bowed to the goddess, reverently lifted her from her bed of cloth, and carried her to the shrine cut into the thick wall. He placed the goddess carefully at the centre of the shrine, where she stood amid similar statues, none of them tall, all garlanded with tokens. 'For now, lady, you may dwell in the King's own personal shrine. And tomorrow we will begin work on a temple for you, a temple in New Troy finer than any in the old.' Again he bowed, and murmured a prayer – and jumped back. 'Ow!'

Milaqa stared. 'What? What's wrong?'

'Something ran over my foot. A mouse!' He came back to Milaqa and the box, reached down, lifted a fold of the purple cloth – and small brown forms squirmed out from under the cloth, out of the box, off the table and went scampering over the floor. He stared at Milaqa. 'Did you see that? Mice – in a gift from the great Tawananna!' He burst out laughing.

She couldn't resist it. Maybe it was the tension, the sheer incongruity. She laughed with him, even harder when one of the little rodents ran over her own leg, and she squealed with shock.

Qirum cupped her face gently. 'You are even more lovely when you laugh, dear Milaqa.' He straightened up and strutted around the room. She saw something like the old energy, the confidence she remembered about him. 'But even the mice are probably a good omen. Well, no doubt I can find a priest who will tell me so. One aspect of the deity the Greeks call Apollo is god of plagues and mice. Maybe the gods are trying to tell us to put an end to this plague of war that blights us. Maybe they are agreeing with Kilushepa, for once! For it's obvious what she intends, you know. By sending you here like this. *Looking* like this. She knows exactly what message she is sending me.'

'I think they are hoping for an alliance.' She took a breath, and plunged on. 'Of the kind you forge between your eastern countries. Where princesses are exchanged to bind nations by marriage.'

He gestured. 'I don't have much of a country. Not yet.'

'And I'm no princess.'

'Ah, you always will be to me, dear Milaqa.' He studied her. 'Look – we don't have to do what they say, you and I. There can be peace whether we marry or not. Or war, come to that. The rules don't apply to us. Do they, Milaqa? They never did, and never will. Whether we marry or not is up to us – nobody else. But that's not to say we can't have some fun, preferably at somebody else's expense.' He clapped his hands, a sharp, shocking noise. 'Woman! Bring wine!'

The senior serving woman came bustling in immediately, bearing a tray of wine and fresh cups. Milaqa was impressed; evidently the servants had learned to anticipate their capricious ruler's moods.

'And send for my head of household. And Erishum. There may or may not be a wedding, but there's certainly going to be a wedding feast. The way the Greeks do it, a pack of curs they may be but they do know how to have fun.' As the woman hurried out, he called after her, 'And musicians! Come, Milaqa.' He held out his hand. 'Will you dance with this humble suitor? For I am going to have to impress you to win your hand.'

She stood, but held back. 'In this dress?'

'Oh, nobody's watching. Well – only an entire kingdom. And I – ow!' He hopped, and slapped at his leg. 'Something *bit* me . . .'

Kilushepa had begun packing as soon as Milaqa had been taken away by Erishum, snapping at her serving women as they packed and repacked bits of jewellery and cosmetics in her boxes.

Teel sat with Raka. They were both drinking Trojan wine, imported by Qirum. Teel was getting drunk, but he suspected Raka wasn't. He watched Kilushepa sourly. 'Do you have any regrets about what we've done, woman? Any at all? If you weren't so busy fussing over *things* at such a time—'

'I certainly regret loading her up with so much jewellery. I suppose it's possible it could be retrieved, once this is all over.'

Teel grunted. 'You will pluck it off my niece's cold corpse, will you?'

'Enough,' Raka said tiredly. 'We all agreed to this, Teel. In fact, as I remember, it was you who persuaded me to accept Kilushepa's scheme in the first place. We are all complicit. We are each of us guilty, or none of us is.'

'But two of us are staying, to share the fate we have ordained for poor Milaqa, and the Trojans of course, but I care not a jot for them. And she—' he gestured at Kilushepa, '—is running away to save her scrawny hide.'

Kilushepa stood so her maid could hang her cloak on her back, and fixed it with a gold clasp at her neck. 'I would take offence at that, Northlander, were you not effectively a dead man already, by your own choosing. Our work is done here. What good does it do to stay? Guilt, you say, Annid? What guilt? Guilt at the fate of Milaqa? You understand that girl as well as I do – I know *you* do, Teel. You see the flaw in her, the emptiness. Let her be useful for once in her life. Or is it guilt at this "dishonourable" ploy? Look – fools like Qirum speak of waging war with honour. But it is all lies. Qirum destroyed your little communities with overwhelming force, there is no honour in that. And when the fire comes, or the storm, or the flood or the drought, no amount of these heroes' precious courage or honour will help them survive.' She tapped her forehead. 'All that will save you is up here. Intelligence. Cunning. And the determination to use it. Which is what enabled your fabled Ana to beat off the Great Sea of legend, from what I've heard of your tradition.'

'You've done this kind of thing before,' Raka said. 'You Hatti.'

Kilushepa sniffed. 'It is in the annals. We have an old prayer to the plague gods: "Shoot my enemy, but when you come home unstring your bow and cover your quiver." The first incident of record was some generations ago, when the King sent donkeys infected with plague into the lands of our enemies the Arzawans. We won the war, and now the Arzawans remember that fever as "the Hatti plague". There have been a number of instances since then.' She spoke dismissively. 'We have experts in these things. The box I brought to Northland is not the only one of its kind stored deep in the royal vaults of Hattusa, like memories of the horrors of the past. There are cages of mice and rats, tended by specially trained priests. Pieces of cloth cut from the bodies of the dead, which in some cases can carry a memory of the disease itself.'

'Weapons of last resort,' Teel said.

'Precisely. And is this not a time for a last resort? After all, that foolish battle you let yourself be talked into waging did even more damage than merely exhausting you. My spies say that before the battle the Trojans were on the brink of fissuring. Sieges are wearing on the besiegers as well as the besieged. But we invited them to battle exactly as Qirum would have wished, we met Qirum on ground he would have chosen, and we enabled him to motivate his men and unite his warring commanders in the process.' She pointed at Raka. 'You boast that this is the oldest civilisation in the world. You boast that you have saved the Jaguar people across the Western Ocean, just as you have saved the Hatti empire from dissolution. Perhaps you have. But that is all in the past. Today, Raka, *you* are Annid of Annids, and if Northland were to fall now it would be entirely your responsibility. And that is why you have allowed me to do what I have done. Because you had to, and don't tell me otherwise.'

Raka simply nodded. 'I have asked Muwa to take back one more message to Etxelur for me.'

'What is that?'

'The name of my preferred successor.'

Kilushepa sneered. 'How noble you both are. I hope it comforts you when the Trojans pursue your shades into the underworld.' She glanced around, as if to make sure she'd left nothing, and without further farewells she marched out of the house.

'Well,' Teel said in the sudden silence, 'at least that's the last we'll see of *her*, and that's a comfort.' He reached for the jug. 'More wine? We may as well finish this.'

64

It took Qirum three days to organise his betrothal feast.

Milaqa spent much of the first day with him. She stayed in his house, at the heart of his citadel. She had her own room, her own little squad of servants dedicated to her, which she found distressing as some of them were clearly Northlander slaves. But she slept alone, and her relationship with Qirum remained chaste, as it had always been. He did not even kiss her, he hugged her only as a brother might. 'For now,' he said, winking broadly.

But on the second day Qirum said he had to attend to the business of his kingdom, and he huddled in his private chamber with his officers, ministers and priests. Meanwhile Milaqa was distracted by a string of visitors, embarrassed-looking officers who showed up in polished armour and bearing elaborate gifts: clothes, cosmetics, jewellery. These were the rival 'suitors' Qirum had ordered to come and woo her, in competition with him. Even Erishum showed up, bowing gravely, bearing a rather pleasing silver pendant.

And it was on that day that she first began to suspect Qirum was growing ill. In the few moments she did spend with him his breathing was rattling and heavy, and he coughed frequently. But he was not a man with the patience for illness, and he ignored the symptoms, while his generals discreetly ignored the spittle he sprayed over their clay tablets and maps, and over their persons.

On the third day the feast itself was set up in an open space in the outer city, beyond the citadel. Everybody was ordered to attend, to watch. There was music, dancing, feasting, tables laden with elaborate dishes from across the Continent, even some plainer Northland fare. The ordinary folk turned up, but there was no sense of joy; Milaqa thought they wore ghastly forced grins, in the presence of a capricious king with the power of life and death. And anyhow there weren't many of them to be rounded up in the first place.

The highlight of the day was the competition between Milaqa's suitors. Qirum asked Milaqa to sit on a kind of throne to preside over the contest, wearing the outfit she had worn when she had come here three days before. The day was comparatively sunny, comparatively mild, but even so it was cold enough that her nipples were hard as stones.

In Qirum's own country and in Greece such contests were conducted in deadly earnest, between princes who might be seeking to win not just a bride but a good alliance for their nations. So it was serious stuff, the tests of archery and slingshotting and spear-throwing, the hand-to-hand fighting with swords and spears – fighting intense enough for wounds to be inflicted, despite the expensive armour on display.

An older man called Urhi, a scribe, was ordered to stand by and make careful notes of the outcomes of all these futile contests. Milaqa thought he looked as if he was going mad with boredom, an intelligent man in a land of brutal young fools, and she wondered what his story was, how he had got here. Qirum had disrupted many ordinary lives in the course of his spectacular career.

And Qirum himself was manic. At first he threw himself into as many contests as he could. But his breath was short, and when he coughed Milaqa thought she saw speckles of blood. So he withdrew, and missed the boxing too, and saved himself for the culmination of the day, his favourite sport, the wrestling.

At a suggestion from Erishum, the King sat out the preliminary bouts, waiting until a victor among the other 'suitors' had emerged to challenge him. That man was Erishum himself. Milaqa could not tell if that was a genuine victory or not.

404

Anyhow it was he who would face the King, surrounded by a crowd of courtiers, warriors, generals, and the common people of the city.

The King stripped to a loincloth, and leaned so his hands were resting on his knees. 'Don't go easy on me, sergeant,' he warned. 'If I think you let me win I'll have your head as a trophy. On the other hand, if you beat me . . .' The sentence tailed off in another coughing fit. More blood speckles, Milaqa saw. Qirum's bare skin was pale, slick with sweat, and oddly mottled with small black marks.

If Erishum was troubled by this impossible balancing act he did not show it. Milaqa supposed he was used to the King's capriciousness, and had after all survived so far. 'I have no doubt you are the better suitor, lord. But you have to prove it first.' He grinned, and crouched.

Qirum laughed out loud. Then he launched himself at Erishum. The crowd roared and clapped as they clashed, heads together, straining, reaching. Erishum got the first break; he twisted, got his arm around the King's neck, and flipped them both over backwards.

And Qirum vomited blood. Erishum let him go in dismay and stood back.

It was in at that moment that Milaqa, in a flash of understanding, realised what had been done – how she had been used, what the true purpose of this expedition to New Troy had always been. What she had done to Qirum's petty empire, and to Qirum himself.

On the day after that, Milaqa's fourth in New Troy, nobody seemed to know what to do with her. She was brought food and drink in her room. The senior woman of the house was attentive to her needs. She was allowed to roam as she would.

She was even allowed into the King's bedchamber, where he lay on a couch.

He was surrounded by soldiers, and by buckets full of blood and stool and piss; the stink was unbearable. She was not allowed to speak to Qirum, but she could not tell if he was conscious anyhow. From time to time he would cry out, as if in great pain. Scared-looking physicians came and went, desperately trying remedies. She heard them speaking of blood in the vomit and the urine, and of painful swellings in his groin and armpits. When they brushed past her, Milaqa saw they were spattered with the King's blood.

She retreated to the King's big reception room. By the shrine with the restored mother goddess figure, the priests intoned steadily, asking Apollo god of plague to put aside his bow. There was nobody else here but the guards, who looked at her with black expressions. Milaqa went back to her room.

That night she could not sleep. The house was full of people coming and going, and it rang with anxious talk, weeping, increasingly angry shouting. I did this, she thought. I brought this here.

In the end she got out of bed and dressed in the pitch dark, in the most practical clothes she could find, and sat on her bed and waited.

Just before dawn Erishum came to her room, bearing a lamp, oil burning in a shallow bowl. 'I will take you back to your uncle.'

'I must see Qirum.'

He grunted. 'Why? To apologise? To finish him off?'

'Erishum, please—'

'You will never see him again. Get ready.'

She clambered off her bed. She glanced back once at the goods that had been brought with her, the Tawananna's jewellery. It meant nothing to her.

He led her through corridors, making for the street door.

'What is happening?'

'Protis is to challenge for the crown. But others oppose him. It makes no difference. Too many others are ill, and the contest is futile until this plague has run its course.'

'Why must I leave?'

'Because there are those who blame you for bringing the plague here.'

'If it's true I did not know, Erishum. I did not know! I have been used. You have to tell him, Erishum.'

He did not answer.

They reached the street, deserted in the dawn light. Milaqa imagined she could feel the fear washing out across the town from the King's house. Erishum hurried her along to the house where Teel and the rest had lodged.

When they reached the house she asked him directly, 'If you think Qirum's death is my fault, why release me?'

'If you are innocent, it is just. If you are guilty, you will take your "gift" back to your own people. And, listen to me.' He leaned towards her, his face hard, dark, grim. 'I am but a soldier; I am no priest. But now I curse you. You and all your cowardly kind, you Northlanders. For what you have done here, your black crime, may our gods destroy you, and may your own gods, the mothers of sea and sky and earth, desert you. And as for you, I will wait for you in the underworld.' And he turned and hurried away.

Milaqa, deeply shaken, ducked quickly inside.

By the light of a single lamp, Teel sat by a couch, on which Raka lay under a heap of blankets. The Annid was unconscious. Milaqa saw swellings on her neck, like those on Qirum's body.

Teel, too, looked waxy, pale, and was breathing heavily. 'This gift of Kilushepa's travels quickly.' He laughed, and coughed.

The world seemed to swivel around Milaqa. 'Then it's true. You sent me to kill Qirum, not to woo him.'

'I'm sorry.' Teel stood stiffly. 'Oh, I am so tired . . . I'm sorry, child.'

Milaqa launched herself at him. He tried to hold her off, but she was stronger than he was, and he could not stop her blows. 'How could you? You are my uncle! All my life you have used me. How could you betray me like this?'

'We had to,' he said. 'Because only you could do it. Only you, child! You with your relationship with Qirum. You with your heart like an empty cup. Only you would go back to the man, knowing what he had done *to your own family*. In a way you're as much of a monster as he is. So we used a monster to trap a monster! It had to be done. Can't you see that?' Coughing, he sat again, clutching his chest. 'Well, remember me, Milaqa, even if you can't forgive me. I'm a sort of anti-Qirum, you know. I don't suppose you'll ever understand that. If a warrior brute like Qirum is the kind his country needs, brave, impulsive, impressive, I am what Northland needs. Cold, manipulative, scheming. I can imagine which of us history will favour. But *you* must remember me, I am the man who gave Northland iron, and changed the world. Ah, but none of it matters. I did love you so much when you were small. I'm sorry that it has come to this.'

She wanted to kill him. She pulled back her fist.

And she coughed convulsively, and her blood sprayed over him.

FOUR

65

The Fourth Year After the Fire Mountain: Midsummer Solstice

The day before the midsummer Giving was set aside for the blessing of the new monuments to the fallen Annids.

The procession formed up in the great Hall of the Annids, deep within the Wall. The grand folk in their fine robes and cloaks of office circulated, murmuring as they got into their rank order. Voro found Milaqa, and here was Mi, blushingly dressed up in a costume not unlike that Milaqa had worn when she had been sent to seduce Qirum's heart, and poison his body.

A blast sounded, on a very ancient deer-bone horn.

Riban took the first steps on the flight up to the Wall's surface, leading the procession. The young priest wore an ornate deer-skull head-dress over purple-dyed hair, with holy words in the circle-and-slash Etxelur calligraphy painted on his cheeks, and his mouth bulged with the ancient wolf's jaw pushed in there in place of his own extracted teeth. He looked the part, Milaqa thought. Riban was head of the House of the Wolves now, somewhat to his own surprise, but he was the most senior priest to have survived the plague, and now here he was leading the holiest of all Etxelur's ceremonial processions, the commemoration of the Annids.

Riban was not the only young Northlander to have stepped up in rank. Possibly thanks to Kilushepa's stern advice about cleanliness and isolation, Hatti taboos imported to Northland, few in Northland beyond New Troy had died of the disease. But even deep within the Wall's recesses some of the oldest and the very youngest, the highest to the lowest, had been taken by the plague. And so many of the great old Houses of Etxelur were led now by representatives of younger generations, and glancing around Milaqa saw that many of those wearing the ornate cloaks were no older than she was. The gathering had a youthful, refreshed feeling about it, she thought.

Even if she would never feel young herself again. Not with all these deaths, in Northland and in New Troy, all of them coming from the opening of the box she had carried to Qirum's chambers: her 'black crime', as Erishum had called it. Few knew what she had done, even here among the senior folk of Etxelur. But she felt as if it must be obvious, as if one of Caxa's great Words had been carved into her chest.

Amid these young people, however, the new Annid of Annids was older than her predecessor, Raka: Noli, who might have taken the post earlier if not for Bren's manoeuvring, and who had now reluctantly accepted the responsibility. Today Kilushepa walked with her, the Tawananna as grandly dressed as Milaqa would have expected.

And Caxa the sculptress walked ahead even of the Annid of Annids, even ahead of Kilushepa, with the priest at the very head of the procession. A proud young woman of the Land of the Jaguar with her big polished mirror-stone hanging over her chest, she looked awed, even nervous. Milaqa knew she preferred to be alone, working steadily at her art. But she seemed to find the patient presence of Riban at her side reassuring. And at least, Caxa knew, she did not have to die today; the plague had taken Xivu, that fretful conscience of the Jaguar kings, and after her work in the war Noli had promised the sculptor her protection.

Behind these principals came other senior figures, Northlanders walking side by side with Hatti. There were many other embassies: wolf-like Albians, priest-like Gairans, warrior-like Greeks, exotic Egyptians with painted faces and towering crowns – even a party from across the Western Ocean, from the Land of the Sky Wolf, proud warriors with tremendous feathered head-dresses and snake tattoos.

There were more Northlanders than usual too, hailing from Wall Districts from the Albian terminus to the World River estuary. The great and ancient community of the Wall itself had almost crumbled under the pressure from the Trojan, and there were apologies to be made, relationships to be rebuilt. But in the end those who had fought in the war had come from end to end of the Wall for the common cause, and that was the foundation for the future.

And towards the rear of the column walked the likes of Milaqa, Voro, Mi and others, too junior for their order of pre-cedence to matter.

They emerged into the air on the parapet of the Wall, before the gleaming new sculpted heads. Out to the north a bank of thick black cloud loomed over a steel-grey ocean, threatening bad weather later.

A breeze blew up, sharp, surprisingly cold for midsummer.

Nuwanza shivered visibly and drew his thick woollen cloak tighter around him. This frail elderly Hatti was the second cousin of Kilushepa who had done so much to secure the Tawananna's successful rehabilitation in the court of the Hatti king. He had rarely travelled outside Hattusa itself before, and had now made a gruelling trek across the Continent all the way to Northland and the Wall. And now this fragile old fellow was to be the husband of Mi, a seventeen-year-old warrior.

'So,' Voro said to Mi, 'how's the boyfriend?'

Mi walked between Voro and Milaqa now, her cheeks painted bright red, her muscular archer's arms folded over her bare breasts. 'Shut up.'

Milaqa tried not to laugh. 'You're a woman who wrestles three-man war chariots. Look at him! You'll probably break him on your first night.'

Mi scowled, pursing brightly painted lips. 'Everybody says it's my duty to marry him.'

Voro nodded. 'It is. Sealing alliances with marriages. It's what they do, out east; it's what they understand.'

'Yes, but why me? I'm no more a princess than she was,' she said, glaring at Milaqa.

Milaqa sighed. 'Maybe not. But I admit you look better in the costume than I ever did. Look, Mi – you'll survive out there. You're tough. Everybody saw that in the war. It's the reason you were chosen, I think. And the old man won't last for ever.' She grinned. 'Not in your bed!'

Mi scowled again. 'Well, I'm taking my bow, and my iron-tipped arrows. Nuwanza has said I could help train their army's archery corps. I think he said that. My Hatti still isn't good.'

'There you go,' Voro said. 'Women have a strong role in Hattusa. The Hatti aren't like the Greeks. Kilushepa herself is proof of that. You'll find a place.'

'And it's warmer in Hattusa,' Milaqa said. 'Besides, you won't have to walk around like *that* all the time.'

'Good.' Mi looked down at her bare chest. 'I prefer to be strapped down, frankly. Helps with the bow action. I hope it's all worth it,' she said, more uncertain, suddenly seeming much younger. 'Worth me giving up my whole life like this. I hope this alliance of Hatti and Northlanders will work, though I can't imagine how.'

'I think it has a chance,' Voro said. 'I was involved in some of the negotiations, with the other Jackdaws. Under Kilushepa and King Hattusili the Hatti empire seems to be stabilising. They are establishing treaties of trade and mutual aid with us. They have done this kind of thing before, as their records show – treaties with Egypt, for instance, sealed by royal marriages. Now they're also talking to the new rulers in Egypt, and in Assyria. And they are sending military missions west into Greece.'

'"Military missions,"' Milaqa said sourly. 'That's one translation. "Invasion" is another.'

Voro shrugged. 'But the Greek kingdoms have all but collapsed. There are already children whose parents were clerks

414

and scribes, growing up in the forests like bandits. Order needs to be imposed from somewhere. We have agreed that we will each have our own domains of influence on the Continent. We will have Albia and Gaira, for instance, and also the Land of the Jaguars and the other countries across the Western Ocean.'

'That's nice of them,' Milaqa said, 'since the Hatti have no ships that can reach those places anyhow.'

'But the Greeks had never sailed into our Northern Ocean either, before they blockaded us. Who knows what the future holds? Milaqa, this is a moment of flux, of change – a pivot of history. Oh, the Hatti are not perfect, but Kilushepa herself remembers how it is to be a booty person. Maybe we can come out of this with a better world, a better way of living.'

'If only we all believe it can be so,' she said cynically.

'Yes,' he said firmly. 'If only we believe.' And he looked directly at her, as if trying to reach her.

From the boy so mortified at being unable to have prevented her mother's death, Voro had grown. He was stockier, graver than he had once been. And he seemed stronger too – or maybe it was just that so much of her own strength had been dissipated by her brush with the plague. He had always cared for her; she had always known that, under her dismissal and contempt. Was she ready now to accept Voro's calm, loyal patience?

But what did she have to offer him? She was a burned-out shell. Kilushepa's surgeons had warned her gravely that survivors of the coughing plague often had difficulty carrying children. And she could never tell him her secret. Never tell him of the black crime.

She was distracted by clouds thickening the sun, a fresh bite in the freshening wind.

'I need time,' she blurted, then instantly regretted it.

Once that would have driven him away. Now he just held her hands. 'I know.'

Beside them, Mi smiled.

Together they turned to face the Wall's new stone heads.

*

415

Riban climbed a platform and, arms outstretched, his face distorted, began gabbling words from a language more ancient, it was said, than the age of Ana herself, who had founded the Wall and saved Northland. But everyone knew what Riban was saying. He celebrated the visages of Raka and Kuma, who had joined the row of those who glared at the ocean that the Wall had defied for hundreds of generations already, and would defy for much longer yet.

Through the long winter Milaqa had watched Caxa and her assistants labour at the heads. They were made not of the local sandstone but of a harder rock, said to originate from dead fire mountains in the north of Albia. Caxa had insisted on using only the techniques traditional among her people; she had roughed out the faces from the ferociously resistant rock with stone hammers, and then had used drills and abrasives, polishing and scraping with ever finer materials, to complete the details. There were markings in the Etxelur script, rings and tails, with the names of the Annids and a brief declaration of their achievement. There was a time stamp too, a string of numbers, a mark of when they had lived and died, recorded in the long calendar of Etxelur. The resulting heads were huge, each as tall as a human being. The faces were stylised in the way of the Jaguar folk, with flattened noses, broad lips, large eyes – yet they were recognisably Kuma and Raka.

And beneath Kuma's head lay a single iron arrowhead, placed there by Milaqa – the thing that had killed her mother, buried for ever beneath this symbol of her eternal triumph.

Riban's peroration was almost done. He raised his hands to the sky, and called in plain language on the little mothers of sea, earth and sky to welcome the Annids to their undying hearths.

And in that instant snow blew in, a sharp, thick flurry that came flying on the wind from the north, off the sea. People murmured in confusion and shock. The snow soon began to gather on the huge profiles of the stone heads, in their eyes, their nostrils.

416

Snow, at midsummer. Milaqa remembered a soldier's curse. *May your own gods, the mothers of sea and sky and earth, desert you.* She turned away, sheltering her face from the sting of the snowflakes.

66

The ice waited in its fastnesses in the mountains, at the poles. Millennia had passed since its last retreat. Human lives were brief; in human minds, occupied with love and war, the ice was remembered only in myth.

But the ice remembered.

And now the long retreat was over.

Afterword

The historical reality of land reclamation from the ocean is almost as remarkable as depicted in this fiction. In the Fenlands of eastern England there is evidence of large-scale water management projects dating back to Roman times (see *Fenland: Its Ancient Past and Uncertain Future* by Sir Harry Godwin, Cambridge University Press, 1978). Using earth dykes, water-pumping windmills and other technologies, from the sixteenth to the nineteenth centuries the Dutch increased their available farmland with reclaimed seabed by a third. However, the management of water by mankind has, of course, a much deeper history. Ancient civilisations including Egypt, Mesopotamia, China and the Indus Valley cultures were capable of tremendous feats of hydraulic engineering (see *Water: The Epic Struggle for Wealth, Power and Civilisation* by Steven Solomon, HarperCollins, 2010).

I have allowed the Northlanders to develop some technologies and techniques precociously. The Egyptians built the first recorded masonry dam some fifteen metres high at Memphis *c.*2900 BC (see Solomon, 2010). To build their Wall the Northlanders used concrete (which they call 'growstone', a word cooked up in a discussion with Adam Roberts on the Latin roots of 'concrete', acknowledged with thanks). We associate the use of concrete with the Romans, but in fact forms of concrete seem to have been in use as early as *c.*3000 BC in Uruk in Mesopotamia (see Reese Palley's *Concrete: A Seven-Thousand-Year History*, Quantuck Lane Press, 2010).

Writing emerged in Mesopotamia in *c.*3000 BC, but in our timeline Britain did not become literate until the arrival of the

Romans. The Northlanders make their own independent invention of a form of writing based on the raw materials of their culture, such as rock art (see *British Prehistoric Rock Art* by Stan Beckensall, Tempus, 1999).

Our conception of cities as dense masses of buildings of stone and masonry is another relic of our civilisation's origin in the arid Near East. The Northlanders' communities, intricate hierarchical networks of communities embedded in a 'green' landscape, are based in part on archaeologists' studies of similar communities in the pre-Columbian Amazon forest. Michael Heckenberger, (see *The Ecology of Power*, Routledge, 2005) interestingly notes that the temperate forests of medieval Europe were studded with towns and villages of similar sizes to those he studied in the Amazon.

Most importantly, my Northlanders are not farmers. All our civilisations have been built by farmers. Modern hunter-gatherer groups surviving in marginal territories are probably not a perfect model of the richness of their lives in the past; given time and a rich environment, hunter-gatherer populations could achieve huge feats, and develop complex societies. The Native American communities of the north-west coast, with towns, aristocracies, slavery, land ownership and patronage of the arts, were arguably the most elaborate hunter-gatherer societies in human history (see *Prehistory of the Americas*, S. Fiedel, Cambridge, 1992). This series imagines a sophisticated, complex, even literate culture developed by a people *without* farming.

Names used here are intended primarily for clarity.

My place names for pre-literate Britain and Gaul (Gaira) are derived in part from mentions in ancient writings such as those of the first century AD scholar Pliny the Elder, which in turn may be based on the reports of such adventurers as the fourth-century BC explorer Pytheas (see *The Extraordinary Voyage of Pytheas the Greek* by Barry Cunliffe, Allen Lane, 2001). I have used the anachronistic term 'Greeks' to describe the contemporary inhabitants of the Greek mainland, known to historians since the nineteenth century as the Mycenaeans. I have used 'Anatolian' for the inhabitants of modern mainland Turkey. The names 'Ilium' and 'Troy' derive from Homer, but according to analyses of Hittite records these appear to be based on the names of territories in the region of Troy: 'Wilusa' which was corrupted to become 'Ilium' and 'Taruwisa' which became 'Troy' (see J. Lacatz, *Troy and Homer: Towards a Solution of an Old Mystery*, Oxford University Press, 2004 (English translation), and chapter 14 of Trevor Bryce's *The Kingdom of the Hittites*, Oxford University Press, 2005). The people of the great Anatolian Bronze Age kingdom we know as the Hittites – because of a link to their nineteenth-century discovery to the 'Children of Heth' of the Bible – seem to have called themselves 'the people of the Land of Hatti'. I have called them 'Hatti' here. In our timeline, by 1159 BC the central Hittite empire had already collapsed. For recent surveys see Bryce (2005) and his *Life and Society in the Hittite World*, Oxford University Press, 2002. I have generally followed Bryce in spelling Hittite personal and place names and other terms.

The old idea that the Hittites maintained their empire through a monopoly on iron-working (see *The Coming of Age of Iron*, ed. Theodore Westime and James Muhly, Yale University Press, 1980) seems to be discredited through a lack of archaeological proof. The Hittites may not have mass-produced iron, but scholars such as Muhly ('The Bronze Age Setting', in Westime and Muhly, 1980) have argued for evidence of carburisation, that is making steel by heating iron in contact with carbon, in the Hittite period. The Hittites certainly manufactured high-quality iron goods, as attested by letters referring to prestigious iron tribute items – most famously given to Tutankhamun, who died in the fourteenth century BC and was buried with iron artefacts that may well have been Hittite. They do not appear to have used iron for weaponry; it was evidently too precious for that. Iron was produced in other areas at the time, but it does seem to be true that it was only after the fall of the Hittites that iron-making, particularly for weapons, became widespread, and the 'Iron Age' began. The main advantage of iron compared to bronze was actually the ready availability of iron ore compared to the scarcity of tin; high-quality bronze weapons could certainly be a match for lower-quality iron weapons. Here I have imagined that high-quality iron precociously developed in Hittite workshops affords a brief advantage to Northland in their conflict with the Trojans.

This novel is set at the end of the European Bronze Age. Just as depicted here it was a time of significant changes across Europe, from the abandonment of high-altitude farmlands in Britain to the collapse of ancient empires like the Hittites in the east, and the onset of the Greek 'Dark Age' in which even literacy was lost. These changes have been ascribed to cultural and systemic factors. But the advent of a new climate regime, punctuated by such events of global impact as volcanic explosions, may well have had something to do with it (see for example *The Long Summer* by Brian Fagan, Granta Books, 2004). In early 2010 a minor eruption of the Icelandic volcano Eyjafjallajokull injected enough ash into the air of north Europe to force airspaces to be closed. Hekla, called here the Hood, is a bigger brother of Eyjafjallajokull. And it did erupt in the year 1159 BC, as depicted here, as proven by ash layers in ice cores extracted from the Greenland ice cap; the resulting injection of smoke and ash into the air seems to have caused several 'years without a summer' which would have ravaged the marginal livelihoods of subsistence farmers. My details of the eruption have been taken from the geological evidence of Hekla's eruptive history.

The use of plague vectors as primitive 'bio-weapons', as depicted here, seems to have a deep history. Plague was used as a weapon by the Hittites as early as the fourteenth century BC (see 'The Hittite Plague, the epidemic of Turalemia and the first record of biological warfare', Siro Trevisanato, *Medical Hypotheses* vol. 69, pp. 1371–4, 2007, and Adrienne Mayor's *Greek Fire,*

Poison Arrows and Scorpion Bombs, Overlook, 2009). The 'coughing plague' depicted here is a variant of the pneumonic form of the plague of which the best known manifestation is bubonic.

My 'People of the Jaguar' are Olmec, a Mesoamerican culture that flourished in an area within modern Mexico *c.*1400 BC–AD 100 (for a recent study see *Olmec Archaeology and Early Mesoamerica* by C. Pool, Cambridge, 2007). I have freely extrapolated details of Olmec culture here. My 'Altar of the Jaguar' is meant to be the site now known as San Lorenzo, preserved from the decline it suffered in our history by the intervention of the Northlanders. As the Vikings discovered around 1000 AD, to sail to the Americas via the Faroe Islands, Iceland and Greenland requires the crossing of no more than 800 kilometres of open sea. Of course the Vikings had the ship technology they needed; I have imagined here a precocious acceleration of ship-building after the first fluked crossings depicted in book one of this series.

In our world, a major feature of the fifteenth-century contact between Europe and the Americas was the devastating transmission of 'herd diseases' such as smallpox and measles to the American populations (see *Guns, Germs and Steel* by Jared Diamond, Vintage, 1998). In my different prehistory I have imagined continual contacts across the Atlantic since the eighth millennium BC, so American populations have had a chance to develop resistance to these diseases.

The plot of this novel hinges to some extent on the (apparently) humble potato, which is brought to Europe by the Northlanders millennia before the post-Columbus explorers of our own history. The potato is a crop that will grow in poor soils and unfavourable positions and climates, it requires only the simplest of implements and techniques to cultivate, and it is tremendously more productive than grain in terms of yield per hectare. Arguably, by fuelling the population growth that underpinned the Industrial Revolution and Europe's rise to economic dominance, the potato changed world history – just as it changes history in this novel (see Redcliffe Salaman's *The History and Social Influence of the Potato*, Cambridge University Press, 1985).

This is a novel, and not meant to be taken as a reliable history. Any errors or inaccuracies are of course my sole responsibility.

Stephen Baxter
Northumberland
Summer Solstice, 2011